— The Vampire Files —

A CHILL IN THE BLOOD

P. N. ELROD

ACE BOOKS, NEW YORK

A CHILL IN THE BLOOD

An Ace Book / published by arrangement with
the author

PRINTING HISTORY
Ace hardcover edition / June 1998
Ace mass-market edition / June 1999

All rights reserved.
Copyright © 1998 by P. N. Elrod
Cover art by Fred Gambino
This book may not be reproduced in whole or in part,
by mimeograph or any other means, without permission.
For information address: The Berkley Publishing Group,
a division of Penguin Putnam Inc.
375 Hudson Street, New York, New York 10014.

The Penguin Putnam Inc. World Wide Web site address is
http://www.penguinputnam.com

Check out the ACE Science Fiction & Fantasy newsletter
and much more at Club PPI!

ISBN: 0-441-00627-2

ACE®
Ace Books are published
by The Berkley Publishing Group,
a division of Penguin Putnam Inc.,
375 Hudson Street, New York, New York 10014.
ACE and the "A" design are trademarks
belonging to Penguin Putnam Inc.

PRINTED IN THE UNITED STATES OF AMERICA

10 9 8 7 6 5 4 3 2 1

With humble thanks to a few of the wonderful people who not only keep me sane, but make life all that much more terrific:

Paul, Julie, & Chris
Susan
Nigel
Glenn, Finni, & Alex
Jackie, and the Teeth-in-the-Neck Gang
Karen
Kim
Sean
Vlad
Rox & Cat
Carole & Sam
Bill & Jody
Sandy
Renate
Jayne
Bill
Jon & the Bell, Book, & Candle gang
Lynda
Max
Mick
Jean, the redhead
Ret & Earlene
Scott
Oleta
The whole gang at ORAC
Teresa
Letha
Brad & Sue
Jean, the other redhead
Kevin—a.k.a. S.I.K.O.
Star
Louise
Quinn, the other, other redhead,
Kathy Bloom for outbidding everyone,
and my fur angels, Big Jake & the Mighty Mite.

Chicago, February 1937

TIRED to the bone, I slumped in the front seat of Shoe Coldfield's big Nash, wedged between him and my partner,
Charles Escott. The car's heater was going full blast, but I
still shivered like a malaria victim. I'd never been this cold
before in my whole life, but that's what happens when you
take a dive off a boat into Lake Michigan in early February.

Coldfield, a large, grim-looking black man in his middle
thirties, glared down at me with a combination of relief and
exasperation, then shifted the glare in Escott's direction.
"Charles, he's half-dead. I'm taking him to a hospital."

Escott bent forward so his pale, sharp-featured face was
more or less in my field of view. The effort made him grunt.
One of his eyes had a bad shiner, the other was swollen shut,
and he held his left arm protectively close to his lean frame.
He'd been through the wars tonight himself, I dimly recalled.
"My dear fellow," he said, addressing Coldfield, not me,
"that really wouldn't be a good idea for any of us, and you're
well aware of it."

In response, Coldfield snarled a ripe curse as he hauled at
the steering wheel. He made a smart U-turn along the beach
road and got us pointed back toward Chicago.

"Jack's a little shell-shocked, but he only needs a warm place to thaw out and rest." Escott went on, peering at my no-doubt-glazed eyes.

"No shit. Then what? We wait for pneumonia to set in?" I got annoyed at their talking over me. " 'M a'right," I managed to puff out through chattering teeth. Bad idea. It made me cough. Escott thoughtfully shoved a handkerchief in my face before I dribbled more lake water onto the overcoat he'd loaned me.

"Like hell you are," said Coldfield. He glared briefly at me again, like all this was my fault—and he was right—then focused on the road and the rearview mirror. I was glad I was low enough in the seat so he wouldn't notice anything odd about the reflection.

"Anyone following?" asked Escott.

"Not yet."

"Let's keep it that way. No hospitals, Shoe, as a favor to all of us. We must assume that Kyler's gang or Miss Paco could have informants anywhere in the city and—"

"Yeah, yeah, well, they won't have any in my neck of the woods. I'm bringing in Doc Clarson to look at you both."

"I can manage without."

"Oh sure, I've seen how well you've managed with those busted ribs."

"They're only just cracked a little."

"Charles . . ." Rising impatience in Coldfield's tone. Couldn't blame him.

But Escott's attention was centered on me. "Jack? Are you up to seeing Dr. Clarson?"

I shook my head. A doctor meant an examination, which meant that the first time he tried to take my pulse he'd find out I was a bit more than just half-dead. In fact, I'm Undead, which was why I'd had such a tough time with the free-flowing water of the lake. Right now I didn't want to bother dealing with anything beyond getting out of my freezing wet clothes and maybe crawling into a nice hot oven for a few hours.

"What are you asking him for?" Coldfield demanded.

"I thought I'd give him a choice in the matter."

"Huh. Shape he's in he couldn't think straight if you gave him a ruler. Same for you."

"I'm also trying to keep the number of people involved in this mess to a minimum."

"Clarson's family, he won't talk."

"I know, but I'd rather not put him to any unnecessary risk."

"It's in *my* territory, I'll be the judge of what's a risk for my people."

"But—"

"Charles, just shut the hell up and let me drive."

Escott subsided. As far as I could tell through my fog of nausea and disorientation, he seemed perfectly unoffended by Coldfield's manner. They were old friends from back in the twenties when they'd both been actors in some touring company in Canada. A decade and then some goes by and now Escott's calling himself a private agent—I suppose it's got more class than "keyhole peeper"—and Coldfield's heading one of the larger criminal gangs in Chicago's Bronze Belt. How they ended up in two such opposite fields and remained friends I was still trying to figure out.

Coldfield drove fast and the car got pretty warm—for them. I was only just starting to feel a little less like an iceberg, but my bouts of shivering gradually shortened, and the teeth-chattering business finally ceased. I could still taste the sour metallic flavor of the lake in the back of my throat, but that would go away if I could make a quick visit to the Stockyards to feed before dawn. Not much chance of doing that with

Shoe Coldfield along; he didn't know about me being a vampire.

I'm not like what you saw a few years back in the Lugosi movie. There're some similarities between me and old Count Dracula, but I don't turn into animals or quake at crosses or silver bullets, flop in a coffin or stuff like that. I do drink blood to keep body and soul together—still have one of those as far as I know—and it's usually animal blood, but *that* little detail can still hit people the wrong way. Because of it I hadn't made up my mind whether to let Coldfield in on the news yet.

Escott knew all about it, of course, and could more easily break it to his friend, but once told me it was really my decision and my job. It would save a lot of trouble right now, but dammit, I was just too tired to open that can of worms tonight. You can't just tell people that you're a vampire and have them accept it, you have to prove it to them and then give out the whole history of how you got to be that way. In my case, I fell in love with a beautiful, but unusual woman, and we exchanged blood. Last summer I was killed by a mobster, but much to his surprise I didn't stay dead. How I got back at him for my murder is another story.

Half an hour or more passed with no one saying a thing. I liked their silent company. It was nice, so very, very nice to be with people who didn't want to kill me. That and the warm air helped me relax until I was as near as I could get to dozing. I don't sleep, not like I used to when I still breathed regularly; at night I'm always solidly awake for the duration. When dawn comes, I'm so close to being dead it ain't even remotely funny. I've no control over it, and lately it's been damned inconvenient, if not downright dangerous. I miss a lot.

I opened my eyes when the car came to a halt, but it was only for a street signal. Coldfield was in the thick of the city now and began driving sedately, easing into the start and stop of the wee hours' traffic, signals with care. Maybe he didn't want to jar us more than necessary, but you could also figure that he didn't want to attract cops. Too many of them were still on the take despite attempts to clean things up since the Feds whisked Capone away on that tax rap, and as Escott said, people like Miss Angela Paco could have eyes and ears anywhere in the town. It was because of her I ended up in the lake tonight, another casualty in her gang war.

"Where we going?" I asked, blinking against a barrage of neon from an all night drugstore's sign.

Coldfield seemed surprised I'd spoken. "Someplace safe and warm."

" 'M all for it. Where's Isham?" He was one of Coldfield's men and had been with them earlier. He'd tried his best to pull me to safety when all hell broke loose at Angela's place earlier this evening.

Escott—bad ribs, shiner, and all—had been her unwilling guest, and I'd snuck into her house to try getting him away, but we tripped a burgler alarm on the way out. Her thugs started shooting at us; Isham started shooting at them, and there was a lot of yelling and noise as Coldfield tore across the grounds in his armored Nash trying to get to us. Isham and Escott managed to reach the car, and I'd almost gotten aboard, but little Angela started throwing hand grenades, which screwed everything up. They'd quite sensibly hightailed it out of there with me weakly waving them on. Coldfield's Nash was tough, but not that tough.

"I told him to get scarce after Charles made his call to arrange to get you back from Angela Paco," said Coldfield.

"She was going to do a double-cross. Try to kill him."

"I'd figured that much by now. You wanta tell us what happened?"

I shrugged, staring straight ahead at the dashboard. "Tried

to walk home from a boat ride. It didn't work so good.''

"The hell you say.''

"Would you care to expand a bit on the subject?'' Escott asked. "We rather lost track of you when Miss Paco lobbed that last grenade.''

And what a sight she had been with her throwing the thing as far as her tiny form could manage, then running flat out in the other direction to hit the dirt a half second before the whole night went up. She'd been laughing the whole time.

"Yeah, Fleming,'' said Coldfield. "We wanted to come back for you. Sorry.''

"I'm not. None of you needed to be there. Angela's her father's daughter and then some when it comes to being crazy.''

"So what happened? How'd you get away?''

It would be much easier if I could give him the truth of it, of how I'd nearly checked out four times over this night. First by getting shot up by a wiseguy named Chaven, which weakened me; I can survive bullets, but can't tolerate blood loss too damn well. Then later, while trying to get away from Angela Paco, I caught a load of grenade shrapnel. The stuff had gone right through me, of course, but it hurt like blazes and weakened me more. The third time, while I was locked up and alone, one of Angela's mugs came to work off a grudge by trying to beat my brains out. I was only just able to stop him, and in the aftermath, I'd fed from him to stay alive. It saved me, until the morphine in his blood kicked in and laid me out flat. That's when Angela, figuring me to be dead, decided to drop my body into Lake Michigan. The only reason I was moving at all was that with my condition I'm a lot tougher than I used to be—though at the moment I was feeling pretty damned fragile.

A real hell night for yours truly, Jack Fleming, and there was still more of it left.

"Kyler had Frank Paco prisoner," I said, trying to sort what to say and what to leave out. "Was going to use him to get full control of the old Paco gang away from Angela. When Kyler pegged out, that lieutenant of his, Chaven, cozied up with her to get her to trade me for her father." And one other hostage, a walking adding machine named Opal who knew how to work the gang's books.

"The hell you say. Why did Chaven want you?"

"He needed a patsy to blame for Kyler's death. Probably pretty embarrassed, what with aiming at me and getting his boss instead when I ducked too fast. After he gave back Paco, he hauled me, Kyler's body, and what was left of a guy called Vic who was playing both sides, aboard the *Elvira* and was going to dump us all in the lake for fish food. I waited until I had a chance, then jumped Chaven. He's dead now. Charles, it was with your gun."

Escott offered me a thin, glacial smile, his face alight for a second. "I'm delighted to hear it was put to such good use, though there might be trouble should the police trace it to me. I suppose I'd best report the gun has been stolen."

"They won't trace anything even if they do find the body. The bullet went right through him."

"How fortunate."

He might not have thought so had he been the one pulling the trigger.

"What's become of it? My Webley?"

"Still aboard the yacht, I think."

He merely nodded. "Who knows, perhaps I can recover it some day."

Escott's got a dark streak in him and it's icy like the lake. Once in a while I run into it. The encounters don't always leave me in a cheerful mood, and I was feeling rotten enough already.

"Are you really all right?" he asked, looking at me as closely as his good eye allowed.

What was making me sick was remembering the *feel* of Chaven's death, not the sound, though that must have been loud enough when the Webley I'd turned on him went off and shot out the artery in his throat. I remembered his hot blood bursting forth, striking me, coating me, the weightless, screaming instant as we both fell into the water and the sudden hellish silence that followed when freezing death closed over my head.

"Jack?"

I huffed out something that was meant to be a laugh but failed. "I guess so," I said, lying. I looked down at my clothes, but the lake must have washed them clean. Too bad it couldn't have done as much with my memory. Turning someone alive into someone dead, even scum like Chaven, made for a black ache inside that no doctor could ever fix. This nightmare would be living with me for a while yet.

"Then what?' asked Coldfield, wanting me back on the subject.

"Then I jumped ship and swam for my life."

"You outta your mind, kid."

"I didn't have a lot of choice. There was another guy there, Deiter, he was all ready to ace me. Between him and the lake I figured I had a better chance in the water." That was total falsehood. Deiter had been too shit scared to even think of shooting, and my ending up in the drink had been a mix of accident and bad luck. Never mind the cold, that's the least of it; because of my supernatural condition free-flowing water and I just don't mix. It's bigger than me and infinitely stronger. If I'd not been able to vanish and float up over the surface soon after going under, it would have been fatal. And that's vanish, not turn into a mist. Another handy talent of mine, but exhausting.

"Deiter, you said?"

"That's what they called him. One of Kyler's boys. His job was to bump off Gordy so Kyler could take over his part of the town, then cut a deal with the New York bosses. With Gordy's rackets in hand he could up their take by five percent and keep the rest. Of course, that was before he got dead. Chaven's not here to pick up the reins, and now I don't know what they're going to do."

"Holy shit." He glanced at Escott, who was shaking his head. "This town's gonna blow wide open once word gets out. Without Kyler to take over Paco's territory—"

"Hey, don't forget Angela," I added.

"What can she do? There ain't a wiseguy in the town who'd let himself be bossed by a woman."

"She's more of a girl, but don't underestimate her. She's using her father as a front man, that's why she wanted him back so bad." Well, to be fair to Angela, she wanted Frank Paco back because he was her father, period, but she still had more ambition than Napoleon and twice the nerve.

"You think she'll be able to take over?"

"I'd make book on it. She's smart, moves fast, and if things work her way she'll have the whole operation's coded account books sometime tomorrow. She sweet-talked little Opal into working for her."

"What?"

"She traded Opal back to Chaven to get Paco out, but Opal's not staying long."

"My God," said Escott, his tone full of admiration rather than dismay. "Between the two of them they could have the city in hand by the end of next week."

I was going to say he was probably overstating things on that point, but shut up. Opal, Kyler's former accountant, was the best soldier in Angela's small army. Never mind all the gun-packing goons, brute force was nothing compared to a balanced ledger sheet showing all the profits, and Opal could do numbers the way the rest of the world breathes—without even thinking about it.

"Let's continue to assume that despite these distractions Miss Paco is still in a murderous frame of mind toward us," said Escott after a minute.

"Toward you," I put in. "She thinks I'm dead, courtesy of Chaven."

"Unless Deiter talks with her."

"He might think I'm dead, too. A swim at this time of year . . ."

"Yes, yes. And we know for certain that it was an obvious trap Shoe and I were driving into."

"Told you so," Coldfield muttered. "If Fleming hadn't been weaving on the road like a New Year's drunk we'd be in the lake by now, too."

"Angela will still have a hit out on you, Charles," I said. "She thinks you're a loose end."

"So I am."

"You're pretty cool about it."

"Part of the job," he said with a shrug of his eyebrows. "Right, I've not shown up for my meeting with her, she'll assume I'm onto her game and expect me to go to ground or to the police, or both, which means she will likely also drop from sight for a bit until things settle. All we need to do is discover where she might go."

"Good luck," said Coldfield with a snort. "What do you do when you find her?"

Escott looked at me. One eyebrow twitched a question.

I sighed. "I'll think of something."

Our drive finally ended somewhere in the middle of Chicago's Bronze Belt, and I was wondering if this was such a good idea. If Coldfield wanted to keep a low profile he was

doing it with the wrong people what with our white skins—
well, Escott's was gone fairly gray by now. I hoped he wasn't
buying trouble for himself taking us in.

The entry to sanctuary was in a trash can–lined alley between some drab structures that must have been built right
after the O'Learys' cow changed all the real-estate values.
Coldfield stopped, cut the engine, and got out, telling us to
wait. As he went up a couple steps to the rear of an old brick
building I checked my watch, but the water had screwed the
works. Damn. I wanted to know how long until dawn. He
came back a minute later, opened the passenger side, and tried
to help Escott out.

"I'm fine," Escott insisted. "Just let me take it slow." But
the wind was cruel, and I still had his coat. He hissed when
the cold hit him and started to double over against it, then
hissed again as his ribs protested.

"Slow is the only way you can take it, you fool."

"Hah," agreed Escott, and allowed himself to be steadied
on the steps. The screen door popped open to receive him.
By then I'd climbed out and shut up the car. The shift from
slouching comfortably in the warmth to standing tall in the
winter air the took me by surprise. Something unpleasant suddenly burbled deep in my belly. I hurriedly staggered to one
side, stopping short at a frozen puddle, and threw up.

Nasty, but mercifully brief. I'd swallowed some of the lake
and my inside works hate that kind of thing. Pain lanced
behind my eyes as I spat out the last of it and wondered how
far we were from the Stockyards. I needed a drink. The right
kind of drink.

"Fleming?" Coldfield waited at the door for me, peering
at what to him would be thick shadows.

I raised a feeble wave. "Coming."

"That bad stomach of yours?" he asked when I joined him.

"Yeah." It was as good a story as any to explain peculiarities in my behavior.

"Ulcers?"

"Don't know, don't care."

We pressed ahead and the screen banged behind me. I shut the inner door and was buffeted by a wall of moist warmth, bright light, and the smell of fish and grease. We were in a kitchen, a pretty big one: three stoves with oversized cooking pots on them were going at full steam and made the air like August again. Some kind of eatery, then, that was either still open from the night before or getting ready for breakfast, or maybe it just never closed at all. Several black people wearing stained white aprons were gathered by one of the stoves, their watchful faces displaying a variety of expressions ranging from alarm to annoyance.

"Sal," said Coldfield, addressing one of the men, "I need you to—"

"The hell you do!"

This came not from Sal, but from a slim black woman in her thirties who suddenly burst in on us like a cavalry charge. She wore a sober, dark blue dress and a no-nonsense, God-help-you expression as she halted in the front of the group, hands on her hips and disgruntlement in every line of her well-shaped body. She treated the whole room to a piercing once-over, then came forward to stand nose to nose with Coldfield. She wasn't nearly his match in height, but made up for it with force of temper.

"Clarence, just what the hell do you think you're doing here?" she snapped.

Clarence? I thought. I caught Escott's eye. He made a small, hasty cutting motion with one hand.

Coldfield offered her a winning smile, holding his palms up. "Just bringing you a couple of strays. It's only for a day or so until we—"

"You know I don't want anything to do with your crap—no offense," she said in an aside to Escott. Brows high, he pursed his lips and gave a minute shake of his head. "You damn well know I run a clean place here and I'm not about to—"

"Please, Tru, this is serious. I wouldn't have come if it wasn't."

She crossed her arms and glared. "Uh-huh. I'm sure you'll have a good sob story all ready for me."

"And you know you'll do what I ask if I ask nice enough, so how 'bout we pretend you've heard it all and I go straight to the please-pretty-please-with-sugar-on-top part?"

My eyes were ready to pop. *This* was Shoe Coldfield?

Tru saw and slapped his arm. "Oh, stop embarrassing yourself in front of the bum. No offense," she added, nodding at me.

"None taken," I whispered.

"He's no bum, he's just had a hard time tonight, and Charles, too. You remember Charles Escott, don't you?"

She rounded on him. "I remember, but he's sure changed. Is that really you under those bruises?"

"Indeed it is, Miss Coldfield. I do apologize for not being in a more presentable state, but as your brother was about to say, this is a rather serious occasion and—"

"It's you all right. Still using ten words when one will do, huh? Well, don't stop, I like that English accent. Come on and sit by the stove. Sal, got any stew ready? Okay, then pour him a cup and get it into him." Sal, a very large man, topping even Coldfield's size by a few inches, instantly stepped forward to carry out this order. "Now, who are you?" She looked at me again. I'd heard a little about her from Escott, and by a roundabout way she'd once sent a case in our direction. Don't know what I expected her to be like, but whatever it was fell short of the reality.

"My name's Fleming, I work with Charles—"

Coldfield interrupted. "Tru, this can wait, the man took a dive in the lake and he's half froze to death."

Her dark eyes flashed fire on him. "You and your—your whatever the hell it is! I don't want to know."

"But—"

"Oh, don't worry, I'll take care of them, but you get out of my way until I stop being mad at you for it."

"How about I go get Doc Clarson?"

Her brows came down and she scowled first at me, then Escott, giving us each a thorough looking over. "Let the poor man get his rest, I can manage these two. They don't seem ready to die just yet."

"But Charles has broken ribs—"

"Only cracked," put in Escott helpfully.

"Shut up, Charles—and Fleming's probably got frostbite by now."

"No I don't," I put in, also helpfully.

"Shut up, Fleming—"

"Clarence!" Her eyes narrowed and she jerked a thumb in the direction she wanted him to go. "Out of the way."

"But, Tru—"

"You run everything else, *I* run this place, *I* call the shots. Those are the rules. Move."

Coldfield put a lid on it and, throwing a quick glare at each of us, found an unused corner and hunched there, shoving his hands in his coat pockets. I had the strong feeling Escott and I would owe him big time for this favor.

Escott, now seated on a stool by one of the stoves and hugging a mug of hot stew to his chest, apparently decided he was at the Vanderbilt mansion for a debutante ball. He cleared his throat. "Please allow me to make proper introductions: Miss Trudence Coldfield, this is Mr. Jack Fleming, my friend and business associate. Jack, Miss Coldfield."

"Pleased to meet you, ma'am," I said humbly.

She rounded on me again, along with another piercing look. She wasn't beautiful in the Hollywood way, but her manner alone was the kind to stop traffic. Maybe not Hollywood beauty, but they didn't know everything. Fine bones, fine smooth skin, really good legs from what I could see of them—she had all the right equipment and then some. Like her brother, she projected an arresting sense of power and energy, but hers was more overt and in motion. Her eyes— well, they were the kind that could look right into you, and when they did you better make sure everything inside was up to snuff or she'd know the reason why. That's how she struck me, anyway, after only ten seconds of her hard scrutiny. What she made of me I couldn't tell.

"Likewise," she said. "Now what happened to you?"

"Fell in the lake. I only need to dry out and warm up. But Charles is the one to—"

She raised one hand. "I'll deal with it, Mr. Fleming. You just come along." She moved past me, motioning toward a door. I followed her through a hall, up some narrow stairs to another hall. The sagging wood floors creaked, but were polished and the paint on the walls was fresh.

"What is this place?" I asked.

She glanced back at me. "Miss Tru's," she answered, as though that was explanation enough.

"What do you do here?"

"Help people who need it."

"Like a soup kitchen?"

"More'n that. Here." She opened the door to a frighteningly clean bath, went straight to the huge, claw-footed tub and twisted the hot-water tap. "Get your clothes off an' we'll dry 'em. You want some stew, something hot to drink?"

"Thanks, but I'm not hungry."

She frowned at me. "All right, I'm going to be rude and

ask you—you got any problems being in a colored place?"

"No, ma'am."

"I didn't think so since Clarence brought you, but I had to be sure. Now strip." She went to a cabinet and rummaged in it. I hesitated and she noticed right away. "Don't be bashful, I'm a nurse, and I've seen more naked bodies than most army doctors. You're not going to surprise me."

"A nurse?" I asked in a prompting tone. I slowly shrugged out of Escott's overcoat and took my time on the rest. Nurse or not, she was still female, very female, and I was reluctant to bare all.

"I got a hospital job, sometimes help Doc Clarson and a few others, and I run this place. I don't know what Clarence was thinking bringing you here; I'm just trusting that he had a good reason."

"You don't like his work?"

"His rackets," she corrected with a sniff. "Says he only provides what people want to have, but I know better. You and Charles will have to leave as soon as you can. Sorry I can't be more gracious, but I won't have Clarence bringing me his broken toys to fix all the time. Next thing I know, this place becomes just another flop for the riffraff, and the people who really need help will be too afraid to come in for it."

"You think your brother's riffraff?"

"Yes, and he should be ashamed of himself. Aren't you out of that wet stuff yet?"

"I'm waiting on the tub water."

She gathered up an armful of bandaging and other medical junk and went to the door. "Men," she said, shaking her head. Her heels made a determined clacking sound in the hall and on the stairs. I carefully eased the door shut and breathed a sigh of relief.

The water was almost too hot. I loved it, stepping gingerly in before the tub had quite filled up. The taps were full on, and I wallowed in the rushing heat. When it was deep enough I held my nose and submerged, scrubbing my hair with my free hand. This was so much better than that damned lake. After a minute or so I noticed a change in the light above and surfaced, shaking water from my ears. Shoe Coldfield had come in.

"How's Charles?" I asked, pretending to puff for breath.

"He's getting his chest taped up right now. Would you believe it, she got him to shut up and sit still."

"I can believe it. She seems quite a gal."

"That she is." He started picking up my discarded clothes. "She's got a half-dozen others to do this, but *I'm* the one she sends up. Her idea of atonement for me."

"She said she helps out people, what's the whole story?"

"That's pretty much it—but she's choosy about who she helps. None of my gang, that's for sure. Women 'n kids come here a lot. She feeds 'em, gets 'em work if she can, or they work here to help pay for themselves. Remember Cal with the shoeshine box? He's one of her projects."

"Who pays for it?"

"She does, with her being a nurse, and people donate, help out."

"You donate, too?"

"She won't take my money. Says it's dirty. She's strict about that."

He left and I resolved to try making a donation myself. This bath was certainly worth a fortune to me. I lolled in the heat, stretched this way and that, moaned and groaned with it. In a little wire rack hanging from the tub I found a mirror and a safety razor. The mirror was of no use to me, but I soaped my face good and had my first shave in I don't know how many nights. Maybe I'd look a lot less like a bum to Miss Coldfield.

Figuring it'd take some time to dry my stuff out, I lay back, prepared for a reasonably long soak. When the water cooled, I let some run out the drain, then topped it off with more hot. Escott had a similar tub, but his water heater wasn't nearly this good. The only thing I needed now was some fresh blood and a bolt-hole to sleep the day away. And some of my home earth. Without it with me I wouldn't get much rest; my body would completely conk out, but my uncontrolled mind would keep running frantically on, usually with a series of bad dreams. Waking up after one of those rides left me more tired than when I turned in. I didn't understand why, but had to respect it, so I always tried to have a bit of my earth with me.

My belt was gone. It was the kind with a hidden pocket for money, only mine was stuffed with some good old Cincinnati soil. Probably Cincinnati mud after my dunking, but I could live with it if there was enough left. I wasn't too worried if it was cleaned out, though, since I had more caches of earth hidden around the city, one up in Escott's attic, one in the attic of the house next to us—they didn't know about that—one at my girlfriend's place. . . .

Time for a stab of guilt as I thought of Bobbi. Last I'd seen of her was hours ago when she was on her way to the safety of a mobster's lawyer's house. I had no name, no phone number, no way to contact her except by talking to the mobster—and I didn't know where *he* was, either. Things had gotten pretty crazy and hurried earlier, but this was ridiculous.

I put it off for as long as my conscience could stand, then lurched out of the water, grabbing a towel Trudence had left for me. The floor was cold on my feet, but the rest of me was a nice cherry red as I dried, wrapped the towel around my waist, and padded downstairs.

Coldfield, overcoat off and cup of coffee in hand, was at ease in the kitchen talking with a couple of women as they worked on food preparation. One of them looked up and giggled at the sight of me in my vulnerable and draft-ridden state. I hesitated and shifted from foot to foot, holding on to the towel for dear life.

"Your clothes ain't ready yet," she said.

"I'll take 'em as is, ma'am, if you don't mind."

"What for, you goin' someplace?" asked Coldfield.

"I wanted to check on my girlfriend and have to make some phone calls. Thought it'd be safer if I made them somewhere else."

"Don't have a phone here anyway. No skin off my nose if you want to catch pneumonia, but Tru might have something to say about it."

"I'll risk it."

"Brave man."

"A worried one—my girlfriend . . ."

"Yeah, yeah, women, I know all about that. Get his stuff together, sweet thing," he said, addressing the giggler.

"You ain't my boss, Mr. Coldfield," she stated, lifting her chin.

His jaw sagged a bit, then he recovered. "Okay, okay, I forgot where I was for a minute." He went to a clotheshorse rack that had been set up before an open oven and yanked my pants free of it, tossing them at me to catch one-handed. If not completely dry, then they were at least not soaking. My leather belt was intact; I could smell the damp earth hidden inside. Good, one less thing to think about.

"What the hell . . . ?" Coldfield held up my shirt and undershirt, which were riddled with holes: four distinct large ones front and back and a number of smaller ones where the bullets and grenade shrapnel had gone through. Most of the blood had washed away, but there was some faint staining. My quite visible hide, however, was all healed up by now.

"It was Charles's idea of a disguise," I said, improvising. "He's got a closet full of things a ragman wouldn't touch."

Coldfield grunted with distaste and threw the stuff at me. I went back to the bathroom and dressed, came down again.

Coldfield pulled on his overcoat. "You'll need a ride," he told me.

"I can walk."

"The hell you can. Show your white ass in this part of town and someone'll take offense at the sight. I gotta protect their sensibilities. Not everyone's as tolerant as me 'n Tru."

"Oh."

"Come on."

The pea jacket I'd worn since the start of this business was still pretty spongy, but I thought I could handle it now that I was warmed up. Most of the time excess heat and cold doesn't bother me, but Lake Michigan was just too damn much at once. The jacket was also marked by a number of holes, but I pretended not to notice them.

The girl giggled again as we left. It might have been fun to go invisible and stick around to see what she and her friend would be talking about for the next few minutes, but I followed Coldfield down the steps and back into his Nash.

"How's Charles?"

"Tru dragged him upstairs to get some rest. Last I saw she was tucking him in and making him swallow a bunch of aspirin. Only reason she's not done more for you yet is that accent of his keeps her hanging around him. He can just open his trap and charm the feathers off a goose without even trying."

"He going to be all right today? Your sister said we'd have to leave."

He hit the starter, fed it some gas. The motor muttered to smooth life and started purring. "She talks tougher than she is, no need to worry about him, but I'll catch hell for taking you out before she's had a chance to check you over."

"Blame it on me." The last thing I wanted was her trying to find my nonexistent pulse.

"Oh, I plan to."

He pulled out of the alley into a larger street. I turned for a look at the front of the place. Still drab, like the rest of the neighborhood, with no sign to indicate what was inside. I asked him about it.

"She runs it like a speak," he said. "You have to know about it to go there."

"Why's that? If she's helping people, what's she hiding it for?"

"Something to do with her bein' a nurse. She thinks if the hospital she works for finds out about it she could lose her place with them, get struck off or something like that."

"But if she's doing good for people, why should they—"

"Because it's an unofficial kind of place. She's trying to get it legitimate, permits and stuff, but it's taking time, and the way she sees it, a hungry baby can't wait until someone in the city office gets off their butt long enough to find the right stamp for the papers. And you don't talk about this, yourself. She worked too hard to get where she is, first one in the family to really go to school and finish it out. She's got more guts than me."

"You didn't finish?"

"I had to make money and my feet itched, so I built me a shoeshine box for a nickel and started walking and working. That's how I ended up in Canada knocking on the back door of a theater there. They needed someone to fix their shoes and Charles talked 'em into hiring me for that, then into taking me on for backstage carpentry work. Don't know how he did it—they didn't exactly want a black hanging around the company, but when that guy makes his mind up to it, he could sell snow to a polar bear. Before I knew what was happening, he had me building sets and reading and memorizing everything from Bertolt Brecht to Oscar Wilde.''

"And Shakespeare?''

"Yeah, him, too.''

"Must have been some life you had.''

He laughed once. "Heaven and hell. Times be that I was the only colored man in the whole territory. Some people would come to the plays we did just to get a look at me like I was some kind of a zoo display, then the company wised up and took advantage of it. Once I got billed as 'the famous Mr. C. Coldfield of London as seen by royal command at Buckingham Palace'—I got good at copying Charles's accent—that was when we did *Othello*. Nobody in the berg knew any better, so we got away with it.''

"Sounds great.''

He made a flat, disparaging snort. "Hell, any idiot in blackface can do the part. I never really enjoyed playing it. What I really wanted was the lead in *Richard the Second*. And don't tell Charles I said that, he busted his ass to get the *Othello* performance set up for me.''

"Ever want to go back to acting?''

"Hell, yes, but I don't see how, the way things are these days. Closest I get is running my club. Besides, I got political ambitions. Ain't no one going to elect an actor to anything important, which is stupid, since that's the one person who knows best how to swing a crowd.''

"All politicians are actors, though, one way or another.''

"Yeah, but the voters don't like having their faces rubbed in it, gives the whole business away for the farce it is when you get an actor up there telling them what they want to hear. Just look at Hitler, the way he hypnotizes 'em. That bastard should be doing opera, not running a country.''

"Opera?''

"Yeah, he's got a beautiful voice.''

"All that screaming?"

"Huh, you should hear him when he's just talking normal. It's terrifying. That big radio of mine picks up Germany and I listen in sometimes. He's got the most compelling, beautiful voice I ever hope to hear this side of heaven, but the stuff he says . . ." Coldfield shook his head. "Got more venom than a cobra and he'd be happy as hell to see people like me dropping dead at his feet, only it'd spoil the shine on his boots. Musta tied his gut up in knots but good when Jesse Owens won all those medals last year." He broke off and chuckled for a while over that one.

"You know German?"

"Enough to listen to. We had a kraut in the company and Escott would get him to talk German in exchange for cleaning up his accent so the audience could understand him. It was really funny trying to do *Hamlet* when King Claudius was sounding more Deutsche than Danish."

I laughed. "This is all new to me, he doesn't say that much about what he did in those days."

"Has a reason for it."

My ears pricked up. "What's that?"

He shook his head. "When he's ready to tell you, he probably will."

Familiar territory there. I wondered what Escott's big secret was. "It have to do with why he's always sticking his neck out farther than what's good for him?"

He shot me a hard glance. "Guess you got some brains rolling around in that head of yours, kid."

We were about the same age. My condition made me look younger. I let it pass. "Guess I do. So what is it?"

"Uh-uh. Not my table. Tell you what, get him drunk some night. Once he stops quoting Shakespeare you might learn something. In the meantime keep an eye on the fool so he doesn't get himself killed."

"Do my best. You, too?"

"My best, though he makes it damned difficult. Always ready to run into a riot. Like tonight, going to see Angela. I knew it stunk, but he talked me into going anyway. I got more sense than that, but once he gets aimed at something . . ."

"I know. Like a train on a track."

He shook his head again, then asked, "Where you want to go?"

"Just drop me near the Stockyards."

He misinterpreted, as I'd hoped. "There's bound to be someone watching Charles's office."

"Just one of the things I want to check on. If it looks clear I'll go in and make my calls, then find a place to flop for the day."

"The hell you are. I'll catch it from both Tru and Charles if I don't bring you back."

Damn. And I was hoping to avoid this. I kept shut until he pulled over and parked. His car had a lot of nice extras, like an overhead bulb that came on when I opened the door to get out. It gave me the light I needed to focus on his eyes . . . and get his full attention.

"Shoe, I won't be coming back until tonight," I told him, holding his gaze steadily. "But that's all right. You can go along to your sister's place and take it easy."

His normally tense expression was relaxed now, almost serene. "Yeah, sure," he murmured in a distant voice.

"I'll call your club around sundown so we can hook up again then. You guys just sit tight and don't worry about me, I'll be fine."

"You got it," he promised.

Then I let my control over him slip away nice and easy. I didn't care much about doing this kind of thing, especially to someone I liked, but I was getting good at it. He had no idea of what had just hit him and would think everything I'd said to be perfectly normal and reasonable. "Make sure Escott gets lots of rest, he needs it. Sit on him if you have to, okay?"

"I'll leave that to Tru, she intimidates the hell out of him."

"Maybe he enjoys it."

I levered from of the car, then turned and put my hand out. "Thank you."

It seemed to startle him, but he recovered and we shook briefly. "Keep your head down, kid."

"I will." I hurried away. He put the car in gear and took the next turn back to his part of town.

Over the last several months I'd gotten thoroughly acquainted with the layout of Chicago's smelliest landmark, the Stockyards. Coldfield had dropped me within a block of the southern end of things. Five minutes later and I'd either walked or passed invisibly through all the various barriers meant to keep the cattle in and the public out and was in the midst of the smaller pens, looking for a likely dinner.

It was noisy, with all that mooing, and it never stopped, like they knew what they were there for. Maybe they did know, since mixed in with the thick farmyard stench and the mud was the smell of blood from the slaughterhouses and processing plants. Unless you were used to it—or craved it like me—it could really ruin your night.

I breathed in the bloodsmell and felt my teeth budding in response. Yes, I'd fed not so many hours ago, but the morphine-tainted stuff had messed me up something bad, had nearly killed me by default. Time now to replace it.

One of the pens had only three occupants, and they looked somewhat cleaner than average. That's an important detail to me, considering what I have to do to get my dinner. I slipped inside and made calming talk with the nearest cow. This was another version of the hypnosis I'd done to Coldfield, but much more basic and less of a blow to the old conscience. I talked and stared and got Bossy to hold still, then eased down on my heels to find the big vein in one of her legs. She remained quiescent as my corner teeth swiftly cut through her tough hide and the first burst of red life hit my tongue.

God, it had been *forever* since I'd had anything this good. Or felt this good about having it.

My girlfriend Bobbi had been a big help to me there. Being a vampire didn't mean I was automatically comfortable with the business of drinking blood. Just talking cold on it and it sounds pretty revolting, but Bobbi finally got it through my thick skull that this was nothing to be ashamed about, especially when it was the only game in town when it came to my continued well-being. I finally stopped worrying about what other people might think if they saw me—fat chance of that since I'm always careful—and just drank it down, having finally admitted to myself just how much I really enjoyed it.

It's hard to explain what the stuff does to me, only that prior to my change I'd never felt anything quite like it before. Sometimes it soothes; others, it hits like a hammer. Either way was fine, more than fine. Since my heart doesn't pump I don't know how the stuff flushes me with that special kind of heat that flows from deep inside right out to my toes and fingers. But it feels great. Better than great. Sometimes when I'm really starved, the tide of it flooding through me is almost as good as sex—but only almost. Making love to Bobbi is something else again.

But I'll talk about that another time.

After a few minutes I had as much as I could hold. Unless I got on Angela Paco's shit list once more and she started throwing hand grenades again, I'd be good for two or three nights now. Usually I made a stop like this every other night to keep myself feeling fit, and I never went more than four nights without feeding, too dangerous. Not that I'd turn into some kind of mad-dog maniac and attack people, but it screws up my being able to think straight and I could get clumsy, get caught.

I pulled back and pinched the vein, blowing on the two wounds I'd made until they clotted over, then I vanished and drifted free of the pen. The animals didn't like that and protested, but by then I was streaming away from the area. Back outside I partially re-formed just enough to see where I was and if it was safe to go from ghost to full solidity. It was. With no one else about, I materialized in a dark patch between two streetlights. Checked the time again, then remembered my watch had stopped. *Have to get it fixed or buy another*, I thought as I got my bearings and pressed on in the direction of Escott's office.

His rent was cheap owing to its location near the yards. He could afford better, but seemed to like this joint. Also, he was the half owner of a tobacco shop backing his place that faced the street on the other side the block, so maybe he stuck around to keep an eye on things. It was convenient for both of us.

I checked the street in front of the office, but saw no stray cars that didn't belong. That didn't mean much, though. I went around the block and entered through the closed tobacco shop, then up its back stairs to a jumbled storage area full of old boxes and junk. One particular crate against the back wall marked the location of the concealed door Escott had installed there. He always excused his indulgence in something so theatrical by saying it was indeed a leftover habit from his life on the stage, but I knew better. He was like a schoolkid about having secret passages and hidden exits handy.

Myself, I just flowed through the cracks in the wall and went solid again on the other side, standing quiet in the tiny washroom for Escott's office and listening.

Nothing to hear. That was a relief. I'd been afraid one or the other of the gangs had sent someone over to lie in wait, but the place was empty. However, I did find that people had been through it pretty thoroughly. Plenty of light came through the broken blinds for me to use. Just as well, because the lamps were wrecked. The back room where Escott stashed a cot for catnaps was all torn up. Someone had kicked everything around: cot, radio, a few books and papers. The front where he received clients was in the same shape: desk overturned, file cabinets open and gutted. Nothing that couldn't be cleaned up and replaced, but it made me want to crack the responsible party's head in just to hear what kind of sound it made. No telling who was behind it, the ex–Kyler faction or the struggling-to-come-back Paco gang. Flip a coin.

The phone was off the hook and making funny noises. I dropped the receiver back in place and righted the desk. The drawers were all out, their contents thrown around. I put them back, found the chair that went with it all, marveling that it was still in one piece. Tried the phone. It clicked a few times, then the tone came back and I dialed the Nightcrawler Club. I let it ring a long, long time.

Everyone was probably asleep, in jail and trying to get out, or elsewhere laying low. Much earlier this night the late, unlamented Vaughn Kyler arranged to have the cops in his pocket raid the place. I arrived just in the nick to keep his man from bumping off the manager, Gordy, who was a friend of mine.

Friend. He was a gangster as tough as the rest, cold as sleet when he needed to be, and I'd once let him beat me up last summer when I'd been trying to learn something from his now deceased boss. Still, he knew about me being a vampire and it didn't bother him, and he was very protective of Bobbi. That counted for a lot in my book. One of these nights I'd have to ask what his other name was.

Then miracle of miracles, Gordy answered.

"Jeez, am I glad to hear you," I said, my voice full of relief. "How's—"

"Your friend's okay," he said abruptly.

"My friend . . . ? What the—" I broke off, belatedly figuring out something was wrong. He would never normally refer to Bobbi that way. He'd use her name. "I'm—I'm glad to hear it. What else has been happening?"

"The bulls are gone, we're just doing a little cleaning up."

"You all right?"

"Can't complain."

"Want me to come over and help out like earlier?"

"It's nothing like that. I'm fine, we're all fine for real, but I don't have a lot to say to you right now."

Bullshit. He had plenty to say and hear, but someone—as in John Law—was tapping his line. "I understand. But I'd like to talk with you sometime soon."

"It's late, maybe you can come by tomorrow just like you did the last time when you surprised me and those other guys."

Right, he wanted to see me, but that I should sneak into the club. "Yeah, I can do that."

"Nothing's going on here, now anyway." A pause, then in a tone more like normal, said, "You okay?"

"Can't complain. Been busy, too. Tell you later." Maybe I could have figured a way to tell him about Chaven's death and that Angela had gotten her father back safe, but Gordy had other methods of finding out stuff like that, so there wasn't much point to it. "And tell my friend . . . send 'em my warm regards. They're really all right?"

"Annoyed, but safe and sound."

"Will I be able to see 'em there?"

"You can make book on it."

"Thanks. Thanks for everything."

"No problem. See you then." He hung up.

I didn't think we'd been on long enough for the call to be traced. Fine by me; I could imagine all too well the fun and games if the cops tried arresting this creature of the night. I'd had enough laughs for one evening.

At least a big load of worry about Bobbi was off my mind. Next to me she couldn't have a better guardian angel than Gordy.

Went to the back room, fiddled with the radio, but the works were all smashed in. No way to tell the time with any accuracy except by instinct and a look at the sky—and Gordy's left-handed warning about it being late. I peered out the broken slats of the blinds and saw things were getting lighter, with more traffic taking up space on the slush-covered roads. Not long now.

Through the washroom wall into the shop's storage. One of the boxes there was much larger than the rest, but you couldn't tell that since only the narrow end was visible. The bulk of it was hidden by others stacked around and on top. Under the raspy dust and the rich smell of the tobacco I could scent my earth. Without disturbing the other boxes, I sieved inside.

Tight squeeze when I went solid, and I hate small spaces. I hoped I wouldn't be awake for long.

Dark. *Totally* black. My eyes can pick up and use the least little shred of light so long as there's some available. Nothing like that here. Didn't help my claustrophobia at all.

I shifted noisily in the damn thing, knees and elbows knocking the sides, until the bag of earth was sitting on my chest, not poking into my back.

And waited.

I hate this part, too, the waiting until the sun comes. It makes me think about death.

The daylight comas are my portion of that long sleep, my payment for cheating it the rest of the time, I suppose. I don't mind them too much, just the waiting for them to happen. At home, in my hideaway in Escott's basement, I'd sometimes put off dropping into my earth-lined bed until the absolute last second. It gave me a moment's illusion that I had some control over the process. No such luxury here. Nor as safe. Once I was out the whole block could burn to the foundations and I wouldn't know I was being killed all over again.

Damn, but I hate—

My eyelids slammed down, and I stopped being me for the day.

2

Jolt of panic when I woke, directly inspired by the absolute darkness cocooning me. In my regular sleeping area I always leave a light on. Muddled, thinking I was falling, I twisted in the narrow box and slapped my hands hard on what should have been an earth-filled mattress. Struck wood instead.

Ow.

Then I remembered. Made myself relax.

Usually, my wakings are quiet and smooth, my daylight rest complete and oblivious, and I pick up exactly where I left off, but this time . . . this time I'd *dreamed*. That wasn't normal. Though not nearly as clear and horrific as the ones that came when I was separated from my soil, these hadn't been pleasant, what little I could recall of them. Escott thought they went on regardless of the presence of my home earth, that it only kept me from being aware of them. His idea was that the earth was some kind of safety valve attached to the larger one of the dreams.

The falling sensation had been me taking another sickening headfirst dive off the *Elvira*, I was sure. I glumly wondered if this was going to be a permanent thing. Maybe my home earth was wearing out, but more likely it was a last shred of the morphine making itself felt, or perhaps too much had happened in too little time and my brain was having trouble digesting it all. Either way I didn't want a repeat come the next evening. Not that there was much I could do about it.

I floated out of the box and stretched. Quietly. From the sounds below, the tobacco shop was still open for business.

Back through to the washroom, where I brushed my teeth with my finger and rinsed with mouth gargle, fighting off the urge to gag before thoroughly spitting the stuff out. I don't care much for the process, but sometimes the smell of blood could linger on my breath after a heavy feeding and be picked up by others. Offensive to my friends, it was also a telltale clue to people who knew about vampires being real. Not that there were many of those around, but I was only doing my part to keep it that way, since my one encounter with them had been a pretty lousy experience. They'd decided I was a public enemy and nearly got me killed. Dammit, Stoker should have written his big book from the vampire's point of view; it might have improved things for the rest of us.

Speaking of revealing smells, I was fairly certain my wool pea jacket was going musty. Damn all this crap. I wanted a real shave, fresh clean clothes, and about five years of vacation. No rest for the righteous—or even those with seriously bruised consciences. Time away from this dog-and-pony show would have to wait until I found out how the day went for everyone else.

The outer office was as I'd left it. I tried the phone, figuring it pretty unlikely for us to be tapped like Gordy, and dialed the private number for Coldfield's club, the Shoe Box.

Escott answered. "Hallo, I thought it might be you."

"Time of day tip you off?"

"More like evening, old man."

"You guys all right?"

"Rested and restless."

"But quiet?"

"If you like that sort of thing."

"Heart and soul."

"Fortunately one of us has his senses. Shoe and I went out to the Paco mansion today."

If I'd had anything like blood pressure anymore, the top of my head would have blown right off just then.

"Jack?"

"I'm here. Charles, in the name of God, what the *hell* were you *thinking*?"

"That I cannot operate in a vacuum of information."

The man was incurable. I beat back all comment wanting to spill out on what an idiot he was and accepted the situation. He'd probably heard it earlier from Coldfield on the drive out. "What did you find?"

"Aside from a few craters and lines of tire tracks weaving over the grounds, nothing. I couldn't persuade Shoe to go very close, but as far as we could determine with field glasses, the place appears to be deserted. After a bit of futile observation we came back to the city and took a detour along Lakeshore Drive and noted that the *Elvira* is back in the yacht basin. She also appears to be deserted. Shoe refused to pursue that one as well. If you were up to it, I thought—"

"Oh, no, I'm not. I've had enough of boats and that damned lake to last me forever. Besides, we both know Angela and what's left of Kyler's mob have probably found holes to pull in after them."

"Actually, we don't know that at all. They could be huddled in the mansion cellar, or have left Chicago altogether. Not likely, but it is unwise to overlook all possibilities. I've asked Shoe about lending a hand in a search, but he is not too terribly inclined to risk any of his people by having them check around."

"I don't blame him for that."

"Nor I. He's more than willing to help *us* get out of town, but that is not a path I wish to take in regard to the resolution of this situation.''

I sighed, pinching the bridge of my nose. ''Yeah, same again here. It ain't gonna go away unless I put my foot into it with Angela one more time.''

''Indeed. The only way out that I can see is if you could privately talk to Miss Paco and firmly request she cease and desist any plans she may have to eliminate either of us.''

''I can do that, but I have to find her first.''

''If you're not enamored of searching the yacht, then perhaps you would not object to looking the mansion over instead. It might provide a suggestion as to where everyone has got to.''

I groused and grumbled on for a minute, just so he knew I wasn't a pushover. My objections mostly had to do with personal comfort. ''This is something that can wait until I'm ready for it. Trudence took one look at me last night and thought I was a bum, and I'm ready to agree with her. I'm going to go by the house first and change.''

''If you feel the need.''

''You're damn right I do. I might as well check the mail while I'm at it. You want anything from there?''

''I left my pipe and a pouch of tobacco in the front room, and you might pull a bit of cash from the safe. Fifty should do it.''

He'd surprised me. ''That much?''

''I don't know how long all this will take and want sufficient funds for at least a few weeks.''

''Jeez, Charles, if this goes on for that long, I'm gonna be bug-eyed crazy.''

''Then we shall have to marshal our best efforts toward concluding things as quickly as possible.''

We meaning me. ''Yeah, yeah. But only after I pull on a

pair of shoes that don't squeak. Gimme a couple hours and I'll come by the club with your stuff."

"I'd be most obliged."

I cradled the receiver. He'd want to hitch along, but on this I'd do my Rock of Gibraltar imitation against getting talked into it. I'd cracked some ribs once—hell, they'd been broken—and hadn't liked it one bit. He was going to rest or I'd save him the trouble of suicide by overwork and kill him myself.

The next call was to Gordy's; he didn't let it ring so long this time.

"It's me, how're things going?" I could take a good and probably accurate guess, but wanted to give him the chance to recognize my voice.

"Not so bad. Your friend sends regards back, wants to talk with you pretty soon."

"It might be a while before I can come over, I got some business to clean up first."

"How about we meet somewhere?"

"Sounds fine. Maybe you and my friend could go out, get some air, then call me at home in about an hour." By then I'd be in a fit state to talk to my beautiful lady.

"Can do," said Gordy, and hung up.

One cab ride later—and looking the way I did it was damned difficult to find one—and I was approaching the house by way of the alley that ran behind the buildings. Things looked all right there, though it's a sad day when you have to act like your own home is a bear trap. A shame, too, since it's a nice enough place, certainly much better than the cheap hotels I'd flopped in since I first began writing for newspapers and found out not everyone, myself included, has Pulitzer potential.

The house was three solid stories of brick. A couple of decades back when the neighborhood wasn't so nice it used to be the local brothel, then Escott bought the empty hulk last year and started fixing the insides up. I had a couple of rooms and a bath on the second floor, and a very unofficial chamber hidden behind a false brick wall in the basement. In its secret and silent fireproof safety I usually slept the day away in reasonable security and comfort. At night it also doubled as my office, so the clatter of my typewriter wouldn't disturb Escott's attempts at overcoming his insomnia.

I always entered this retreat using my sieving through the walls gimmick, but there was also a concealed trapdoor under the kitchen table. Escott used it to duck down to my room the other night in order to hide out from yet more of Kyler's men. When they couldn't find him, they ransacked the place and hung around waiting for me to turn up. It wasn't to present me with a bunch of posies.

Because of me, Vaughn Kyler had missed collecting the payment on an important gambling debt. He had one solution for those interfering in his rackets: make the poor bastards disappear forever. He was too crazy for me to hypnotize and knew about my own kind of vanishing act, which made him a major threat to me and mine. While I was still trying to figure out how best to deal with him, Angela Paco had dropped herself into the fight like one of her own grenades and with about the same effect. Her game was getting her kidnapped father Frank back along with the control of his gang, and she didn't much care who she had to kill to do it. Since Kyler had felt the same way about her it was a hell of a mess for me, the cops, and all the other gangs in the city. Though Kyler was safely dead, the dust had yet to settle. I could figure everyone who had a hint of what was going on was waiting to see what would happen next between his lieutenants and little Angela.

Just put me at the head of the line.

All was dark and quiet now as I circled the area of the

house, just the usual cars parked in their usual places, including my dark blue Buick out front. Escott usually kept his Nash (a secondhand purchase from Coldfield) in the garage out back, only now it was in a shop somewhere getting fixed. The motor was fine, but when the cops see a car drive past with the glass starred and cracked and the body pocked with a hundred or so bullet dents along one of its extra-thick steel sides—all courtesy of Kyler's goons—they get curious.

The back door to the house was locked; I left it that way and slipped inside nice and quiet, re-formed in the kitchen, and listened.

Nothing to hear but more quiet. The place had a hollow, deserted feel to it that I didn't like. My back hairs were up, but I wasn't sure if it was for something real or imagined. Hard for me to tell the difference after all I'd been through, my nerves were much too sharp, the edges ready to cut. A man shouldn't have to live like this. Grimacing, I shrugged the stiffness out of my shoulders.

We hadn't had a chance to clean up much since all hell broke loose. I'm not as demanding as Escott when it comes to keeping things neat, so that wasn't the problem so much as the fact the house had been invaded. Someone had broken into my private territory and the violation hit me the same as with the office: I wanted some skulls to bust, preferably those of the ones responsible, except they were already dead. Guys like Chaven, Vic, Hodge, Kyler . . .

Had to stretch once more as my shoulders stubbornly bunched up again. I was giving names to roaches, and who in their right mind feels guilty about a dead roach? It was past time to stop doing this to myself or I'd be ready for the loony bin like Frank Paco.

Walked slowly into the hall, still listening. Nothing. Good. Went to the front door, unlocked and opened it, and pulled a wad of mail from the box, got the papers, too. My arms were full when I backed inside, kicked the door shut, turned, and abruptly came nose to muzzle with a gun.

I don't know who was the more surprised, me or Deiter.

Escott's Webley, I thought a split second before disappearing again, mail, papers, and all. Having been shot several times too many I didn't care who saw.

Through my distorted hearing I heard Deiter's sharp cry of horrified shock. He'd been on the boat last night, had pulled the tarp from my apparently dead body and dragged me toward the edge of the deck ready to roll into the water. Chaven, repeating what Kyler had said, had told him about my being able to vanish; until now Deiter had no reason to believe him.

Great, another loose end to tie up. Well, I'd put a bow on this one.

"Where are you?" he said, his voice all shaky and hoarse. "Where?"

He had guts. Given the same circumstances, I'd have hoofed it out of there and kept on going.

I floated around him to the front room where he wouldn't see me and went solid only long enough to drop everything on the couch. No need to move after that, hearing the noise of it, he came to investigate. He walked right through me, which was not so much fun for him because the air gets real cold in the space I occupy. According to Escott, the chill goes a bit more than bone deep, as in right down to the soul.

"Where are you?" Deiter demanded, still sounding like a kid whose voice had just broken. You could almost feel sorry for the bastard.

I reappeared right behind him, grabbed the gun with one hand, and snaked my free arm around his neck, lifting him clean off his feet. Being tall enough, I got away with it slick as sweat. He choked and struggled, and managed a kick or two to my shins, but never really had a chance, and I think he knew it. I wrested the gun away, firmly tapped the side of his head with the grip, and felt the sudden sag of his weight. His heels making long black marks on the wood floor, I hauled him around, dropping him on the couch with the other junk.

Listened again. Nothing. Not at first.

I tiptoed into the hall and noticed the door to the understairs closet was open. He'd been hiding there, being particularly quiet, and slipped out to shoot me—Escott really, since I was supposed to be dead—while I'd been busy with the mail.

Time to close my eyes and really concentrate. Now that I was focusing on it I could hear them, like rats in the walls. I'd almost rather have the rats, they're smaller and harder to catch, but they don't pack any heat. Had to assume the human vermin lurking upstairs were all armed—they'd sooner be caught with no pants than leave their guns at home. Couldn't blame 'em for it, it's a rough world.

I checked the Webley. Deiter had reloaded it, though where he'd turned up the .455 ammunition I'd like to find out. Escott often complained about the stuff sometimes being too scarce for him to target-shoot regularly.

Tempting as it was, I left the Webley on the hall table. I wouldn't really need it this time. Too noisy. No reason to disturb the neighbors, after all. Besides, Escott did have a number of other useful weapons lying handy around the house. Left over from his acting days were a few working crossbows, spears for the spear carriers—stuff he'd made as stage props. There were other, more practical items tucked away in odd places and overlooked like old pencil stubs. I tried the drawer on the hall table. Pencil stubs. Also a dried out fountain pen, scrap paper, rubber bands, a bowie knife that needed sharpening, and a couple of blackjacks—normal stuff for this joint. Grinning, I picked out and hefted the larger blackjack, liking the feel of it.

Near as I could tell from their breathing—the one sound

besides their heartbeat they couldn't stop—there was a guy in my set of rooms and another in Escott's down at the end of the hall. They must have heard the business with Deiter, but hadn't moved. Cagey bunch. I wondered how long they'd been waiting for Escott to come home. I was pretty sure from seeing Deiter's raw amazement that I was not their intended target. That led to the question of who sent them. Had Deiter taken over things from Chaven? Was he trying to pick up where he and Kyler had left off? Escott wasn't much of a threat when compared to Angela, so why still be bothering with him?

I'd get the answers shortly, first I had to flush out some rats.

Ghosting upstairs and thus making no sound at all, I vanished completely to enter my rooms. The door was nearly shut with the guy hiding behind it, probably peering through the crack to watch the upper hall. It didn't take much to put him out of business. I went solid and whacked him behind one ear with the blackjack. He dropped with a very satisfying thump. Son of a bitch, but I was actually getting my wish about busting some skulls.

Listened. The other guy held his place. I kept grinning, deciding to let him do all the work.

"Psst! I got him!" I whispered, putting some excitement into it. He took the bait and rushed out to see, but by then I'd vanished and got behind him. Whack again. At this rate I'd be breaking Babe Ruth's record for hitting 'em home.

No lights were on, so I remedied that for a closer look and was surprised to recognize them both. They'd tried this hide-and-hit game the other night during an attempt to kidnap Bobbi from her dressing room at the Top Hat Club. She'd helped me get the drop on them, then the club bouncers took it from there.

The big one was Chick, and the shorter guy with the

scraped face was Tinny. Much more of this and there wouldn't be any of the Kyler gang left to play with. I relieved them of their supplies of deadly hardware and went down to the front room to check on Deiter. He was still inert, but there was no need to take chances. I found some rope and trussed them up good, using dust rags I found under the sink to gag them.

Then I stopped, stood back, and took stock of the situation. All three were downstairs now, tied up snug—and me with no idea on what to do with them. I couldn't exactly take them to the cops. The more I thought of it the more exasperated I got, which was not a good state for me to be in when I started with the questions that were already bumping around up in my head. The last time I'd done the hypnosis stuff when I was angry had been with Frank Paco. That was why he went nuts, because my temper got away from me and tore things up in his mind. I didn't want to do that to anyone else, even if they were rats.

But the longer I thought about them and how they'd been waiting here to kill Escott, the worse I got. I needed time to cool down, to get in control again.

So I said to hell with them and went upstairs to do what I'd come here for in the first place.

By the time I was clean, properly shaved, and in fresh clothes, I felt a whole lot better about me vs. the rest of the world. My captive goons didn't have it so good. Chick had woken up and nearly spit out his gag—couldn't blame him since it smelled (and tasted) like dust and furniture wax—but I stuffed it back in place despite his mumbled and no doubt obscene protests. He started to thrash around, so I fixed him with a look, and when I had his undivided attention told him to take a long nap. He instantly dropped off.

No need to worry about Tinny, he was still out to lunch,

but Deiter was starting to come around. He was taking his time, though, so I went to the kitchen and called the Shoe Box again.

Coldfield answered.

"Something happened," I told him. "Three of Kyler's goons were at the house to jump Charles. I got 'em all quiet, but I don't know what to do with them. Any ideas?"

He said "shit" a few times then demanded details. There weren't that many to share—well, that many I *could* share—but I filled in the blanks a bit, giving their names. He repeated the whole thing to Escott, then finally turned the phone over to him.

Once more I said I didn't know what to do with them.

"You can't let them wander loose." His voice went faint as he turned from the receiver. "Shoe, do you think—"

"Uh-uh, I'm in as deep as I ever want to get. I ain't playing zookeeper to Kyler's leavings."

Escott came back to me. "Give me a little time and I'll see what I can arrange." He hung up just as I heard Coldfield start with another objection.

It looked like we all had a peachy night ahead.

I got a glass, put some water in it, and went to the front room, sitting on the coffee table to face Deiter. Pouring the water on his face had been my initial idea to wake him, but Escott would only get all pained over having a damp couch. Instead I dipped my fingers and sprinkled. It had about the same effect. Deiter squinted and groaned and tried to move out of range, then his eyelids flew open.

After that he just didn't have a prayer.

He went under fast and hard, and I pulled out the gag, certain he wouldn't shout the house down. His eyes were as empty as a dead man's. I didn't like the look, but tough knuckles and all that.

"Deiter, we're going to have a little talk. You want to tell me everything. When I ask a question you will answer. Right?"

His jaw trembled and went slack, matching the rest of his expression. "Uh-huh."

"Now tell me what's going on with Kyler's people."

"Kyler's dead."

"I got that, what are his people doing?"

"Keeping low."

"And who gave you the bright idea of coming over here?"

"Frank Paco."

That stopped me short. Frank Paco was barely in shape to dress himself, let alone order a hit. "You mean Angela Paco?"

"She was just passing Frank's orders."

So, she was bulling through with her game of using her father as the front man, enabling her to run his mob. "You're working for Paco now?"

"He made us a sweet deal."

"I just bet he did. Did he hire all of you away?"

"Some. Others are holding off, see what happens."

"You expecting something to happen?"

"New York's sending a guy out to pick up the slack."

"What guy?"

"Sullivan, Sean Sullivan."

The name meant nothing to me, though Irish mobsters were not rare and as tough as they come. While the others would kill you for a reason, the Irish would ace you just for the hell of it. "What's he going to do?"

"Pick up the slack."

"Yeah, I got that part, but what's he going to do about Paco?"

"Don't know."

"What's Paco going to do about him?"

"Don't know."

Deiter was, after all, just one of the soldiers, why should Angela let him in on the big decisions? Or maybe she didn't know what to do herself.

Yeah, fat chance of that. She'd moved in one big hurry today, hiring on muscle from Kyler's leavings before they could scatter too far. "You were supposed to come here and kill Charles Escott for Paco?"

"Uh-huh."

"Where is he? Where's Angela?"

"Flora's Dance Studio."

"Where's that?" He didn't have the number, but gave the street name and that it was close to a movie theater. I realized the latter was an all-night place I'd been to a few times. I dimly remembered seeing a sign in the area advertising dancing, but the joint was always closed by the time I came around to catch a late feature. "How many people does she have with her?"

And so it went, with me finally taking notes to keep it all straight. Angela still had her core of insiders: Doc, Newton, Lester, and, of course, Daddy Frank. No news of Opal, though. She hadn't arrived by the time Deiter left with his friends to settle Angela's accounts with Escott.

"When does she expect you to report in?"

"When the job's done."

"What, later tonight, tomorrow?"

"When the job's done."

I was getting a headache. Too much of this eyeballing stuff makes me feel like I've got a rope twisted tight around my temples.

The phone rang. I told Deiter to take a nap. Maybe Escott had a solution for me. Only it wasn't Escott, but Bobbi. My headache lifted.

"Hi, sweetheart," I said. It was so great to hear her voice

again I wanted to hug the phone. "I've missed you. Is it safe to talk?"

"Yeah, Gordy drove us to a drugstore not far from your house. We can be over in a minute."

"Hang on, there're complications." I gave her the short version about my new guests and got some rather unladylike language back. "Easy, this ain't my fault."

"I know, Jack, but how much longer is this going to go on? Oh, don't answer, it'll only aggravate me more. Look, can you blindfold these jerks or something? I want to *see* you."

I tried to think of a good reason for her to stay away, and did, several of them, but talked myself out of 'em. In their present state Angela's goons were no threat to Bobbi. "Okay, but come in by the back way. Gordy can put the car in the garage."

"We'll be right there." She disconnected fast, maybe worried I'd change my mind.

One minute, then two, with me waiting in the kitchen peering out the window every few seconds before I saw the car lights turning into the alley. Like Kyler, Gordy favored a Caddie, and I had a bad moment before I got a good look at his big form behind the wheel and could relax. He slowed and stopped long enough for Bobbi to slip out, then eased the car into the garage while she sprinted up the steps to the porch. I had the door open already and she nearly knocked me backward onto the kitchen table when she threw herself into my welcoming arms.

"Easy, baby," I said, laughing, "it hasn't been that long."

"It's been years," she said, then fastened her lips onto mine as if to make up for lost time. It was better than great until she had to come up for air.

For someone who had been dragged without warning away from her club engagement and forced into hiding for the last few days, she looked wonderful. Short platinum hair shining, hazel eyes bright, and a smile that made my knees go weak every time I saw it flash in my direction, I knew without a doubt I was the luckiest s.o.b. walking the planet. When I last saw her she'd been in her stage costume, a white satin safari outfit with patent-leather riding boots, incongruously topped by a fur coat and hat. She still had the latter two on, but had turned up a less showy pair of dark pants tucked into ankle-high hiking boots, and a red plaid flannel shirt.

"What's this?" I asked, holding her away for a look. "You going off to a cabin in the woods?"

"Only if you come, too. The wife of Gordy's lawyer loaned them to me. She loves to ice-fish."

"Well, the wife of Gordy's lawyer has a helluva figure. You keeping okay?"

"I'm fine, but you—" Her turn to look. I collected a frown.

"What?"

"You've been through the wringer—backward. Three or four times."

How did she always know? I pulled her close, just wanting to hold her. "Guilty. But I'm feeling better by the minute."

"Glad to hear it," said Gordy, filling most of the doorway as he came into the kitchen. I lifted one hand away from hugging Bobbi and put it out to shake his. He always seemed a little surprised at the least sign of friendship from me. "Want to tell us your side of things?"

"My side? What have you heard from others?"

"Just rumors and not much of them because of the wire. I gotta find me some bright boy who knows phones and can clean this one's line. It's cramping my business."

"You need a vacation," Bobbi told him with a crooked smile; it went away a second later. "Good grief, Jack, what happened here?'' She let go of me as she got her first glimpse of the mess.

"Kyler's men came by the other night and threw a party. Then three of 'em came by again tonight for another one. They're in the front room with the sandman for the moment.''

Gordy strolled through the dining area to the front and looked over the casualties. "I can take care of 'em for you. This time tomorrow they can be part of the nearest WPA project, canal repair, maybe a new highway.''

I'd have laughed, but he was completely serious. "Charles is already working on something. He'll call when he gets it all arranged.''

Gordy shrugged. Stuff like this was no skin off his nose; he was honestly trying to be helpful.

"How are things at the club?'' I asked, wanting to change the subject.

"Same as before, but with less broken glasses and more lawyers. Should have it all nailed together and running tomorrow.''

"You in any trouble with your bosses because of this?'' I knew he had to answer to people higher up.

"They're not happy. A raid they don't worry about; a raid started up by one of their own boys on their own place, they get annoyed.''

"So they know Kyler ordered it?''

"Pretty much. He'd be in the stew now if he wasn't already busy feeding fish.''

"What's your place in this fight with Angela?''

"They want me to stay out of it while they settle things their own way. I wouldn't be here now except to keep an eye on Bobbi. Be hell to pay with her when it's time to leave.'' His gaze slid in her direction and a smile barely showed itself on one side of his mouth. She made a face back at him.

"To your lawyer's place again?'' she asked.

"Yeah."

Bobbi shook her head. "But not before I get some magazines to read. All they have are law books and stuff on sports."

"Can do," he said, all affability.

"And we give the phone number to Jack."

I found some paper and scribbled as she dictated. She was in the home of a mouthpiece named Anthony. It sounded familiar. "Do I know him?"

"He's the one who got Madison Pruitt out of jail that time."

Bobbi's friend Pruitt, a dedicated communist, had the misfortune to be born into a very wealthy family. He took every opportunity to publicly live down the shame of having tons of bucks coupled with a long pedigree. A few months back he'd been arrested while helping some of his red brothers at a sit-down strike turned riot at an auto plant. The muscle working for the factory owners broke his arm, and he was still having trouble keeping his eyes focused after a hit on the head with a club. Soon as he was out of the hospital, the cops grabbed him, then Pruitt's mother stepped in with lawyer Anthony and posted bail. She'd reportedly whisked her wayward son off to a private island on a lake somewhere in upstate New York and was spoon-feeding him lots of castor oil to make him behave. No one in Bobbi's group had seen him in a while, but they didn't mind, since he was a bore. He was an even worse bore when talking politics, his only real passion besides food.

"Has Charles got coffee here?" asked Bobbi. "I could use some about now."

"Try the fridge," I suggested.

She gave me a "you must be crazy" look. "He keeps his coffee in the icebox?"

"Says the beans stay fresher. I wouldn't know, so don't ask me."

She poked around the kitchen until she turned up the necessary items and started making a pot for herself and Gordy. Usually, any odors to do with food and cooking made me nauseous, but coffee was the single exception to that rule. I couldn't drink it, but it still smelled fine, made me wish I could have a cup.

As the stuff brewed away I filled her and Gordy in on all the fun and games from last night, and discovered I was getting real tired of talking. Repeating things made me remember them, when I really wanted to lock them all in a box and lose the key. On the other hand, I could tell them the whole story. Last night with Coldfield I had to remember not to mention certain supernatural details, and it was a strain keeping things straight.

"Sullivan?" said Gordy, when I got to the part about questioning Deiter.

"You know him?"

"Not personally, but I heard a few stories."

"Such as?"

"He wasn't directly in on it, but he smoothed the road out so someone could bump his brother."

"Why'd he bump his brother?"

"Sullivan wanted his spot in the organization. Word was the brother was skimming off the top and would have been scragged anyway, but Sullivan made sure the right people heard about the scam. One funeral later and he steps into his brother's shoes while they're still warm. He didn't raise a stink about the hit and that's how lotsa guys figure he helped it along."

"Nice fella. His own brother."

Gordy shrugged. "It's business. There has to be some trust or everyone gets the screw."

I didn't smile at Gordy for talking about trust in his line of work. It was an important part of successful organized crime. Without it, the body count hits the ceiling. "So he's someone I need to avoid?"

"You and everyone else. He may not know about you or Escott yet—"

"I'll try to keep it that way. I got my hands full with Angela."

"Yeah, what's she like?" asked Bobbi.

"Cross-eyed, bowlegged, and covered in warts."

"She must be some cute dish, then. Do I need to be worried?"

"I'll tell you something I heard Chaven say, 'I'd rather sleep with a tarantula.' " Actually, he said he'd rather do that than trust her, but Bobbi didn't need to hear the rest. Angela was a cute dish all right, very attractive and exciting, but then so's a box of dynamite on a bonfire.

The phone went off. It was Escott.

"I've arranged something with a friend of mine," he said.

"Not Shoe?"

"He's helping to some extent. Can you load the goods into your car and transport them to another location?"

"I guess so. What's the deal?"

"My friend is a federal agent, but I would prefer not to have him or his cronies seen near the house. Being part of an official group, they might attract the attention of the papers and—"

"Don't have to draw me a picture, I know what a reporter can do with this kind of story. Where do you want me to take 'em?"

He gave me an address and said to knock on the back alley exit door.

"I'll meet you there shortly," he added.

"Wait a minute, you're supposed to take it easy. Hello? Hello?"

He'd cut the connection. Maybe I'd have to break my private rule about leaving friends alone when it came to hypnosis and give him a fish-eye whammy about taking a rest.

Gordy asked what was going on, and I told him, then he offered to help me shift the bodies.

"I can manage," I said.

"My car's already in the back. What were you gonna do, haul 'em out the front door so some old lady walkin' her dog sees and goes into fits?"

Okay . . . I let him talk me into it.

But we didn't get a chance to do anything about it right away. First Bobbi all but shoved him onto a kitchen chair and made him have some coffee, to keep her company, she said. I think it was more so she could keep an eye on me, get me to talk about other disasters than my own. The ones going on in the rest of the world made my troubles seem small, like the Ohio River flooding. It washed half a million people out of their homes, killed over two hundred, was turning Cairo into an island, the WPA and CCC were up to their asses laying down sandbags, and more rain and snow were on the way. I wondered if I needed to be worrying about my folks and the rest of the family in Cincinnati. The city was well downstream from things, but not all that far distant, and the water had to go somewhere sooner or later.

But even with this bleak stuff for a topic it was good to just sit and gas on about it all with friends. It was something normal, and I really needed a big dose of normal, a moment of quiet before the rest of the night jumped on my back and started beating me up. Of course, it might not be that way, but recent events were to the point I was starting to always expect the worst.

Not a good way to live.

As for the wider world, Bobbi wondered what Escott thought about the way things were going in Europe. I didn't have much of an answer since we'd not really had a chance to talk politics lately, and what was the problem, anyway? Turned out that the Germans weren't giving the British a straight answer on making a lasting peace—when they even bothered to answer. The fracas seemed pretty far away until I thought about Coldfield's radio bringing Hitler's voice right into his living room.

"Think it'll be war?" Bobbi asked.

I shrugged. "You know more'n I do about it."

"They keep talking about peace all the time. The British."

"Which means they're scared shitless," said Gordy. "Every fight I ever been in with the wiseguys in this town always happened right after the bosses arranged for an understanding. You think it's gonna be the usual business, just start to breathe easy, and next thing you know bullets are flying."

Which wasn't exactly reassuring to me, what with my hopes of getting Angela to lay off and be nice. I stared at the scarred surface of the kitchen table, idly picking at some splinters around a hole that happened when Escott and I had to fight a crazy man wielding an ice pick. The place got quiet, and when I finally noticed, it was in time to see Bobbi and Gordy both looking at me like I'd sprouted a third ear.

"What?" I asked.

"Think about something else for a minute, why don't you?" Bobbi suggested.

She never lets me get away with anything, especially when it's not good for me. Well, if she wanted me to think about something else, we'd have to find a polite way of asking Gordy to leave us alone for a while. That wasn't too likely, so I settled for gently bumping my knee against hers under the table until she smiled.

"I'm done," Gordy abruptly announced, standing and putting his coffee cup in the sink. "Let's get this show on the road."

Bobbi washed things up while he backed the Caddie out, spinning the wheel this way and that until the car was close to the door. I kept my eyes open, but no neighbors got curious enough to take a look. Maybe they were all cozy by their radios listening to *Lum and Abner*, or whatever was on tonight. Too bad I couldn't do the same.

I slung Deiter over my shoulder like a sack and carried him out to the car. My frame's not as large as Gordy's, but I'm a lot stronger, so it was no hardship. Besides, I enjoyed the look on his usually phlegmatic face as I shoved Deiter into the backseat like he was a two-year-old. Twice more and the Three Stooges were ready to roll. I made a quick trip to the basement safe to get that fifty out and shoved it in my pocket with Escott's pipe, tobacco pouch, and Webley. Then I pulled on my long overcoat, third best hat, locked the house up—for all the good it seemed to do—and piled into the front seat of the Caddie. Bobbi sat in the middle and snuggled hard against me as Gordy drove to the address I'd been given.

It was near the edge of the Bronze Belt, an aging vaudeville house turned film theater, though the movie title up on the marquee was new to me. I thought I knew 'em all. Gordy passed it, made two turns, and rolled into the brick-lined alley behind the place. He cut the lights, but left the motor idling. I got out, found the back door, and rapped it a few times. On the other side I heard music and dialogue from the show that was running. It sounded like a drama.

The door opened and a flashlight beam caught me square in the kisser. I winced against it.

"Easy, brother," I said, putting my hand up.

The light stayed put. "I ain't your brother 'less you gone color-blind in a big way." I could guess the voice belonged to a black man, and he didn't sound too happy.

"Keep that in my eyes and I'll go blind, period."

That got me a single dry cough of a laugh and he aimed the light at the floor.

"My name's Fleming, I was told to come here."

"I know. I'm Mr. Delemare."

I stuck my hand out, but he didn't take it.

"Boss said you had a few bundles to store, but not for long."

"That's right. I'll keep a watch on 'em until someone comes to take 'em off my hands."

"Okay, but you have to be quiet. The audience is here to see the movie, not hear you banging around."

"No problem," I promised. "Where do you want the bundles?"

"Ten miles southeast of Halifax, but since that ain't gonna happen, you can put everything just inside the door. I'll hold it so it don't slam shut."

"Thanks," I said, and went out to the car and gave the news to Gordy. He nodded and cut the motor as I opened up the back. I did the hauling again, though he helped pull them out. Delemare watched, dark face made darker still by what seemed to be an expression of perpetual annoyance. It could have been for me specifically or for the whole world in general, no way to tell, yet. He didn't seem to be in the least surprised that the bundles were three unconscious white men. Most of his concern was for maintaining complete silence, though I didn't see how anyone could have heard us above the movie.

"I knew you'd come back, Johnny," a woman with a silken voice whispered above us.

"But I can't stay, doll. I'm in trouble—bad trouble," a man, presumably Johnny, rumbled in reply.

"Oh, Johnny!"

The music soared dramatically. From it, I got the impression they were kissing. Couldn't see anything of the screen, I caught only a few vertical slivers of light coming through a thick velvet curtain hanging behind it. Its purpose seemed to be to keep the screen before it from being backlighted and thus spoiling the film's projected image.

I wanted to see more, but Delemare was in a hurry to lock up again because of the draft coming in. He said it was twenty degrees out, and I believed him as I returned to the car to say good-bye to Bobbi. Gordy was pretty decent about giving us some time and strolled a few yards off to have a smoke in the cold. I slid into the front seat next to her.

"Can't we wait around a little longer?" she asked.

"Too much of a risk for Gordy. He's in enough hot water helping me this much. He can do without calling special attention to himself by having Escott's fed see him. Don't worry, after I deliver this bunch, I'm going to try to wind things up with Angela tonight."

"If she's at this Flora's place."

"I'm willing to bank on it."

"Just don't get killed."

"That's at the top of my list."

"I mean it, Jack. When you were telling us about what happened last night I could tell how much you were leaving out so you wouldn't scare me. Well, it didn't work."

"Next time I'll have to try harder."

But she didn't think that was even remotely funny. "You wouldn't say such things if you could see your eyes."

I glanced at the rearview mirror, touched it. I made a fingerprint smudge, but raised no image. "Don't think I want to, I probably wouldn't like it much."

"I sure as hell don't. I want you to come back in one piece—inside and out. Don't let this kill your soul, Jack. I've seen it happen to others."

"What others?"

"Gordy for one. The things he does, the people he deals with, that's what got to him."

"But Gordy and I are different."

"Then what about you and Charles?"

"Charles? You trying to tell me his soul is dead?"

"Or so buried it might as well be. Haven't you figured that out by now? You told me how cold he can be at times. He wasn't born that way, life did something to him and hollowed him out. All the stuff he does now is to cover that space up so people won't see it or ever guess it's there."

"Bobbi, this is—"

"*Not* crazy talk."

"I wasn't going to say that."

"The hell you weren't. You can think it's crazy, but trust me, I know what I'm saying on this. I don't want you ending up like Charles. He's charming, he's fun, and he's smart, but think about what's underneath all that. I don't want the same thing happening to you, taking you away from yourself."

"Nothing's going to take me away."

"Oh, sweetheart, don't you know?"

"Know what?"

She touched the side of my face, looking as sad as a crucifixion angel. "It's already started."

3

GORDY and Bobbi were long gone; I sat in the darkness behind the theater screen feeling worried about myself at a time
when I didn't want to feel worried about myself. I had enough
trouble on my hands not to be borrowing a fresh batch by
looking into a mirror for something I couldn't see in more
ways than one.

Along with singing, one of Bobbi's many other talents was
for slicing through the fat to get straight to the bone; she was
right about Gordy, and my instincts said she was right about
Escott. As for being right about me, well, thinking about it
gave me the creeps, so I tried not to and failed, of course,
pacing around in the small space looking for a wall to climb
if it got bad enough.

For distraction I checked on the Stooges, but they were all
quiet, if probably cold and uncomfortable on the bare concrete
floor, but too bad for them. I wondered when the hell Escott
planned on coming; I wanted to be shed of this pit and away
from my thoughts, to be doing something. Deiter had given
out with a possibly hot lead that could take me straight to
Angela, and it needed checking before tomorrow arrived.

The movie kept my impatience at bay for a time, but the
voices were unfamiliar and I wondered who was in it; I
thought I'd seen and knew 'em all. Since my charges were

tied up safe, I used a narrow passage that Delemare had taken earlier to go out front and followed it, eventually finding a peephole in the thin plywood wall that looked into the auditorium. What lay on the other side brought me up short.

I expected the audience to be black, but not the actors on the screen. I'd heard of such pictures, but never actually seen one with an all-black cast. Now and then you'd spot a performer doing a specialty number in a film, like Bill Robinson or the Nicholas Brothers, but not a whole movie like this. I was fascinated. Except for the Cotton Club in New York and the Shoe Box here in the city, there wasn't a lot of mixing going on between the races, and people on both sides of the fence often actively discouraged it.

The plot was about a guy accused of murder who had to prove that a gang had done the dirty work. It was no worse than others I'd seen along the same lines and this one had, surprisingly, worked musical numbers into the story, only they looked like they belonged to a totally different movie. The thing wound itself up with a gunfight and a deathbed confession; the guilty man had done it to remove his rival and get the girl. As she and the hero had a final closing clinch, the music soared, faded, and was replaced by the authoritative tones of a newsreel. The news was all about white people. The audience began pulling on their coats and hats and filing out, except for a few staying on to see the show again.

When the film started up with the opening fanfare, Delemare came back and found me getting absorbed in the story.

"What the hell you doin'?" he demanded.

"Shh," I said, whispering. "You want them to hear? I'm watching the show."

"But that's an all colored movie."

"I had noticed."

"What is it? Some kind of curiosity for you like *Believe It or Not*?"

"Huh? I was just trying to see how they did the frame against Johnny."

"What the hell for?"

Then someone in the audience told us to shut up. I shrugged and went back along the passage to the backstage area, Delemare right behind me.

"Why you watchin' a colored movie?" he still wanted to know. I got a better look at him now, medium in height and build, balding, gray hair at the temples, age anywhere between forty and sixty. He had a set-in, grim expression that may have been the result of the hard times or just the natural bent of his personality.

"Why not? I like movies and that's what's running. I'm going nuts waiting back here in the dark. You got something against me watching the show? I'll pay for it if you want."

"I don't need your money."

"So what's the problem?"

"Just ain't natural, I'm thinkin'."

"What? For a white guy to watch a black movie?"

He grunted and it could have meant anything from contempt to an affirmative or maybe both.

"Well, it's interesting to me. Where'd it come from?"

"Hollywood, where else?"

"Yeah?"

"Yeah. This is what gets shot when the white crust is put away for the night."

"And there's no white people in any of 'em?"

"You see many black people in the white films?"

"Good point. No wonder we're so pig ignorant about each other."

"Oh, jeez, you're not gonna start about how them actors are a credit to their race and all that crap, are you? If there's one thing I can't belly it's some do-goodin' social soldier—"

"Whoa there, I'm not—"

"—out to raise me above myself an'—"

"You've got the wrong—"

"You comin' in here an' staring bug-eyed—"

"Now just a frigging minute—"

"Makin' judgments about what you don't know—"

Then several people on the other side of the screen told us to shut the hell up or take it outside. Delemare and I glared at each other for a moment, then he made a shrugging, throwing-away gesture and walked off, though he didn't get far. Someone knocked at the back exit. He beat me to it, brought up his flashlight, and opened the door a crack. It was Escott. Delemare blinded him with the light, then grudgingly admitted him to the inner sanctum.

"Mr. Coldfield sends his regards," he said to Delemare, who was unimpressed.

"You tell that snot-nosed kid he's gettin' too big for his britches, an' I'm only doin' this for his sister, for her being such a lady."

"I'll be sure to pass that along to him."

"You do that. Now get this trash outta my theater."

"Immediately, sir."

Delemare shot him an annoyed look, but Escott was all sincere respect, then moved off down the passage again.

From what I could see in the faint and shifting illumination filtering through from the screen Escott looked better than the night before. He wasn't moving around as freely as normal, but he was moving, and his expression, though still bruised, was sharp with interest rather than dulled out with pain. Trudence Coldfield must have worked a small miracle on him.

"Interesting fellow," he observed when Delemare was out of earshot.

"If you like rabid wolverines. You got here just before another Great War broke out."

"Indeed? He must have liked you."

"*Liked* me?"

"Oh, yes, Shoe mentioned that Mr. Delemare enjoys a good fight more than anything else, but only indulges in one if he likes a person."

"Jeez, I stay here much longer and he'll put me in his will."

"Then we shall delay no more. I didn't see your car outside, how did—"

"Gordy came by the house and helped load the goods, offered me a lift."

"That was most kind of him."

"I don't think kindness was what he had in mind. He also offered to bury these guys in the next WPA project, but I told him you had first dibs."

"Thank you, I think."

"And there's some more stuff: now that Kyler's out of the way New York is sending in a heavyweight called Sullivan to take his place."

That caught his attention. "Sean Sullivan?"

"According to sleeping beauty over there." I motioned at Deiter.

"I've certainly heard of the man, a rotter by all accounts. What else have you learned?"

I quickly filled him in on what I knew from Gordy and what I'd gotten from Deiter.

Escott gave a slight head shake. "From the sound of this you may not be required to do anything at all, simply sit back and see what develops."

"I don't have to see, I know. Angela's going to put up a fight and more people will get killed."

"If the Hydra we're facing wants to chop off a few of its own heads I think it is in our own best interests to move out of the way and let it get on with the business."

Well, I already knew about his streak of darkness, but what Bobbi had said about him came back to me, and I found myself staring at his battered face, trying to see what was behind his eyes. For right here and now it looked like a wall made of ice-cold iron bricks.

"I'll try my way first, if you don't mind," I murmured.

"As you wish. Best get going, then, our transportation is waiting."

"What is it exactly?" Needing something else to think about, I poked my head out the door and caught sight of a dark panel-sided truck that had somehow squeezed into the alley. The Stooges wouldn't lack for room in it.

"I contacted a federal friend of mine, a Mr. Adkins. It took him a bit to make the arrangements, but he's come through for us, as you can see."

The name tripped a breaker in my brain. "Adkins? As in Merrill Adkins?"

"The very one. My, but his fame does seem to be spreading."

"Well, yeah, when you mount a plow on the nose of a truck and charge into a distillery with machine guns blazing it does make for headlines."

During Prohibition Merrill Adkins created a name for himself by busting up more stills per week than any ten treasury agents put together. When Repeal came he shifted into tracking down federal fugitives. Last I'd heard he'd taken part in the gangster hunt and shoot-out disaster that had enabled Baby Face Nelson to escape capture sometime back. It had been an all-round embarrassment for everyone. After that he'd dropped from sight.

"He hardly ever does that sort of thing anymore," said Escott. "Much too noisy."

"What's his connection to you?"

"We share a common interest in fighting the Hydras. I met him a year or so back on another case."

"So you're bringing him in on this? It's important enough to get noticed by the feds?"

"By this particular one, at any rate."

"On what kind of charges? Even if Deiter and his pals intended to commit murder, breaking and entering's not exactly headline stuff these days." Adkins had always been there for the newsreel cameras, looking closemouthed and modest.

"Not to worry, Adkins is more than willing to take things in hand at this point."

"What do you mean by that?"

"Oh, he shan't interfere with anything you have planned, particularly since he doesn't know that you have plans, but he will relieve us of the responsibility of these three burdens."

"And do what with them?"

Before Escott could answer Adkins himself walked through the door. It's a bit of a jolt to be face-to-face with someone you've seen in the newsreels and all the papers. This guy had even gotten into *The New York Times,* which is some trick since his line of work was more suited for the Hearst rags. He was in them, too, a lot, a real somebody who had done things to deserve the fame, if you could believe the reports. I tried to match the black-and-white shadows I'd seen in the reels to the reality.

You know exactly what celebrities look like, what they're doing that made them famous, even admire them for it, and there they are with you, close enough to touch. You want to but you don't because of the combination respect and bashfulness reflex most people get when they have a brush with a big shot. They don't know you from Adam, and probably have no reason to correct the oversight, but because they're famous, you want them to know *you,* you want to matter to them in some way. Even if it's just for a minute, it ends up being *your* minute, your little piece of them to take away. Nutty stuff, but that's human nature, and I was no different from anyone else on it, and even with all this in mind I found myself straightening my hat and touching my tie.

Adkins was less formally attired in a short hunting jacket, a striped scarf wrapped around his neck, and a sweat-stained newsboy's hat. He seemed about my age, had a thin hard face, small mouth, heavy lids over slightly protruding black eyes, a determined, unsmiling expression, just like in the reels. Not handsome, but he didn't have to be. Escott introduced us and we shook hands. I said it was a real pleasure. Adkins gave a noncommittal grunt for a reply and didn't bother removing his work gloves.

"This it?" he asked, gesturing at the Stooges.

Escott nodded. "Three less heads for this Hydra to turn upon us."

"We'll take care of 'em."

By that I understood he had friends waiting outside. "You want a statement or anything from me?" I asked.

He gave me a once-over glance, shook his head. "Don't need to right now."

That didn't sound kosher. Government guys were sticklers for paperwork. "When, then?"

"Later, we'll let you know."

"Where you taking them?"

The glance was turning into a stare. "Out of the way."

"Out of the city? Out of the state?"

"You don't need to worry about it, kid, they won't be sneaking up on you anytime soon." There was more than a hint of condescension in his tone.

So my restored youth was working against me, that or he was a career asshole. I shoved whatever hero worship I might have had in a deep pocket and put on an expression of earnest relief. ''Well, golly gee, I sure am glad to hear it. I wouldn't want to have to hurt 'em all over again.''

His small mouth got smaller, and I wondered for a moment whether he'd try punching mine. If so, then he'd only get the one attempt. But his gaze flicked around me and to the side the way you do when you're dismissing something way beneath your notice, and he told Escott he'd be back with help, then went out.

''He always like that?'' I asked.

Brows high, Escott went innocent. ''Like what, old man?''

''Forget I asked. Think I'll go find Delemare again so we can have a nice cozy race riot.''

He had time for half a chuckle then held the door open as Adkins returned with two more men dressed like himself. They ignored me and went about the business of hauling Stooges out to the truck. I didn't offer to help; I'd done my share and figured to have more work ahead tonight.

''You're going to look for Miss Paco?'' asked Escott, only just loud enough so I could hear him over the sound from the movie.

''And find her, if what Deiter gave me was straight.''

''You might want to consider holding off a bit until Sean Sullivan gets settled in.''

''Uh-uh, I'm finishing things up tonight. She's not going to be so busy with him as to cancel the hit on you.''

''My thought was to spare you undue disquietude. You gave me to understand that you're not quite comfortable about employing your persuasive talents on young ladies. By holding off and waiting, you need not distress yourself at all.''

A few nights back I'd told him about a still-too-fresh crisis I'd had when hypnotizing a woman to get some information. While she was under my influence I'd started taking her blood, way too much of it. That loss of self-control had scared the hell out of me. I was still scared, of myself, of my questionable ability to keep my own dark side in check in the future. I hoped I was scared enough.

"Can't get out of it, Charles. I'll be careful."

He looked at me like he wasn't all that convinced of my assurance. His cautious attitude didn't offend; it just made for two of us. "You may avoid any problems altogether by waiting a day or so."

I cocked a sharp eye at him. "You know something I don't?"

"Only a bit more about local gang politics. Even if Angela does manage to get Kyler's account books the other mobs are not going to want to deal with a woman. If they don't already know, they will soon find out about the pretense of her using her father as the front man and won't stand for it. She will soon be brushed aside."

"Translated, that means a gang war."

"Fewer heads on the Hydra. Angela Paco is only one of them. The world has thousands more. When a war breaks out they only kill each other, so I say why not let them get on with it?"

There was that cold streak again, and it made a kind of crazy sense up to a point. "I'm all for it, but we both know innocent people get hit in the cross fire. And if you get scragged who's going to pick up my laundry?"

No answer for that one.

Adkins and his boys got the last Stooge tucked away in the truck. He came over to speak to Escott.

"Can't give you a ride back," he stated. No apology in his tone. No emotion whatsoever. I didn't have to wonder what Bobbi would have made of him.

"I'll find other means of travel. Should there be any new developments will I be able to contact you at the same number?"

"Yeah, sure, something will get through to me." If he didn't watch it his piss-and-vinegar enthusiasm could sweep us off our feet. Maybe Escott found him useful, but to me he was about as charming as a dead mackerel three days gone. Adkins jumped in the cab of the truck with his buddies and the thing trundled out of the alley, gears grinding, exhaust billowing and stinking the place up before the wind got to it.

"You going back to the Shoe Box?" I asked Escott, shutting the theater door on the parade.

"Not right away. I thought I'd take in the show, then see if Mr. Delemare won't give me a ride."

That'd be a good trick, but then Escott was a genius at talking people into things. I fished out his requested pipe, tobacco, and the fifty bucks and gave them over.

"Excellent," he said, pleasure evident on his face. "Cigarettes are a quick convenience, but there's nothing quite like a pipe for a real smoke."

"And here's a bonus." I hauled his Webley-Fosbury automatic revolver from my coat and presented it to him, enjoying the expression on his face.

"My dear fellow, you are a miracle worker. Wherever did you find it?"

"Deiter must have taken it as a war prize. Sure you want it back? The last two guys who had it weren't exactly lucky."

"My delving into the realm of myth and superstition is strictly limited to the theatrical profession, not cases like this." He checked the cylinder and muttered a grudging approval for the ammunition it held.

"What about me? Ain't I a myth?" I vanished and reappeared a foot to his left to illustrate the point.

"You," he said, not looking at all impressed, "are merely a scientific puzzle that wants a bit more research."

"Thanks a heap."

He put the Webley away in his overcoat pocket, wincing at the movement.

"Shouldn't you be someplace safe and quiet? Resting?"

He made as expansive a gesture as his taped ribs allowed. "Who would look for me here?"

"You're kind of noticeable, pale face."

"Not to worry, I'll sit way in the back and not make any trouble. Hopefully, Mr. Delemare will vouch for my good behavior should anyone take offense."

I got out my little notebook and wrote a number, ripped the sheet free, and handed it over. "This is where you can reach Bobbi if you need to. She'd probably like to hear from you."

"Is she all right?"

"Worried, wants all this finished and done." Another reason for me not to delay. "Oh, and if you need to talk to Gordy, it can't be to his club, there's a tap on the line."

"Does he know what you're going to do?"

"He didn't exactly ask and I didn't exactly say. Maybe he talked some with Bobbi and has a notion about things from her. He gives me the idea he's waiting to see what happens and then will go from there. His New York bosses told him to stay out of it, presumably to give Sullivan some elbow room."

"Or to provide reinforcements should they be required. I'd advise you to be cautious with him, not rely on him if you can at all help it. Gordy may be helpful now, but if push comes to shove . . ."

Gordy was a businessman, and he wouldn't put himself out for anyone if it jeopardized his spot in the organization. He was too fond of breathing. "Yeah. Tell me about it."

"I was rather hoping that would be unnecessary."

* * *

To avoid drawing more attention I left by the back door and started walking until I found an L-train to take me to the neighborhood I wanted. Chicago is a hell of a sprawl, swallowing up little towns one by one, making them part of the big one. My destination was one such spot. At the turn of the century it was probably a rustic delight, but the boom brought on by Prohibition had turned it into a square mile of brothels, gin joints, and burlesque houses, blocks of 'em only occasionally interrupted by an eatery, a grocer's, or some other more ordinary business. The population lived cheap and died young, usually just a few steps ahead of a landlord with his hand out for back rent. Oddly enough, the Depression hadn't hit here as hard as in other places, since people could always be counted upon to have enough money to spend on their vices.

Just on the edge of things was the all-night movie house that was one of my regular haunts. I was usually out this way a couple of times a month when I got tired of staring at the walls of my room on those evenings when I didn't have a date with Bobbi. For other people, when the bars closed down and they still didn't want to go home, this was the place to spend the rest of the night. During the winter, if they could scrape up a dime for the admission and not spend it on booze, the bums would come here to get a warm place to sleep. They could stay at one of the rescue missions for nothing if they wanted, but most preferred watching a movie to being preached to, and second runs of a Shirley Temple feature was close as they wanted to get to redemption. I was here often enough that they knew me by sight and that I wasn't a soft touch for drink money. Once in a while if it was really bad weather, I'd pay the way in for a regular or two, but I handled the tickets to keep them from being traded off for a share in a bottle.

The neighborhood didn't appeal to me beyond the movie

house, so I'd never paid much mind to it beyond the attention necessary to avoid getting mugged. This time when I strolled along the sidewalk from the L-stop, I had more eyes for my surroundings. Sure enough, there was Flora's Dance Studio across and down the street just like Deiter said.

Passing the theater (it was a Marlene Dietrich film tonight), I walked unhurriedly along until I was opposite my goal. For a cold, windy night they seemed to have plenty of business going for them. A dozen or so men were gathered under the bright lights of the entry, and whenever the doors opened I heard the brassy tones of a live band banging out a fast version of "Melancholy Baby." Once past the glitter, I saw an old, rambling two-story structure that must have stood duty for dozens of other businesses over the decades; you could see where past signs in the wood had faded and been painted over. One of the current signs read FIFTY—COUNT THEM!—FIFTY BEAUTIFUL GIRLS WHO WANT TO DANCE WITH *YOU!* Lights showed on the top floor, but the blinds were down.

I crossed the street and joined a line of men in front of a ticket kiosk. So it wasn't an instructional studio, but a hall for taxi dancers. The men paid out one or two bucks for a string of ten or twenty tickets, then a bouncer pretending to be an usher motioned the way inside. I bought ten tickets and followed the rest through the door. To the right was a place to check your hat and overcoat, but some of the men kept theirs, leaving them draped on chairs lining the sides of the hall. I left mine on, same as a few others who weren't trusting in the integrity of their fellow citizens not to steal. My reason had to do with the fact I didn't know how long I'd be staying, and if I had to leave in a hurry I'd rather have my property with me.

It was a pretty big place, with a low ceiling held up by thin metal columns at regular intervals. The noise was high over the music, shuffling feet on the scarred wood floor, a woman's artificial laugh, a man's hopeful voice, muttered conversation everywhere between strangers holding each other in an imitation of passion. Everyone was well behaved, though, there were lots of bouncers to see to that. For some of the customers this was the closest contact they could manage with a woman, and they weren't about to screw things up for themselves by getting thrown out. I saw men of all ages and backgrounds, and just standing there heard five different accents asking the girls variations of "what's your name?" and "will you dance with me again?" Most had taken the trouble to dress themselves up; even if the suit was twenty years old, it was brushed clean. I saw little old guys with hair parted in the middle like they did when the century turned, and gangly kids that were all pimples and buckteeth, hair slicked back with half a jar of Vaseline in hopeful imitation of George Raft.

The girls were mostly young, some were even pretty, but moved slow on obviously sore feet as the evening was not new. A couple of girls still kept their energy up and it was making them money. When a song ended—none went on longer than two minutes—it was time to rest or change partners, or dance one more time with the same guy. Signs on the wall declared you could only dance with a girl twice in a row, then had to switch. I suppose it was meant to keep you from becoming too attached. Jeez, you could fall in love with her and suavely sweep her away from all the glamour to a fifth-floor walk-up and half a dozen kids neither of you could afford. Couldn't have that.

The music stopped and a girl with frizzy yellow hair and a bored face came over and asked if I wanted a dance. Her satin dress needed to retire; she'd tried sprucing it up with some paper flowers, but they were crushed now, probably had been for days. I gave her one of my tickets and caught a flash of leg as she lifted her skirt hem and shoved the bit of pasteboard into the top of her stocking along with a wad of other tickets. Other girls across the floor were doing the same. You could tell who the popular ones were by the size of the distending lump on the front of each thigh. I wondered how much of that ten-cent ticket they were allowed to hang on to for dancing with the customers. Enough to keep them in paper flowers, no doubt.

A slow waltz started up and I took my gal in hand, and in deference to her sore feet led her around a few snail-like turns so I could get a better look at the place. The band had a trumpet man, a snare drum, piano, fiddle, and a couple others I didn't catch right off, all playing loud so they could be heard on the other side of the hall. Around the edge of the dancers were guys holding tickets waiting for the number to end so they could cut in and get the partner they wanted. There were few wallflower girls, none were shy about going up and asking a guy to dance with them. Anyone acting coy here wouldn't make the rent for the week. Even if the girl was plain as an unpainted barn, her offer was usually accepted; you could practically smell the loneliness coming off the men, mixed in with the scent of bay rum.

Plenty of bouncers stood around keeping an eye on everyone, but it looked to be a quiet night. Compared to some of the other Paco businesses, this was as respectable as a church picnic. I knew for sure now that it was connected with Paco, because with no small satisfaction I spotted one of his men going up some stairs at the far side of the hall. His name was Newton, and I would have recognized him for a ringer no matter what. The difference between the regular bouncers and Angela's professional killers was pretty obvious if you knew what to look for, kind of like being able to tell a peashooter from a machine gun.

Now that I'd seen one of them, I noticed there was a lot of coming and going on the stairway, all men, some in cheap

flashy suits and loud ties, others apparently just finished with
their jobs in drab work pants and oil-stained shirts. None
matched up with the would-be Fred Astaires I was rubbing
elbows with.

More went up than came down and this was where the
bouncers were really concentrated to keep out the unwelcome.
Quite a mixed crowd it was, and I had a pretty good idea
what was drawing them together, but wanted confirmation.

"What's upstairs?" I asked the girl.

"I dunno," she mumbled through her chewing gum.
"Manager's office, I guess. He's always up there."

"He must have a lot of company. Who are all those guys
going up?"

She shrugged. "Customers, I guess."

"For what?"

"I dunno. Dance lessons maybe."

She wasn't holding back as far as I could tell; it's hard to
fake that kind of supreme disinterest. The waltz finally ended,
and I gave her the rest of my string of tickets, which woke
her up.

"Hey, I can't dance with you for all these," she said.

"Pretend," I said with a wink, and walked on toward the
stairs, losing myself from her in the general crowd.

There was a men's room along the same wall, which was
a bit of luck. I waited until another dance started and pushed
in, standing in line for one of the closed stalls. My idea was
to go in, vanish, and find my way up to the second floor, but
now it didn't seem so hot. The next guy in line might start
wondering why I didn't come out. Then he'd check and find
I was gone. Not that he could do anything about the mystery,
but it was better to keep my head low and unnoticed for as
long as I could get away with it.

I obligingly let others ahead of me and moved to the back
of the line. A fast check to make sure none were looking my

way and I vanished with nobody being the wiser for it. As far as I could tell, I got away with it since there was no immediate reaction. That gave me a pretty smug feeling, being able to pull something like that off. I let it carry me as I filtered through the porous resistance that was the ceiling to emerge onto the floor above.

Since I'm blind in this state it's always an adventure trying to get my bearings. Hard enough to attempt in familiar surroundings, it could be a real circus for my brain in strange territory like this. I bumbled along a wall, found a corner, turned, and soon turned again, bouncing lightly against oddly placed surfaces. There didn't seem to be anyone about, so I chanced partially forming again and found my ghostly body floating about a foot off the floor in the stall of another men's room placed exactly above the first. No big surprise there, it was probably for the convenience of the water pipes. I drifted down to the floor and went solid.

Someone in the next stall flushed and left. The rest of the place was happily clear, so I eased out to hear better. Music and the drone of the crowd came from below, efficiently masking over anything useful I might pick up. I opened the door a crack and peered out into a hall. Cheap wood panel gone dark with age halfway up the walls, the other half all peeling paint and water marks, with light fixtures hanging by rusty chains. I swear some of them were still sporting their old gaslight fittings. Lots of men milling around or waiting to get into certain rooms, but no sign of Newton, at least from this view. I chanced poking my head out to check the other end of the hall. More doors and crowd. Okay, so where was the big attraction?

Then I picked up the unmistakable sound of slot machines being worked and a roulette wheel spinning. Great, I'd guessed right, give the man a cigar.

No one paid any mind to me as I stepped out for a better

look around. What conversation I picked up had to do with every conceivable sporting event going on that week and how much to lay out on which risk. The numbers were pretty low, a reflection of the general poverty of the neighborhood and the times, but there were plenty of bettors to make up for the lack. I was in the wrong business if I wanted to make money. Maybe I should invest in a good solid, tried-and-true gold-plated vice, then sit back and watch the dollars roll in until I had my own mansion and twelve-car garage. Of course, there'd be the tough part of explaining it all to the tax man, but that's where accountants like Opal come in, making fancy with the bookkeeping until it looks all clean and sweet. But then there's other guys in the same vice business, your rivals, all trying to take the butter off your toast, so you either make a treaty or shoot 'em, simple as that. Then you hire lawyers to keep you out of court, or have enough dough to pay off the judge when they can't, or buy off the whole goddamned jury when . . .

I shook my head. Too much trouble. When I wound all this up I wanted to go back to my battered typewriter and make up nice simple stories about man-eating spiders, and then maybe Bobbi wouldn't worry so much.

Being just another face in dim light I had no problems making my way from one side of the hall to the other. Everyone was more concerned trying to figure a new angle on how to get some free money than to notice a fake in the crowd. The bouncers were another matter, though. As I worked my way around I checked each one against my memory on the theory that if I knew one, he'd know me, then it'd be time for my vanishing act again and the hell with the consequences.

There were a few closed doors at the far end of the long hall, one held a sheet of pebbled glass that had a light showing through. Maybe it was the manager's hiding place. Might as well start there. I did the same as in the men's room, put my back to a wall, waited until no one was looking my way, and disappeared again.

Invisible now in a forest of feet, I slipped along, keeping the baseboard on my left so I wouldn't get mixed up until striking the end wall, then it was a matter of pouring through the gap where its door didn't quite meet the threshold.

Unlike the other mugs out there, this was my lucky night. The first voice I heard was Angela Paco's. I found an unused corner, took up post there, and waited and listened.

"They should have called in by now," she snarled. She seemed to be moving, probably pacing back and forth. This was one gal who didn't know how to hold still.

"Every hour on the hour," added a man in an agreeable tone. I recognized the voice as belonging to Doc, a joyfully inebriated crony she'd inherited from her father. Whether Doc was a real lieutenant with power in the organization or just a sometimes useful hanger-on, I still hadn't figured out. Last night, when some morphine-laced blood I'd been forced to take to keep alive knocked me flat, he'd pronounced me to be deader than Dixie, which decided Angela about dropping me in the lake. It was no reflection on his medical abilities—not that I had much trust in them—but when I'm out for the count and unable to speak or move, anyone could mistake me for dead. Depending on how things went tonight, Angela was in for a hell of a shock.

"Where are they?" Another snarl from her, and it sounded like she'd been asking that same question for some time now.

"You can try calling them."

She muttered and grumbled out a negative reply. "If he's pulling a double cross on me with Sullivan, I'll string 'em both up by their balls."

So . . . she definitely knew about Sullivan coming into town and was obviously not happy about it.

"Now, now, you know your daddy doesn't like such language."

"You and I both know he hardly notices stuff like that anymore. Why the hell don't you do something about him? You're supposed to be a doctor."

"Indeed I am, good for busted bones, lancing boils, and patching up the odd bullet hole or two. Frank needs a head doctor to fix him, not a quack like me."

"They're all quacks with their hands out for cash and none of 'em doing him a damn bit of good as far as I can see. I had him in that sanitarium for months and all they did was make him worse."

"They got him so he could dress himself and eat okay."

"He's like a kid, I don't want a kid for a father, I want my dad back and running things like before."

"I know, girl, but sometimes we can't get what we—"

"For God's sake, Doc, don't give me that load of crap again or I'll start screaming."

Doc subsided, and I heard Angela's heels clacking on the floor as she walked back and forth.

"Where the *hell* are they?" she repeated.

This time Doc made no attempt at an answer. I wished he'd take a trip to the john so I could do something about her; I was getting tired of concentrating to stay invisible.

"Where?" A loud crash across the room as a heavy object hit the wall. I got the impression she'd thrown something.

"I do want to remind you that this is not your office and that was not your property," said Doc.

"Screw it. With the money he makes here, Dunbar can buy himself another bowling trophy. I know he skims off the top, they all do. As soon as Opal gets herself set up I'm going to nail the whole pack of 'em to the wall to dry out in the sun."

Someone knocked and the door opened. "Angela . . . ?" Another man's voice.

"That's Miss Paco to you now."

"Uhh—yeah, Miss Paco. What's wrong? I heard—"

"Nothing, you heard nothing."

"Yes, Miss Paco. Ahh, as long as I'm here, you got a minute?"

"What do you want?"

A shuffling as the owner of the voice and several others came into the room.

"What is this, a convention?" she demanded.

"We really need to talk to you, Miss Paco." He sounded more confident, probably because of all the people backing him up. There seemed to be seven or eight of them.

"What about?"

"The way the business is going."

"Last I looked it was just peachy. Those roulette wheels are still spinning and the slot machines are raking in more dough than a bakery. You complaining?"

"I don't mean what's in here, it's the rest of it."

"Which isn't exactly your concern."

"We don't think that way, Miss Paco."

"Oh, you're thinking now. Please enlighten me, Mr. Dunbar."

"Well, it's like this, we know that Big Frankie ain't feeling so good lately an' that you been running things for him."

"So?"

"So we wanted to know how long it would be going on."

"Only until Big Frankie's better."

"But how long?"

"As long as it takes. I'm not making you poor, am I?"

"Well, no, but it just—it just ain't right for a girl to be doing this kinda thing."

"Says who?"

Dunbar hemmed and hawed, then finally came out with it.

"We know that Sean Sullivan's comin' in to take over for Kyler. There might be trouble."

A long silence on Angela's part; then: "And you boys don't think I can handle him?" Her voice was low, clear, and very cold.

"Maybe if Big Frankie was—"

"Answer me, Dunbar."

"You're—you're just a girl, Miss Paco."

A very brief silence, then a gun went off. Loud, but not too loud, like a balloon popping. A .22 perhaps, great for indoor work. I heard a thud as a body hit the floor, a man's drawn-out cry of extreme pain, then a series of grunts and groans mixed with cursing.

"Any of you other bastards think I can't handle myself?" she asked, her voice even, like she'd commented on the weather. "Come on, talk to me about it."

Not too surprisingly there were no takers.

"All right, now I'm going to give it to you straight: Sullivan's coming into town, and yes, he'll try to make some trouble, but you can make book that I'll be able to dish back anything he throws at us, but doubled. Anyone got any doubts, then have another look at Dunbar."

"You damned bitch," said Dunbar, apparently through pain-clenched teeth.

"You're right about that," she said. "I am a damned bitch through and through and you're one lucky bastard. You caught me in a good mood tonight or I'd have aimed higher and changed your voice the hard way. As for the rest of you, if you plan to give me any grief, then you'd better put that out of your heads right here and now because I've got no belly for it. This is a steady, profitable organization that's made you a ton of money and will continue to do so while I'm running things for Big Frankie Paco. Nothing's changed and nothing will change. Got that?"

"But—but what about Sullivan?" asked one brave soul.

"We treat him the same as any other asshole trying to muscle in on Paco territory. Kyler tried and failed, this won't be any different, because I'm going to run it the same as Big Frankie, which means I need you to do your jobs same as before. I've got all the account books, and you know they mean I've got the world by the short hairs. I'm not afraid to give 'em a yank when it's needed."

A murmur and a nervous laugh of approval for that one.

"When my father's all recovered I'm handing the whole caboose back to him, and you can bet that I'll have a list in hand of anyone who turned chicken and let him down. You want to face that? I didn't think so."

I heard more shuffling and murmurs. No one seemed ready to disagree with her.

"All right. I'm not saying things are going to be smooth. I'll need every one of you helping out before the dust settles, but when it does, you won't find me ungrateful. I'm thinking a hundred-dollar bonus for each and a couple of free nights at the Satchel with all the booze you can handle might cheer you up. All I ask is that you don't break the girls, 'cause I'll need 'em for the regular customers later."

That garnered the start of a general laugh. "Sure, Miss Paco," someone said.

"That's better. Big Frankie'd be proud. Now, a couple of you get Dunbar out of here, he's making such a mess I'll have to call for the night maid."

Another short laugh, followed by movement. Dunbar cried out again as he was carried away.

"Doc?" she said when they were gone.

"Don't worry, girl, I'll get my bag. I swear, you keep this up and I'll run out of bandaging."

"I do whatever it takes."

"That you do, that you do. You put this fire out well

enough. You impressed the hell out of this bunch by making sure Dunbar ain't gonna be bowling again for the rest of his life, but what about Sullivan? You won't sweet-talk the likes of him out of town with a promise of free booze and broads."

"I told you: whatever it takes."

"Huh. I'd warn you not to get carried away, but what's the point?"

"That's right. A dozen down, three to go."

"What?"

"Deiter, Tinny, and Chick. Finding out what the hell happened to them. If I don't hear from them in the next five minutes I'm going over myself to see what's wrong."

Invisible and formless, I still managed to grin. Good luck to her in trying to find her missing stooges.

"Be better if you send someone else."

"You think I can't—"

"You can handle it fine, girl, I was thinking it might make you look too anxious if you go yourself. Don't want the others to get the idea that you're worried about a routine hit on some nobody."

I'd better not tell Escott that Doc thought of him as a nobody or he'd be hell to live with at the slight.

Angela didn't care much for Doc's recommendation and told him so.

"Like it or not, your best course is to always ask what your daddy would do in the same situation. My guess is he'd send someone else to check on the problem for him. Let the rest of 'em see that you're just as big and busy as he was, too big and busy to be bothering yourself with small-fry stuff."

"I'll think about it."

"Good. Now, where'd I leave my bag?" His voice faded as he left.

She called after him. "Doc? Find Opal when you get a chance and send her in."

He grumbled back an affirmative and was finally gone. I heard the door shut.

Alone at last. But I hesitated at re-forming.

A mistake, since it gave me time to think.

My lover Maureen, the woman who, with the exchanging of our blood, gave me the possibility of living again, had talked to me about her ability to hypnotize people, about how dangerous a thing it could be if it got away from her control. Back then it had only been a distant concept for me and might not ever happen since neither of us knew whether or not the exchange would work. If I did become like her and returned, I fully expected her to be there for me to guide me through everything and keep me out of trouble, but life never hands you what you expect. Five years later I returned from death all right, but was very much on my own, and soon discovered firsthand what could happen when my unnatural concentration locked hard onto a vulnerable human mind while my own was fogged over by strong emotions.

The first result was the total shattering of Frank Paco's sanity. I saw it in his eyes, watched the devastating change take place when my white-hot rage slammed through him like a train.

It didn't mean much to me at the time, even seemed to be a kind of justice for what he'd done to me, but then I didn't want it to mean anything more than that because of my hatred for the bastard for killing me. I still hated him, but now more for what he represented than what he'd done. He was a re-minder of my ignorance, of a lapse in judgment and loss of self-control. A living reproach.

The second incident was when I found myself alone with that woman I needed to question. It started the same as others before her: just get the information, then leave was the plan, but it didn't work out that way. She was temptingly attractive to me, and I was hungry. Even as I hypnotized her I got caught up and lost in her total vulnerability to me, with the heady realization I could do *anything* I wanted to her and get away with it. Then I gave in to that temptation and started kissing her throat.

It was like someone else was running things for me. I knew it was wrong and did nothing about it until it was almost too late. Instead of pulling back, I bit hard and began taking her blood into me. Seductive, irresistible, and entirely illicit, it was the best I'd ever had, and in my greed I wanted all of it—even if it killed her.

My conscience tardily kicked in, waking me out of the fever in time to stop. She was weakened, but never knew what really happened, of how close she'd come to dying. I did, and it made me ashamed and disgusted with myself and terrified of repeating the experience.

And here I was, alone with another attractive, tempting woman.

I'd killed before, but not by draining another's life away to feed my own, to feed something as ephemeral as appetite and desire. I'd come close, too damned close already. Those other deaths were hard enough to live with, I didn't want this hovering over my shoulder as well.

But what else could I do? I had to hypnotize Angela and make her call off the hit on Escott. An easy job—unless I killed her.

The assurance I'd given him about my being careful now seemed like so much hopeful bullshit.

4

It's a hell of a thing being a vampire with a conscience; maybe I wasn't so far gone as Bobbi feared.

And I'd better stop thinking so much and do something quick about Angela before anyone came in.

What hit first when I faded back into the real world was the bloodsmell. Dunbar had bled a sizable smear all over the floor. While my corner teeth didn't automatically bud, it was still a lousy distraction, exactly the wrong kind for me, considering the situation.

Next I took in a glimpse of the room: a small, seedy office with all the usual furnishings except for the bloodstain and a broken bowling trophy lying under a dent in one wall.

Finally there was Angela herself. Her back was to me, and she had one hand on a desk phone, but hadn't picked it up yet. Maybe she was just thinking about making a call. Right by it was a nickel-plated .22 semiauto, and I could guess that the muzzle was still warm from the shot. Must have been Dunbar's, I knew Angela usually favored a much larger caliber.

A tiny young woman wearing a dark print dress, she was delicate of bone and body, but with the soul of a grizzly bear and twice as mean. I could tell myself that in my brief contact with her I'd only ever seen her bad side, but it was such as to make me wonder if there were any others. There might not be room for them. Sure she cared about her father, but it was hard for me to balance that one good point against her easy willingness to kill people and still try to make it all come out even. My very first sight of her was to stare in disbelief as she put the muzzle of a .45 to the back of a man's head, pulled the trigger, and blew his brains over the street. For all the emotion she showed then and afterward, she might as well have been filing her nails.

Then there was the business of last night, when she'd been tossing hand grenades around like firecrackers. The shrapnel had nearly been too much for me on top of all the other damage I'd taken, and even with me trying not to look like I was dying and failing miserably, she'd not batted an eye except to flirt in an attempt to get information from me. She was cold as that damned lake where she'd arranged to have my apparently dead body dumped.

Yet for all that, she was cute as a ladybug, small features, short dark hair that curled around the edge of her face; she had Frank's big heavy-lidded eyes, but on her they were attractive, bee-stung mouth, and a little mole just over there. . . .

She turned. Saw me. That sweet mouth opened in shock. Her hand scrabbled for the gun.

No more time to think. I drew a fast breath and locked my gaze hard and fast onto her dark brown eyes.

"Don't move, don't speak," I whispered, all urgency.

She forgot all about shooting me and rocked back on her heels from the force of it. Her eyes went too wide. I eased off from full pressure and waited, but she did nothing else. Her face ceased to express fear and went all blank. Not a comforting sight, but better than before. I realized my emotions had started to get in the way, emotions like my own inner terrors, just what neither of us needed.

I took another shaky breath and a few more besides. Found

my shoulders were hunched up almost to my ears. Forced them down again. It was enough to make my concentration slip and I was too spooked to grab it back again.

Angela shook her head like a drunk trying to get sober fast. "You—you're not . . . what the hell . . . ?"

"Never mind that, just be quiet."

"No, you—"

"Angela, you will be quiet and listen to me. That's the most important thing you can do right now."

Another head shake. She was really fighting this; I wasn't used to such resistance. She either had a hell of a lot of will-power, had been drinking, or I was going too easy with her.

The last, I thought. If I wanted to get anything done, I'd have to hit it harder than this. After a moment to collect myself I moved in close until we almost touched. She had to look straight up to see me, making a long graceful line of her throat. I could hear her heart. . . .

Don't go there, buddy.

But I didn't have to do anything; all on her own she put both her hands on my chest. They were so small, but even through my clothes I could feel, or thought I could feel, the quick pulsing of her blood just beneath the pale flesh. Sweet Jesus, I could smell it and tell the difference between the dead stuff staining the floor and the living stuff rushing through her veins.

No.

Backward step, my own hands out to keep her in place. From the floor below, the band struck up a slow tune. We could have danced to it. She even followed me a pace or two until I ordered her to hold still again, my voice thick and hoarse. I backed up more and kept going until the desk was between us. Might have felt silly about doing it but for the fact my teeth were out; we were both in danger. I looked anywhere in the room but at her and caught myself shuddering with a perilous combination of fear and arousal.

Dammit, but this was too much. It was past time I got square with myself again on this once and for all. I wasn't a mindless, ravening animal; I wasn't a rapist. I didn't have to give in to this kind appetite; I didn't have to lose control. Hypnotizing men sure as hell didn't do this to me, only women, women who attracted me, and all this was because I *knew* I could get away with it.

Taking all her blood would be great, the finest, I'd had enough of a sampling from the other woman to know just how fine it would be, but then I'd have to live with myself and the consequences for a very, long, long time. A few minutes of ecstasy followed by God knows how many years of regret. I had enough of those already from the normal events of living to be making new ones to throw on the pile.

Yes, indeed, it's a hell of a thing to be a vampire with a conscience, but then why not? Better to have a brief twinge of it now than decades of it eating away at my soul later, of wishing I could undo things. Better not to indulge to start with.

I took a long moment to mentally catch my breath, and it seemed to work. I got a lot calmer inside. My teeth gradually receded. The next time I looked at her I had myself all reined in, but she was half-awake and still fighting.

"Angela."

She stopped blinking and shaking her head, her attention arrested on me. I looked hard for a few seconds, then stared past her. That helped. So long as I kept the contact brief with pauses in between I might just be able to get away with this.

"Saw you . . . saw you dead," she whispered.

"I know you did, but it was a mistake. You're going to listen to me now."

"No . . . why . . . should I?"

I said her name again. Damn, but she was a tough cookie.

"Because you have to." Which was a pretty lousy reason to give, so I improvised a better one. "Because it will help your father."

There, she stopped fighting me so much. The part of her that was still thinking was all attention. "How?"

"Just listen and do as I ask. First off, I want you to cancel the hit on Charles Escott. I want you to forget he even exists."

"Escott?"

"Charles Escott, the tall, skinny guy with a big nose, you're gonna leave him completely alone. Far as you're concerned he's nothing and nobody, not worth your time. And tonight you tell your boys to do the same. Got that? Tell it back to me again."

She did so, but it was a struggle. I made her go over it twice more, then a third for good measure, until she was saying it smooth with no faltering. Only then did I relax with a sigh of relief. The really important item was finally out of the way; the rest was going to be my own personal ingenious plan. Not that *it* wasn't important, but I had some doubts about being able to force it through. With this kind of hypnosis you can get anyone to do anything, and I mean absolutely *anything,* right up to jumping off a building to admire the view on the way down. The normal kind used by doctors and in sideshows you can't take so far because it'd be against the nature of the person you put under. That was something I never had to worry about, but my version only lasted for a short while; any orders I gave against a person's basic instincts would wear off with time unless I reinforced them.

On the other hand, if I found a way of getting around a person's natural objections, so they wanted to go along with me on something, then it's back to anything goes again, and I already knew what angle to try on Angela.

"Now, about this Sean Sullivan and what you're planning to do . . ." I began.

Commotion downstairs. Couldn't ignore it, not when the music suddenly stopped and the shouts and screams started. Didn't know what the hell it was, a fight between the patrons, a fire, or worse. I told Angela to stay put and went to the door to see.

In the hall outside were a bunch of other men like me, craning their necks toward the source of the noise, trying to figure out what was happening. A few of them decided not to wait and were moving fast toward exits. The shouts got louder and at the far end of the hall I spotted a knot of bouncers tearing up the stairs, pushing men roughly out of their way. They were closely followed up by another knot. Those boys were in dark blue coats and carrying fire axes.

"Raid!" someone yelled a fraction too late. Maybe Angela had skimped with her payoffs to the cops this week. Everyone had the idea by now and was trying their best to escape. A dozen of them stampeded right at me. I tried shutting the door, but they bulled in, cursing and breathless, heading for a second door at the back of the office.

With all this going on, Angela woke right up and made a grab for the .22 on the desk. I swatted it out of her hand before she could bring it to bear. It thumped against the wall without going off and landed by the bowling trophy.

"None of that, sweetheart, we're getting out of here," I said.

She replied with a ripe and very unladylike word or three, the general meaning being for me to get out of her way. Her usual method of handling emergencies would put people in the casualty wards, so I slipped a quick arm around her waist, lifted, and threw her over my shoulder, intending to carry her out like a sack of potatoes if necessary. She swore and squirmed and clawed and kicked, but I gave her behind a couple of stinging swats and told her to shut up and behave. She squawked with sincere outrage and called me a really nasty name, adding in more verbal vitriol for good measure. At least I assumed as much from her tone of voice since she was cursing me in fast Italian now. I didn't know any of it, but was willing to bet hers weren't the kind of phrases that would show up in a Berlitz course.

With her under control, I joined the growing crowd flowing through the office. They oozed into another hall and stairway, which were both choked with flailing bodies trying to get out. Some of the escapees were trying for the fire exit and crowding around an open window. Cold air blasted its way in, mixing with the stink of sweaty desperation.

"Not this way, you idiot," Angela snarled at me, beating a fist on my back to get my attention.

"Where, then?"

"Toward the office."

I looked. "We are not gonna get in there again."

"Not *in* the office, toward it. Put me down and I'll show you."

What the hell, why not? I thought, and did so. She eeled through the bodies, heading upstream with me right behind her, but instead of the office, she veered to the right and yanked open a door sporting a sign that read JANITOR. Maybe she was figuring to hide out there until the worst of the fuss was over. Seemed a fine idea to me. We could block ourselves in, and if there was any kind of light inside, maybe I could finish what I'd started with her then call it a night.

Crashing, splintering noises, and an odd, out-of-tune ringing sound. The cops with fire axes were making short work of the slot machines. Funny, you'd think they'd hold off on that for later. The usual routine was make arrests first, then chop up the property for the reporters and their cameras so the paper-reading public could see they were being well protected from the ravages of vice. More shouting, but no gun-fire, not yet. All I had to do was keep Angela out of things and maybe it would stay that way.

She dove inside the janitor closet with me at her heels. I slammed the door against further interruptions. The place smelled dank and dusty from the mops, buckets, and brooms. Angela found a switch and flicked on a twenty-five-watt bulb overhead. I looked for some kind of inside latch or lock, but had no luck there, just an empty keyhole. I'd have to jam a foot against the door and lean on it.

Angela glanced up at me, her face alight from the excite-ment of the moment. Oh, but didn't she remind me of Escott and the way he liked living on the edge? He should be the one alone in a closet with her, not me. She bent, reaching for a thin cloth rug to drag it out of the way. *A rug?* Why would anyone put a rug in here? She twitched it to one side, re-vealing the rectangle of a trapdoor.

"Help me pull it up," she said.

"Where's it lead?"

"Where do you think? Jeez, were you born yesterday?"

I hauled at a rope handle and the thing came up on its hinges. Not as smooth or subtle as the one in Escott's kitchen, but it worked well enough. Within was a glimpse of steps going down into utter darkness. Even my eyes couldn't get past it. Unhesitating, Angela swung her legs into the narrow space.

"How far?" I asked.

"Find out," she answered, going in.

I followed, thinking this was a really lousy idea, especially with my claustrophobia trying to kick up. The walls were so close here I barely had room for my shoulders to squeeze in. Once away from the dim illumination of the closet above, I felt a fist going all tight around my heart. God, but I hate small dark places.

"How far?" I repeated. There was a distinct whine in my tone.

"Don't be such a baby. Hurry."

I could hear her clattering away from me. Had to take the stairs by feel now, couldn't see a damned thing in this pit.

Then she stumbled. That's what it sounded like. Thumps, heels cracking on the wooden steps. She cried out.

"What?" I called.

"Help!" she called back, desperation and pain in her tone. "Oh, God, help me!"

I pressed forward, heart galloping up to my throat. Going too fast and likely to stumble myself. "I'm coming, hang on."

Something solid caught me around the ankles and pushed up hard and fast. It was too quick, too unexpected; I toppled forward. Hell's bells, I was falling. Panicked, I lashed out with my arms to try to stop my momentum, but there was no banister to grab, I just slammed them into the walls. The solid thing pushed higher against my legs, and I tumbled headlong. At the last, the very last second, I managed to vanish so I wouldn't crush her when I landed.

Damned convenient talent, but invariably disorienting. I spun faster than before, couldn't get out of that part of it just yet. Damn, damn, damn—

The spinning slowed, I got myself in check, finally stopping to bounce lightly between the walls, trying to figure which end of me was up. My first guess was wrong as I floated one way and concluded I was heading toward the ceiling. Wanted to call out to her, find out what had gone wrong, but no voice in this state. A moment later I located the regular right angles that marked the steps. No sense of Angela, though, I must have floated well back up above her or had gone ahead and was below wherever she was. One way to find out. If she noticed anything odd I'd fix it later.

I materialized cautiously. Dark piled on top of dark met
my eyes. I looked up, saw a very faint dim light. Rectangular.
The trapdoor. Then it suddenly slammed down and the darkness got as bad as it could get without my actually being in
hell. Ironically, that's when the dawn started to break in my
brain.

It was muffled, but I heard her triumphant, exhilarated
laughter coming through the trap, the same kind of laugh as
when she'd been throwing hand grenades.

"You goddamned little bitch!" I found myself shouting as
I finally figured out what she'd done: faked a cry for help,
dropped into a ball to trip me as I rushed to the rescue, then
shot back up the stairs while I was still playing avalanche. If
I'd been a normal man I could have broken my neck in the
fall. She sure as hell hadn't stuck around to find out.

Using my hands to climb, I charged up, vanished halfway
along, and smoked through the trapdoor. Went solid. The
closet was empty. Damn, but she was fast. Eased open the
door to the hall for a peek. The place was still crowded with
dozens of men, all in a sweat to escape. I joined them, trying
to spot her small figure in the press.

Like I said, fast. She could be halfway to Cicero by now,
dammit.

Milled around looking for her, but my heart wasn't in it,
besides the cops were starting to make real headway into this
part of the building. It seemed a good time to disappear again.
I could find a quiet corner, wait until the fuss died down, then
maybe grab one of Angela's inside boys to get a clue on her
next bolt-hole, if she had one. Probably did. She was one
lady it didn't pay to underestimate.

The janitor closet was still as good a place as any to lie
low. Small, but not like that damned passage, and I could
leave the light on. If anyone opened the door to check inside,
I'd have plenty of time to not be there for them. Went back

to it—none of the other men had noticed it yet—and closed myself in and listened, putting one eye to the otherwise useless keyhole. More of the same riot going on in the hall, then the cops really started in, ordering everyone to shut up and make a line. No one was in a mood to cooperate just yet and punches were thrown. Fresh outbreaks of yelling, cursing, I heard Irish accents dominating the rest; it was a real donnybrook for everyone.

Then my peephole was abruptly yanked away as someone opened the door. I backed up and straightened; a small figure charged in, slamming hard against me before I could disappear.

Female, but not Angela, not nearly small enough. For an instant I thought she might be one of the taxi dancers and changed my mind as soon as I noticed the baggy woolen clothes and galoshes. She looked up and there was the familiar pinched face and thick glasses.

"Why, Opal, what a pleasant surprise!" I said, grinning down at the Paco's bookkeeper.

Alarm washed over her features; she expressed it with an inarticulate chirp and tried to back out, but I had firm hold of her, dragged her in, and kicked the door shut with my foot. She went all fists and feet, hitting hard, but I caught her hands, looked into her eyes, and told her to knock it off. She did exactly that.

Okay, so I'd lost Angela, but Opal was the next best choice, having very quickly become Angela's fair-haired girl of all numbers. Of all the people in the Paco mob, she would probably know where her boss lady would run for cover.

"Where's Angela?"

Mouth open, Opal shook her head. "Dunno."

Well, I could trust the truth of that, not just from my brief influence over her but from her very literal mind. I broke off and she woke right out of it to stare up at me.

"They said you were dead," she stated in her flat voice.

"They were wrong, then."

A scowl for me. "You *should* be dead."

"Stop, you're hurting my feelings."

"Because you're so mean. And don't make fun of me!"

"Okay, okay, I'm sorry, I apologize. Let's start over again."

"I don't want to. Just go away and let me by."

"Taking the scenic route out?" I gestured at the trapdoor.

"No." She gave me a look like I was prize pupil for the dunce's corner. "The stairs."

"Fine with me, I'll help you."

"I don't need your help."

I got out of her way and let her wrestle the trap up. "Where will you go?"

"None of your business."

"It's really dark in there, be careful."

Another withering look. She opened her huge purse and pulled out a flashlight, switching it on. Down she went into the passage, a real Girl Scout, prepared for anything. I followed, pulling the trap shut behind.

"I don't want you to come," she grumbled.

"Too bad." The place was still too narrow for my comfort, but the bobbing beam of light made me feel almost brave. "Not much you can do about it."

No reply, maybe she was trying not to slip around in her galoshes.

The walls were bare plywood and threw back what noise we made with interest. It was like walking around in a drum. She reached a tiny landing and tried the doorknob. It turned, but the door wouldn't budge more than an inch. She pushed against it. Two inches more, but it tuckered her out.

"Lemme try."

She pressed herself small into a corner to avoid all contact with me. I put my shoulder to the cold metal of the door and shoved. With a scraping sound something reluctantly gave on the other side. Another effort and we had enough space to squeeze through.

"Some escape tunnel this is, when you need to be King Kong to get out," I said.

"I'd have gotten through."

"Oh, yeah, in a week or three."

"Lemme past."

"After me," I said, going first to check things. I nearly tripped on a hunk of wood sticking out; it was incongruously attached to the lower part of the door. I saved myself by grabbing the jam.

An alley. Strong icy wind whipped between the buildings, rattling an army of dented trash cans waiting in hope for someone to empty them. One had been pushed in front of the door to block it. The can's base was partially eaten away by corrosion and had been patched over with a small load of cement, about a hundred pounds' worth. Opal could have moved it and maybe even Angela, but not easily. There'd have been hell to pay with the fire marshal, but someone had painted a "no-entry-no-exit" sign on the door. A couple of two-by-fours had been bolted across it, top and bottom, the lower one having caught my ankle. The effect, when the door was closed, was to make it look completely boarded up. Pretty clever.

Opal slipped out and started walking down the alley.

"Hey, wait up!"

"No!" She kept going, her purse banging hard against her hip. She brought it around and dropped the flashlight in.

"You got no choice in the matter, lady. You're stuck with me."

"I don't like you."

"Your loss, but I'm coming with you no matter what."

"Why?"

"Because I need to talk with Angela, and sooner or later you'll lead me to her."

"No, I won't, so leave."

"No."

She growled something and walked faster, but I kept up the stray-puppy routine.

"It'll be all right, Opal. Angela and I were talking just before the raid hit. All I want to do is finish our conversation. Angela wants the same thing. Of course, if you can tell me where to find her, then I'll go away so fast you'll feel the draft."

She had plenty of time to answer, but didn't give me one. Another confirmation that she didn't know where Angela was just yet. She probably knew how to contact her, though. "She wanted to kill you."

"Nah, we worked it all out, we're all roses and sunshine now."

That one got me a snort of disbelief. Couldn't blame her. "You were sick the other night. Really sick. I saw."

"I got better, honey."

"Don't call me honey!"

"Whatever you say. Where you going?"

No answer. She got to the end of the alley. It was a different street from the one across and down from the all-night theater and looked a lot nastier, but there was no commotion of cops and paddy wagons here. I noticed a number of hard-looking men hurrying along, keeping their heads down when they weren't glancing behind. They must have been lucky escapees from the raid.

Opal brought her purse around again and began digging in it. I heard the jingle of keys. She cut left onto the sidewalk and approached a parked Cadillac. From the smoked windows I recognized it as having belonged to the late Vaughn Kyler.

As new as it was, no one had put so much as a finger mark on its fresh wax job, let alone attempt to hotwire and steal it. The locals knew better.

She unlocked the driver's door and climbed in; I hitched a hip next to hers and slid her over.

"Get out!" she screeched.

"No!" I shouted back. "No more arguments, lady. Just give me the keys and tell me where to drive."

She fumed, breathing hard. Not really enough light coming in for me to bring her around to my way of thinking, but it turned out to be unnecessary. She slapped the keys into my open hand, scooted as far as she could over to the passenger door, crossed her arms, and stared straight ahead, disgust showing in every line of her body.

I found the ignition, the starter, got the motor turning, and fiddled with the gears and clutch. "Where to, ma'am?"

She looked too mad to talk and only jabbed her index finger in a forward direction. Probably too much of a lady to use a more obvious digit, that or she didn't know to use it in the first place. Her worldly education had some gaps in it, I knew.

I pulled sedately away from the curb. Smooth ride, quiet and secure as we all but sailed along. I could get used to it real fast, and the crazy thought flitted through my head that maybe I could talk Angela into giving the Caddie to me as a gift. After all the shit I'd been through with her, it was the least she could do. Escott's bullet-pocked Nash was in for repairs, he could drive my Buick until . . .

Corner. "Left or right, Opal?"

She pointed left. I brought the steering wheel around and drove us well away from the dance-hall area. Cop cars passed us, going the other way. It'd be a busy night in the holding tanks. I wondered if they chopped up all the gambling equipment. Usually they kept some intact for evidence, but from the sound of things, they weren't being all that careful.

"What happened back there?" I asked. "Did some big shot downtown decide he wasn't getting paid enough to look the other way?"

Opal shrugged.

"You feel okay?"

"No."

"You're not hurt, are you?"

She shot me a quick look. "No."

"Good. That's good." I sneaked another gander at her, but she seemed all right. In her young twenties, but with a hard face, I wondered what it would take to make her soften up and smile. Maybe she didn't know how. She knew squat about the social graces; the only thing that mattered to her were numbers. Vaughn Kyler had discovered her performing math miracles at an eatery, saw the potential of her bizarre genius, and hired her away to bigger and better things than collecting tips for parlor tricks. She did the books for him until his death, then switched sides to go to work for Angela. The last I'd seen of Opal had been on the yacht *Elvira*. Maybe she was intellectually short in some areas, but she must have had the instincts of a Houdini to get herself and Kyler's coded account books away and clear. My hat was off to her.

"You want to tell me where we're going?"

"No, I don't."

Damn, but I'd have to get used to her literalness all over again and watch how I phrased my questions. "All right, but I'm gonna have to know sooner or later or we'll just drive in circles until the gas runs out."

After a moment she said, "I don't have the address, just how to get there."

I told her that was fine with me and she fed me directions as needed. The blocks sped by, getting newer, more respectable, then decaying again. We reached a kind of halfway point between two such areas when she ordered me to stop at a run-down hotel.

"This is it?"

She nodded.

"You live here?" I remembered that Angela had promised to pay her fifteen hundred a month to keep the books. She could do a lot better than this joint.

"No, I'm supposed to go here when there's an emergency."

"Does it come with a parking space?"

Apparently not, so I had to find one. I finally nabbed a spot across the street, but only after making a quick and illegal U-turn. No cops around to notice. Maybe they were still at Flora's studio primping to get their picture in the morning papers. I levered out, holding my hand toward Opal to help her. She glared at it and slid across the seat without assistance. I locked the car up and kept the keys.

She jaywalked over to the hotel entry, me sauntering close behind.

Once upon a time there had been a doorman out front, but he'd either retired or died a long time back and no one had bothered to take his place. The closest they had now were a few winos huddled over a steaming grate. Opal sped briskly past them and pushed through a door with an etched-glass panel. The glass was cracked.

The inside lobby was all faded glory. What had been beautiful at the turn of the century looked pathetic and used up now. The once proudly polished brass of the showpiece staircase was dim and dark with neglect. The patterned marble floor was scarred, stained, and dull with decades of dirt. The rest of the place, from the reception desk with holes kicked into its front, to a cobweb-decorated cage elevator, told the same sad story.

The place was strangely busy, though. Three or four men

were lined up at reception. One impatiently slapped down a
dollar, grabbed the key the old clerk offered him, and took
off up the stairs. I saw no sign of a registration book, but you
didn't need a genius brain to figure out why. Waiting for the
man at the first landing was a tired-looking woman with too
much makeup, fighting middle age with every dab of paint
and powder she could muster. She'd squeezed her ample body
into a tight satin skirt, gaudy polka-dotted blouse, and topped
it with a fancy hat. Her heels were much too high for normal
walking, but then I was guessing she wouldn't be on them
for the next little while. The man caught her arm, and she
tottered the rest of the way upstairs with him.

"Nice place for Angela to put you," I commented as we
paused just on the threshold.

"It's safe," she said, and pushed past me toward the reception desk. The old manager blinked at her.

"Angela sent me," she stated.

"Huh," he replied, checking her over. She didn't look like
she belonged anywhere but at a library, sorting through the
decimal system. Certainly she didn't fit into this place. He
nodded, reached to the wall behind, and took a key off a hook
separate from the others, handing it over. "Stairs, second
floor, straight down to the end of the—"

"I know the way."

"I'll bet you do, girlie," one of the men in line said, all
bloodshot nose and leering mouth. "How 'bout you show
me?"

She kept her eyes down and moved away. He made a grab
for her. I stepped in and caught his arm before he connected.

"The lady," I said, "ain't interested, bub."

He was just drunk enough not to take the hint. He swung
at me with his other hand, but I hardly felt it. In fact it only
made me grin. I caught hold of his coat and lifted until his
feet cleared the floor. He was too surprised to do anything

but gape. He wasn't as tall as me, but considerably wider, and I shouldn't have been able to hoist him up like a baby.

"Hey, no trouble, no trouble!" cried the manager.

Yeah, there wasn't much point in my breaking some drunk in two. He'd only forget about it the next morning, if he lived that long. Hell, his hangover would do worse things to him than I could. I eased the guy back down and thoughtfully dusted his shoulders.

"No trouble," I repeated, still grinning. "Right, bub?"

"R-right." He backed off a few steps, falling against some of his friends in line. Half of them wanted to see a fight and egged him on, the other half told him to get out of the way so they could go upstairs. He disappointed them both by holding his place and plopping his dollar down on the desk.

Opal had watched at the foot of the grand staircase. When she saw I was finished and coming toward her, she started scuttling up.

"Nice place," I said again, hurrying fast to catch her.

"It wasn't like this earlier."

"When was that?"

"Today. I met Angela here."

"With all her muscle around to keep you safe from the patrons, I'm sure things were just dandy. It's always a different story at night. All kinds of creeps are out then."

"I know," she said, pausing to give me a pointed look.

"Hey, unfair."

"You're a creep."

"Yeah, the creep that saved you from getting groped."

"I can take care of myself."

Never argue with a lady when she says that, even if she is a half-pint in galoshes. Bobbi usually carried a blackjack in her purse, and God knows what Opal could stuff into the junior suitcase she was hauling around. "You must really trust Angela," I said.

"Trust?" She looked like she'd never thought of that one before. "I'm doing what I'm told."

"And if she tells you to run in front of a machine gun, will you do that?"

"She wouldn't tell me to do anything that dumb. Anyway, she needs me to do the books."

"So she has Kyler's account books now?" I already had the answer, but wanted to get her to talking on nice and steady. Maybe then she'd let drop something useful I didn't know.

"That was part of the deal we made the other night. I kept them, so now I work for her."

"How'd you swing getting away with them?"

"Why do you need to know?"

Good point. It didn't really matter how she'd done it, so long as it was done. Angela had the world by the short hairs all right.

Once on the second floor, Opal went straight to the door at the far end of the hall and tried out the manager's key. It fit the lock without a hitch.

"Angela got this set up just for you?"

"No. She does a lot of business here, she said. This was where she told me to bring the books."

"The books still around?"

"No."

Well, it was really too much to hope for, but I did have to ask. As she opened the door we had a little dance routine when she tried to slip in and slam it in my face. I was wise to that and sidestepped her. She looked pretty annoyed, but I was used to that by now.

The room was a cut above the rest of the joint. The furnishings weren't new, but not nearly junkyard leavings yet, and it looked like someone had cleaned it within the last week. It was a suite, or what passed for a suite at the turn of the century; it was small, but we had a sitting room with sofa, chairs, tables, radio, even a phone. Striped curtains covered the windows. I took a quick tour of the bedroom and found all the necessaries, including its own private bath. Very cozy. Once upon a time this must have been *the* place for honeymoons. It still wasn't all that bad except for the noisy neighbors. I could hear several of them through the thin walls making a night of it—or a quarter hour of it, anyway.

"Get out of here," Opal stated, holding the door open.

"Not yet. I have to talk with Angela, and that hasn't changed. The fastest way you can get rid of me is to call her." I nodded at the phone, making an "after you" gesture.

She shut her mouth hard, thinking things over. "It's not *right* having a strange man in my room."

"Honey, in this place strange men in the room is normal."

"Not for me."

"I get the idea, but you don't need to worry about my harboring designs on your virtue. All I want is to finish my business with Angela and then you'll never see me again, promise."

She didn't look like she believed me. I thought about giving her a little mental push, but she saved me the trouble and closed the door. Nearly closed it. She left it ajar a few inches, probably so she could scream for help if she felt the need. Not that anyone here would bother to come running.

I got well out of the way so she could get to the phone. She dialed a number and waited, biting her thin lower lip. I could hear the faint ringing on the line, but no one answered. She waited a full two minutes before giving up, then looked at her watch.

"I'll try again in a little while."

"Okay," I said, dropping into a chair. "Want to call room service and order champagne and sandwiches?"

"Stop making fun of me, I know this place doesn't have room service."

"I wasn't making fun of you, Opal, that was a joke."

"Oh."

"It wasn't much of one," I admitted.

"I don't like jokes."

"Maybe I don't tell them so good." The radio was within reach. I turned it on and waited for the tubes to warm up. "You like music?"

"Sometimes."

No music just then, but I found some comedy show, to judge by the laughter. She didn't crack a single smile through the whole thing. It was painful to watch. Any other time I'd have left the radio off and toughed it out, but the moans, grunts, and squeaking bedsprings I was picking up all around us were distracting. Everyone in the joint was having a good time but me. And possibly Opal. I was sure her idea of a good time had to do with a balanced ledger sheet.

The radio-audience laughs died away, and after a cold-remedy ad the announcer introduced a band that did a catchy number I'd not heard before. That was saying a lot considering how much time I spent with Bobbi; she knew all the new music.

"Ever go dancing?" I asked.

Opal stared like I'd sprouted a new nose. "No, I haven't."

"Should try it sometime."

"I don't know how."

"That's easy enough to fix. Why don't you let me teach you the fox-trot while we wait?"

"No."

I hadn't expected her to give any other answer, but there was no harm in trying. "Then what do you do for fun?"

"Fun?"

"When you're not doing numbers and playing with the books, what do you do?"

"I read."

"So do I. What kind of books you like?"

She shrugged, bored with the conversation.

"I like magazine stories myself, stuff like *The Shadow*. You ever hear his show? It's pretty good."

No comment to that one. She looked at her watch and dialed the phone again. This time she waited at least three minutes before giving up.

"Nobody home, huh? Where you trying to call? Maybe I could drive you there."

"I do what I'm told."

"In other words, you don't know."

"I'm not stupid!" she shrilled, startling me.

"Whoa, I didn't say that." I must have hit some sensitive phrase she'd heard too many times before. "Of course you're not. Anyone says otherwise and I'll punch 'em for you."

She snorted. More disbelief, but she settled down a bit. "What's your name?"

"I thought I told you the other night."

"I forgot it. I'm not stupid, I just forgot."

"That's okay. I'm Jack Fleming. You do remember the car ride?"

"The one that made me throw up? I remember."

"Uh, well, sorry about that. I didn't intend any harm."

"Yes, you did. You're mean."

From her point of view I was exactly that and beyond redemption. "If I'm so mean, how is it you can work for someone like Vaughn Kyler and now Angela? They gotta have me beat six ways to Sunday."

Opal continued to stare at me like I was a particularly ugly bug.

"You must know what's going on, the kinds of things she

does. She kills people. Those were hand grenades she was throwing last night, not rice at a wedding. Why are you mixing yourself up with this crowd? Sure, the money's good, but there's another side to think about. It could get you killed.''

Opal swallowed, brows down with concentration as she struggled to release an answer. "She . . . she . . .''

"She what?''

"Angela respects me.''

I traded stares with her. "Respects you?''

A lift of her chin. Defiance. "Yes. And so did Vaughn.''

It made sense. Opal probably didn't get a whole lot of regard, high or low, from most people. My guess was, if not for her weird talent with numbers, she'd be nothing much at all to anyone, which was a damn sorry state to be in. Even with her talent, she was more likely to be viewed as some kind of a freak rather than as a person with feelings. Having someone's respect, even if that someone was Angela Paco, would make for a very strong loyalty.

"Respect is a good thing, but what happens to you if Angela goes out of business?''

"She won't, business is good.''

"Other people think so, too, they want to take it away from her.''

"Like Sean Sullivan?''

"So you know about him?''

"I heard them talking. I met him once when I was with Vaughn.''

"What was he like?''

"A jerk.''

"You know he's going to try taking over Angela's territory?''

"They won't let him.''

"It could happen. The mugs here won't want to work for a girl, even if she is Big Frankie Paco's kid.''

"She's just filling in until he's better."

"They won't believe that story for long, and when she runs out of payoff money, the whole setup will come apart."

"She won't. The daily receipts give her plenty to work with. Then Vaughn had a big packet of cash hidden away."

"He did? How much?"

"About seven hundred thousand. He didn't let me count it exactly, but that's my estimate based on the subtractions he had me—"

"Seven hundred thou—" That's as far as I got as all the air rushed out of my lungs for the next few moments. "Good God in heaven. Where is it?"

"Someplace safe." She was pretty smug, which I took to mean she knew exactly where.

"How'd he get so much together without his bosses finding out?" With that kind of money I could figure he had to keep it all very quiet. The mobs didn't mind taking from other people, but thieves within the organization were just begging for an early funeral.

"He had me fix it for him in the books. I did a good job."

"I'm sure, but it's not something you want to talk about to just anyone."

"Doesn't matter. Angela's going to get it soon."

"You're turning it all over to her?"

"It's not mine."

"But you helped Kyler steal it. If the boys in New York find out what you've done, they'll kill you."

"I was just doing what I was told, why should they?"

"They shoot cookie-baking grannies just for the hell of it, Opal. If I'd been one of Sullivan's men, you'd be scragged right now."

"No I wouldn't. You'd want to find the money first."

"Which wouldn't be too hard. They know how to hurt people and they would hurt you to make you tell."

Her face darkened. "I don't want to talk about this anymore."

"It ain't gonna go away just because you don't like the
subject."

She crossed her arms and stared at the floor, mouth set.

I shrugged. "Right, have it your way, but do yourself a
favor, Opal, and don't mention that money to anyone else.
Not even to Angela's lieutenants, one of them might start to
get big ideas and then you'll all be in the soup. You got
that?"

She finally glanced up. "I got it."

While we were looking at each other I did a little hypnotic
push on her and waited until her face went blank. "Where is
the money hidden?"

"At the roadhouse," she said with hardly a blink.

"The one where Kyler died?"

"Yes."

"And Angela's not gotten to it yet?"

"No."

Well, glory hallelujah. I just found something that I wanted
more than Kyler's used Caddie.

"Where in the roadhouse?" I asked.

"Basement. Behind a panel in the wall."

"How about you draw me a picture of what to look for?"

"All right."

I fished out my notebook and gave her a pencil. She went
to work and soon had a fairly clear sketch I thought I could
follow. When she'd finished I went back to my side of the
room, tucked the book away, and told her to forget all about
the artwork. She went back to stewing and glaring at the
telephone, and I shut my eyes and let the numbers for seven
hundred thousand float across my brain.

What an awful lot of zeros.

Sure, I could do the honorable thing and disdain all that

dirty, ill-gotten cash, but I wouldn't be human if I didn't at least learn more about it. What went through my mind was that in reality I didn't stand a chance in hell of getting it, but the mere thought of it was very much of the mouthwatering kind, and I might as well pursue it as sit here and twiddle my thumbs waiting. With that kind of money I wouldn't have to wait for a magazine to buy my stories, I could get myself a whole frigging publishing house of my own.

Or I could buy my own nightclub and make Bobbi the permanent headliner if she wanted.

Or put my parents—my whole family—on easy street for life.

Or . . . a hundred other quite wonderful things.

Of course, there'd be hell to pay with the taxes, but I could think of some way to smooth it over. Or pay someone to do it for me.

That was how I spent the next half hour as Opal kept trying the phone over and over again. Very pleasant stuff, if on the daydream side. Maybe I'd get the cash, maybe not. It wasn't exactly real to me and probably wouldn't be until I actually had it in my hands. And that couldn't happen until I got things wound up with Angela tonight.

"Try again," I said to Opal after another wait.

Until now I'd been Mr. Patience himself, but after her initial surprise wore off, she dialed. Another full minute of ringing and the start of the next.

Then someone picked up the other end. I heard their faint hello.

Opal sat up straight, identified herself, and asked for Angela. A pause and she had the boss lady herself. "I'm at the hotel like you said, but that man Jack Fleming is here with me. He wouldn't go away. What do I do?"

5

GOOD thing for me that I didn't mind having Angela wise on where I'd gotten to; in fact, I wanted her to know I was keeping Opal company. Then she might be more inclined toward setting up another face-to-face talk, and I could put this whole circus to bed in a few hours and go back to my typewriter.

I shut off the radio to better hear the other side of the conversation, but apparently Angela was as fast at giving orders as she was at making escapes. When I turned again it was to find Opal in the process of drawing a gun out of her purse. She aimed it square at me, one-handed, as she held the receiver in the other. My own hands slightly raised with the palms out, I tensed and waited to see if she was going to shoot. A dozen of her fast heartbeats went by with neither of us moving or blinking.

"You know how to use that?" I finally asked. It was a short-barreled .22 revolver, apparently double action since she didn't bother to cock it, one of the easiest guns in the world to use. Just aim in the right direction and pull the trigger like kids do when they play cops and robbers; it wouldn't have much of a kick and the balloon-popping noise of the shot would go unnoticed or ignored in this kind of joint. The bullet might not even go through the walls.

"Angela taught me," she said.

Opal had enough confidence in her manner to make me think twice about trying any quick moves. I could go invisible and get the drop on her, but decided to let things play themselves out. If she was going to shoot me, she'd have done so by now.

"I've got him," she said into the phone.

"Okay, put him on," said Angela, her voice thin through the wires. "Don't let him get close enough to make a grab."

Opal set the receiver down, backed off a few paces, and told me to pick it up. Too bad Angela hadn't told her to search me; I'd lifted a .38 off Tinny at the house and tucked it into my coat pocket just in case things got hot tonight, but didn't see much advantage to it right now. Besides, I was beginning to like Opal in spite of her associates, so I obliged her and said hello into the phone.

"Fleming?" Angela made it more of a demand than a question. She sounded pretty fed up.

"None other, Miss Paco."

"You're getting to be a pain in the butt."

"I do my best."

"You lay one finger on Opal and I'll skin you alive with a dull knife."

"She's safe. Besides, with that gun on me I'm much too scared to do anything."

Opal gave me a "go to hell" look, but I was used to those.

Angela made a growling sound in response. "What do you want?"

"Just to finish our conversation."

"You've got a hell of a nerve after leading the cops in and breaking up my place."

"Hey, that was nothing to do with me."

"I don't believe you."

"If I'd been with the cops, then I'd have had Opal down

at the local station house answering a lot of questions right now, not sitting in this dump waiting for you to haul your act together. I'm sure they'd be fascinated to find out what Big Frankie Paco's little girl has been up to for the last few days.''

"You—" She broke off into rapid, and probably very rude, Italian. The connection faded, followed by a sharp and loud clunking sound. My guess was she'd slammed the phone against something hard. The lady had a short fuse tonight.

"Hello?" I said patiently, eyes toward the ceiling. "Hello-hello?"

After a few minutes, where I heard a lot of raving and swearing in the background, she came back on again.

"What do you want?" She still sounded mad, but was in control of herself.

"To continue the little talk we were having before all hell broke loose."

"So talk."

Fine and dandy with me, but you can't hypnotize people over the phone. I can't, anyway. "Set up a meeting place, anywhere you like, and I'll be there. Or you can come here yourself. You can be certain that Opal's not going to let me go running off."

"I don't have time for this tonight."

"Make the time, Miss Paco. Your prize bookkeeper is standing here and not too happy about things. She's under the impression that you're going to take care of her. You wouldn't want disillusionment to set in, would you? It'd be very easy for something like that to happen in an outhouse like this."

"You say one word—"

"I know, the dull-knife routine. So put some grease on the wheels, Miss Paco, and get things moving. We'll be waiting for you."

I hung up.

Opal squawked and for a second I thought she'd shoot, not in anger but from reflex, since she seemed to forget all about her gun. I got my hands up again and backed hastily away, making calming noises.

"What'd you do that for?"

"Seemed like a good idea at the time. I can see it was rude of me. Did you still have to speak with Angela?"

"I need to know what she wants me to do."

"Keep me covered just like this, but I'd appreciate it if you didn't shoot until after your boss and I have had our talk."

No more than a minute went by before the phone rang again. I'd expected Angela to call back with more instructions for Opal and I was right. Opal grabbed the phone up and they talked close. I didn't let on I could hear both sides. The upshot was no surprise: She wanted Opal to sit tight until a couple of her boys came around for us.

"What about the car?" Opal asked.

"One of them will drive it back for you."

"Angela . . . ?"

"Yeah, what?"

"I—I sort of accidentally told him about the money at the roadhouse."

"You what?"

"I didn't mean to, it just came out."

A long silence from Angela.

Opal got nervous. "I'm sorry, it was an accident, please don't be mad at me."

"Okay, okay, calm down, lemme think."

Opal waited, chewing her lower lip. "It was an accident."

"Yeah, yeah."

"He was asking a lot of questions and it just came out. Then he told me not to talk about it or I might get hurt."

"I'll just bet he did. Okay, don't worry about it. I'll take care of it for you. Just don't say anything to anyone else.''

"I won't, I promise.''

"And make sure he keeps shut about it, too.''

Damn. Maybe I should have told Opal to completely forget she'd mentioned the money in the first place. Now Angela had a whole new reason to kill me. Again.

A few more reassurances from her boss got Opal to feeling better, then Angela asked for me. Opal backed away and once more I said hello to Angela.

"So you know about Kyler's little nest egg?'' she asked sweetly.

"Not nearly enough. Your girl shut up before she got too detailed.''

"Uh-huh, but the damage has been done.''

"What? Are you thinking I'm going to run out to chase down buried treasure? She's got a gun on me.''

"You're a smart operator, you could get away from her if you really wanted to.''

"But I don't want to. We need to talk.''

"That's what you keep saying. I want to know why. What's so important that you want to take such a risk?''

"No risk, Miss Paco,'' I hedged, trying to think of something that would hold her attention. The truth wouldn't do here.

"Well?''

The something I needed jumped into my brain just in time. "I want to go to work for you.''

Silence, then a bark of laughter. "You what?''

"Chaven's dead, a lot of your boys were probably arrested tonight, Deiter, Chick, and Tinny ain't coming back—yeah, I took care of them—and Doc's gone with the booze most of the time. With all that working against you, I'm thinking you can use all the help you can get.''

She sputtered, actually sputtered. "Like hell I—''

"Especially since Sean Sullivan's coming into town to take over Kyler's spot."

That completely shut her up for a moment. "How do you know about him?"

"You said I was a smart operator. Who am I to argue with a lady?"

"I don't believe you," she repeated, but her tone didn't go along with her words. She had some doubts, and plenty of them.

"Your loss."

"Why would you want to work for me after I've been trying to kill you?"

"Because I figure if you'd really been trying, I'd be dead by now." It wouldn't hurt to throw a little flattery at her, but it had to be the right kind. Telling her she had beautiful eyes wouldn't work in this situation.

"You're right on that," she said, sounding warmer.

"But maybe after your boys haul me around to see you, I can convince you of my sincerity. As a sign of my good faith I won't mention that seven hundred grand to them on the trip over."

"Or I can just have them kill you when they get there before you even open your mouth."

"I'm willing to take that chance," I said dryly, trying to imitate Escott. He would have done it better with his accent, but I wasn't half-bad. I made her laugh.

"Okay, Fleming, Doc was right, you've got balls."

"And they're at your service."

Another laugh. "Don't get fresh. My boys will be there in about half an hour."

This time she hung up. I didn't mind, she was due a turn.

"We've got some waiting to do," I told Opal, and gestured at the silent radio. "Sure you don't want to change your mind about those fox-trot lessons?"

"Angela's going to hire you?" She looked like she'd just bit a bad lemon.

"With any luck."

"I don't believe it."

"The boss lady said about the same thing, but she'll come around."

"I think it stinks. Besides, if it's so bad for me to be working for Angela, why is it okay for *you* to want to work for her?"

Oops. Damn good question. Not one I could answer, either. As I had Opal's full attention, it seemed a shame to waste the opportunity. "Opal, you need to forget that. Don't even bother to think about it. Okay?" The bad-lemon look went away as I concentrated on her.

"Okay."

Funny thing, or maybe it wasn't so funny, but I didn't have the least temptation to take Opal's blood while I was putting the eye on her. It would have been about as exciting as kissing one of my sisters. Just as well for both of us, I suppose. "Why don't you go to the other room and freshen up? I'll be all right here. Take your time and don't pay attention to anything I do. Just put the gun down. It'll be here when you get back."

"Okay," she said, her voice flatter than usual. She left the gun on a table and went into the bedroom, then the bath. Before the door had shut I was dialing Shoe Coldfield's number. He caught it halfway through the first ring, must have fairly pounced on it.

"What the hell's going on?" he wanted to know.

"I got a little sidetracked. Hasn't Charles checked in? I thought that movie would be done by now."

"Yeah, he called from the theater. He'll be back soon, but you—"

"I'm still working on things. I got started hammering out a truce with Angela—"

"A truce? With her?"

"—then the cops raided the joint. . . ." I filled him in on the rest of it, and not without a lot of argument. He didn't want to believe me either, and I couldn't blame him for it. One of these nights I'd have to sit him down and tell him some important details about myself, then I wouldn't have to work so hard trying to persuade him about my ability to get things done. Of course, if it all worked out the way I wanted in the next few hours, I wouldn't have to, since Escott and I wouldn't need his help and protection anymore. Speaking of Escott . . . "And you can tell Charles I got her to call off the hit on him."

"You must be a miracle worker, kid."

"I didn't say it was easy, but we should all be back to normal pretty soon."

"Normal? There ain't nothing normal about this shit and don't try to tell me otherwise."

"Okay," I said cheerfully, knowing he couldn't take a slug at me over the lines. "But pass all this on to him when he gets back and tell him to give my girlfriend a call for me so she won't worry so much."

"Can do. Just how were you able to get Angela to—"

"Charm and good looks go a long way with her."

His comment to that was somewhat less than polite, and grinning, I had to hold the receiver away from my ear.

"I wouldn't worry about it," I said when he paused for breath. "I gotta go now, sounds like Opal's coming back." Which wasn't strictly true, but why take chances? I hung up and paced around, shutting and locking the entry door almost as an afterthought.

Opal came back after a minute or so, picked up the gun again, and resumed scowling at me. If she'd powdered her nose I couldn't tell. I sketched a wave at her and turned the radio back on. I was feeling pretty damn cocky with myself and needing to work off the energy. The dance music was still playing, and I made a few turns with an invisible partner.

"You're nuts," said Opal, eyeing me with disdain.

"Maybe so, but I have fun. Come on and give it a try." I turned again and tried a dip.

"Angela told me to keep you covered."

"Hey, we're practically business partners now, so all that's off."

"Not until Angela tells me so."

The gun routine was boring me, and besides, she looked like she never had a good time in her life. I fixed her with another look. "Relax, Opal. Put the gun down and come take a dance lesson."

She blinked, then put the revolver back on the table. As a subject for suggestion, she was a dream. Maybe what I was asking of her was very much in line with what she really wanted. She came over and I waited until the blankness in her expression cleared.

"It's easier than it looks," I said. "I'll just hold this hand, then you put the other one here, and you start off counting one-two-three-four, one-two-three-four. . . ."

Her feet seemed glued to the floor and no wonder, with the galoshes still on her shoes. Good grief, we were both still in our coats and hats. I decided to ignore them and make the best of it. After a minute she relaxed and the glue came slightly loose; she actually followed my steps, albeit on very stiff legs, staring down the whole time to watch where she was going.

"There, you're dancing, girl," I said after a minute, thinking she could use the encouragement.

Then she raised her head just enough to look at my tie and smile—a twisting of her lips that was there and gone in an instant. The muscles of her face probably weren't used to such acrobatics. Maybe I was wrong and it was a only twitch of concentration or maybe a wince of pain, but I hadn't stepped on her toe or kicked her shin.

I kept counting. She got confused, so I slowed down, and told her she was doing fine, just relax and listen to the music. She couldn't seem to do both at the same time, so we didn't magically turn into a poor man's Fred and Ginger, but I could tell she was really trying. I didn't repeat the hypnosis stuff; there are some things in life that it just won't work on and this was one of them. If Opal was going to dance, it would be on her own.

The song ended and I stepped back and made a little bow. "You ain't half-bad, ma'am."

"I was terrible," she stated. "I watched the dancers at the studio. I know."

"Ahh, give yourself a week and you'll be dancing circles around 'em. You're supposed to be so good at numbers, right? People good at numbers always make great dancers."

"They do?"

Well, I didn't know for certain, but assured her of the truth of it. "Hey, they're playing a waltz, and that's even easier. Hand here and here, one-two-three, one-two-three." More clumsy steps from her, but I'd been just the same years back. My mom, God bless her, made me take lessons when I'd been in short pants. I'd hated dancing then and had gotten into fights about it with some of the rougher boys at school. Then I changed my mind when I realized it was a great way to spend time with girls. Most boys go through a girl-hating stage; mine was remarkably short-lived.

"Oh! I'm sorry!" She landed square on one of my toes.

"Never mind, keep going." I got her to the end of it without either of us crashing to the floor. A coal commercial came on, interrupting the music. "There, we're not exactly Vernon and Irene Castle, but we could do okay at the Stardust Ballroom."

"We could?" she sounded doubtful.

"Well . . . maybe with a little more practice."

She nodded. Honesty was the best policy with her. Then her face twitched again. No, it was a definite smile. Gone in a flash, but real. It did nice things for her, but I chose not to comment about it. She'd smiled to herself, after all, and it seemed better to wait until she was ready to share before I intruded any opinions on her.

"Did you like it?" I asked.

"I guess so."

She was usually much more decisive when expressing opinions. "Only guess?"

"I . . . my . . ."

"What?"

Her face was all screwed up until she finally managed to blurt it out. "My—my aunt told me if I danced with boys I'd have a baby."

I was very careful not to laugh. She'd flushed deep red at this confession. "Well, one thing can lead to another and maybe it could happen, but if *all* you do is dance, then you don't have to worry about having babies. What other bright things did your aunt tell you?"

She shrugged, eyes down.

"Your aunt raise you?"

"Yes. She didn't like me much."

"I'm sorry to hear that. You have a tough time with your family?"

"I don't want to talk about them."

Answer enough. "Okay. Then how about telling me about the last book you read?"

"Why?"

"To fill the time until Angela's boys get here. I know I'm fascinating, but it's your turn to talk."

A suspicious look. "Is that another joke?"

"A half-assed one, but yes." I dropped into the chair by the radio, throwing one leg over the thinly cushioned arm. "Okay, about that book . . ."

I lived to regret it. Instead of a popular novel, she'd last pored over some thousand-page cure for insomnia that had to do with mathematics. For ten minutes she nearly quoted chapter and verse to me of the whole damned volume while I tried to make sense of it and look interested. I wanted to keep up the encouragement with her, figuring she didn't get much, but every man has his limit.

"Whoa," I said, finally raising a hand. "What are you doing here? Why aren't you at some college teaching this stuff?"

I got a blank look for my question, and she wasn't under my influence. "Because I couldn't pass the entry exams."

"They're not that hard. I mean, if you can get this math down so solid—"

"That's *all* I can do. English, foreign languages, history, I don't know that stuff. Just numbers."

"Pretty one-sided."

"It stinks."

"Yeah, but it's fixable. Learning stuff just takes practice, like dancing or playing the piano. Ever learn piano?"

"No."

"Maybe you should try. I bet you'd be good at it, it's all numbers, y'know."

"It is?"

"My girlfriend could find you a teacher to get you started. In a few months you could be the life of the party with your playing."

She shook her head. "That's not for me."

"How do you know until you've tried?"

I could tell from the way she scowled at the floor she was about to come up with another negative kind of answer, but someone banging on the door interrupted her. She went all alert and scrabbled for her gun.

"Who is it?" I bawled out. It was too early yet for Angela's goons to have turned up. I put my hand in my coat pocket to assure myself the .38 was still there.

"The manager," a man called back. I recognized his reedy voice.

"What's the problem? Don't tell me we were making too much noise."

"I have a message for you from Angela."

I glanced at Opal, who was equally puzzled. "This is fishy," I whispered. "Go back to the bedroom for a minute."

"I can take care of myself."

"Yes, you can, but I need you to cover me in case there's trouble. Angela doesn't want either of us turning up dead if we can help it. Is there a fire escape at the window? Good. Get it open nice and quiet and be ready to run."

"To where?"

"You know the all-night theater across from the dance studio? If we get separated I'll meet you there."

"What about Angela?"

"Call her later. Now get behind that bedroom door. If you hear me say the word *kosher*, get the hell out and don't look back. Promise?"

She nodded, chewing her lower lip.

The manager knocked again. "Open up or I'll use my key."

"Awright, awright, keep your shirt on." I took my time to give Opal a chance to take care of the window. She came back and nodded from her shelter behind the bedroom door. I slipped the bolt, pulled the entry door two inches toward me, stopping it with my foot, and peered through, trying to put on a disgruntled face. It wasn't hard. "What's the problem?"

In the slice of hallway within view I could see the manager was ghost white and sweating. The smell of his obvious fear put me instantly on edge, but I didn't let any of it show. Behind him stood several men in blue uniforms. What the hell? Another raid? Or had some alert member of the Chicago police force tracked us all the way here from the studio?

"Let us in, Mack," said one of the cops.

There were three of them and another guy in plainclothes. "What's this about, Officer?"

"You'll see," answered the plainclothes man. His voice was sharply familiar, then I got a look at his face, knew him: Lieutenant Calloway, one of the cops who had been square in the late Vaughn Kyler's pocket.

"What's going on here?" I said loudly, drawing inside a bit and putting a hand up as if to rub my eyes. "You got a warrant to come in? It ain't kosher unless you got a warrant."

"I'll give you kosher," the first cop said, and started to shove his way past the door.

"Son of a bitch," said Calloway, grabbing his friend's shoulder and staring at me. "It's *you*!"

He and I had had a run-in the other night at Gordy's club when he'd still been working for Kyler. I'd won. When he woke up out of the sleep I'd put him in, he'd been plenty sore. Right now he looked like he wanted to pay me back for the humiliation. With interest.

He pushed the uniform and the manager out of the way and started to bull in. I let him come. In fact I grabbed his arm and dragged him in, swinging him around like a square-dance partner as I slammed my weight against the door to stop the others. I shot the bolt, which might buy me a whole five seconds of time until they broke through. I heard thumps and cursing on the other side.

Calloway had his gun out, but I was moving fast now, lots faster than he could follow. I slapped it from his grip, then got his skull between my two hands and made him look at me.

"Take a nap," I whispered with as much force as I dared. His eyes rolled right up in his head and he fell like a brick. As his friends started banging their shoulders in earnest on the door and the hinges began to rattle loose, I took an instant to roll the man's body up against it. Maybe it would buy a few more seconds.

I shot through to the bedroom and was happy to see Opal was already gone. Good, good girl. Now I grabbed the iron-framed bed and hauled it around to block this door. More time for us.

The window was open, the curtains flapping in the strong cold breeze. I clambered out and shut it behind me, then looked for Opal. She'd made the street and was clumping toward the Caddie.

Damn. She'd forgotten I still had the keys.

I went invisible and slipped down the stairs without a sound, going solid again as soon as I reached the sidewalk and began running toward her. She heard me coming, and glanced back in panic.

"It's me," I called. "Keep going!"

She kept going until she got to the car and tried the door, but I'd locked it earlier. I got the key out, opened it up, and all but bodily shoved her in. No squawks of objection this time. Jabbed the key in the ignition, hit the starter . . . and nothing happened. I cursed and tried again, checking that the gears were right. Nothing.

"They must know the car and have done something to it," I said. "Get out and keep moving. Hurry!"

She did just that on her side, and I did the same, catching up with her in a few long strides.

"Put your gun in your purse," I told her. "We don't want to attract attention."

She shoved it out of sight. "What's going on?" she demanded, all breathless as we hustled along the walk.

I looked back at the hotel and saw cop cars blocking the street, their lights flashing in circles, bright red patches moving against the surrounding buildings. "I think some of Sullivan's boys are wise to this place and decided to check on it. My guess is that he's the one behind the raid on the dance studio. They had no real reason to bother otherwise, there's no election coming up just now."

"Sullivan? But those were cops at the raid."

"Kyler had some on his payroll, didn't he?"

"Yes . . ."

"So Sullivan just moved in and picked up the reins. Jeez, he must work as fast as Angela."

"But those were *cops*." She looked like someone had just told her the truth about Santa Claus.

"Bad apples in the barrel. The ones on the take sometimes do things for the mob. I thought you knew that."

"I just know numbers." She stared straight ahead, a stubborn set to her mouth.

Right. Another subject she didn't want to talk about.

"We have to call Angela," she said. "Have to tell her what's happened."

"I'm all for it, kid."

"Don't call me kid!"

"Okay, I'm all for it, Opal, but first we get clear of all this and—"

Two cops stepped around the corner and stood right in our path. They were smiling, not at us both, but specifically at Opal. She wasn't hard to miss, and for all I knew the whole Sullivan mob had a description of her right down to her wire-rimmed glasses. They'd probably been beating the bushes for her since she disappeared with the books.

"Hold it right there," one of them said, drawing his gun.

"No need for that," I said. "Calloway told me to get her back to the studio."

"That's not what he told us."

He was too far away for me to chance jumping him, but at least his attention was on me, not Opal. "He changed his mind."

"Since when?" Great, now his partner had his gun out.

"Why don't you ask him? In the meantime I've got to get her—"

"I don't think so, wise-ass," said the first one. "Turn around and start walking back. We'll all ask him when we get there."

I tried focusing on him, but nothing happened. We weren't close and the light wasn't good enough for him to see my eyes clearly. Opal began to slip her hand into her purse, but I put an arm around her shoulder to stop her. "Take it easy. I'll get this worked out." She shot me a worried look. I winked back, but like the cops she seemed not to see in the darkness.

"C'mon, you an' your girlfriend head back to the hotel."

"I'm *not* his girlfriend!" Opal snapped.

They just laughed, which made her madder. I tightened my grip and muttered to her to calm down and do what they wanted. As our little parade proceeded along the street, Opal shrugged hard to shake my arm loose. I obligingly let go.

"What'll we *do*?" she whispered out of the side of her mouth.

"I got a plan," I lied. "Just let me do the talking." That seemed to settle her for the moment; as for myself, it only made my palms itch. The cops here could scrag me if they wanted—for all the good it would do them—but I wasn't sure of their intentions toward Opal. To anyone with brains she was more valuable to Sullivan alive since she had information on where the books were, but who said any of these mugs had brains? Maybe Sullivan was looking to make an example of her on what double-crossers could expect from him.

Sullivan . . .

What the hell, since I couldn't talk to Angela, then Sullivan was my next best choice. If I worked things right he could be a whole new cat to skin and nail to the wall. My date with Miss Paco would just have to wait.

The cops urged us toward the hotel until we reached its street entry with the cracked glass on the doors. Calloway was outside now, fully awake again, standing next to one of the squad cars, hands on his hips, looking both worried and disgusted until he caught sight of us. Then he looked delighted. On his face it was not a pleasant expression.

"Caught 'em at the end of the block, Lieutenant," said one of the cops.

Calloway was all but licking his lips over Opal, then he focused on me. "Fleming." What a load of bright hatred the man could put into one word. That the one word was my own name did nothing to ease my worry about the situation. This might be a lot harder than I'd anticipated.

"You know this bird, Lieutenant?"

"I know him. Kyler told me a thing or two. You keep your heaters on him, and if he even tries to look cross-eyed at you for a laugh, plug him."

While his friend held his gun in my face the cop slapped me down and found Tinny's .38 in my coat pocket. After that they seemed to relax, thinking they'd made me safe to be around. They didn't even bother to search Opal or her purse. "He was with the girl. Tried to pass himself off as being with us. Thinks he's smart."

"We'll see how smart. Bring 'em inside."

The lobby had two cops in it, neither of them doing much to lift the tone of the place. The pale manager was off to one side, still looking scared. I didn't see any signs of the hotel's customers. Maybe they were making use of the fire escapes themselves.

"In there," said Calloway, pointing across the lobby to some double doors. They'd probably once sported etched-glass panels to match the ones out front, but the glass was long gone, leaving sad, gaping openings into darkness. One of the cops pushed ahead and hit the light switch. It looked better in the dark.

Opal and I were herded into the hotel's radio room, but the radio wasn't on and probably hadn't worked in two decades or so, it was that old a model. The chairs and sofas meant for the comfort of its listeners were as worn and dusty as the rest of the place, and the ancient rug was so thin, patches of drab flooring showed through in spots. I wanted to take a bulldozer to the joint and put it out of its misery, preferably with crooked cops like Calloway and his friends still inside.

Calloway was a stocky man but with a strangely thin face, and one ear stuck out farther from his head than the other. Put that with sallow skin and cigarette-yellowed teeth and he was anything but leading-man material. He lit up a smoke, then gave Opal another lip-smacking once-over, probably already spending whatever reward Sullivan had offered for her return. "You the bookkeeper?" he asked her.

"Yes. Who are you?"

"Never mind." He looked at me. "And what are you to little Miss Opal the bookkeeper, Fleming?"

"I'm just looking out for her."

"Uh-huh. Well, you ain't doing such a good job, are you, kid?"

In here the light was just fine. I focused on him, not too hard; I didn't want his boys getting wise. "What are you going to do with us?"

His face went a little slack, but it couldn't be helped. "Take you to see Sullivan."

"And where is he?"

Then one of his very helpful friends in uniform stepped in and slammed a fist into my right kidney. My change had toughened me up, but he was big and it was a hard enough hit for me to feel it. My legs buckled from the impact; Opal gasped and grabbed at my arm. I didn't quite make it to the floor, but it was a near thing. She kept me shored up until I could stand without wobbling. That son of a bitch had bruised me good.

"The lieutenant asks the questions here, Bo," the cop belatedly informed me. I remembered him from a couple nights back, Calloway's partner, Baker.

Any reply I might have had wouldn't have endeared me to him, so I kept my mouth shut and rubbed my bruise.

"You're not with Paco," said Calloway. He'd snapped right out of it, but I could put him back under as soon as it suited me. "I know most of Frank Paco's people, and you're not one of them either."

I kept shut.

"So who the hell are you, Fleming? And just why did Kyler think you were so dangerous?"

I threw a sideways look at the cop who'd hit me. He was grinning, indication that it would be his positive pleasure to pop me again. He wore brass knuckles. Jeez, no wonder he'd hurt me. "Kyler was nuts, not like Big Frankie, but nuts all the same, right? I just rubbed him the wrong way is all."

"You rubbed him out is what I heard."

"Not me, Chaven did the honors. Thought he could take over running things. He planned to work something out with Angela Paco, but she didn't want any of it."

"And how do you know that?"

"I heard things. Last night I was in the room when he put four slugs into his boss."

"You were, huh?"

"Yeah. Followed you and Baker from the Nightcrawler Club after you missed your chance to take out Gordy."

He'd been drawing a long pull on his cigarette and suddenly choked. Smoke came out of his nose and mouth. One of the cops started to thump him on the back, but Calloway waved him off. "You—"

"Yeah, me." I pretended to look around at the others. "Oops, did I let any cats out of the bag?"

The guy behind me. I caught the start of a movement from the corner of my eye, whirled, and sidestepped out of the way of his fist at just the right moment. He missed me and it threw off his balance. He recovered fast and looked ready to make another swing, but Calloway nixed him.

"Can it! Let him talk!"

Baker subsided, eyes full of hate, all aimed in my direction. He resumed his post behind me. I could hear his breathing.

"So you heard things at Kyler's?" Calloway prompted.

"This and that. Not too much because Chaven was in a hurry. He corked Kyler, but before he could plug me next, I jumped through a window and ran like hell." Not exactly, but the truth wouldn't do me any good with this bunch.

"And how do you know about Angela Paco's plans?"

"I was also at what was left of her daddy's mansion last night."

"Busy boy."

"I was—wasn't I, Opal?"

She nodded, looking serious.

"I had my ears open; I heard plenty. Angela took a shine to me and hired me on."

"To keep an eye on Opal?"

"Something like that." I hoped Opal would stay quiet until I played things out.

"Well, I'm firing you for her."

"Not a good idea, Calloway."

"Whyzat?"

I spread my hands, looking confident. "Because Sullivan's gonna want to know what I know about Angela and what she's got planned for him."

He thought about it, then shook his head. "And I think you're just gassing on to keep yourself alive."

Time to try again. "Listen to me, Calloway. I'm telling the truth and you know it."

His face went blank again, just for a few seconds. It was enough. Then his brow furrowed. "Listen . . . to you?"

"Yes. The best thing you can do is leave Opal where you found her, clear your men out, and take me to see Sullivan."

It must have been the complete opposite of what he really wanted to do, because he didn't fall all over himself trying to obey me. His expression clouded up as he struggled against it.

"Lieutenant, listen to me. . . ." I put on a little more pressure, but it must have spooked Baker; the bastard popped me in the same place. This time I did hit the floor. Just to my knees, but it shattered the fragile link I'd made.

"Like hell I will," Calloway said somewhere above me.

Opal had dropped back this time; maybe she'd seen this kind of thing before and knew that she couldn't help me.

I *should* have told him to do one thing at a time, like having him get rid of his men first, then I could have gone full force on him. Live and learn.

"Now, what's the real story, punk?"

"It's what he just told you," said Opal.

We both looked at her in surprise. Calloway because she'd not been much of a participant until now and me because I didn't think she knew how to lie.

"Angela wanted him to watch me, like a bodyguard. I don't like him, though."

"Stop, my heart's bleeding," he said.

"I don't like you either. You'd better let us go or—"

"Or what?"

She bit her lower lip. "You'd just better, that's all, or there'll be big trouble."

"The only big trouble is the kind coming to you, four eyes."

Opal flushed red again, but from anger. "Don't talk like that to me!"

I lurched to my feet. Baker braced himself for an attack, but I hobbled over to Opal instead. "Take it easy," I murmured, touching her arm. "He's not worth it."

She shook me off, glaring.

"He's only trying to provoke you, don't give him the satisfaction. Just keep quiet and—"

"And what?" asked Calloway.

I turned back to him. "And give me a chance to get things worked out with your boss. You *are* planning to get us to him sometime in the next month or so, aren't you? So how about you leave off taking cheap shots at the lady and start things moving?"

He looked ready to belt me one himself, but held off, his bloodshot eyes going all hard. Then that unpleasant smile of his came back. "Okay. It's gonna be a positive pleasure. I can't wait to see what Sullivan does to you."

No reply from me, I knew when not to push my luck.

"Where's the phone in this dump?" he demanded.

"One at the desk," someone answered.

"Keep these two on a leash till I get back." He stalked out. I could see him through the empty panels turning his charm on the cowed manager at the desk. He got the phone he wanted and made a call. I could guess it was to report in to Sullivan.

Opal tugged hard at my coat sleeve, getting my attention. She didn't voice any obvious questions, but her face was eloquent. She was scared and mad. I knew the feeling. I patted her hand.

"Don't worry," I whispered. "They're not going to hurt you."

Baker polished his brass knucks on his shirt and laughed once. I wanted to pay him back for that and a couple other things, but it'd have to wait. The other three who'd followed us in all had their guns out. I wasn't about to tackle the whole team with Opal still in the room.

Calloway didn't take long and was full of orders when he got back. He sent one of his men out to fix the Caddie and his return signaled our general exit from the premises. I hoped the next joint would have better atmosphere. Before we'd quite got through the lobby, he made us all stop again and ordered another man to cuff me and Opal together.

"Hey—no need for this," I protested as he latched my right hand to her left. Opal gave out with a similar set of complaints, to no avail. They told us to shut the hell up and get moving.

"This stinks," said Opal.

"Goes double for me, sister," I grumbled as her big purse bumped against me. I thought about the .22 she had in it, but thinking about it was as far as it went. There's a time and place for stuff like that, and it wasn't here and now. The right moment would come, preferably when I was with Sullivan, and then I wouldn't need a gun. If he wasn't loony like Kyler, I'd be able to deal with him, then Opal and I could both climb out of the jam pot.

Two cops held the front doors wide for us, and out we went into the cold wind. Opal shrugged down in her coat.

Cars in the street: noise, exhaust, bright headlights. A big Packard that must have wandered into the seedy neighborhood by mistake swung around the corner and prevented us from jaywalking to the Caddie.

I saw what was wrong the same moment as the others and grabbed Opal, dragging her down. She yelped, the only human voice I heard before the machine-gun fire blotted everything out.

6

I yanked hard on Opal's arm and we half dropped, half fell on the unforgiving concrete, then I rolled on top of her. It was pure instinct, my body wouldn't stop a bullet now, and God knows there were plenty of them flying. They cracked and thundered all around us, and I pressed my face against Opal's shoulder and prayed for it to be over. It took me back to the War, to the one time I saw any fighting, and I'd moaned a similar prayer then when I'd crouched in a ditch while a bunch of strangers in a machine-gun nest tried to kill me. The noise had gone on and on and on and there'd been an unending supply of it, and that's what was the worst: the sound hammering into my ears as if to beat the brain from my skull. I got the insane thought that maybe if they actually shot me and saw the blood, they'd finally stop the damned noise.

It was like that all over again, only without the ditch. We had no cover at all and didn't dare try for any. I glanced up and saw the slow passage of the Packard as it swept regally by, though it must have been going a good clip. My terror turned it into a snail's crawl.

Calloway and the others were also caught up in the crawl as they ducked and tumbled or tried to run clear. The ones who had their guns out returned fire, but I couldn't hear the smaller cracks of their pistols against the fire-spitting roar of a full automatic.

It tore up chunks of pavement; it splintered the hotel doors; it scattered frightened men; it did everything but shut the hell up.

And when I was ready to start yelling just to try drowning out the bedlam, it was suddenly gone.

If there was silence, I couldn't appreciate it. My ears felt stuffed, like I had a cold, and seemed to ring like a phone on the fritz. Down the street the Packard's red taillights vanished around the corner. It could come back, no reason why it shouldn't. Calloway's men were no match for it, that was for damned sure.

I checked on them. One was down on the walk and not moving, two rushed past trying to catch up with the car, firing as they ran. The others were out of sight. Calloway was just in front of me and starting to stand; he yelled at the pursuers to come back, sounding like he was behind a brick wall. I could hear him, but not too well.

"Opal?" I knew I was talking too loud; it was all reaction.

She didn't answer right away. I looked down, trying to read her pinched face. Her glasses were half off. I straightened them for her with my free hand. Her eyes were squeezed tight shut and she was half-curled on her side. I told her it was over and tried to coax her up, but she wouldn't move.

"Hey, honey, you okay?"

All she did was groan.

Bloodsmell.

Oh, damn. Oh, goddammit. Couldn't tell where she'd been hit, her coat was dark.

"Calloway!"

He turned, looked down, and took it all in, then started cussing.

"Call an ambulance, you bastard!"

"Screw it!" he yelled back, and stalked over to his fallen man. It didn't take long to check him out; at twenty feet I could tell he was dead. One of the others had caught a slug in the leg, and was limping back, supported by a luckier friend.

Opal whimpered.

"Calloway!"

He twitched as if from an electric shock and rounded on me. Had his gun in hand. Three quick steps and he brought it level with my eyes, inches away. The fast movement surprised me, but the real shock was his expression.

I'd heard about blind rage, knew all about it from feeling it myself, but this was the first time I'd actually *see* what it did to anyone. His face was distorted, teeth bared, eyes wide and blank, all the cords and veins showed through his mottled red skin. Unrecognizable. I stared right up the barrel of his .45, the hole in that yawning muzzle blacker than hell. It was a meaningless tool. Nothing was more dangerous than the man himself. I tore my gaze from it to his sightless eyes and knew what birds know when they freeze just as the snake takes them.

Before I could vanish, he pulled the trigger.

My heart jumped into my throat, a cold ball made of iron and ice that made me choke. It slammed back down into my gut again. No time to brace for the pain.

But . . . nothing.

Used-up round in the chamber.

He tried three more times before the idea penetrated that it wasn't going to work, then I thought he'd throw the revolver at me. One of his men bellowed at him, and that seemed to help. He came out of it by degrees, but very fast. One moment trying to kill me, the next shouting back at his man and getting reorganized, and in between he visibly hauled in his fury hand over hand to shut it away for later. It had to be for later. A man doesn't get crazy mad like that without having a lot of it stored up inside.

Then Opal made another pain-filled sound and I got mad again myself.

"Calloway, stop screwing around and take this kid to a hospital."

"I'll take you both to hell!"

"She's no good to you dead!"

Baker put in his two cents' worth. "We gotta scram, Lieutenant. We can't explain this."

Calloway said "shit" a few times under his breath while he was thinking. "Okay, we'll scram, but not all of us. Get the Caddie and bring it over here. You and you are with us." He pointed at the cops who'd tried chasing the Packard.

Baker gestured at the dead and wounded. "What about—"

"They stay." He looked at the wounded man's partner. "You're both going to cover for us. Here's the story: You heard something at the raid about this place, that the Paco gang might have holed up here, so the three of you got ambitious and came to check it. Before you could get inside, the shooting started. Blame it on Paco. You leave everything else out, understand? The rest of us weren't here."

The men wearily nodded. One looked down at the dead cop on the sidewalk. "Lieutenant . . ."

"I know, but it's done. You cover for us and you're covering for him. You're going to give him an 'in the line of duty' finish. Make him a hero and no one touches the rest of us, got that?"

"Yeah." They nodded again.

"Now get in and fix it with the manager, make sure he knows what's good for him. You two stick together and just follow normal procedure. Do the job right and I'll see to it

you get extra this week; botch it, and we're all in the can.
Go.''

They hobbled off.

He turned to me. "How bad is she?"

"She's bleeding, Goddammit, how bad does she have to
be for you to do something?"

He didn't bother to answer, just came close and knelt. He
pulled Opal's coat open. The white blouse underneath was
stained with bright, fresh red. He undid the buttons and peeled
back the right half. There was a hole just under her collar-
bone, seeping more red at an alarming rate. The blood made
steam in the cold air. He pulled out a folded handkerchief
and pressed it against the wound, then rose and nodded at his
two remaining men. "Get them in the car."

"Where we going?"

"Sullivan's."

Baker got the Caddie started and swerved it in against the
curb. Calloway climbed in the front, and the other two helped
me get Opal in the back. I told them to take the cuffs off to
make things easier, but no one listened. Wedged between
them, I held Opal on my lap. She wasn't big, but completely
limp, making her strangely heavy. I pulled her coat close
around her, hoping to keep her warm, and kept up the pressure on the sodden handkerchief.

"Hey, Opal, come on, sweetheart, wake up."

She made a protesting sound. God, she was pale.

"Hospital, Calloway," I said as Baker hit the gears and
pulled into the street.

Calloway looked at me over the seat. Didn't say a word.

"Hospital." I was focused on him, but didn't think there
was enough light.

He jerked his chin at the men. "Keep him quiet."

"She's bleeding to death, you—"

The cop on my right cracked me across the forehead with

the side of his revolver. Not full force, but enough to hurt, to get my attention. It made a white flash under my eyelids, and my head snapped back over the top of the seat. I blinked at the padded cloth of the ceiling for a few seconds before straightening.

"Quiet," the cop said, pointing with one finger like a parent to an especially backward child.

I glared at him. "This girl is bleeding, dammit, it ain't gonna stop just because—"

His partner got me from the other side. More flashing lights. More pain. No vanishing for me, it wasn't to that point yet, but would be the next time I opened my mouth. I weighed the pros and cons of vanishing. It would throw these two for damn sure. I could get in the front seat, take out Calloway, and get Baker to . . . no, bad idea. He was going over the limit just now. Any surprises at this speed could be fatal. I'd have to wait until we got to a stop signal.

Checked Opal. Her lids cracked open.

"Hey, sweetheart, come on and talk to me." No hits from my friends for this. They only took offense if I tried speaking to them. "Opal?"

She winced and shifted in my arms, then made a soft cry.

"It's all right, we're getting help." I looked at Calloway for some crumb of confirmation, but saw only the back of his head.

"It hurts," said Opal.

"I know it does, honey. Just hold on for a little bit."

"My shoulder burns . . . it hurts."

"*Calloway*—"

The guy on my right put his gun to my temple. "This one's all loaded again. You can shut up on your own, or I can do it for you." The look on his face told me he wasn't even remotely kidding.

It wouldn't do Opal any good if they shot me. I'd just

disappear, and whatever happened next would be out of my control until I finally recovered. Best not to push them or pull any supernatural surprises until an opportunity occurred. If only they'd put the inside light on; I'd whammy them so fast they wouldn't know what hit them.

But Baker kept up the driving, sliding illegally through stop signals. Never a traffic cop around when you needed one, not that getting pulled over would change things. All Calloway and the others had to do was show their badges and move on. He had plenty of rank to get away with nearly anything. He must have been one hell of an asset for Kyler; now he was Sullivan's man, and that made me wonder what Sullivan was like. I was getting a good idea from watching Calloway, though. Before, with Kyler, Calloway's attitude was that of any worker for his boss, respectful, but impersonal. Now he was showing a lot of anger, but it was of the kind that meant underneath he was really afraid.

The tension in the confined space was smothering. They were utterly silent, which wasn't right; people always have to talk. On the other hand, one of their own had been killed right in front of them. Any of them could have caught that hit. That sort of thing was a tough deal to approach no matter what direction you took. No wonder they wanted me quiet.

Not that I gave a tinker's damn for what they were going through. Opal was my only concern. I tried to get her to talk again, but she'd only shake her head and mumble about hurting. All I could do was keep the pressure up on the wound. My right arm was curled around her to hold her close. Before too long I noticed a warm wetness there. Blood, of course. It had soaked down from her shoulder. The whole car reeked of it.

Had to take a risk. I kept my voice low and even. "Calloway, she's bleeding to death from this. It's no flesh wound. It's serious. She needs help."

He looked over the seat again, sending a silent signal to his men not to hit me. "We're taking her to help, pretty boy."

"She needs a hospital. Get us to one. I'll give your boss anything he wants on the Pacos, I help him put them right out of business, but this girl has to come first."

"Can't do that, but she'll get help, I promise. Now shut the hell up." He turned away. The guy on my right wore a face that was just waiting for me to say one more thing so he could shoot.

The signals thinned out, as did the traffic, and we were on a long dark stretch of road that was almost but not quite in the country. The city was growing in this direction, and stores and gas stations were making steady headway against empty fields. A lot of the businesses had gone bust because of the crash, though. The remaining ones were most certainly tied to the mobs and had another, hidden business on the side, like the dance studio. You could tell which ones, too, they just had that look.

I recognized the route. We were going to Kyler's roadhouse. Unlike Angela, perhaps Sullivan felt he had no need to keep his head down. Or maybe he knew about the seven hundred grand hidden in the basement. Opal's diagram was still folded away in my little notebook, safe for the moment. They'd only checked for guns earlier.

A few minutes more and Baker hauled the wheel around, turned into a discreet unpaved drive, then we pulled into a graveled parking lot. It served a big joint, two sprawling stories of brown brick with white trim, a wide porch going all the way around the front and sides. In the summer tables and chairs would be there for the patrons to enjoy their drinks and food while counting the stars. No one was out now. The place was closed tight, all the windows dark, the outer doors shut, the lot itself empty and bleak. Quite a change from last night, when everything was jumping like New Year's Eve.

We drove around to the back. Three cars were parked close by the delivery entry. A single cold blue light glowed over the metal door. It looked to be hard to get through. All the windows on this side were webbed over with metal lattices. If anyone wanted to break in, it would have to be elsewhere on the building.

Baker braked and cut the motor. My hearing had fully recovered during the trip; I tried to listen and pick up Opal's heartbeat, but the others made too much noise piling from the car. They ordered me to get out and I did so, trying my best not to bump Opal around too much. She whimpered and cried again, holding weakly to me with her free hand. I carried her up half a dozen wood steps to a loading platform, where Baker and Calloway were just going in the back door.

A good-sized kitchen. I had a feeling of dèjá vu, but only for a moment. Trudence Coldfield's place had been full of light, warmth, and company; this one was dim, chill, and crowded with seven or eight hard-looking men. A swell welcoming committee, if you didn't mind all the iron they were packing under their armpits.

The shadows here were big; a single light shone at the far end over one of the stoves, but it looked to be enough for me to work with—if I was careful. Calloway was edgy; Baker, alert and ready for trouble, was right behind me along with the other two cops. Crooks and cops, each group eyed the other warily.

A slight-figured, greasy-haired man with pale, cold eyes behind tortoiseshell-framed glasses stepped forward. He wore a silk shirt, suspenders, and a neatly done up bow tie. He looked me and Opal over with mild interest, then turned to Calloway. "What happened?"

I caught a whiff of sweaty fear from Calloway as he hesitated over answering.

Opal didn't have time for this.

I pushed forward past all the men, past Calloway. "Are you Sean Sullivan?"

He quirked his lip and lifted his chin. "I'm Maxwell, Mr. Sullivan's secretary."

"Well this is his bookkeeper. She's been shot and needs a doctor."

"You're Fleming? Calloway told me about y—"

"Later. You just get some wheels moving."

Cold eyes on Calloway now. Leisurely. "How did this happen?"

He shifted once on his feet, visibly uncomfortable, then gave a succinct report of the basics. "I think it was Paco's people."

"Hitting their own place?" Maxwell shook his head, amused. "Why would they do that?"

I bulled closer, this time to make eye contact with him. "Talk about it later. You need to help this girl. Now. Nothing's more important than that."

He rocked on his heels.

A couple of his boys stepped toward me. I felt something cold and hard pressing on my temple. Calloway had his gun on me. "Shut up, pretty boy."

Maxwell wobbled again like I'd slapped him, then recovered his balance. He came out of it, raised one hand. "That will be enough, Lieutenant. He's perfectly right. We really must see to the welfare of the young lady."

Calloway shot me a murderous look. "What did you do to—"

"Later," snapped Maxwell, suddenly all bustle and business. "Put her on that table. One of you find a pot, get some water heated. Find some towels."

The whole troop stood stunned for a moment by this change in him, but Maxwell told them to move again, and that did the trick. Finally. They scattered to obey his orders.

I eased Opal onto a big, white-painted preparation table. She was very heavy now; she'd passed out.

I focused on Baker, held up my cuffed wrist. "Key. Use it."

He started to reach for it, but Calloway put a hand out to stop him. "What do you think you're doing?"

Baker shook out of it, and couldn't come up with a good answer. They both glared at me, Calloway all puzzled anger until Maxwell stepped in.

"Yes, unlock those things," he said.

Baker looked first at Calloway, but got the nod from Maxwell. He unlocked the cuffs. Opal's skin was marked red where the metal had bit, but that was the least of her worries. I tried to be gentle as I wrestled the coat off her; the wet, folded handkerchief dropped away to the floor, spattering blood as it landed.

Her coat had soaked up a lot of it, but more was coming out. One of the men found towels; I grabbed one and pressed it against the hole. At least it wasn't pulsing, otherwise she'd be dead by now.

Maxwell told one of his men to go upstairs and get someone. Another man was busy at a sink, running hot tap water into a big pot, the rest, including Calloway, just stood about and stared hard at me. Probably wondering what I'd done to put the corncob up Maxwell's ass. Let 'em wonder.

"Get some light in here," I said.

Someone found the switch, brightening things instantly. The man with the water pot put it on a massive stove and turned the gas on. Blue and yellow flames licked high, hissing. It was the only sound besides their breathing until I caught a double set of footsteps coming our way. One heavy, the other shuffling.

Maxwell's errand runner came in, holding the arm of a thinner, slightly older man. He was stooped over, like a fighter guarding his belly, and had a sizable shiner forming around his left eye.

What the hell?

It was Doc.

They must have grabbed him at the raid. Worked him over a bit, too, to judge by his faltering walk. I didn't think he was in shape to treat himself, much less another, but any port in a storm.

"Doctor, your services are required," said Maxwell, gesturing him toward the table.

Doc squinted against the light. Took in me first. Mouth wide. "Son of a bitch. I thought you were—"

"Can it," I snapped. "You were drunk and made a mistake."

He scowled. "Wouldn't be the first time."

Next he'd be asking me how I'd got off the yacht alive. Best to change the subject. I pointed at Opal. He squinted again, rubbed his good eye, and came closer.

"Sweet Jesus, what'd you do to her?"

"She caught a forty-five. She's bleeding bad."

"No shit." He tsked over her.

"You sober enough to work?"

"Yes, unfortunately. I do better drunk. Now get outta my way." He went to the sink, started running the hot water, and soaped up his hands. They were trembling.

I turned to Maxwell. "Get him a drink. He's no good to her if he's got the shakes."

Calloway stepped forward. "Listen, you punk—"

But that was as far as Maxwell let him get. "Another time, Lieutenant."

A quiet order from him sent a man off to play waiter. The rest stared at Maxwell, astonished. Calloway stared at me, still murderous. He didn't know exactly what was up, what I'd done, but he didn't like it. I'd let too much show, but didn't care.

"Clear out, the rest of you," said Maxwell. "Give the man some room. Lieutenant, please come upstairs with me."

"But what about—" He gestured in my direction.

"I'm sticking here," I said, ready to give a push where it was needed.

"He'll be fine," answered Maxwell in a gratifyingly normal tone. "I'm sure his concern for Miss Opal will be sufficient to keep him from wandering off, and there will be a man here on watch. Come along, Mr. Sullivan is not very patient."

The mention of Sullivan's name had its own special influence. Calloway holstered his gun and went quietly with the rest.

"My, but don't you have a way with people," said Doc, witnessing their exodus out of the corner of his eye as he scrubbed. We were alone except for one man left behind on guard. I could take care of him easily enough and bolt now if I wanted, but didn't see much advantage to it at the moment.

"It's just a knack. What about getting her to a hospital?"

"Fine with me, but not yet. She's likely in too tender a condition for moving around. Lemme get a look-see first."

"Got your bag?"

"Nope. Just have to make do with what's on hand. Not much difference between a kitchen and a surgery, though, the tools for cuttin' are just a sight bigger."

Another man came back with a couple of bottles of booze. Doc ordered a triple whiskey, neat. I poured it out, then had to hold the glass so he could keep his hands clean while he drank. He took in a sizable jolt, squeezed his eyes shut in reaction, and shook his head.

"Hoo now, but ain't that the cheap stuff? Thought they'da

drunk up all the deer piss left over from before Repeal. Okay, put the rest here.'' He held his hands out from the running tap. I dumped the glassful over them. Doc scrubbed in it, then held his hands high, inspecting them. ''Lorda mercy, any germ alive after a shower of that rotgut gets my respect. Now, let's see what's wrong with the little gal.''

I took away the top towel and pulled open Opal's stained blouse. He studied the damage. The hole looked too big, too ragged.

Still bleeding.

''Huh. She got lucky. Missed her lung. Might have some bone fragments. Have to clean her up some first. Not just a bullet in there, might be some fabric inside from her clothes when it punched in.''

''What about getting her to a hospital?'' I asked.

''Not just yet. Bleeding's not too bad now, but she don't need any more moving around if we can help it. You start opening drawers and let me see what I got to work with.''

Me and the other guy did so while the third watched. Doc picked out what he wanted and had us dump them into the pot of boiling water. From his choice of instruments I was very glad Opal was out cold. Just looking at the things made me go all queasy.

''Could use some tweezers,'' he said. ''Rubbing alcohol, sterile dressings, blankets, a pillow.''

I turned to the man. Pushed. He went off to search.

Doc hadn't missed what I'd done. ''Y'know, my granny used to do what you do,'' he muttered, barely moving his lips. ''But then she was older'n God an' a lot more strict, so folks did what she told just to avoid her fussing at 'em. But somethin's different about you. Ain't natural for a punk kid like yourself to get those kind of men to tuck in their tails so easy.''

''No need for you to worry about it.''

"Maybe not, but you just keep doing what you're doing and maybe we can get out of this alive. 'Less you're on their side." He gave me a narrow look.

"I'm on my side, but I'm all for getting out of this alive. They take you as a hostage?"

"S'pose they did, for all the good it'll do 'em. Angela's a spunky gal, she won't lose any sleep if something happens to me so long as she keeps her daddy's organization solid and running."

"She's crazy."

"Pragmatic's the word, my boy. Oh, she'll spit and holler when they hold a gun to my head, but she won't give an inch to Sullivan. When the smoke settles she'll shoot a dozen of his men to get even, then give me a beautiful funeral."

"If we both get out of here with Opal, no one has to die."

"Suits me even better. I'd sure like to get a lot more drinkin' time in before I check out."

The man came back, arms full with a white bundle. "Don't have no blankets here, just tablecloths."

"Bring 'em over," I said. I tucked them around Opal, then stood back, watching, feeling drained and helpless now that I was out of things to do for her.

"You're wanted upstairs," the man told me as I went to the sink to wash the blood from my hands. It was all over my coat, especially the sleeve.

"Doc?"

He waved me off. "Go on. I don't need someone breathin' down my neck the whole time. You can't do nothing here."

But I probably could do something upstairs. Once I got to Sullivan I could have an ambulance, doctors, and maybe even some cops not on the take swooping in like the marines. They'd find the whole nest of roaches asleep and ready to cart away.

I left Doc and his guard and was guided out of the kitchen

and through a darkened dining area where all the chairs were stacked on the tables. Deserted stage for the band, empty dance floor, the kind of opulent decor that only vice money can afford. It should have been filled with lights, music, and laughter, but not even the ghost of a past customer stirred the place. I was glad when we left it behind.

Upstairs was more of the same, with carpeting so thick and soft a hummingbird would have sunk in up to its beak. Some of the crowd from the kitchen had congregated in the hall, smoking and talking low. They stopped doing both when I came into view. Everyone watched as we walked between them toward a door paneled with fancy wood inlay at the far end. There was a brass sign stuck to it with the word MAN-AGER cut into the metal in curving script letters. My escort opened the door and motioned me in first, then kept close behind, an armed shadow, ready for trouble if I even thought about stepping out of line.

It was the room where Kyler had died. A big place, de-signed to impress the peasants. Lots of money in the trim-mings, but not enough to take the bloodstains out of the pricey carpet. Dried out and gone dark, they were still where he'd dropped.

Maxwell stood attentively next to the vast desk at the far end, hands loose at his sides, looking on everyone with ap-parently benign interest. Calloway, Baker, and the two other uniforms were in front and turned as I came in. The man seated behind it didn't bother to get up.

"That's close enough," he said when I was still a good thirty feet from them. He looked at Calloway, who must have given him an earful about me while I was busy downstairs. "Satisfied?"

Calloway licked his lips, staring at me with intense hate. A glimmer of the rage he'd shown before at the shooting lurked in his face, and he was aiming it in my direction. "Blindfold him. Put a sack over his head."

"Later. I like to see a man's face when I talk. Helps me to know when he's trying to lie."

"You Sullivan?" I asked, already knowing the answer this time.

"That I am." His accent was more of Boston than of Ireland, but that didn't mean anything. The Irish gangs had had a firm hold all over the East Coast for years, what with their rumrunning during Prohibition. Hell, some of them were even starting to put on respectable airs and sending their kids off to places like Yale and Harvard to learn polo. Sullivan looked to be one such example of the coming generation; he was younger than I expected, early thirties. His conservative and costly suit draped a stocky but solid frame, topped by brown hair with a red cast to it. The stockiness extended to a square face with a cheerfully pleasant expression, and he was probably handsome to the girls except for those hard eyes. They were flat as paint. I couldn't read a thing from his expression, a natural-born poker player. He gave me a long, careful looking over. If he was trying to make me uncomfortable, he was already too late. I was way past being either intimidated or impressed by his kind, all I could feel was a weary disgust. Just when you think all the roaches are gone, another one turns up.

"Fleming, is it?" he asked, also already knowing the answer, if I could tell anything by his tone and self-assured manner. If I thought of him as a cockroach, then he must have pegged me for a dung beetle. This was going to be interesting.

I nodded once. Calloway kept watching, damn him. If I so much as winked, he'd probably plug me one. Didn't matter. I was too far away from him and Sullivan to do anything fancy. Just have to wait for the right moment when it came.

Sullivan indicated his pet cop. "The lieutenant here says you're working for the Pacos."

"I was just looking after Opal." There, not exactly a clear answer, but not really lying, he could take it any way he liked.

"Didn't do too well at it, did you?"

"Out of my control."

"Why were you two at the hotel in the first place?"

"Everyone scattered after the raid. We were to wait there for Angela to call us so we could hook up with her someplace else."

"And did she?"

"Yeah. Told us to lay low until she could send someone for us, only your stooges got there first."

"And who do *you* think is behind the hit?"

I had a very good idea and hated it, but wasn't about to say anything. The situation was dangerous enough. Shook my head. "The Pacos have a lot of enemies. Maybe some smaller bunch wants a cut of their pie. Maybe the hit was meant for Calloway, and Opal and I were just unlucky to be there. Anyone at the hotel who was wise to the situation had plenty of time to call for friends to come over and get a job organized. Calloway and his boys weren't exactly subtle."

"Calloway seems to think it was the Pacos."

"Making a hit on their most valuable asset? Oh, sure, that makes lots of sense. They need Opal to decode the account books for 'em. Without her, they're useless."

"Maybe they didn't want her coming back to work for me again."

"Could be. Of course, you could have done it yourself to cripple the Paco operation."

He went frozen-faced for a moment, then chuckled. "Maybe I did. But she's back with us now, so it's all under the bridge."

I threw a quick glance at Calloway, who was looking at

Sullivan and trying to keep from showing anything but a blank face at my latest suggestion. Apparently there wasn't a whole lot of trust built up between either of them yet. Fine with me; I could play the divide-and-conquer game. Let him wonder if his new boss set him up.

Sullivan arranged his face to display the smile of a reasonable man. "What I need now are the books Opal took away to little Angela. Oh, and don't think any of us are fooled by her scam. We all know Big Frankie's not the man he once was."

"Angela's just as dangerous. More so."

"That's why we want her out. She's too flashy. She draws attention into areas we would rather have go unnoticed."

That was for damn sure. "And you want the books in exchange for . . ."

"I don't buy back my own stolen property, Fleming. But I am willing to return Doc to her, if she chooses to be sensible."

"What makes him so valuable?"

"He's been with Big Frankie for years, practically another father to Angela. I'm not above using her sentiment against her."

Gave him a nod. This wasn't the time to tell him he was following the wrong trail with that ploy.

"Doc's other value is that he knows where all the bodies are, so to speak. I'm figuring a little persuasion and he'll be too glad to tell us all of the Pacos' hiding places, then I send my boys in to smoke 'em out one by one. The books are bound to be somewhere in the rubble."

"Not a good idea, Mr. Sullivan."

Brows high. "Oh?"

"It'd take too long and you'd lose a lot of soldiers. Operations like that are expensive and make noise. It draws the kind of attention you say you don't like. This ain't the same wide-open town Big Al ran a few years back. You make enough of a stink and the reform crowd gets ants in their pants and start putting on the pressure to the politicians. You may have a lot of them in pocket, but not all. They'd have to do something. Then there's the federal side of things. Nasty bunch of Boy Scouts is what I hear about 'em, and they can play tough and dirty as anyone. And don't forget the tax people. You won't want them checking up on your income records any more than Capone did, and all that and more would just be for starters. I'm thinking the bosses who sent you here would prefer you to go completely unnoticed by any of that crowd.''

Elbows on the desk, he clasped his hands together and rested his chin on them, amused. "Got it all figured, have you?"

"It's pretty obvious."

"Then how would you recommend I get my books back without drawing all this disaster and grief down on my head?"

I was hoping he'd ask. "Let *me* get them for you."

That made everyone laugh except Calloway.

Sullivan recovered first. "And how do you plan to do that?"

"I talk with Angela, feed her a line about you setting up a hit on me and Opal—she'll be thinking that anyway because of you being behind the dance-studio raid—then tell her she needs to scram before Doc spills his guts. She's stubborn, but not stupid, she'll find some hole Doc doesn't know about and take me along. She'll have the books with her, so—"

"You know a lot for some punk who just started working for her," said Calloway.

"It only makes sense. Without them, her whole business is crippled, so she's gonna keep 'em tight as her own skin."

"And you think she'll just hand them over to you?" asked Sullivan.

"She'll raise a royal ruckus—unless I can promise her some additional compensation besides Doc's safe return. I can talk her into it, but she'll want money."

"I don't buy back my own—"

"I heard you the first time, but you're gonna have to bend a bit on that point. You gotta give her something so she thinks she's saved face and come out ahead on the deal."

"Bend how far?"

"Give Angela enough so she can take Big Frankie off to some sanitarium to get his head shrunk. I heard Switzerland has good doctors for that kind of thing."

He gave a snort and derisive shake of his head.

"Her father is what all this is about," I said. "What she wants from the Paco territories is money to get him well again—which probably ain't gonna happen, so you won't have to worry about him coming back. One or two days at the most and they're both out of the country, out of your hair, no one gets killed, and the papers and reform groups don't have anything to kick about because nothing's happened."

"Except for me being out of a ton of cash."

"A week's receipts for the territory at most. Compare that to a full-blown war—and she's ready to fight it—and you've got yourself a bargain. Think of the expenses saved on funerals alone."

Calloway sneered, but Sullivan slapped the desk and burst into laughter again. "You got balls coming in like this and telling me how to run things, kid."

"I'm just making a suggestion or two for everyone's benefit, Mr. Sullivan."

"And don't be pulling that 'aw, shucks' routine on me. We both know you're a smart operator or you wouldn't have lasted this long in the business."

I gave a noncommittal shrug.

"What I'm thinking is you're trying to go into business for yourself. Maybe you've figured a cute way of arranging for me to hand over this compensation to Angela, and then it disappears and so do you."

Shook my head. "How you make the payment is your problem. Work it out with Angela, use your own people. Just give me the chance to convince her and the rest is your game. I want no part of it."

"I almost believe you. What makes you so special that she'll listen to you?"

Gave a laugh this time. "Well, she and me . . . we got us a sort of understanding . . . if you know what I mean."

"The hell you say." He exchanged a look with Maxwell. "First I've heard of it. How 'bout you, Calloway? You know about this?"

"No." He was watching me like a rattlesnake.

"Maybe we should ask Doc what he knows."

"Go ahead," I told him. I was willing to gamble that Doc would tumble to things and play along. He was a drunk, but an instinctive survivor. "But let him take care of Opal first before you start dragging him up here to play twenty questions. Oh, and if you want to make sure she stays around so she can decode the books once you get them back, get someone better than Doc to look after her. You must have somebody who knows of a safe place she can go for proper treatment and no questions asked, otherwise . . ." I raised one hand and made a casting away gesture. Anything more would have been too much for this crowd.

Maxwell looked at his boss. There was a very, very slight change in his manner, an indication of my earlier influence on him. I only noticed because I was looking for it. "Shall I see to that task?"

Sullivan cocked a brow at him. "You think?"

"The young lady was in a bad way, I assure you. Doc can patch her up for now, but I doubt that he can keep her alive given the limits of his circumstances."

For a long moment I mentally held my breath.

Sullivan watched me the whole time. If I knew what he wanted to see, I'd have given it to him. He finally quirked a corner of his mouth and nodded. "Okay."

Let out the mental breath. But didn't show it. I still got the feeling that Sullivan noticed.

Maxwell went past me to the door. I caught the scent of bay rum coming off his hair. Put him in seedier clothing and he could have been any of the lonely hearts cooling heels at the dance studio. He spoke with the men outside for a moment, asking for information, then issuing quiet orders. He didn't raise his voice beyond a murmur, but he initiated a lot of movement in response. Either he had hidden depths to inspire such swift obedience or it was enough that he spoke for Sullivan. No matter to me so long as it got help to Opal that much faster.

"Fleming." I turned back to Sullivan. He'd gotten up from the desk and crossed to the bar. He browsed through the various bottles, but couldn't seem to find anything to his taste. "It's time you told me what it is you want from this deal."

"To get out of it with a whole skin."

He shook his head. "We all want that, but what else is there?"

"I just said."

"Uh-uh. Everyone has an angle, especially smart operators, and that's you."

I'd have to throw him something. "All right. What I want is after this is all settled for you to forget I was ever here. I got mixed up in this by accident and want to get clear, completely clear of all this. You and yours pretend that you never heard of me and I promise to return the favor."

He put his back to the bar, leaning on it to regard me. The crease on his pants was fresh, his shoes were new and well polished. And he was still too far away for me to do anything constructive. "That's all?"

"I'm a smart enough operator to know when it's time to leave the game."

"You leave the game when you're ahead."

"I'm ahead if I leave this one alive. I'm way ahead if I'm anonymous to the other players and team captains. They can go on without me."

That raised another chuckle. Maxwell took his spot by the desk again and continued with the benign expression. I wondered if he'd look so harmless without the glasses and bay rum in his slicked-down hair. Easy subject for hypnosis or not, there was something about him that was starting to make my skin crawl.

"Ready to leave your girlfriend, are you?"

"Don't worry, I'll let her down easy."

More laughs as Sullivan returned to the desk, too, and motioned for Calloway and his group to move off. They came to stand near me, but not too near. Calloway made it obvious that he didn't like my getting on with his boss. Maxwell leaned forward, head cocked in a listening pose. Sullivan murmured very quietly so no one else could catch any of it, but I had no trouble at all hearing the conversation, only with keeping my face composed while they talked.

"Can't trust him," said Sullivan. "Not the whole way."

Maxwell was probably good at poker. His lips barely moved. "No, but if he could do the job, it would save you a lot of effort."

"He's too confident. He should be scared."

"Indeed he should be."

"Hasn't even broken a sweat. He's worried about the girl, but that's all. He's got another game running. You think?"

"Maybe."

"He talks to Angela, sure, but then does a double cross and turns on us. Leads her right back here for a hit."

"Endangering Doc?"

"That's what I'd do to get rid of a threat like me. Position she's in, she can't afford to have friends in this business."

"It would endanger Opal, too."

"I don't think she's that important. Not as important as getting me out of the way. So what if the books are coded, we just find someone to figure them out for us. She could do the same."

"Have to get them back first," Maxwell pointed out.

"So I should use this punk?"

"As long as he's on a leash. Opal can be the leash. Let him run and see what he does."

"You think she matters that much to him?"

"I saw how he was downstairs with her. Since you can't trust him, your best bet is to trust the soft spot he has for her."

"God knows why."

"Some people take in stray cats and get quite silly about them. I expect the same thing has happened here; that, or he thinks he's some kind of knight in armor trying to save the damsel."

"Yeah, he looks the type," he said, tossing a sidelong glance my way. Apparently Sullivan wasn't too impressed by common human decency. He didn't look the type. "Okay, watch my dust." He turned to face me, smiled like a carnival barker, and waved an open hand at the phone on his desk. "Okay, Fleming, I'll buy your goods. Let's get things started. Call Angela."

First check and a bad one, but I had an answer ready. "I don't have the number. It was Opal's department."

That garnered a snort from Calloway. "He's been lying his

head off. He doesn't have anything going with her or he'd know where to call."

I looked at Sullivan "Hey, I can't help it if the boss lady plays her cards close. She's cute, but careful. Do you give your private number out to every guy you hire for muscle? Do all your girlfriends know where to find you every minute of the day? What I can do is ring the hotel and leave a message with your number for her to call, but that would let her know where you are. Besides, it's the long way around things."

"And the short?" asked Sullivan.

"Have someone drive me back to the hotel. She'll have the place under watch—"

"It'll still be crawling with cops investigating the shooting."

"I can get around them."

"How?"

"I got a phony press pass." Actually, it was real, left over from my time as a reporter in New York. One of these nights I'd have to clean out my wallet.

Head shake. "I'm thinking you'll want to slip away for good instead."

"Why should you think that?"

"Because that's what I'd do."

I hate it when guys like Sullivan measure me against themselves, against their own personal standards. It's never complimentary. "You mean if I'd asked for money as well, that would give me a reason to hang around until things got cleared with Angela?"

He smiled. "Exactly."

"But I've asked for anonymity with that freedom. If I took a walk now there'd be nothing to stop you from coming after me. Take it as the other half of the deal that will keep me in line."

"There's a better way."

"Yeah?"

"You do exactly what you've promised and I won't dump Opal in a field somewhere."

I pretended to choke. "What? You can't, you need her to—"

"No one's that important, Fleming. I've other accountants to take her place. Losing her would be inconvenient, but not a disaster."

Struggled to pull the anger in. Though I'd known what bluff to expect, it wasn't hard to believe in it, so my reaction wasn't all pretend. In fact, for Opal's own good, I'd better believe his threat whether he was bluffing or not. "You lay one finger on her . . ."

He kept up the smile. I was feeding him exactly what he wanted to hear. "She'll be safe, so long as you behave."

"You've got my word on it. I'll swing this deal for you."

"Good, because if you don't, if Angela turns up here and tries acting cute, Opal is crow food."

"I get you. I still have to see Angela to make this work."

"That I can believe," muttered Calloway.

I spared him a glance. "Have Calloway and his men take me back. You know he'd never let me out of his sight."

"Damn right I wouldn't. But we cuff and blindfold him first."

Sullivan gave a half snort. "He's really got you spooked, hasn't he?"

"I'm not shitting you on this, Mr. Sullivan. There's something really weird about this bird. He can get people to do things, all he has to do is look at 'em."

"If that's true, then maybe he can get Angela to play ball with us. Do whatever you want, then. Max, give the kid our number."

Okay, so my idea of putting them all to sleep and calling

in the marines didn't happen. I knew my limits. If it had just been me alone, I'd have taken the chance, but there were too many of them, and she was too vulnerable. Doc as well.

Maxwell drew out an oversized fountain pen and wrote something on a slip of paper, blew on the ink, then walked over to hand it to me. "When you've got things arranged, call. You'll have until midnight to make an initial report. To us. After that and we won't answer to Opal's safety."

I automatically checked my watch, but found my wrist was clean. There didn't seem much use to wearing a broken time-piece, so I'd left it on my bureau at home. "How long till then?"

"A couple hours."

"It may take more than that to fix things."

"Nonetheless, you will call in."

Focused on him. Light. Casual. Didn't want to give any clue of it to Calloway. "Take care of Opal, would you? Like she's your own kid sister."

Maxwell blinked behind the glasses. Wasn't sure if I got to him or not, but I didn't dare do more. He stepped out of Calloway's path; he and his cops closed on me, and I was hustled downstairs.

Out through the kitchen again. The bloodsmell was mixed with the sting of rubbing alcohol and the sour smell of cheap booze. Opal lay small and forlorn on the table, covered to the chin with white tablecloths, her skin nearly the same color. I tried not to think about how much the sight reminded me of a corpse in a morgue. Doc sat on a steel stool next to her, drink in hand and a mournful look on his face.

"How is she?" I demanded. If she was dead, then all bets were off, and Sullivan and his crew were just so much cold meat.

"She's hanging on. I've done as much as I can with what

I've got. She could use a transfusion. Might help her chances."

"Talk to Maxwell. He's supposed to be arranging things to get her to a better place."

He sipped from his glass, winced and hissed in reaction, then looked at me. "You must be some kind of a fancy talker, kid. What's going on up there?"

"Never you mind," said Calloway. He found a spare tablecloth and used his pocketknife to cut a wide strip from it. While Baker pulled my arms behind and cuffed me once more, Calloway tied the strip tight around my head, cutting off my vision except for a slice of floor I could just glimpse if I lifted my chin and looked down far enough. Insofar as hypnotizing anyone went at the moment, I was out of the running.

"Take care of her," I called as they pushed me toward the exit. "I'll be back."

Calloway laughed once.

▲
7
▼

THEY held to the blindfold routine all the way into the city. I didn't care much for it, but if they felt safer and left me alone, then I was willing to put up with the farce. It spared me from having to look at the drab streets again, but I found myself fighting an unexpected and embarrassing bout of car sickness. The vehicle's motion was silk-smooth, swaying only at the turns, which was enough to set me off. It had to mean I was tired, not so much physically, but certainly in the mind and soul. The night had been too busy already and wasn't nearly over yet.

A quiet bunch for the first few miles, Baker, who was driving, finally broke the silence. "You trust this Sullivan?"

Calloway didn't take much time to answer. "No. Can't trust any of 'em."

"Then why work for him?"

"Because we don't have a choice. We're in too far."

"What about the boys at the hotel? What if they screwed up or tip on us?"

"Then we say we don't know what they're talking about and stick to it, no more and no less. You guys got that?"

The men on each side of me in the backseat murmured agreement. I kept my trap shut and didn't join in the chorus. Now wasn't the time to play wiseacre. Swallowed some of my spit and took a deep breath, hoping my guts would settle soon. I'd read someplace that dizziness had to do with your ears, so why was it that your stomach was always the focus of all the misery?

"What about the punk, then? Sullivan doesn't trust him, why should we? All he has to do is blab in the wrong ear."

"Our word against his. We're safe. You hear that, Fleming?"

"I heard. I'm not gonna make trouble for you. I was straight up with Sullivan. All I want is out of this mess with a whole skin."

Another one of his short, unpleasant laughs. I knew I sounded like a sucker to him, but didn't give a tinker's damn for his opinion. He'd also just given me confirmation that letting me go free and clear wasn't going to happen if he had anything to do with it. Once the books were back with Sullivan, I'd be written up in them as a new liability vs. an old asset. Though I could hope to avert a major war between the gangs, I couldn't kid myself into thinking either side would let me loose with what I knew on them. The one thing in my favor was that Sullivan didn't quite buy Calloway's suspicions about me. All I had to do was ditch the cop, corner Sullivan alone for a private talk, and the world would be mine again, with me in charge for a change.

Of course, first I had to talk to Angela, since the same and more went for her. At some point before I saw her, Calloway would have to let me go, if only to avoid getting shot by her as a turncoat to Daddy Frank, then I could really get the show on the road. Well, something like that was easily arranged, just wait until he was off guard and jump in with both feet. He looked like he could use a long nap.

We slowed and stopped once or twice, probably for traffic and signal lights. My dizziness eased during the pauses. I tried to guess where we were, then gave it up. So long as the trip

ended at the hotel I didn't need to trouble myself on details—
except where it came to time. I had only until midnight. I
wondered if there was a reason for that particular hour, or if
Maxwell was just being dramatic.

Final stop. I could tell because Baker set the hand brake
just before cutting the motor. A door was opened and the rush
of chill air brushed away the last of my nausea. Next time
I'd ask to travel in the front seat with the window slightly
cracked.

"You might want to take this thing off me, Calloway," I
said, indicating the blindfold. "It's a little too noticeable."

I heard some shifting around and one of the cops pulled
the cloth up over my head, nearly taking my eyebrows along
for the ride. Had to blink a few times against what seemed
to be sudden brightness to me, though the inside of the car
was still in normal darkness. The first thing I focused on was
a gun muzzle hovering a few inches from my nose. Calloway's. It was all loaded again. I could see the rounded nubs
of the bullets tucked inside the chambers.

His face was ugly, his tone worse. "You try anything fancy
and you'll wish to God you hadn't. You understand me?"

Mouth dry, I nodded. I've survived getting shot, but would
just as soon go on living without further experiences of that
sort.

"Okay. Get him out, but take the cuffs off. I don't want
anyone asking about him. Fleming . . ."

"I'm not gonna make trouble."

"Just try, and see what happens."

It took a minute for us all to trade the shelter of the car
for the cutting wind of the sidewalk. Baker had parked half
a block down under a broken streetlight and now stood behind
me with Calloway, who kept his revolver jammed against my
back as a constant reminder to be good.

We made a slow approach. They must have wanted to

make sure it was safe for them, but there was no need to worry. By now most of the fuss from the shooting was over. The trip out to the roadhouse and back and all the talking in between had chewed up a lot of time. Whatever police investigation had taken place here was mostly gone now. Whether any of Angela's goons were hanging about we had yet to see. I tried to check the darker nooks along the street, but that gun in my spine was a hell of a distraction.

The front of the hotel still showed some light and life. Sawhorse barriers had been set up around it to keep people clear. A single cop car with two men inside was parked right at the curb. They were in sight of the bloodstains and the chalk outline where the body had fallen on the pavement. Someone had forgotten to sweep the street: Brass shell casings from the machine gun were all over the place. Maybe tomorrow the morbidly curious would have their chance to collect a memento.

Calloway left guard duty to Baker and walked ahead to the car to speak with the officers. From his manner I couldn't tell if they were in on the take with him or not. They didn't bother to get out into the wind. I strained to hear, but they were too far away even for me to pick up a stray word. Calloway gestured at the mess on the walk once or twice, looking serious and sympathetic. The driver glanced back at our group and shrugged, nodding. Calloway had apparently convinced him we had business at the hotel; there was no hitch about any of us going in.

The bullet-pocked entry doors were in the same condition as the ones in the radio room now, gaping wide and empty with the etched glass gone, only it was much draftier as the winter wind slipped through. The old manager, in an ancient coat with a tattered wool muffler wrapped around his head, had a box of thumbtacks in hand and was busy pinning flapping layers of newspaper over the openings. He also had the nervous twitches, looking up fast the instant he heard us coming. He recognized me and the boys right off, if I could judge anything from his terrified expression, and got out of the way to let us pass. No questions for us, though. Probably too scared.

Broken glass from the doors and windows was scattered all over the marble floor, which also showed damage. Stray bullets had created brief plow lines in its surface where it hadn't cracked apart altogether. Wherever you looked at eye level from the street, you could spot bullet holes in the walls, along the stairs. They only went up so high, like some kind of rock stratum, indicating the limits of the range of fire from the street. The killers had sprayed the place pretty good, though. It must have been some kind of big kick for them to blast the hell out of something and too tough for anybody who'd been in the way.

I wondered if the shooting would hurt or help the business. Probably the latter, once word got out. When the feds and the East Chicago police had taken down Dillinger a couple years back, the Biograph Theater had done a boom in ticket sales. Of course, anyone making the pilgrimage had to stop after the show to stare at the alleyway where he'd fallen and look for blood. Nothing of it was left, though; previous souvenir hunters had seen to that, sopping it up with handkerchiefs, scrap paper, and bits of torn cardboard, or so Escott had told me.

On the other hand, the dead man for this one wasn't John Dillinger, but a crooked cop who'd run out of luck. By the time the papers came out tomorrow, the world would know the truth or honor him for a hero.

Calloway motioned for the manager to come in and we all gathered at the front desk. It was at a right angle to the street, parallel to the bullet paths. No holes in the wood except for the ones already there.

"Yeah?" The manager shifted on his feet and looked like nothing would please him more than to be miles away from us.

Everyone stared expectantly at me. "I want you to call Angela Paco," I said. "Tell her Jack Fleming's back and needs to talk. I'll be in the same room as before."

"Huh?" As an imitation of lack of comprehension, it was awful.

"You know what I mean. If you don't have her number, you'll know someone who does. Make whatever calls you need to contact her, but do it fast."

He shook his head, gaze darting nervously over us all, silently pleading for me to go away. "I don't get you, mister."

Calloway showed him his gun. Shoved it up under the old man's chin, in fact. The lobby was empty of patrons, but I knew he'd have done the same thing with or without witnesses. "You get this, Pops? I thought so. Go do what you're told." He lowered the muzzle and signaled to the two uniforms. "Stay with him and see to it he doesn't get funny. I don't want Angela doing a repeat of what happened here."

"So you think she was behind the hit?" I asked him as we trudged up the stairs.

"Who else would have a reason? Probably still pissed that we stuck with Sullivan instead of her after Kyler bought the farm."

"What about your new boss? Could have been him. You see the look on his face when I mentioned it?"

A hesitation. Then: "Why should he?"

"Human nature. Every job I've ever had, whenever they changed the top men, they'd fire the workers and bring in their own people to take their place. Don't tell me you've never been through those hoops."

"It ain't like that here. Not with this setup."

"Sure about that? Maybe Sullivan was thinking of trim-

ming the fat so he looks good to the New York bosses.
What's a few cops more or less to him?''

"Shaddup," said Baker, who was just behind me.

I shut up. Since I'd gotten a rise out of him it meant he'd
been thinking along similar lines. Now he was thinking that
way again, maybe both of them, since Calloway's jaw was
visibly clenching as he ground his teeth. Didn't know what
good it might do me to throw down a false trail, but having
them off balance and even more mistrustful of Sullivan
couldn't hurt.

We reached the door at the end of the hall. It was half off
its hinges where they'd broken through earlier. I'd left Calloway right up against it before hightailing out the fire escape,
so you could make book that the bruises he took were probably giving him twinges now that there were fewer distractions. Have to allow he'd be in a bad temper from the
discomfort, maybe even find a way to take advantage of it.

Inside, the room was the same as before, but much colder.
Apparently no one had troubled to close the window I'd used.
Calloway covered me, keeping his distance, and sent Baker
to take care of the problem and look at the heater.

"It's on," he reported from the back. "Just not working
so good."

"What's the time?" I asked.

Calloway checked his watch. "Half-past ten. Better hope
your girlfriend wants to talk soon. Or else."

"Maxwell didn't say anything about an 'or else.' I'm just
supposed to call him then." I dropped into the chair by the
phone. Calloway, gun in hand, tossed the blindfold in my lap.
"Put it on."

"Jeez, are you kidding? What the hell do you think I—"

"I don't know, but until I do, you're gonna wear that. Put
it on."

Arguing wouldn't have gotten me anywhere, so I wrapped

it loosely around my head, tied off the ends, and sat there feeling like an idiot.

"What the hell's this?" asked Baker, coming in.

I turned my head in his general direction, crossing my arms. "Haven't you heard? They're making a talkie of *The Sheik* and I got the lead."

"You're cute, so cute I should drop you off a bridge. Can we do that after this is done, Lieutenant?"

"Maybe if we ask Sullivan real nice," answered Calloway. I didn't need to see to know about the smirk on his narrow face. The whole of it was in his voice. He should have been on radio.

Baker groused on. "God, but I hate punks like him."

"Who?" I asked with bright interest. "Punks like me or punks like Sullivan?"

"No one's talkin' to you."

"Just wanted some clarification is all," I said, all injured innocence.

"That's what I'm talkin' about. Smart-ass bastards like him coming out with the five-dollar college words and pretending to be so tough. Well, you ain't so frigging tough, pretty boy. You don't have any idea what tough really is."

"Calloway, make him stop, he's scaring me so bad I wanna puke."

"Both of you lay off, before you give me a headache," Calloway snarled.

Baker growled something under his breath I didn't catch, but it must have been aimed at me since Calloway didn't take exception to it. I kept shut and let him have the last word for now. My turn would come later, after the blindfold was off.

Sitting around listening to them breathe was only slightly less boring than actually watching the process. That I was spared from seeing their faces for the time being was another consolation. Calloway would just throw me more hate-filled

looks, and then I'd probably sniff and rub my nose the wrong
way, and Baker would try hitting me again. Try. Now that
Opal was out of the reckoning, I was more or less free to
take some chances.

God, I hoped she'd be okay.

Just have to wait on that one. Find out later. Bide my
time—what there was of it until midnight came or Angela
called—and take my best chance when it offered itself.

Soon now. Maybe.

Calloway had the right idea with the blindfold. There's a
lot of power in the eyes. You don't need to be a vampire to
influence others with a stare, just have to have the knack for
it. Some people are naturals, others learn how to control it.
How much is bluff and how much is real depends on the individual and how others react to them. I had a reporter friend
back in New York who once saw Hitler in person and said it
was the look in his eyes that grabbed people first and pinned
'em to the wall. You either fell under his spell and loved him or
came up with an instant and irrational urge to shoot him. My
friend wanted to shoot, which he found to be extremely up-
setting since he'd been raised a Quaker.

Maybe Calloway, now that he'd had a sample of my unnatural talent when I'd gone overboard using it, was having
a similar reaction to me. Only in this case he didn't have any
objections to using violence based on his religion, or based
on anything else for that matter. If Sullivan gave him the go-
ahead, he'd scrag me willingly enough. Nuts to that, he'd do
it without a go-ahead, like he'd tried in front of the hotel,
only this time there would be bullets in the gun.

I gave a shudder in spite of myself.

"Whatsamatter? You cold?" Baker turned it into a jeer.

I wasn't but said I was. "Must not have done such a great
job with the heater."

"I'll give you heat, you—"

"He's right," said Calloway. "Go turn it up."

"It *is* turned up."

"Then check it again and see what's wrong. I can see my breath hanging in the air."

Soon.

I leaned my head back as though to rest against the wall. It allowed me to just see under the bottom edge of the blindfold. A slice of floor and Calloway's feet slid into view. He was in the chair by the radio I'd used earlier when I'd been here with Opal.

Heard Baker tinkering with the heater, muttering to himself.

He'd be back any second.

No time like the present.

Calloway had suspicions about the hypnosis, but not a single clue about my other major talent.

Vanishing.

One instant in front of him, solid and real as an anvil, and the next gone and on the move, leaving him an abruptly empty chair to gape at.

In this state a blindfold is a pretty useless hindrance against me, since I can't see anyway. I used my memory and what sense of touch remained to whip around behind Calloway. It happened so fast he had no time to react either verbally or physically. He was still seated and trying to take in the impossible when I re-formed, tore off the cloth, snaked a hand around to cover his mouth, and used the other to fix his gun in place.

Now he did start a ruckus, kicking and flailing like a crazy man. He rose high out of the chair, making it crash over. I dragged him clear, then spun him around and did the same as before, focusing on his wide-open eyes and telling him to take a nap. He slowed, but didn't collapse. Too on guard against me, I guess. He got out a couple of sobbing sounds—

it was fear, absolute terror—and tried to wrest his gun free. My hand was closed tight around the cylinder, else he'd have fired it by now; I'd already felt his trigger finger making the attempt.

Hypnosis was out, but another fighting instinct kicked in, and I tried a less exotic but highly effective fist on his jaw, my arm going too fast for him to follow. Kept the punch pulled, though; I didn't want to kill him. He thumped straight to the floor, a bag of rags.

Baker was next on my list of chores. From the bedroom he'd heard me dancing around with his pal and charged in all ready for the worst. I went semi-transparent, which isn't easy to maintain, but is great for avoiding bullets while still being able to see the shooter.

He froze, absolutely froze, mouth sagging, eyes popping. Couldn't blame him. Suddenly being able to look right through a guy to see the room beyond must be pretty hard on the old rational facilities. Must have been especially hard on Baker; from the expression on his mug his brain must have completely closed down for the winter. Or maybe even until further notice. Since I didn't have that long to play games I got within a yard of him and gradually went solid. His whole horrified attention was on me, so I had an easy time convincing him to hand me his gun, go back to the other room, and climb into the bed for a nice nap.

Oh, yeah—I told him to forget all about my imitation of a ghost. It was for his own good. That kind of inexplicable thing is hard for a person to live with, better for everyone that he not remember any of it.

I surveyed the battlefield—no permanent casualties and me with all the weapons—then gave myself a mental pat on the back. Damn, but it felt *good* to be in charge again.

*   *   *

Just to give myself something constructive to do until Angela called, I righted the toppled chair and dragged Calloway's extremely unconscious body into the other room to get him out of sight. While I was at it I lifted his watch from his wrist to mine. It was a cheap thing. Whatever money he got on the side, he was smart enough not to give away easy clues to it like wearing something pricey from the Boston Store. No heirloom, so my conscience didn't chafe much. He could afford a replacement—that is, he could if Sullivan still wanted him on the payoff roster after this latest failure.

I watched the minute hand of my new property shift from one marking to the next a few times and wondered how long before Calloway woke up so I could whammy him like Baker. My idea was to make sure their stories matched—the details of which would depend on the outcome of my talk with Angela.

Who was taking her own sweet time.

Full of nervous energy again now that I was back in control of this little piece of my world, I paced around as before to work it off. Didn't feel like dancing, though. No partner. I circled the room, chewed the inside of my lower lip, and offered a prayer or two for Opal. God, she was only a kid with a raw deal on life, so raw that she didn't really know how to live yet. The potential was there, if only she could have the chance to see it, reach for it. Sullivan had damned well better be taking good care of her or I'd take it out of his Harvard hide.

Wanted to make some calls, but didn't dare. Talking to Escott and Coldfield would have to wait to keep the line free.

Line. What if it wasn't working? Picked up the receiver, very quickly. Heard the reassuring hum of the dial tone. Okay, the phone was fine. Good, great, wonderful. Now everything depended on the scared old man below. I couldn't run down to check on him, to make sure he'd done his phoning, not with the other two cops on duty. Kept telling myself there was really no need. If there'd been a problem, one of them would have come up to report it to Calloway by now. I almost wish they would so I could get the drop on them. That would simplify my exit from this joint when the time came.

Checked the hall. Empty. Pushed the door more securely shut. If anyone knocked, chances were it'd fall down from the force of the raps, but I wanted the feeling of privacy a closed door imparted. It's all in the mind, like most things, the same as pulling blankets up over your head to keep out the bogeyman. If he really wanted to get you, he would, but until that time came, you were safe under the covers with your illusions.

Phone.

I let it ring a couple times, then picked up.

"Fleming, you son of a bitch, what the hell kind of scam are you pulling?" Angela yelled in my ear.

Things were off to a flying start. "So nice to hear from you, too, sweetheart."

"First you pull a raid—"

"Not me, I told you that was Sullivan's—"

"Then a hit on the hotel. You were trying to set me up."

"And did a piss-poor job of it since you weren't anywhere around when it happened."

"You were trying to get me killed."

"Get sensible, I was right in front of the guns while they were shooting, not you."

"Fleming!"

So the lady wasn't interested in making sense just yet. She'd probably been storing this up for hours and needed a release. I was just the man to help her do it. "Angela, calm down, count to ten, and then I'll be glad to let you know what's been going on between me and your Irish friend."

"You're a dead man, you bastard!"

I bit my tongue so as not to tell her she was way too late for that and waited until she'd cooled enough to talk. After a minute her curiosity would win out over her temper, and I could begin the preliminaries.

"Well?" she demanded after a stretch, when I'd stopped responding to her cursing and threats.

"First off, Opal's still alive."

"Alive?" That changed her tune. "I thought—"

"She took a bullet, but they have Doc looking after her."

"What? Doc's supposed to be . . . he hadn't called in and I thought he'd gone on a drunk."

"Nope, they snagged him at the studio raid. Roughed him up some, but he's alive, mostly well, and drinking as usual. I think the idea is to use him as a hostage like Kyler used your father."

She gave a snort. "Doc's not my father, and he knows it. What about Opal?"

"She's not feeling so good, no thanks to the hit on the hotel, Doc's pretty worried about her. You should have sent your boys to collect us faster and we might have avoided a lot of trouble."

"Don't go blaming that on me, you frigging snake. Sullivan's the one behind it."

Right, so Sullivan thought Angela had made the hit, and unless she was lying she thought him to be responsible. That left one other possible player, and I still hated the idea: Gordy. Damnation. Escott was right. When it came to this kind of cold-blooded business, no one could be your friend. I still hadn't figured what specific advantage killing Opal would gain him, but in general terms it would throw both sides off balance. The fact that I might get hit in the process, too, was part of it, and that made me want to punch holes in the wall, or in him. Gordy, along with very, very few others, knew I could survive such an attack.

"I'll have that Irish bastard's balls on a meat hook before this is over," said Angela, still going on about her new competition.

"And he sends you his love, as well." No point in mentioning Gordy to her right now. I'd have to take care of him later.

"All right, Fleming, what's your angle?"

"That's where it gets complicated. I need to talk to you face-to-face. You never know who might be listening."

"I'm sure. You're just trying to finish what he started."

"If that was the case then I'd have a much better story to feed you than the truth, which is pretty grim, lady. Doc and your wizard accountant are in Sullivan's hands and the only person who has a chance in hell of getting them clear is me—with your help."

A very long pause.

"Angela?"

"Yeah, okay." She sounded more subdued. "What is it you want?"

"Just a little talk so we can get some stuff straightened out."

She laughed once, a hard metallic sound. "I'm not gonna let you within a mile of me. You're stooging for Sullivan and just looking for another chance to finish the job. The manager said you walked in with those dime an hour cops like you owned the place."

"So I did, but your manager missed the fact those cops had a couple of guns jabbing into my back at the time. He's too scared to notice much because they're watching him."

"And how is it you're able to—"

"Oh, I *was* under guard, but these mugs have mackerel for brains. Two of them took me upstairs to wait to hear from you. I grabbed an opportunity and got the drop on them. They're having a nice snooze in the honeymoon suite.''

"Uh-huh." By her tone she didn't believe any of it. Too bad.

"All I have to do is slip out the back way and meet you anywhere you name. Bring all the muscle you want, make it public or private, let 'em search me to the skin, and you call the shots. I'm telling you I just want to talk."

"Anywhere, huh?"

I was gambling that it wouldn't be over running water, like the lake. Had a way clear of that hitch, though. "There's one thing: I gotta be able to get to a phone. I'm supposed to call Sullivan at midnight or he starts playing hardball with Doc. He could also get mean with Opal, but she's too far gone to notice."

"You mean she's dying?"

"I don't know. Doc didn't look too happy. They promised to take care of her, but I don't trust 'em much. The faster we get things resolved the better, otherwise Sullivan promised to dump her in a field."

"Where are they?"

"I'll tell you that when I see you."

"You'll tell me now."

"So you can hit him back and get them killed? I don't think so."

Another long pause.

"Angela? I know this sounds fishy as hell, but this is all I've got to play with."

"Then it's not enough. For all I know, Doc and Opal are dead and you're setting up a trap for Sullivan to get me as well."

"Don't be a sap, Angela. Use your instincts, you must know I'm not that kind of a player."

"Mister, I don't know who the hell you are. You talk a

good line, but my dad taught me that those are the ones to watch out for more than any of the others.''

"And any other time he'd be right. Come on and fix a meeting, on your terms, wherever you want.''

"Over the phone or nothing at all.''

"No can do.''

"He must be paying you a bundle.''

"He's paying me jackshit. All he's done for me is keep me alive a few more hours, and I don't know how much longer that's going to last if you don't want to listen to—''

"I can listen right here and now.''

Had to stop, take a breath and let it out slow. I knew she'd be stubborn about a meeting, but hadn't anticipated that she'd be so irritating as well. "Look, I'll tell you what I told Sullivan: I'm only trying to get out of this with a whole skin. *He* was the one who decided I should be the go-between so you two can settle your differences before things get even more out of hand than they are.''

"This after he raids my place and shoots Opal?''

"On his terms he was just flexing his muscles. Don't tell me you wouldn't do the same given the chance.''

"I'll tell you what I'll do to that—''

"And I'm sure it involves the use of hand grenades, but they're not the answer to everything. Just give me the chance to tell you what he has in mind.''

"Sure, go ahead.''

"In person, sweetheart, in person. It's too risky on a phone. The cops might be listening in and we've said much too much already.''

"Then find another phone to call from.''

"You'd have to give me a number, which could give away your location.''

"So would my giving you directions on where to find me.''

"Okay, okay. How about I just leave the hotel and start

walking? You can have someone pick me up while I'm on the move. I won't kick a fuss.''

''No thanks, you're too anxious to deal, Fleming.''

''I'm not exactly in a real good spot not to be! I got two unconscious cops up here, two more downstairs I have to get past, Sean Sullivan ready to scrag me if I screw this up, and you've already told me you want me dead—you're damn right I'm anxious!''

''Then why not leave town, disappear?''

I shut my eyes a moment. God knows walking away from this was looking better and better. ''You wouldn't believe me.''

''Uh-huh. You've got that pegged. What's this midnight call to Sullivan about?''

''It's so I can let him know what's going on. He's given me that long to find out if you wanna play ball with him or not. What I tell him is gonna affect Opal and Doc. The way things are going now, they're both gonna end up in a field with no headstone.''

''I figured that already.'' She didn't sound like it mattered all that much to her, either. ''Okay, if you're not in his pocket, why should he pick you for this job?''

''I had to do some fast talking to stay alive, so I made him think we had something between us.''

''You and me? That's a laugh.''

''Sweetheart, you're hurting my feelings with this talk.''

''And I'm choking up, too.''

''The idea was to help me stay alive; it worked and I'm only trying to keep it working. So come on and let's get together and—''

''It's not gonna happen, Fleming. If you can't do business over the phone—''

''What about Opal and Doc?''

"You're so worried about 'em, you tell me. Phone or nothing. It's in your hands."

"You'd let 'em die?"

"If I have to. Sullivan wants to play tough, then that's the way it is."

Jeez. I wasn't talking to a human being, but to a block of ice.

"Fleming, I'm not saying I *want* them to die, but I'm not risking myself for anyone. You want to take chances, go right ahead."

"But they're the ones who—" but I cut the rest off. No point talking in circles. She'd made up her mind and was willing to throw away two lives to keep from changing it. Apparently she didn't mind noisy fun and games like the raid or tossing grenades around her backyard, but to stick her neck out in the cold on purpose was something else again. Too bad for Doc and Opal. I'd have to stop pushing the personal-interview stuff and try a different angle.

"Okay, Angela, there's gotta be a way we can work something out here. You at least want to get Opal back, without her the books are useless."

"The books. I wondered when you'd get around to them. That's what this is all about, isn't it?"

"Sullivan mentioned them, yes."

"Well, he's out of luck. He's not getting them."

"He's willing to buy them from you."

"What's his offer? I can use another laugh."

"Enough to put you and your father up in style. Enough to allow you to afford the best head doctors in Europe to treat him, get him better again."

Long silence for that one. I let her think it over.

"Europe?"

"Maybe take him to Switzerland. They got more shrinks

than mountains there. You could get your father help—real help—for what's happened to him.''

"And when he's better he'll have nothing to come back to. The business he spent his life building gone, sold for a song by me? I'm not gonna do that to him.''

"It's got more going for it than the road you're on now.''

"What's that supposed to mean?''

"It's stuff I heard at Sullivan's. The New York bosses think you're too flashy and dangerous. Even if you dump Sullivan down a drain, they'll just send out someone else to take his place and another one after that and another, until you end up on a slab and your father is wrapped tight in a straitjacket in some state institution for what's left of his life.''

"No! You shut the hell up!''

"That's how the world works, you can't change it, but if you're smart you can fix things so you're sitting pretty, play it dumb and everyone loses, especially your father.''

"No!''

"If something happens to you, who's gonna take care of him? He'll be in a white room somewhere with some guy spoon-feeding him oatmeal three times a day in between basket-weaving sessions—''

"No!" A real shriek. She didn't hang up, but did slam the phone down hard on something. Several times.

As Escott could have said, I'd touched a nerve. A mighty sensitive one to judge by the crashing sounds and her language. It was a few long minutes before she came back. At least she had a chance to rant and blow off steam. I had to sit still and hang on to the line, feeling like a dog on a short leash tied to a bomb.

"Fleming.'' She sounded breathless.

"Yeah?''

"God damn you to hell." Now she sounded tired. Very tired.

"No doubt."

"Fleming?"

"Right here."

"What's . . . what's that bastard's offer?"

Bowed my head. Tried not to get too hopeful. "I don't know, but the two of you can negotiate it, set up a delivery."

"Why should he even bother paying me off?"

"Because it's not as noisy as a war and a lot less expensive. The boys in New York don't like that kind of noise."

Pause on her end. A long one. I tried not to fidget.

"Fleming."

"Yeah?"

"You said you could get Doc and Opal out?"

"Maybe I could."

"Then you do that. I'll deal with Sullivan on condition I get them back."

"He won't give you Opal. Not willingly. He needs her to decode the books."

"Doc, then. I'll trade Doc for the books and the payoff. As a sign of good faith."

I didn't want to trust her. That little double back she'd pulled on the stairway tonight left a bad taste in my mouth. "You'll stick to any deal you strike?"

"Not just any deal, this is only if I get enough cash."

Words were easy to say, and neither of us had mentioned that seven hundred grand sitting in the roadhouse basement, either. She probably didn't want to remind me of it, and I sure as hell didn't want her going there, though it was a surety that she'd run out and try to pick it up before the dust settled.

"Get Doc released, and I'll hand over the books for the money," she said.

"It'll take time for me to work this." I wanted plenty of

maneuvering room as far as the ticking clock went.

"I'm in no hurry."

"And I'll need a better way to contact you than to keep coming to this dump. Something more direct."

"If you get Doc out, he'll do that for you. He knows what places to find me."

"Come on, Angela."

"You just get Doc and he'll take care of it; otherwise, no deal. That's all you need to worry about."

It was more than enough.

"You want some muscle, some guns?"

I thought about it. Asking for them just might put me next to her. "What if I do?"

"Then I'd tell you where to go to get them."

Cagey girl. "Nah, I'll be fine without."

"What'll you say to Sullivan when you call him?"

"That you're willing to deal, but it won't be easy. I'll make you look good."

"I don't need your help for that, and you're damn right it won't be easy. If he doesn't cough up enough money to suit me, he'll have a fight on his hands."

"I'll make sure he understands."

"You do that. And one other thing, Fleming." Her voice came back stronger, like it was from the start, but darker and sleet-cold. "You pull anything cute, I mean *anything,* and I'll hang your carcass from a meat hook right next to Sullivan's. You won't be able to hide from me; no matter how this turns out, I'll come after you and make it happen. Take that as a promise."

"I believe you, lady," I whispered.

Calloway was awake finally, sort of, if you didn't mind him looking like he was having an open-eyed cataleptic fit. Before I could call Sullivan I had to have his stooge up and ready to talk. I got tired of waiting for him to come around naturally and tried the cold-water-in-the-face routine along with some hard shaking and a few face slaps. They worked just fine, and while he was still in a highly receptive state for it I gave him my best evil-eye. Now he was sitting in the chair by the phone, quiet as a cat and ready to do a bit part in *White Zombie*.

I'd primed him with a bogus memory of my conversation with Angela, then gave instructions on exactly what I wanted from him in reaction. I hoped it would cover every point Sullivan might raise, but the effort had given me one hell of a headache. It felt like someone had tied a tourniquet to my skull and was squeezing it too tight. I vanished once to see if that would make the pain go away, but it didn't seem to have much effect, which was a disappointment. Usually that cleared up things like cuts and bruises pretty fast; maybe I needed to not be solid for a longer period. No time to experiment. It wasn't near to midnight yet, but I didn't want Sullivan to get the sweats waiting. He'd seemed confident when I'd left, and I wanted to bolster that feeling with an early report of success.

I dialed the number Maxwell had given me. Two rings and he answered. Low voice, as well modulated as a radio announcer, very civilized.

"Yes?"

"It's Fleming. Is Opal okay?"

"She was when I last saw her."

"What's that supposed to mean?"

"Just what I said."

"Did you bring in a real doctor for her?"

"She's being carefully looked after in a very safe place, I assure you."

Didn't know how much of that I could believe, if any. Sure I'd been able to give him a last order, a slight push in the right direction, but was uncertain whether it'd taken a solid enough hold in his mind to do Opal any good. I'd find out soon enough, though. "I've talked with Angela. You want your boss to hear the news?"

Apparently he did. The next one on the line was Sullivan.

"What have you to say?" Cultured, with that flat Boston accent. A Boston roach. He was probably a real pip scuttling around the football field. Or maybe it was polo.

"I think I've got a deal for you."

"You only think you have it?"

"I'll know for sure once I meet with the lady. She's pretty skittish after all the fireworks tonight. She wants your guarantee you'll lay off for the time being, call a truce."

"So she has a chance to hit back?"

"At the moment she's got very little to hit you with and no idea where you are. I'm going to meet with her, but Calloway's kicking a fuss about letting me out. She won't talk if I've got fleas on my tail. I wouldn't put it past her to plug me if she thinks I've turned and gone over to your side."

"Nice girlfriend you've got."

"It's the same as for any girlfriends you might have. Would you let one of them stand between you and the organization? Didn't think so. She's soft for me, but only to a point."

"Smart gal."

"I've always thought so. Now how about calling off Calloway so I can get some work done?"

"What sort of work?"

"I'm gonna meet her at some place on the road in Indiana. No one else knows about it. No address, I just know how to get there. It's gonna take a while, too; I won't be able to call until morning, if that soon."

"That's too long."

"She's a stubborn gal. I'm gonna have to do a lot of sweet

talkin' to get her to come around to your way of seeing things. If I'm not careful about this she'll dangle me from a meat hook. *Talking* her into dealing with you means I get out of it alive.''

"Sounds like you're trying to skip."

"I'm not trying to—"

"Put Calloway on."

"But—"

"Put him on, Fleming."

I grumbled and growled for effect, then passed the receiver over. Calloway pressed it against his ear. No worry from me. He was my creature, I owned him. His voice sounded perfectly normal, but his face was still quite blank. Creepy.

"Yeah, Mr. Sullivan?"

"What's this deal about him meeting Angela?"

"I listened to both sides, he's on the up-and-up with it far as I can tell. She wants to see him, but I still don't trust him. He needs to be watched."

"Of course he does, but from a distance might be better. Can you trail him?"

"Yeah, I can do that."

"Very well. Don't be caught or things could get complicated."

"I won't."

"Put him back on."

He handed it over.

Sullivan sounded reassuring, like a teacher with a not too bright student. "I got things straightened out with the lieutenant, so you won't have any trouble from him now."

"That was easy. Maybe too easy. He swallowed that without any choking."

"He knows what's good for him and how to obey orders. I'm hoping you do as well."

"We both want the same thing, Mr. Sullivan. You hold to

your part and I'll hold to mine and then everyone's happy. But if Calloway screws this up for me . . ." I thought I'd give him a chance to adjust things. If I really did have a meeting with Angela, Sullivan's orders to Calloway could get us both killed.

"He won't."

Why did I even bother to hope he'd smarten up and play square? Okay, to hell with him and all his cousins. "All right. I'll call in the morning around ten."

"That late?"

I gave a snotty chuckle, the sort he'd expect from someone who was quite a bit less than a gentleman. "Well, Angela's a pretty hot little twist. I may have to be sleeping in from all the—"

"Eight o'clock, Fleming," he said in a world-weary and rather patronizing tone.

"Hey, I can't—"

"Eight, no later." He hung up. Probably thought he'd scored a point or two. Fine, far be it from me to disillusion him. By this time tomorrow, if I had any luck at all, he wouldn't even remember my name.

8

JUST to be neat about things, I led Calloway back to the bedroom and tucked him up nice and sweet with his friend Baker,
who I had to wake briefly in order to give him new instructions. It made my headache worse, but everything went
smoothly. They'd come to in the morning and swear up and
down that after the call to Sullivan I'd knocked them cold
and escaped, which was more or less the truth. Certainly Calloway had the physical evidence of it forming on his bruised
jaw. This way, no matter how the night turned out, they'd be
in the clear. Maybe. If Sullivan even knew what they were
talking about. No matter, I could fix him just as easy.

I also planted the idea in them that they should start to
back off playing stooge to the gangs. Not quit suddenly,
which would get them dead fast, but to be less available in
the future. It might not last long, but for that time they'd have
something to think about, perhaps act upon.

Yeah, I was being too soft on 'em. Call it conscience. Or
rather it had to do with what Bobbi had said to me. Gordy
would have killed them, or made them disappear, which was
pretty much the same, and Escott would have let them swing
in the wind. Because of what I'd become, I had a third choice
open: Let them swing, but give them a way off the rope.
There was a pretty good chance they wouldn't take it, Cal-

loway thought they were in too far, but what the hell, it was worth a try, even a half-assed one.

That finished, I got the car keys from Baker's pocket and went out the fire-escape window again.

Didn't bother to open it this time.

I don't care much for sieving through glass, but cared even less for bumbling my way through the lobby to get past the two cops on watch there. Besides, having done this before, I was familiar with the territory. The regular angles and struts of the metal stairs were an easy path to follow, so down I went to re-form on the street, pressing myself against the hotel's shadowed outer wall.

Now I could take my time for a good look around. The cops in the patrol car were still on watch. There was no knowing why they were just sitting there all but asking to be targets; if another Packard tore by spitting lead they wouldn't last two seconds.

Except for them, the rest of the street was empty and cemetery quiet. No sign of Angela's goons, or even Gordy's. The party had shifted elsewhere, and I was ready to move my own part of it.

I slipped right past the patrol cops. Even if they'd known where to look and when, they'd have had a hard time trying to spot something as invisible as the wind—which was affecting my progress. Maybe I wasn't solid in the normal sense, but a strong breeze could still push me around if I let it. I fought the stuff, trying to estimate how far I'd come. Groping blindly forward, I could only rely on my vague sense of touch to keep on course. With the hotel on my right and the sidewalk below, it wasn't too hard, but you'd think I'd be used to the disorientation after all these months. One good thing, a few dozen yards later when I went solid again, my headache was all gone. I'd traded it for a wave of weariness, though, like a runner after a brief sprint. At this rate, tomorrow night I'd have to hit the Stockyards for an extra feeding to make up for all the work I was doing.

The street was unchanged, only my view of it had altered; I was well behind the cops and a few steps from the Caddie. Keys jingling, I unlocked it and got in, starting her up. The motor was beautifully quiet. Keeping the lights off, I shifted her into reverse, gently backing along the curb to the next corner and around, well out of sight. One quick U-turn later, I had the lights legally on, and was on my way to the road-house.

Not much traffic at this hour, though there were some patches around theaters and late-closing eateries. No car sickness for me, but then I was in the front seat, could see where I was headed, and had the driving to keep me occupied.

Thinking it over, I suppose I could have taken care of the cops in the lobby and questioned the manager about Angela's whereabouts. She might be laying low for the present, but was still a loose cannon ready to go off. Getting to her first would have eased my mind quite a bit. But finding her . . . the odds were high the old manager didn't have a direct line to his boss, only to a middleman whose job was to pass on information to someone higher up. It'd be futile for me to try taking the same route. She'd just get annoyed, be more on guard, and find a hole to drop into that even Doc didn't know about.

But on the other hand Doc would *give* her to me wrapped in a bow—with a little push applied in the right part of his mind, that is. I just hoped he wouldn't be too drunk to co-operate.

And most importantly, I could see Opal, check on her; another reason to let the problem of Angela go look after itself for now.

The miles flowed under the tires. The neighborhoods got drab again, thinned out, turned into semicountryside. The scenery grew monotonous, and the corner I wanted snuck up on me; I nearly missed the turning. I hit the brakes only just in time and swung into it a little too sharp for safety, but the big car landed back on all four wheels without much complaint, bounce or swerve. If I'd tried that in my smaller, lighter Buick, I'd have ended up sideways in a ditch.

The unpaved drive led right to the house, and the only cover was a thin line of scraggly bushes that had lost all their leaves. I wanted to park close enough for a fast getaway but not to the point where my car would be spotted. Soon as I made the turn I cut the headlights to lessen that chance, but still felt exposed and vulnerable. If they were on the ball, someone would have seen me already.

The darkness was reassuring, though. No moon showed, lots of clouds masked the stars, and we were out far enough not to have any glimmer of the city's glow reflecting back to the ground. I had to remind myself that though it was like diffuse daylight to me, to everyone else it would be solid murk.

I spotted some trees farther along the drive, but those were up well past the house. They would conceal the car, but if I had to make a quick exit, there was a chance of being cut off before getting to the main road.

What the hell, why not? I thought after some hemming and hawing. It wasn't like Sullivan's people could prepare themselves for anyone like me. How can you fight the next best thing to a ghost?

Lights still off, I eased along the drive, glad of the well-tuned hush of the engine, and the wind. The latter would cover the sound of the tires crunching along the dirt surface. Still, I had to pass fairly close, and because I was moving, I couldn't tell if any curtains twitched at those windows overlooking the lane. At most, I could hope that it was well traveled enough so that an occasional passing car would be ignored, but if anyone glanced out and saw *this* one easing by with its lights off, I couldn't expect them not to be curious. They might think Calloway had run into trouble—which he had—and then do something about it.

Too bad I couldn't make the whole damned car invisible.

The trees, once I reached them, were ideal: nice thick evergreens with low branches all bunched together between me and the house. I found a spot to pull in, did some fancy wrestling around with the steering wheel to turn the car so it pointed outward, then shut it down and waited, listening to the wind, eyes wide for any and all movement.

If you could call a difference of five feet in elevation high, then I had the high ground. My perch, such as it was, overlooked the rear and part of the right side of the place. When I'd come in with Calloway, I'd noticed three cars parked in the back lot; now one was missing, and I couldn't recall offhand which, not that I'd noticed their make or plate numbers at the time. I wondered how many men had left in it. The fewer soldiers inside the roadhouse to deal with, the happier I'd be.

Lights showed on the second floor. People were still awake and moving, but I didn't expect them to be up the whole of the night, especially since Sullivan thought I wouldn't be calling again until morning. Sooner or later they'd have to slow down and sleep. When that happened, then I would see what to do about getting Opal and Doc away. For the time being I had to wait until things got settled and quiet, which might take a while, but I knew how to keep busy.

After making sure the other doors were unlocked, I got out of the Caddie and closed the driver's side gently, just enough for it to latch. I checked my overcoat pockets to see that the guns I'd taken from Calloway and Baker were still in place. The revolver on the right, Baker's semi-auto on the left— with the safety off. I probably wouldn't need them, but you never know when you might have to use a more normal kind of intimidation on someone than forced hypnosis. Another thought occurred to me, and I went around to the passenger side to check the glove compartment. It held the usual trash and a tattered road map, but I got lucky and turned up a flashlight. The batteries were less than new, but its feeble light would be like a search beacon to my sensitive eyes. So long as there was some illumination for them to pick up, they worked just fine, but I was anticipating a very dark place indeed, ahead.

Feeling ready for nearly anything, I walked to the edge of the trees, got a firm fix in my mind of the direction and distance, and vanished. Flowing fast along the ground—and still fighting the wind—I sped toward the right side of the house where I'd seen a line of small basement windows. When my now amorphous body bumped up against something large and solid, which could only be the building, I re-formed just enough for a quick look around.

The nearest window, like others I'd seen, was latticed over with a thick metal grate to keep out intruders. A good effort, but useless against me. I did my specialty act again and eased through the cracks.

Now I was floating blind in completely unknown territory. All kinds of obstacles loomed close as I bumbled around getting my bearings. One advantage of this state was I couldn't knock anything over or collect bruises from hitting them. Some of the objects were of a regular shape and height, probably crates, most likely liquor boxes. When I found a clear space in their midst, I went solid again.

Dark, as I'd anticipated. I was well away from the windows. Just enough of their outside light came through for me to see I was in an aisle formed by boxes stacked shoulder high on either side of me, and I'd been correct about their alcoholic content, though it was beer bottles not booze. Empties on one side, full ones on the other, I catfooted along their length, going farther into the shadows.

It was a pretty big place, probably taking up the whole foundation of the joint, and had more than one stairway. The one I was looking for needed to lead to the kitchen.

When it got so thick even my eyes couldn't work, I switched on the flashlight. It was a risk, but I'd listened carefully and determined that everyone was safely upstairs, leaving me the free run of this area.

More odds and ends sprang out of the dimness, stacks of chairs and tables, some broken, boxes of Christmas and New Year's decorations, bags full of dirty tablecloths ready to be trucked off to the laundry, and junk like that. As I went deeper the inventory gradually changed, and I was walking between cans of lard and sacks of flour. Roaches scuttled boldly over the dusty floor. The stairs here went straight up to a closed door and a thin line of light showed along its base. I'd found the way to the kitchen.

Cutting my flash, I vanished and floated up, slipping through the slender opening under the door. It was like squeezing through the narrow neck of an hourglass and seemed to take ages before I was completely clear, but it was better than pushing my way past the more resistant material of the wood. All was quiet on the other side as far as I could tell with my blunted sense of hearing, so I went solid.

The kitchen was empty and clean, really clean. The table where I'd put Opal and the linoleum around it had been thoroughly scrubbed down. Lingering in the air was the astringent bite of some kind of harsh soap. The sting of it reminded me of hospitals. Every sign of what had happened earlier was quite gone.

Maxwell had said she was all right, and I'd wanted to believe him, but she could be dead. My guts twisted hard at the thought, but it wouldn't go away. If she hadn't made it, they'd have taken pains to clear out all evidence that she'd ever been here.

Heart heavy, I went to the door leading to the rest of the house, intent on finding out what was going on.

After a cautious quarter-hour of partial to fully invisible poking around, I determined that not very damned much was going on at all.

I counted ten men populating the upstairs, and no one anywhere else. Five were gathered in one of the larger rooms playing poker, the others scattered around the rest of the floor, two listening to a radio, two sprawled asleep on sofas, and one on a phone away from the others negotiating for a date with someone he called "Sugarbun." The big office was empty. Of Sullivan, Maxwell, and Opal there was no sign, but I did find Doc. By accident. I materialized in a windowless storage area for a moment to think through the situation and discovered his semiconscious body in the same small closet.

I sensed him first by his breathing and the nearness of his heartbeat, and that made me jump, but fortunately the place was coal-mine dark. Flailing my hand about, I found the pull cord to the overhead light and gave it a tug. The dim bulb revealed lots of shelves crowded with cleaning supplies, rags, and similar junk. Most of the floor was taken up by a gigantic vacuum cleaner . . . and Doc.

He was curled on his side on the bare wood, knees drawn up and a bleary grimace on his face as the sudden glare caught him. He shaded his eyes and squinted up at me.

"What the hell are you doing here?" His voice was thick. Drunk, drugged, or roughed up by Sullivan's clowns, take your pick, he wasn't in very good shape.

"Where's Opal?" I whispered, dropping to one knee.

"They took her away. Sullivan, some of his boys. Tol' 'em not to . . ."

"Where'd they take her?"

"Damned if I know, son. Little bit after you went they came and got her." He pushed himself upright and rubbed his face.

"How was she doing?"

"Poorly. I got the bleeding stopped, but she needed a blood transfusion and other kindsa stuff I couldn't do for her. If'n I'd had my bag with me—"

"You got *any* idea where she is?"

He shook his head.

"Didn't they say anything, give any hint?"

"Wish I could tell you otherwise, but they wasn't much for talking. They were bein' careful with her, though. Wrapped her up warm and pulled the car right up to the door so she wouldn't get bumped around too much being carried out."

That sounded better than I'd expected, but not all that satisfying. "How many of them? Who?"

"Sullivan, a couple others."

"What about Maxwell?"

"Don't recall, maybe. He's not the sort you notice much an' they were hustling me back up to this hole at the same time. What the hell're you doin' here?"

"Keep your voice down."

Lower tone. "What the hell're you—"

"I'm going to try getting you out—in one piece."

"Well, son, then I'm on your side. What do you want me to do?"

I stood and tried the doorknob. Locked, as I'd expected, which was why I'd covered the action with my body so Doc wouldn't notice and wonder how I'd gotten in. Now I put an ear close to the jam and had a long listen. Heard the radio down the hall and the occasional mutter from the poker players farther on, the guy on the phone had hung up. The rest were too quiet for me to know what they were doing; still snoozing, I hoped. No one seemed to be immediately outside the closet. Good.

"Is the coast clear?" he asked. He'd been holding his breath.

"Not just yet. Our best chance is to wait until they're all asleep. It may take some time. Do they check on you often?"

"Not since they threw me in here after Sullivan left with Opal. Wish they would, I gotta take a leak."

I pointed toward one corner. "There's a bucket. Don't draw their attention if you can help it, I want them to forget about you for the time being. I also don't want them knowing I'm here, so keep shut."

"Can't blame you for that. How'd you get inside anyhow?"

"Jimmied a lock."

"I mean in here."

"Slipped in under the door."

"Smart-ass. Why you being so helpful to me?"

"While I was gone with Calloway, I had a talk with Angela and we made a deal. If I get you out safe, she'll think twice about a war with Sullivan."

"Musta been some talk. Nice of her to care."

"When we're clear of this joint, you're supposed to take me to her."

"She say where?"

"She said you'd know, so you tell me."

"Not so fast. You *could* have struck a deal with Sullivan an' be joshin' me. I'm not gonna be the one to get her in front of a bullet by—"

"Doc." I dropped to my heels in front of him, fixed a hard

look on his lined face and baby-blue eyes. "Tell me where
to find Angela."

He blinked a few times and squinted mightily. "Fleming,
no offense, but you can go to hell."

I tried again, but it didn't work. There was too much booze
in his brain for me to get past.

"What do you take me for?" he growled. "You must
know I've got no reason to trust you, no matter what you
say."

"Angela has pretty much the same outlook," I said sourly.

"Smart girl."

"All I'm trying to do is keep her and Sullivan from
blowing this town apart—"

"And a mighty fine sentiment it is, to be sure, but I'm not
sayin' anything until I have the go-ahead from her." He put
a stubborn set on his mouth and crossed his arms.

Nuts. I'd just have to wait until he was sober or more
willing to talk on his own. To achieve the latter, I'd have to
get us away from here, which shouldn't be too hard, but I
wasn't all that happy over the prospect of hypnotizing ten
guys into slumberland. I could do it, but it would be a whale
of a chore and certainly bring back my headache. If some of
them had been drinking like Doc, things could get even more
complicated. My goal was to duck in and out of the roadhouse—Doc and Opal in tow—with no one the wiser, then
clearing the mess with Angela and Sullivan long before the
sun came up. Now I'd only get half of it accomplished. It
was damned inconvenient for Sullivan to have gone running
off, even if his intent was to help Opal.

"Okay, Doc, never mind. You got any idea whether Sullivan's coming back tonight?"

"Nope."

"I'll have to leave you here and scout around for the best
way out. It could take a while."

"How long a while?"

"I don't know, an hour or two, maybe more, till they fall asleep."

"How 'bout I just come along and keep an eye on what you're doin'?"

"Too risky. I need to keep low and move fast and know where you are when the time's right so I can get to you."

He shot me a sour look. "Yeah, I get it."

"Not yet, you don't; I'm coming back for you, because that's part of my deal with Angela. You just take a nap until I get back, you need the rest." I wanted to force one on him, but spared myself the effort and likely disappointment. He was three-quarters gone, if I was any judge of degrees of inebriation, and would probably conk out five minutes after I left, anyway. I gave the light cord another pull and the closet went black again. "Stay put and keep quiet," I said in parting, then vanished and re-formed just outside.

"Fleming?" he whispered urgently. "Fleming?" He made grunting noises as he heaved to his feet. The light came on; I saw its glow through the crack at the base of the door. He tried the locked knob. "Hey—!"

"Shut up!" I snarled back.

"How'd you get out there? I didn't see the door open."

"Tell you later. Now keep quiet."

He made noises to indicate his dissatisfaction with my reply, but offered no more arguments. I again listened hard for any reaction from the men down the hall, but none came.

Time to go to work.

My first choice was to find the guy who had been on the phone. Separated from the others, he'd be the easiest target. I swept through the room he'd been in and came up empty, which bothered me. I didn't like not knowing where he'd gone off to, since he could turn up at any given inconvenient moment.

Another invisible sweep. He wasn't anywhere on the floor. I went downstairs, thinking he might be after a drink at the bar, but that area was locked up.

Kitchen. Someone clattering around there.

Better and better. None of the other mugs would hear us this far away. I eased in and concluded by the sounds that he was fixing a meal. Drifting past his area, I took up a spot as far away from him as I could get and very slowly reappeared.

He worked using only the small light over a stove, but it was plenty for me. If I kept still and quiet, he wouldn't notice me right away while I got a look around. He had an icebox door opened wide and was very absorbed in deciding what food to take out. A fat block of cheese was already on the table, along with some bread and mustard. Nobody else was around. This would be my best chance. I went invisible for a moment, long enough to close the space between us, then solid just as he straightened with three eggs in one hand and an onion in the other.

Maybe I should have waited until he'd put the stuff on the table. He gave a terrific yelp of suprise at my sudden appearance and the eggs and onions went flying.

Some minutes later I had him thoroughly under my control, and the first thing I made him do was clean up the mess. If we got interrupted I didn't want anything to look funny, so I kept nervous watch as he got the broken eggs off the floor and retrieved the onion from where it had rolled.

The second thing he did was to tell me where Sullivan had gone, except he couldn't, since he didn't know. I made a thorough job of questioning him and could trust what he said, but it was still nothing worth knowing. He was just another soldier and not one with any kind of rank. He could only confirm Doc's story that Sullivan was gone with the girl to parts unknown and there was no telling when he'd be back.

But I already knew when: eight o'clock the next morning. Lousy for me since I wouldn't be making the promised phone call at that time. At least Doc would be out of the line of fire, and maybe I'd have Angela in a sweet-talking frame of mind by then, so the night wasn't going to be a complete water haul, but it could have been better. Nobody else was cooperating; I was starting to get into a bad mood from it.

Well . . . there were ways to fix things more to my liking.

Not wanting to interrupt his meal, I told him to continue with whatever he had in mind, but when he'd finished eating he would get very sleepy and take a nice long nap. He took the suggestion—along with the one to forget all about me— very well and got on with his preparations. It looked to be an egg-and-onion sandwich.

I vanished away from there before the onion stink got to be too much and floated back under the cellar door, materialized at the foot of the steps, then got out the flashlight. Next I fished out my notebook and flipped it open to the map Opal had drawn. Facing away from the steps, I walked about five yards along, stopped, and turned right toward the wall. It was fairly clear of clutter, compared to the rest of the place, just some old paint cans and a broken broom, exactly what she'd said would be there. I moved them out of the way.

My flash picked up the unpainted wood boards no different from those covering the rest of the wall. Halfway up, one of them sported a small knothole that had been knocked through. I hooked a finger inside it and first pulled, then pushed to work the latch mechanism.

Someone had done a great job of carpentry; a two-foot-wide, six-foot-tall section swung inward on a special concealed hinge. Escott would have loved it. I shone my light inside and was surprised to see a sizable chamber within. It seemed clear of booby traps and alarm wires, so I stepped in sideways.

With a low ceiling like the rest of the basement, the room was maybe five feet wide and twenty long and completely walled up except for the narrow hidden door. It looked to be part of the original layout of the foundation, but sectioned off from the rest by the phony wall. Comparing outside measurements to inside ones might reveal its existence, but there's not many who would bother with such a detail.

The stuffy air smelled of machine grease, wood, and excelsior. Some long crates lined one side. I found an open one and checked it, discovering a fine collection of brand-new shotguns and ammunition. A second box turned up a carefully packed Thompson machine gun with all the trimmings, a third revealed a number of hand grenades nestled all snug in their wood shavings. Vaughn Kyler had apparently been prepared for all kinds of fun up to and including an assault by the United States Marines Corps. Angela knew about the money; I wondered if she knew about all the weapons. She'd have one hell of a field day with those grenades.

Toward the back was an old cot, a lantern on the bare floor next to a pack of cards, and a scatter of dusty magazines with lurid pictures of half-clad girls (usually screaming in reaction to some grotesque menace) gracing the covers. Damned if one of them wasn't a copy of *Spicy Terror Tales*—I'd been trying to write a story to sell to them for weeks. Its latest page was still languishing all abandoned on the desk in my own basement sanctuary at home. I felt like years had passed since I'd last worked on it.

With all the guns at hand I knew the place wasn't meant to be a prison cell. My guess was when a member of the gang needed to lay low, this was where they took him. If the cops raided the joint all the person had to do was duck down here and fill the time in with reading or solitaire until the law got tired of searching and went away. If you didn't know where to look to get in, then too bad.

Enough of a chill hung in the air to let me know this was probably not a popular spot to visit and linger unless you absolutely had to, adding to its security. There was no real lock for the entry, just the trick of the latch, so few people would think to look here for anything really valuable other than the guns. It was secret, but not too secret. Whatever Kyler chose to keep down here would be safe from his own gang members.

At the farthest end of the room were four innocuous, unmarked crates piled on top of one another, no different from all the others. If Opal hadn't told me what to look for, I'd have passed them by.

Instead, I went straight to them. They were covered with dust, unremarkable, each about a foot high and two wide, maybe a yard long, with thick rope handles, and had most likely once held weapons the same as the other boxes. I tried to lift the topmost one and found it heavy, even for me, then got a good grip on the nailed-down lid and hauled sharply upward. The nails squawked against the wood as they reluctantly parted company. The case lid came suddenly free in my hand. I peered inside, holding the light high.

I don't have much need to breathe now, but caught my breath all the same. Couldn't help it.

Holy shit.

Crammed within were fat bundles of fives, twenties, fifties, and hundreds, row after row of them, an obscene amount of cash smelling of old paper, ink, and the hands that it had passed through. No way to tell how much of that seven hundred grand was in this one box alone, but it was still a hellacious amount of money before me, and all I could do was stare.

A lot of fast thoughts were rushing around in my brain, though. Embodied before me on these bits of paper was the potential of a dozen different futures for yours truly, all of them featuring extreme comfort and luxury as the main theme. Sure I was a vampire, but like everyone else on the planet I'm still only human. The idea of driving away from this place with all that cash packed into the trunk of the car seemed like the most sensible thing in the world I could do for myself.

My conscience chafed, though. It was, after all, dirty money, collected from countless brothels, gambling houses, the numbers trade, loan-sharking, protection payoffs, and the other varied rackets going on in this city. An unbelievable pile of cash came from those sources. The only thing more incredible was the fact that this cache was less than a fraction of a fraction of what was being moved through this city every month. Misery money. Every last dollar of it. Who was I to enjoy it?

On the other hand . . . who was I *not* to? Better me than some gangster, right? And it wasn't like I'd never done this sort of thing before. Only a few months back I'd lifted a briefcase with ten grand of Frank Paco's money inside and had split it with Escott, hardly thinking twice. We were still living well on it. At the time he'd said that a free agent was entitled to any reward his conscience would permit. After looking at all this cash ready for the taking, mine was getting more and more elastic by the minute.

But ten grand wasn't anything compared to seven hundred thousand. Dealing with that much money was bound to make for trouble. Vague thoughts of coming to a bad end because of its dark origins clouded my enthusiasm. It was too good to be true. I knew for damn sure that my mom wouldn't approve of this kind of thing at all.

I could just shove the lid back on and walk away from it . . . save myself a lot of trouble and maybe grief.

But only saps in the movies did that kind of thing. I wasn't that saintly or that nuts.

I kept staring and hoping some flash of enlightenment would clear away my sudden doubts, but none came. It was just too much to take in, and I had other things to deal with tonight.

Finally I gave a shrug. What the hell, I'd take it now and work out the moral problems later when there was more time for them; my immediate problem was figuring a way of getting the whole shebang out of here.

Lifting the crates was easy, I was more than strong enough, but I couldn't vanish and bring them along for the ride; they were just too big and bulky. I'd have to get creative. While I considered possibilities I broke open a big bundle of hundreds and began shoving the smaller bundles of bills—one thousand in each—into the various pockets of my overcoat, suit coat, and pants pockets. The stuff went away surprisingly fast and didn't take up that much room. This admission to bare-faced greed did have a practical inspiration: If I got interrupted, then I'd at least have some "spare change" to carry away. Call it a tip for all the trouble I'd been through up to now. There was no point in counting it just yet, but I knew it to be several thousands. I collected enough in the next couple of minutes to live high on the hog for a considerably long time to come.

God bless America.

The dam broken for the moment, I gleefully went to work. Slipping back outside the hidden room, I located the bags stuffed with table linens. No one would miss a few of these; I emptied one after another onto the cold concrete floor. A quick retrace of my steps and I was stooped over the crate, busily transferring cash into the laundry sacks. I divided it into thirds, roughly estimating that was how much I could disappear with in order to safely carry it out to the car. The estimate proved correct when I took a moment to test it by vanishing, hugging one of the heavily loaded bags close to my chest. It came along without a hitch.

There were nine of them in all at the end, and they took up a lot of space, and nine trips to the car and back took a hell of a lot of effort and energy from me. It did go pretty fast, since I can move very quickly once shed of the normal barriers of corporeal travel. No stumbling or noise and I can flit through brush and trees like smoke. Each jaunt left me feeling thinned out and more tired than the last, but soon the Caddie's trunk was full, with bags left over. The rest I shoved onto floor of the backseat, tired to the point of dizziness by the time I'd finished. Maybe I was better suited for sprints instead of marathons and sat on the running board for a time to catch up with myself and see if a little rest would help.

I was pushing things, but judged this onetime effort to be worth it. How many chances does a guy have to pick up this much money in one evening? Something less than none, so I'd take mine while I had it and deal with the physical consequences later at the Stockyards.

Before I completely quit the hidden room I put the empty crates back into place, their lids pressed down more or less as I'd found them. If by some chance Angela did manage to come here after the money, she'd know who had it, then it would be meat-hook time for me. Only I wasn't going to let it get that far.

Checked my watch, it was nearly two—how time flies when you're getting rich—and not a peep from upstairs. While I kept myself busy with something far more rewarding than just twiddling my thumbs, the house had settled for the night as I'd hoped.

Time to get started with the next stage.

To conserve strength, I went up to the second floor solid, ears wide open for any sound. Nothing but snoring from a couple of the rooms, even the poker players had given up for the night. I catfooted to the storage closet and tried the knob, putting some elbow grease into it, twisting it right from the wood. It made a couple of sharp snapping noises, but not enough to disturb anyone enough to wake up for a look. Still, I counted to a hundred before taking out the remains of the latching mechanism and pulling the door open.

Doc was asleep and muttered unhappily as I shook him. The flashlight batteries were nearly gone, but I flicked it on a moment so he could see, then helped him to his feet.

"What now?" he whispered.

"Down to the kitchen nice and easy and out the back door. I got a car up in the trees ready to go. I'm not figuring on trouble, but if we get interrupted, you duck and let me take care of them."

"You're welcome to it, son."

He hung on to my arm to keep steady, and I guided him carefully along the hall, thankful for the thick carpet. I was still dry-mouthed the whole way, feeling very vulnerable, mostly for his sake. He couldn't disappear if he had to.

The graveled lot was the same, no new cars. I got us moving forward across the highly exposed stretch of open ground as fast as Doc could take it. He picked up some speed toward the end, if only because I was half carrying him, but he was puffing loud.

We finally made the cover of the trees, and I paused to look back while he wheezed and gulped, trying to catch his breath. No new lights, no sign of movement at the windows. By God, we were going to get away clean on this one after all. Once inside the car I could gun it to hell and gone if I wanted and nuts to them.

Turning back to the car, the first sign I had of trouble was a glimpse of a shiny new green roadster parked in the trees just a bit farther up the rise. If my eyes had been human normal, I'd never have spotted it. The thing hadn't been there on my last trip out, and I didn't think it belonged to a courting couple looking for a quiet spot to neck. I stopped us cold, but by then it was too late to do anything.

Four of them emerged from where they'd been crouching behind the Caddie. They must have seen it while driving down the road from the other direction or I'd have heard them pass the roadhouse. Maxwell, wrapped in a brown suede raincoat, was in front, and so confident he didn't bother to take his hands from his pockets. The dirty work was for the other three mugs closing around us. Their hands were out and full of guns.

"Oh. Shit." Doc summed up my very thoughts.

"Why, Mr. Fleming, this wasn't part of the agreement you made with Mr. Sullivan," Maxwell informed me in his radio announcer's voice. A gentle, unpleasant smile tugged at his normally bland expression. "You're supposed to be persuading Miss Paco to—"

"All right, can it. You caught me, we all know it. So now what?"

"So you and the doctor step away from each other and hold still long enough to be searched, then we'll all go back to the house."

"Where's your boss? Where's Opal? Is she okay?"

He didn't answer, only gave the nod to one of the gorillas to check us for weapons. Doc was clean, but I was loaded down, and not with what they expected. The first pocket the gorilla checked was full of bundles of hundred-dollar bills. He pulled one bundle free from the rest and held it up, trying to see better.

"Hey, Max, lookit this. The guy's a frigging bank."

Their eyes all widened as they moved closer. Nothing like the sight of large sums of money to bring about a feeling of true reverence in a crowd.

I put my left elbow into the ribs of the guy behind me and

slammed the side of my fist into the gorilla's belly. Both men doubled over. The last guy had his gun out and ready, but I was moving too fast for him to even begin to react. He hardly had time to look up before I clocked him one in the chin and sent him and his .38 flying.

As for Maxwell, he had only an instant to do a quick imitation of Harold Lloyd being surprised and then he was out for the count.

Doc, surprised as any of them, surveyed the bodies. "Hoowee, boy, remind me not to get you riled."

I stooped to pick up the bundle of cash. The homemade paper band holding it together was labeled with the amount. I'd used ten grand for a distraction, money well spent, I'd say, especially since it was going right back into my pocket.

"What is that?" asked Doc, peering.

"Never mind, get in the car before more of 'em show."

The two men I'd punched were starting to recover. I rudely interrupted, making sure they wouldn't be waking up any too soon, leaving them just where they dropped on the bare ground. It was too much to hope that they'd freeze. The air was cold, but not that cold.

I opened the rear door while Doc hobbled around to the passenger side and got settled.

"Now what?" he demanded.

I grunted, busily hefting Maxwell into the backseat. The floorboards were all full up with bulging laundry bags. "He probably knows where Opal is. When he comes to I'll have a few questions for him." He didn't make a sound as he flopped loose over the chill leather upholstery. After a quick search, I lifted a .22 semi-auto from his inside coat pocket. Either he relied on the gorillas to keep him safe or he was a good enough shot with it to be comfortable with a small-caliber gun. That, or anything larger messed up the lines of his suit. I shoved his legs in and slammed the door to stop them from slithering out.

Gave the house a glance, worried that someone had heard the noise, but it was so far so good for the moment. I hopped up behind the wheel and worked the key and starter. The motor made some sound coming to life, then eased back to its usual soft purr. Getting to like this car would be a very easy thing to do.

No need to spin the steering wheel much since we were already pointed in the right direction, so I hit the gears and gas and headed her easy does it down the rise toward the road so as not to draw attention from the house. The bigger the head start we had before the gorillas came to, the better.

We made it to the main road and I gunned it.

Doc sat halfway turned around to face me and to keep an eye on Maxwell in the back. "Well, I owe you one, Fleming."

"You sure as hell do."

"And you've got something in mind about how I should pay it off, don't you?"

"Just get us both to Angela tonight and I'll call it even."

"I'll think about it."

"You'll what?" The car swerved as my attention shifted toward him.

"Watch the damn road!"

I gritted my teeth to keep the bad language in so the air wouldn't go blue around our ears. When I had some control back I said, "You'll *think* about it?"

"You heard me. Getting out of there was just too easy. Great Aunt Hattie, three armed guys against just you?"

"I'm stronger than I look."

"They dropped mighty easy, maybe a mite too easy."

"You think it was a setup? A show? Why don't you check on Maxwell? See if his eyes are uncrossed yet."

"So maybe you didn't pull all your punches."

Actually, I had done just exactly that so as not to kill anyone, though God knows I'd had enough provocation for one night to forget myself.

"Maybe you got a feud goin' with Sullivan's watchdog and—"

"Oh, for cryin' out loud, can't you believe what you see with your own eyes?"

"Not since the last time the shakes got me and I had rats coming out of my shoes to dance the polka." He was absolutely serious.

"Then how about I turn back around and drop you on their front porch? I'm sure Sullivan'd love to see you again. When it comes down to it I don't really need you to find Angela, my guess is she'll find me, sooner or later."

"You're right on that one, boy, but I suspect it'd be a lot better for you if you found her first."

"There might be a few less bullets and grenades in the air, yes. It'd be better for everyone."

"Made an impression on you, did she? Quite a gal." He chuckled.

"So? Are you gonna tell me where to drive?"

"Just head on like you're doing and give me some thinking time."

There wasn't a whole hell of a lot else to do, so I shut my mouth and drove, keeping us steady and within the speed limit. The last thing I wanted was a cop pulling me over with an unconscious man in the back lying on top of all those bags of cash. It wouldn't be a problem to send him or anyone else along with a conveniently altered memory, but I just didn't want the bother or headache.

The cross streets slowed us with their signals. I was a little worried Doc might bolt while we were stopped, but he sat at his ease, occasionally glancing at Maxwell. I checked on him as best I could in the rearview mirror, but only saw part of his brown raincoat.

"Suede," I said, shaking my head.

"Huh?" said Doc.

"Why in hell would anyone want a suede raincoat? It shows all the water marks."

Doc considered the question and shook his head, too. "You got me there. Why not ask him when he wakes up?"

"I just might. You make any decisions about taking me to see Angela?"

"Up to a point."

"Which is?"

"I'm wondering what you plan to do with four-eyes back there."

I'd been thinking about that myself, but was fairly certain Escott could help with that problem. All I had to do was find a phone. Luck was against me as there didn't seem to be any all-night drugstores in this area. The ones I knew about were miles away. A gas station, then. Jeez, but this part of town was deserted. Lonely spots like where we were driving always gave me the creeps. Crowded during the day and a ghost town at night, it just wasn't natural.

"Fleming?"

"What?"

"Maxwell. What you got planned for him? Hey . . . you okay?"

"Yeah, I'm peachy." It was catching up with me, all the strain of the last few hours and the ones before them and the ones before them. Maybe I should make a stop at the Stockyards before I stretched myself too thin. Not much chance of that unless I could get Doc to take a doze while I went off to feed. Maybe he'd sobered up some and I could work with him.

"What about Maxwell?" he prompted again.

"He stays with me, Angela doesn't get him."

"But she might find a use for him in dealing with Sullivan."

"I'm sure she would—before plugging him once and dumping him in the lake."

Doc didn't contradict my prediction, only made a throwing-away gesture as if to agree with me. I felt a sharp pang in my chest, right over my heart where the bullet had gone in and changed my world forever. Angela's father had plugged me and dumped me in the lake not so very long ago. Perhaps it was a family tradition. Now and then the memory would still flash up in my mind, inspiring either a wince or a shudder, depending on my mood. This time I just ground my teeth some more and took one hand off the wheel long enough to rub the spot till it stopped tingling.

"It'd sweeten her up some to have Sullivan's secretary," Doc said after a moment. "He'd make a mighty fine lever against that Irish bastard."

"What I've learned tonight is when the wrong side has you, your so-called friends start putting in orders for the funeral wreaths. She wasn't going to budge an inch for your sake, so why should Sullivan be different from her?"

"Good point," he admitted.

"And why should you want to cozy up with her again, anyway? She was willing to leave you to them."

He shrugged. "Because that's just how things are. Since you don't seem to understand it—"

"I understand all right, I just don't like it."

"Then the best thing for you is to get out while you're still in one piece. Whyn't you just drop me off by one of the L's and I'll find my own way from there?"

"Uh-uh."

"I'll tell her you left town for good. She'd believe it comin' from me."

My head wanted to hurt again. "No. We're going to find a phone, and after I get some help with Maxwell, you're going to call Angela and persuade her to set up a meeting place for the three of us. Tonight." Whether Doc was sober enough for it or not, I'd make it happen.

I finally found a phone and dialed Shoe Coldfield's number.

Escott answered right away, and if he'd been asleep, his voice didn't sound like it. "Are you all right?"

"I've been better. Things have changed since I talked to Shoe. . . ." God, how long ago was it? I gave Escott a rough idea of what had happened since I'd been optimistic enough to tell Coldfield I was fixing up a truce with Angela. Not once did I make any mention of the seven hundred grand in the laundry bags. Doc stood hunched next to me just outside the booth and could hear everything. He wanted to wait in the car out of the wind, but even with the keys in my hand I didn't trust him enough to leave him alone in it. "I got one of Sullivan's top boys with me and need to put him on ice for a couple hours until I'm squared away with Angela. It needs to be someplace quiet, and you shouldn't have any trouble with him. He's out cold right now, but bring some rope and a gag, just in case."

"Done your Svengali act on him, have you?"

"More like a right cross, but I do have to talk to him, find out where they've taken Opal. Doc says she's being looked after, but I don't trust any of them."

"That goes without saying. I'm sure I can make some sort of arrangement."

"Can you come meet me? I don't want Doc seeing anything he shouldn't." Better for us all if he didn't know where Coldfield hung his hat. I gave him the name of the street and the nearest cross street. After backing the car into an alley, Doc and I had walked the dozen or so steps to the phone on the corner by a closed gas station. We were right under a lamp. It made harsh blue shadows on his creased face, aging him, and probably wasn't too flattering to me, either, not that I gave a damn. I heard Escott repeating the names aloud and Coldfield rumbling a reply in the background.

"Shoe knows the area. We should be there in about a quarter hour, perhaps a bit more."

"You in any shape to come?"

"I'm well enough."

He was probably lying so he wouldn't miss anything. Wouldn't his eyes pop once he saw what was in the laundry bags? He could watch Doc while Shoe and I shifted them. I wasn't about to take that Caddie with the cash anywhere near Angela.

"What about yourself?" he asked.

"I'm . . . tired." Escott didn't speak for a moment, maybe trying to figure out how much I wasn't saying because of Doc's presence. For me to admit I was less than perfect physically and in just that tone meant more than if anyone else said it. Escott knew how much it took to seriously knock the wind out of me. "Just get here as soon as you can and take this guy off my hands for a while."

"We will."

"Things been quiet on your end?"

"Like a church."

"What about that friend of yours we met at the movie house?" No need to mention Merrill Adkins in front of Doc, either.

"What of him?"

"Think he'd be interested in taking in another boarder once I'm finished with him?"

"I'm sure he'd be delighted."

"But only after I'm done."

"Of course."

"Great. See you." I hung up.

Doc was shivering in the cold, so I led us back to the car and started it up to get the heater running. I let it idle for five minutes to take the chill off then shut it down. The only thing interrupting the silence was the wind whispering outside, the engine ticking as it cooled, and the sound of blood being pumped through two living bodies. Doc's breath grew harsh and sometimes uneven. He had the fidgets.

"I need a drink," he finally announced, looking miserable. "You got a flask?"

"Nope."

"What about him?" He nodded at Maxwell.

I shrugged.

"Think I'll check him and find out."

"Leave that to me." I leaned over the backseat and slapped him down again and gave Doc the bad news.

"Damn."

On the other hand, Maxwell was awake. I sensed the change in him; something about his breathing and heartbeat tipped me off. I shook him good and told him to stop fooling around and sit up.

His eyelids dragged open, and after a minute he pushed away from the seat and looked around. Being new in town, he probably didn't recognize the area. If he was used to civilized ivy-covered walls, then this spot would be anything but comforting to him. He was in a bad place, in more ways than one, once he got a look at my sour expression.

"Where's Opal?" I asked.

He blinked a few times, coughed, and rubbed his bruised and swollen jaw. Taking stock, probably.

"Where?"

Now he took off his glasses, fumbled for a handkerchief, and cleaned them. He carefully did not look at me now, but let his gaze check out everything else, the doors, the alley walls, a glimpse for the laundry bags.

"I know a stall, Maxwell, so don't push it. Tell me where Opal is and I'll leave you all your teeth."

He gave me that gentle smile. The unpleasant tinge in it was gone, replaced by a touch of genuine fear. I hoped it would make him sensible. "Yes, I'm sure you're quite capable of that sort of violence, Mr. Fleming. I just wanted time to think things over."

It must be catching, I thought, sparing a glance for Doc, who gave an amused snort. I worried that he might notice something if I had to put the eye on Maxwell, but maybe hypnosis wouldn't be necessary. Max seemed willing to talk. "Got everything worked out, I hope?"

"Sadly, yes, and I will cooperate so long as you refrain from further mayhem." He lightly touched his jaw.

"Deal. Where's Opal?"

"She is in a safe place and being very well looked after. Mr. Sullivan was quite upset about her injury, so he is seeing to it she has the best care at his disposal."

"Where?"

The smile went all chagrined. "This is something of an embarrassment. I know how to get there, but I didn't take an exact note of the address. I'm not all that familiar with the town, you see."

"Uh-huh. Doesn't make you much of a secretary, does it?"

"An oversight that won't happen again, I promise."

Stalling again. I was ready to put him into zombie land.

He must have picked up on my loss of patience and raised an unsteady hand in mild protest. "However, I can give you directions on how to get there. I'll write them down. It's sort of a clinic, not too very far from the roadhouse."

I looked at Doc. "You know of any place like what he's talking about?"

"Well, now that he's bumped my memory, I think I do. One of Kyler's projects I heard tell of, but I figured it to just be one of them stories that goes around."

"What is it exactly?" I asked Maxwell.

"Something like a way station for men who wish to drop from sight. They get a chance to rest and think while they put a new face on their situation, you might say."

"What—like plastic surgery?"

"If it's necessary. Very expensive, of course, but worth it if it successfully puts the police off your track."

Doc shook his head, amazed. "Well, if that don't beat all."

Maxwell fairly glowed with pride. "Oh, yes, and it's quite up-to-date. None of the old chamber of horrors makeshift and hope for the best. The place has a nice little operating room, very clean, and a qualified surgeon. Mr. Sullivan notified him of our problem with Miss Opal, so he was more than happy to make himself available to see to her care."

"Who is it?" asked Doc.

"Oh, I doubt that you're acquainted with him," he said with a sniff. "Our man managed to graduate from medical school."

"You son of a—I'll have you know I—"

"Put a lid on it," I said. "Okay, Maxwell, give with the directions."

"I've pen and paper in my pockets, if you'll allow me to—"

"Allow away."

He fumbled with his coat, searching. His hands brushed the pocket that had held his .22, but if he was disappointed at it being empty, he covered it well. "The light here is very bad."

I turned on the small overhead bulb.

He hauled out a little leather-bound notebook and tore out a page, then produced his fat-bodied fountain pen. Pricey stuff, I noted. Probably had it custom-made, though he wasn't vain enough to have his initials stamped on in gold lettering.

"Here now," he said, starting to scribble a rough map. "You go up the lane behind the roadhouse . . . oh, damn. What a time to run dry." He fiddled impatiently with the pen, making a face. I wondered for an instant if he was going to be stupid enough to try squirting ink in my eyes, but he made whatever adjustment he wanted and tried writing again. "I'm terribly sorry, but the blasted thing is—have either of you a pen or pencil?"

Doc snorted in disgust and leaned back against the door to pinch the bridge of his nose. "I really, and I mean *really* need a drink."

Keeping my eyes on Maxwell, I reached into my inside coat pocket and found a pencil by touch, held it out to him over the seat.

"Thank you. I'm afraid all this activity has me a bit rattled. Usually I'm not like this."

"Just write," I said.

"Yes, yes, of course," He nervously reached for the pencil, pen still in hand.

He should have put the pen away. The movement suddenly became too aggressive, too fast, and it was over and done before I even thought about reacting. He caught me right on the inside wrist with the pen, only instead of a stab with the blunt point of a nib, it was something sharp, stinging.

I snarled and yanked my arm back like I'd been burned, dragging the pen with me. It startled Doc, who looked up, eyes wide.

Maxwell hit the latch on the door and scrabbled clear of the car.

The pen stuck up at an incongruous angle from my wrist and hurt like blazes. I figured it for some kind of a retractable stiletto, as there was a long needle coming out of it that he'd buried in me. Nasty little weapon. I slapped it free like swat-

ting an especially ugly bug, and madder than hell shot out of
the car to chase Max down. He hadn't gotten far, was probably still rocky from the punch I'd given him earlier. I caught
up with him in ten steps, snagged his coat to haul him into
range of my fist, and gave him another sock to remember me
by. He dropped.

Leaned wearily against the side of a building, my head
spinning. *Jeez, what a night.*

I checked back to see what Doc was doing. He'd levered
from the car as well, but was coming toward us rather than
attempting to escape. He probably knew better than to try in
his shape, since I'd be able to catch him just as easily. He
had the pen with him, but held it gingerly between his fin-
gertips like it was some fragile piece of glass.

"Holy hell, you ever see anything like this in your life?
Wonder where he got it?" he said, looking down at Maxwell.
"What a little weasel. I think I owe him a kick for that crack
about my not graduating."

"Let him be, he's not going anywhere. What is that
thing?" I took the pen from him for a closer look. I didn't
care much for what I saw. The needle was hollow, a hypodermic. I examined my wrist. There was a hole in it and a
little blood. Nothing to worry about, I hoped, except that there
was now a knot under the skin, which felt very cold.

"Lemme see," said Doc, squinting at the damage like a
fortune-teller. He clamped his fingers above the knot with one
hand, then gently squeezed it. I didn't feel a thing. A very
small amount of clear fluid came out the hole, then nothing
as it swelled shut. He bent low and sniffed my skin. "Gimme
that pen again."

I held on to it, but let him check things. He worked some
tiny mechanism in the fat barrel with his thumb and a drop
of fluid appeared at the end of the needle. He sniffed that,
too.

The cold was starting to travel up my arm, fast. "Something's wrong. . . ."

He shot me a sad, worried look. "What d'you feel?"

"It's gone all numb." My arm was too heavy to move. It drooped from my shoulder, a deadweight.

"Sit down, son. Take it easy."

"What the hell'd he stick me with? Morphine?" But it didn't feel like morphine.

"Just sit down," he insisted.

I didn't want to, but my body gave me no choice. The cold blossomed out from my shoulder, spread over my chest, down my legs. They also went numb, and abruptly Doc was supporting me, easing me onto the hard pavement. I tried to take a breath to speak, but it felt like my lungs were stuffed with cotton.

"Easy, now," he kept saying over and over. Whatever was wrong with me, it had to be bad to get that sort of reaction out of him. You're only kind to your enemies when they're dying.

"Doc?"

"It's nothing I can do anything about," he said, but he sounded like he was telling that to convince himself, not me.

"The pen—"

"It's full of something nasty."

No shit, I thought as the numbness swooped down my other arm. I was cold, very, very cold inside.

"Just take it easy . . ."

"Wha—" I managed to gasp out with a last little bit of air. Kept staring at him, desperate for an answer.

"Got a smell to it. I think it's some kind of cyanide. You know what that is?"

I knew. With the numbing cold came paralysis. My sight clouded over. Tried for more air. Nothing. Tried to move. Nothing.

Saw a shifting blur above as he felt for a pulse in my neck. Couldn't find one, of course. "Oh, Lord, but I'm sorry for you, son. It's hell, but there's harder ways to go."

True, but this one was bad enough.

Couldn't move, couldn't think. Could hear, but not react. It was like being caught away from my earth for the day. Part of my mind was conscious of activity around me, but utterly unable to do more than absently note it down. I should have been silently screaming in my brain from the panic, but I couldn't remember how.

Another blur, then darkness. He'd shut my eyes with his fingers.

I heard other sounds from him. A long, sad sigh, a soft grunt as he stood up, a curse or two, his shoe soles scraping as he slowly walked away. Farther off, the clunk as he shut the Caddie's door, the motor turning over and catching. A stuttering grind as he struggled with unfamiliar gears and fed it gas. The tires whined against the road as he turned them, then the wind and exhaust from the swiftly passing car washed over my cooling body.

9

I didn't drift in a hazy mental fog as when I'd accidentally taken in a dose of morphine. That might have been pleasant. For this I was absolutely ironed flat to the ground, each of my bones weighing tons, the skin and muscle hanging from them dragging even heavier. Movement was impossible, as was thinking. The inertia enveloping me was complete and perfect.

If I could have thought about anything, I might have wished for total unconsciousness. Better not to have this sort of blind helplessness than be even a little aware of it and its attendant terror. But I did have that much left to me, more's the pity, the first feeling to come when we're born and the last to linger when we die, if we're given enough time in the dying to recognize it.

And with the terror was the stunning cold. I was only sensible of it because of a contrasting band of warmth stubbornly clinging to my midsection. It wouldn't go away. If that was bad or good I couldn't work it out. Couldn't even shiver.

Wind against my face, ruffling my hair, plucking at my clothes. It felt warm, too, compared to the iciness within my stilled flesh.

Hard pavement. Strange that it didn't crumble and collapse under my body's infinite weight.

Sound. Wind curled around my ears, whispering. Hollow clank and rattle as it pushed a tin can along the street. Mournful song as it slipped between the phone wires high above, making them hum in turn.

All this went on and on. No way to tell the time. No real time to tell. No real time. Nothing and everything at once and forever. The fear and the cold and the wind, no beginning, no ending.

And that one little spot of warmth.

A car came along and screeched to a stop. Voices. Questions. A hand on my brow. A hand lightly slapping my face.

"Jack? Wake up. Jack?"

"Damn it, Charles, you can't leave this kid alone for five minutes. And who the hell is this mug?"

"Probably that Maxwell person Jack mentioned. How is he?"

"Out for the count. What about—"

"He's out, too. We can presume some misadventure overtook them both after Jack called in. Perhaps Doc got the drop on them, then escaped. I don't see the car anywhere."

"Presume fast then, we gotta get these guys off the sidewalk before someone else comes by."

"Or Doc returns with help. Come on, then."

"No you don't. You're not doing anything with your ribs the way they are. You just hold the door open, I can get 'em in."

So saying, someone hauled me roughly up. He must have been amazingly strong to be able to handle my leaden form. I was lifted and lugged and eased down and pushed into place. Sitting at first, then I heeled right over. Leather upholstery. Softer than the pavement.

Sound of another man being lifted and the car rocked on its springs a little once he was inside. More rocking as they got in, two breathing men on either side of me. They pulled and pushed me upright, but my body kept wanting to slide sideways and down. Doors slammed shut.

"What's that?" the second man, the amazing weight lifter, asked.

"Found it on the walk. It slipped from Jack's hand. I think it's supposed to be a pen, but—careful!—that's a needle, and there's some kind of fluid in it."

"Does he take dope?"

"Certainly not, but this may be part of the misadventure that befell him. Get us home, Shoe. I've a very bad feeling about this."

Starter, gears, forward motion. Two breathing men on either side of me, a shard of dim consciousness trapped alone and silent in a dead body.

"It can't be safe coming back to this place," said the one called Shoe. "They been here twice now."

"I rather think it will be, since they failed twice," said his friend, Charles. "At least for the moment. Jack did get Miss Paco to call off the hit on me."

"As far as he knows. The shape he's in, anything could have happened since then and she could be behind it. He's an honest kid dealing with a bunch of pirates. You can't play fair with them and win."

"Even so, he needs to be home for me to be able to help him."

"What's here that we can't get at my sister's place?"

"Just some odds and ends that she won't have. Don't worry about it."

"I'll worry if I damn well please. Now go hold the doors."

More lifting, more carrying. Lots of carrying. Another soft place for my body to rest. A pink brightness against my eyelids as a light clicked on.

"Charles—Charles, hurry in here, he's bleeding."

"Where?" Footsteps, coming close, pausing. "Dear God."

"I don't see any cuts, but look at it! It's all over him." Fear in the voice.

Fingers brushed across my forehead. "This is very interesting. It seems to be coming right out of his pores."

"What's the matter with him?"

"I'm not sure, but that bizarre hypodermic . . . perhaps he was poisoned."

"What the hell kinda poison does that to a man?"

"I'll work on it later. Can you carry him up to the bath?"

"Bath, nothing. He's going to a hospital."

"Shoe, we cannot take him there."

"Yeah, I heard that speech last night, but—"

"This has nothing to do with the Paco gang spotting us, it's something altogether different."

"What, then?"

"There's no easy way to explain it. Jack has a rather rare physical condition, it's similar to catalepsy, but quite a bit more complicated. I know how to help him where most doctors could not. You have to trust me on this."

Long pause. "Charles, it's the kid's life that's at stake, not my trust in you. Are you sure?"

"I may strain that trust in the next few minutes, but, yes, I am sure. This is going to get a bit strange, my friend."

"How so?"

"Just get him up to the bath for a start. You'll find out."

A grunt as I was again lifted. "Goddammit, I *hate* it when you go all Mr. Mystery on me."

Steps, lots of them, another light clicking on.

"Put him in the tub," said Charles.

Hard surface, slick.

"Hm. Right. Here, I want to check his eyes." Fingers prying open one of my eyelids. Blurs, bright blurs. Release back to the pink-tinged shadows. "His pupils are reacting to light, that's something." Fingers tugging at my upper lip, pushing it back.

"What the hell . . . ?" More alarm in Shoe's tone. "What's wrong with his teeth?"

"It's all right, in fact, I'm glad they're like that. I know for certain what to do now."

"Then do it, but what about his *teeth*?"

The fingers pressed my lips back into place. "It's his condition. I said it was complicated, and I promise I'll explain later."

"You're gonna explain all right."

"When I have more time. I have to hurry."

"Yeah, he's bleeding bad. Soaking right through his clothes."

"Then get them off him. This looks like it will be very messy." Footsteps retreating.

Hands, pulling at my clothing, tugging. Then an abrupt pause. "Charles." The voice, sad, tired.

"What?"

"There's no need to hurry. He's . . ."

"He's not dead." Statement, not question. A very firm statement.

"I know dead, Charles. And that's what he is."

Footsteps returning. Cloth across my face, wiping it clean. "Just watch for a moment. There, see what's happening? It's still coming out of him like sweat. A dead man does not bleed."

"Maybe the poison did that to him, thinned his blood in some crazy way."

"Or his body is getting rid of it. I told you this could get strange."

"This is way past strange, this is goddamned *weird*!"

"I agree, but I've no time to commiserate with you on it.

Whether you think he's dead or not, will you stay here in the
house with him?''

"Yeah, sure, for what it's worth.''

"And don't forget our friend Maxwell downstairs. See to
it he's well trussed up, and some sort of blindfold wouldn't
be out of place, either. I've an errand to run, so—''

"You can't drive.''

"I'm able to and will.''

"Where do you think you're going?''

"To see a man about a cow.''

More argument, voices fading downstairs. A door shutting.
Someone coming back. Hands on me once more peeling away
my sodden clothing. Coat, shirt, belt, pants. When the belt
slipped away from my waist, the only warmth went with it.
The grinding cold encompassed me, and with it came the final
comfort of absolute oblivion.

I'd had this dream before, the one where I surprise myself by
waking up, the one where I've got a tube in my nose that
makes it possible for blood to drip down my throat and directly into my stomach. The dream doesn't last long, just a
flash of it on those very rare times when the sun comes and
I'm away from my earth. There are always other, much worse
dreams to take its place. If it lasted longer than a few seconds
I'd consider myself lucky, since compared with the rest it's
not all that bad.

Then I really did awaken, fast, with a startled yelp, strug-
gling to sit up, banging my elbows against the sides of something hard, and I thought for an instant I was in that damned
box over the tobacco shop.

"There now, it's all right, you're safe,'' said Escott, trying
to be soothing, I suppose.

I clawed at my face and found the tube and started to pull
it out, but that hurt so I forced myself to stop and look around.

The upstairs bathroom. Escott sat on the closed toilet lid, informal in an unbuttoned vest and rolled-up shirtsleeves, his face all pinched with concern, bruised eyes red for lack of sleep. Shoe Coldfield filled up most of the doorway, eyes wide, jaw sagging, and looking like someone had just twisted his nose. I was in the bathtub, cold in my shorts and undershirt, and covered, completely *covered* with blood.

I gave another yelp and Escott, talking louder to get through my fear, told me to take it easy. I couldn't make myself speak; nothing coherent wanted to come out. Held my arms away from my body, smearing more blood against the sides of the tub, adding to the stuff already there. It was on my face, my eyelids, my hair, dried flakes snowing down whenever I moved, and I sat in a thick icy puddle of it, could follow the threads of flow where it had slowly made its way toward the drain.

Escott kept talking, saying my name until after a moment I got hold of my panic and could do better than just sit and shiver and fight the urge to jump up and run off—something I *really* wanted to do.

"Get this . . . get this thing outta me," I said hoarsely, gesturing at the tube with trembling fingers. One end of it was in me, right up my *nose,* for God's sake, the other led to a bottle hanging from a metal stand. The bottle was nearly full of blood.

"Right, you should have had your fill after all this. Lean back and relax."

The next few seconds were really boring, but over and done with fast enough, and I felt better, more in control once it was out. He wound the tubing up so it wouldn't drip and put it and the bottle into the sink. Coldfield just watched and said nothing. I didn't want to know what he was thinking, but it couldn't have been good, to tell from the frozen expression on his face.

"Sorry," I said to the general air. Crazy thing, apologizing when I hadn't done anything wrong.

Escott snorted, dismissing the whole business. "How do you feel?"

I lifted my arms again. "Disgusting." I was also still cold through and through, had to keep blinking trying to clear my cloudy sight, and couldn't quite shake the impression I weighed a ton and a half more than was normal.

"You up to bathing, then?"

Nodded my head. Ready or not, I had to wash clean again. "How'd I get like this?"

"I was rather hoping you'd tell me. What happened after your call to us last night?"

"*Last* night?"

"You've slept the day away."

"Oh, jeez, I don't remember."

"Yes, well, I did put this in with you just before dawn." He reached and pulled out one of my bags of earth where it had rested against my feet. The bag was all bloodstained, of course.

I glanced up at Coldfield.

Escott followed my look. "Not to worry. I took the liberty of explaining everything about your condition to Shoe. Considering the extraordinary circumstances, there was little choice in the matter."

Now we both looked at Coldfield, who looked back at us, mostly at me. He was shaking his head.

I started to say something to him, but it wouldn't come out. I just didn't know what to say.

He stopped shaking his head, kept staring. Finally pointed at me. "You . . . you're a vampire."

"Shoe, I . . ."

Continued to point. "*You're a vampire?*"

Then his frozen expression cracked wide open and he doubled over laughing.

There was a gas heater built into the bathroom wall. I asked Escott to light it since my case of gooseflesh didn't want to leave just yet.

"What's so damn funny about *me* being a vampire?" I groused as his match caught and blue flames filled the grating.

Coldfield had to go downstairs so he could roll on the floor, slap his sides, beat the furniture, and hoot all he wanted without my having to witness the spectacle.

"He's just venting some of the tension. We've all had a bit of a stretch on this one."

"Some venting." I could still hear laughter coming up through the floorboards. "If he doesn't slow down he'll need an oxygen tent."

One of Escott's eyebrows bounced and he cleared his throat. "Look, get yourself cleaned up, you'll feel much better for it."

"Yeah, yeah."

"Then Shoe and I would very much like to hear what went on last night. Perhaps you can explain about all that money we found in your overcoat pockets."

"Money? Oh, yeah, that stuff."

"It is not an inconsiderable sum. Sixty-eight thousand, three hundred dollars in various denominations and nonsequential serial numbers, and so far as I'm able to determine, it is not marked or counterfeit. I've put it in the basement safe for the time being."

"Thanks, but if you think that's a lot then wait till . . . wait . . . the car—the stuff in the Caddie . . ." The memory popped back of Doc driving away. Off he'd gone, probably straight to Angela, looking after himself once he figured my part in things was finished for good. Off he'd gone, along with the balance of that seven hundred grand, and not even knowing he had it.

"The car?"

"Oh, God," I groaned as it overwhelmed me. My loss was horrible and heartfelt, right down to my toes; it hurt so much I was within a hair of actually breaking down and crying.

"What?" Escott demanded, all anxious.

I pulled myself together and waved him off. "Gimme a few minutes. I can't talk about it now."

He took his leave only very reluctantly. From his view of things, it must have seemed crazy: He reminds me of a fortune in my coat and I go into a fit of instant misery. It couldn't be helped, I had some serious mourning to do. I sat in the tub, head bowed and moaning and feeling very sorry for myself. I'd found and lost an ungodly amount of money in a laughably short time, and whining excuses about none of it being my fault weren't cutting any ice with my sense of greed.

I mentally kicked myself until the chilliness of my physical condition finally got through to me and demanded some attention. By then I was ready for a distraction and cautiously stood to get a good look at the mess I'd literally been sitting in. There was no knowing how Escott had been able to stand it, since he'd mentioned his squeamishness to me more than once in the past. I wasn't too happy myself; the sight of all that blood practically painting me was pretty damn revolting. The smell wasn't so great to my sensitive nose either, being something like almonds mixed with old rust and raw meat starting to go bad. Ugh.

The poison must have sweated its way out of every pore in my body. I was glad now that Escott had had the wisdom to replace the lost blood, or God knows what kind of shape I'd be in. As it was, I felt fairly fit, but dry in the throat, from thirst or irritation from the tube, I didn't know. I reached over to the sink and got the bottle, removing the stopper and tube from the opening, and gave the contents a sniff. Cow's blood. Gone cold, and not the same as taking it fresh, but still very drinkable. I gulped freely and let the stuff work through me. It took its own sweet time, but gradually the chill started to recede from my bones, and I didn't feel so weighted down as before. With the last swallow sweeping away the last of the cobwebs, I turned on the tub water, letting it run until it got hot.

I usually prefer a bath, but wasn't about to sit down again until the tub was clean, so I pulled the lever to get the showerhead going and yanked the splash curtain around. Running water was no friend of mine, but this kind I could handle without problems. Took off my shorts and undershirt after the water soaked the fabric from my skin, then soaped and scrubbed away until all the red was gone. Finishing off with a shave and dressed in fresh clothes, I felt like I could face the world again and maybe even Escott and Coldfield, so I went downstairs.

They were holed up in the kitchen, sitting at the table. Escott had a big cup of tea, Coldfield some coffee, and between them was a bottle of whiskey, which they must have used to give their respective drinks more of a kick. On the counter by the sink were several rinsed-out bottles similar to the one I'd emptied, plates, and the remains of some Chinese-food cartons. Escott hated to cook, even to make a sandwich. I'd seen him eat the bread and meat separately right out of their wrappers just to avoid the bother of putting the two together.

"Better?" Escott inquired when I came in.

"Yeah. Sorry I went a little nuts there."

"I'm sure you had an excellent reason."

"You don't know the half of it."

"Then please tell us." He shoved a third chair out with his foot as an invitation to sit.

Coldfield glanced at me once, looked away, and stifled another grin.

I glared at him. *"What?"*

He snickered and tried to turn it into a cough, then gave up and started laughing again.

"Why don't I come back in a few hours when he's got it out of his system?"

Escott looked pained. "Really, Shoe, it's not all that amusing."

"It sure as hell *is*. I mean, *him* being a vampire? He's the last person I'd pick."

"Thanks a lot," I said sourly, dropping into the chair.

"I don't mean it bad, but it's taking some getting used to."

"No kidding."

"I can see why you want to keep this kind of news to yourself, so I don't blame you for not saying anything to me. I thought Charles had lost his mind when he brought in that sack of dirt and all those bottles of blood and put the tube up your nose and—"

"I think Jack would prefer to skip that part. I know I would."

"I don't usually drink it out of a tube," I added. "Where'd you get the stuff, anyway?"

Escott shrugged. "I struck a deal with a night watchman at a slaughterhouse."

"No questions from him on why you wanted the stuff?"

"I said it had to do with a practical joke against some antiunionists. He was all for it."

"I'll bet. What about the bottles and all the rest? Where'd you get those?"

"After your last escapade I thought it a good idea to acquire some for an emergency rather than borrow from Dr. Clarson again.''

"What escapade?" asked Coldfield, all interest.

I didn't want to go into the business of how I'd been staked in the heart and promised to tell him later. A lot later, I hoped.

"Least now I know why you always had a bad stomach when it came to eating. So that's it for you? Drinking nothing but blood?"

"Yeah."

"Huh. That must get downright dull."

"Well, it saves me from a lot of dishwashing."

Coldfield chuckled, but managed not to succumb to another fit of hilarity. "You want to tell us just what happened to put you out like that? I thought vampires were supposed to be damn near indestructible."

I resisted enlightening him further on the subject and told them about last night in all its grim detail, from the raid at the dance studio to Doc leaving me for dead on the sidewalk.

"He's gonna be in for one hell of a shock when I turn up again," I concluded.

"No doubt," Escott agreed. "Then you plan to try recovering that money?"

"Damn right I do." They'd been properly impressed by the amount when I'd gotten to that part of the story.

"How?"

Shook my head. "I'll figure something out, but I gotta know what's happened today. You hear anything? You guys must have had your ears open."

"Nothing new from my bunch," said Coldfield.

"I called Merrill Adkins," said Escott.

I snorted, not much liking his government friend.

"He was unable to talk freely since I am not a fellow agent, but I gathered that all the law officers in town are up in arms about the shooting of the policeman at that hotel."

"Yeah, he was one of Calloway's men and working for Sullivan," I said. "What lies did the papers print?"

"Oh, he's a hero destined for sainthood. The later editions mention plans for a public memorial service. Oh, and there's to be a major crackdown on crime in the city."

"Well, that's nice and general. I'll bet the citizens are feeling safer already. Any suspects?"

He grunted. "Now you know why it's so general. But still, it would be wise if you avoided the area for a time, say a decade or two."

"No problem." It was one of Gordy's favorite phrases, and reminded me that I wanted to call him. Maybe he had some news. "Where's Maxwell?"

"Safe in the basement. Shoe put him near the furnace, so he should be warm enough."

"What? He's been tied up there all day?"

"With a few comfort breaks and some food. He's full of questions, but not too very forthcoming with answers. Seems rather mystified on how he got here and who we are in the play of the game. He's promised us a vast reward for his safe return to Sullivan's camp. Several times."

"Must be fresh out of poison for his pen."

"Yes, remarkable little toy, that. I've since rendered it harmless. No more ill effects from it?"

"I think it's all sweated out. Little weasel got me right in the wrist." I pulled back my sleeve, but any sign of the needle jab was long healed over. "Doc said it was cyanide."

"Indeed, a very nasty batch of it, too—I had a sample analyzed today by a chemist friend. Had you been a normal man, it would have dropped you within seconds of the injection."

"Jeez."

"Indestructible," Coldfield muttered, taking a swig of coffee.

"Only barely," I added. "It didn't feel so hot. Thanks for helping me, both of you."

They shrugged.

"I mean that. Look, when this is finished, how about I take you out to Hallman's?" It was one of the swankiest restaurants in Chicago. "I know it's not much, but—"

"I'd say it was a fair trade, a meal for a meal—even if you weren't awake for it," said Coldfield. "That is, if they let me in again. Charles got away with it once. . . ."

I grinned. "Gimme five minutes with the management and I can make sure you have a regular table at the joint anytime you want."

"Using that hypnosis gag? Sure, why not? Sign me up."

"It's a deal." Maybe he didn't completely believe I could do it. I'd prove it later. I was glad he didn't remember my giving him the same business the other night. Getting caught's embarrassing.

The phone rang.

"I think I know who that might be," said Escott. "Shoe, let's give our friend a bit of privacy and adjourn to the front parlor to finish our drinks."

With that for a hint, I knew who it might be, too, and hurried to grab the receiver as they left. Bobbi's voice hit me like summer rain on a dry field.

"You all right?" she asked. "Charles said you'd got back late and would call when you could, but I just couldn't wait any longer."

I was glad he'd not told her about the poison. She had enough worries. "I'm sorry, I should have done that first thing, but there's been so damn much going on. I'm fine, really."

"Are you finished, then?"

"Not yet."

"Not even close?"

"Baby, if I could tell you that, you'd be the second to know after me."

"Rough night?"

"Yeah, that's what I'd call it, I'll give you the whole story some other time. Tell me how things are with you. Still at that lawyer's house?"

"Uh-huh, the Blooms have been wonderful. We haven't a thing in common, but they're good at not letting it show, and Cathy has been so sweet—that's his wife. . . ."

I prompted her with more questions, just to keep her talking. It didn't matter what she said, I needed to hear her saying it, to know there were still normal people with normal lives around. Well, fairly normal. This lawyer's best client was a gangster, after all.

Then Bobbi must have figured out what I was doing and stopped the flow. "Are you sure you're fine?"

"I'm a little rocky, but this is what helps it, hearing from you."

"It's even better to see me."

"I know, and I will as soon as I can. I promise you I want this finished. I miss you."

"Not half as much as I miss you," she whispered. "It's been so long since we've been together that my neck's all healed up."

"Uh . . ." I felt my ears going red at this news and the thoughts it inspired and checked to see that Escott and Coldfield were well out of earshot. It's not easy trying to hold an intimate conversation with a beautiful woman while standing at a wall phone, but I did my best.

An indecently long time later, after some hot flirting we finally said reluctant good-byes and I went into the parlor. Coldfield was alone listening to the radio and flipping through a paper. The headlines screamed outrage at the cop-killing.

"Must be quite a woman you got to put a look like that on your face," he commented.

"Yeah, she's really something. Where's Charles?"

"Went down to the basement to check on his guest. He said you'd have to give the guy a special talking-to."

"Yeah. Might as well get it over with."

"What, you don't enjoy 'clouding men's minds'?"

Great, Escott had told him how much I liked *The Shadow*. "Not especially. It can be dangerous."

"Okay if I watch?"

I gave him the nod and led the way. The lights were on down there, all of them, and Escott was over by the furnace talking to Maxwell. His whole head was covered by a thick black sack and he was securely tied to a very sturdy chair— which had fallen over, so he lay sideways on the cement floor. It couldn't have been comfortable for him.

Thinking about the jab he'd given me with that damned needle, I found myself grinning.

"I think you're acquainted with this gentleman," said Escott, turning toward us.

"Looks like he's been trying to escape again," Shoe said wearily. He effortlessly righted the chair, Maxwell and all. "Now we've already had a long talk about this, Maxie, I don't want to have to warn you again."

"It was an accident," Maxwell said.

"You surely do have a lot of them. 'Course, if you *like* crashing onto the floor all the time, I'm thinking we can—"

"Very well, but you must understand that this is quite trying for me. Perhaps I've not yet made it clear to you gentlemen how very grateful my employer would be to have me returned—unharmed—to his organization."

"How much is he up to this time?" Coldfield asked.

"Five thousand dollars," answered Escott.

"Same as last."

"For each of us."

"Well, now, that *is* just starting to impress me. I think it means he's getting a little more scared than he was. Maybe a lot more scared."

"Indeed. And he has every right to be fearful."

Maxwell was probably wanting to ask for some clarification on that point, but kept his trap shut. Couldn't tell if it was out of caution or if he really was afraid, he was good at keeping control of his voice.

I motioned for Escott and Coldfield to come away out of his immediate hearing range. The furnace was running and the sound would mask our talk. "Has he seen either of you?"

Escott gave a decisive shake of his head. "No, but he's certainly heard us. We have been careful not to use our names."

"That's good. This stuff works, but it don't last forever. The less he needs to forget, the better. I'll need to fix the lights before I start."

He made a gesture to invite me to fix away.

"Watch this," I told Coldfield, and walked to a blank and very solid brick wall, the false one that covered my hidden sanctuary. While he stared, I vanished, and went right through it. When I came back I had my desk lamp in hand, and he had a look of flat-faced shock all but tattooed on his mug. I could have been nice and tried to prepare him, but I wanted a little payback for all that laughing.

"You—" He pointed at me. He gaped at Escott, still pointing at me. "He—"

"I know," said Escott. "I did warn you."

"He—"

"Yes, it always unnerves me a bit when I'm not expecting it. Enough showing off, Jack, let's get on with things."

I started to walk past Coldfield, but he stopped me. "Do that again."

Shrugging, I partially vanished.

He put his hand right through me. "Jesus, hallelujah."

"Only one free show a night," I said, re-forming after his hand was out of my midsection. "After that I sell tickets."

"Shit." He flexed his hand, working to warm it up.

Maxwell's head came up in a listening pose as we closed on him. He must have sensed some kind of change in the air and that it might not be especially good news for him. "What is it? What are you planning to do?"

"Nothing fatal, Maxie," I answered. I found a couple of cans of paint left over from Escott's efforts at fixing up the house and stacked them, placing the lamp on top.

He went very still. "Who are you?" A tremor infected his usually smooth voice. If he'd recognized mine, then he had a right to be worried, since I should have been dead.

"Guess."

There was a wall outlet close by and the cord just reached it. I clicked the lamp on and angled its flexible neck so the light would strike Maxwell right in the eyes. A high sign to Escott and he and Coldfield shut off all the other lights; the only one left was the glowing cone focused on our seated and trussed-up friend. He wouldn't be able to see past it.

I took the black sack off his head and let him wince, blink, and get used to things. He looked even more deceptively harmless without his glasses, which were tucked in his breast pocket. I removed them and put them on him.

His eyes went wide with recognition combined with fear.

Good. For talks like this, fear is a very good thing. It makes a person vulnerable.

Without distractions like being stabbed with fancy fountain pens or people like Doc watching over my shoulder, I got all the information I wanted and more from Maxwell, and this time I got the truth.

The plastic-surgery joint was real, but he'd lied about its

location being behind the roadhouse. He and his bushwhacking friends had been paying a visit to quite another kind of house located a few miles farther up that lane when they'd returned, spotted the Caddie parked in the wrong place, and decided to check it out.

As for the surgery, at least as of last night, Opal had been there and was being looked after, but the place was actually in the city, and not all that far from a real hospital. I wrote down the address. With Escott sometimes making suggestions, I also made notes about all the places where Sullivan might be found, how many men were with him, and what his likely actions would be at the news of Maxwell's kidnapping and Doc's escape with my help.

It didn't look good for Angela. Maxwell's guess was that Sullivan would blame her and try for another hit. The hitch in the plan would be not knowing where she could be found. The solution: bribery. A thousand bucks to anyone who pointed out her hiding place, a grand in a town with hard times where most people would do it for the price of a hot meal.

"Not the best news in the world for Miss Paco," said Escott, shaking his head. It was safe for him to talk. I was finished with Maxwell, having told him to completely forget everything that had happened since the first time I knocked him out behind the roadhouse. He was thoroughly asleep now and would stay that way until someone said his name three times and clapped their hands. I'd seen my share of stage hypnotists.

I rubbed my temples. An easy session, but still headache-making from the effort. "Yeah, but Angela's probably good at pulling holes in after her, since you haven't heard of anything all day."

"Doesn't mean much if Sullivan got to her and was quiet about it," said Coldfield.

"Believe me, if he did try for a hit on her it wouldn't be quiet. She'd make sure of that."

"What'll you do?"

"First I get Opal away from him. Maybe she might have an idea on where I can find Angela. If she's able to talk." *If she's still alive.*

"And if not?"

"Then I go take Sullivan out of the fight. Him I know where to find."

"Doing like you just did here with this guy?" Coldfield gave Maxwell a sideways look, perhaps worried he'd wake up. Fat chance of that.

"Pretty much. Then I'll try the dance studio for Angela, and if necessary that crappy hotel—don't worry, no one's gonna remember me being there. Someone at one of those places will know where she is."

"Along with all that money in the car?"

"I hope so." I was assuming the worst, that once Doc was back with friends, sooner or later somebody would get curious and take a peek in the laundry bags and declare it was Christmas all over again. Come hell or high water, I wanted the dough back. Sure, I'd walked away with a nice bundle, but that was nothing compared to the balance.

But first things first: I had to take care of Opal.

"The place looks too damn respectable," said Coldfield, scowling over the wheel of his Nash.

"Which is probably why its shadier activities pass unnoticed by the police," said Escott.

I didn't feel like adding anything and just looked out the passenger window as our big car slowly cruised by. The three of us were shoulder to shoulder in the front seat again, but with Escott in the middle for a change. I wanted them to stay out of this, but they ganged up on me and insisted on coming.

Besides, Escott wanted to make a surprise delivery to his
charming friend Adkins a little later, which was why Maxwell
was tied up nice and cozy in the trunk. Good thing he was
oblivious or he'd have had plenty of justifiable complaints
about the travel accommodations.

The address he'd given us was a surprise, being a neatly
kept red-brick house in one of the better neighborhoods of
the city. It was larger and much more expensive than Escott's
area, but very similar in looks, quite genteel, and, as Coldfield
had accurately observed, respectable. A tasteful sign featuring
a caduceus on the wrought-iron gate told people that it was
the Balsamo Clinic and gave the hours it was open. There
was no clue as to exactly what sort of treatment it offered,
only that it was supervised by Dr. Joseph Balsamo, his name
followed by a string of letters to show how well educated he
was and to hint at how much his services might cost his clients. According to Maxwell, he was the one Sullivan had
called in at a moment's notice for Opal's emergency.

"We're too late for an office visit," I said.

"But lights are showing on all the floors," said Escott.
"There may be a houseful of patients."

"That's what I'm afraid of, people getting caught in the
cross fire."

"You expect to do some shooting?"

"All the time with this crowd, but I won't let things go
that far. No one's going to get hurt if I can help it." Well,
not unless they really deserved it.

I asked Coldfield to take us around the block again. The
house was on a corner lot, with a short driveway on the side
leading to a separate garage that was closed down. You
couldn't tell if the doctor was in or not.

When Coldfield began his third circling of the block, I
asked him to pull into an open spot by a fire hydrant. It com-
manded a view of the front gate. We gave the place a good

long study, with special attention to doors and windows, and Escott recommended I try one of the latter to make my entry. It was in the back, up on the third floor, and dark.

I shook my head.

His left eyebrow shot up. "You can't just go in the front door."

"Why the hell not? I'm tired of sneaking around, of not being able to see where I'm going."

"She's sure to be guarded."

"They won't know what hit 'em." I opened the passenger door. "Don't know how long this will take, but be ready to roll."

"Keep your head down, kid," Coldfield advised.

I grunted, making a mental note to tell him what my real age was sometime, then shut the door gently. There wasn't much wind tonight and the sound would carry.

Through the gate, up the walk to the porch to ring the bell and wait. The foyer light was on, but I couldn't see any movement through the sheer white curtains covering the diamond-shaped window set in the door. All I heard were my shoes scraping on the welcome mat. Rang the bell again, then knocked. Nothing, and I was starting to get chilled in my short jacket. Maybe some of that damned poison still lingered in me—that or I was starting to get nervous. I'd have worn my long coat, but it needed to go to the cleaners.

Another ring and knock, along with a sigh of exasperation. They had their chance to answer a dozen times over by now. I just might have to do something.

What the hell, why not? I thought, and faded out, passing through the cracks around the door and going solid inside.

I didn't surprise anyone on watch. The foyer was small, with arched openings leading to the hall stairs and a waiting room. Everything was as nice in as it was out, tasteful, even elegant, with a fancy spindly-legged reception desk and velvet curtains on the waiting-room windows. Balsamo made a mint at his work and wasn't shy about showing it.

Except no one else seemed to be here to enjoy the decor. I went very still and listened hard and didn't hear so much as a mouse with asthma.

Another chill hit me that had nothing to do with the weather. This sort of silence wasn't right. It was well and truly a dead silence, too similar to the kind I endured the other night while in that coffinlike box over the shop.

My fear steadily growing, I searched the place, tearing into every room, every closet, from basement to attic. Nothing and no one. The lights were on for a reason, the best one being to keep someone like me busy watching here instead of looking elsewhere for Opal. Sullivan knew Maxwell might talk and had had all day to find a new parking place for his prize bookkeeper. I hoped to God that was what he'd done, then went all over the house again, this time looking for some clue as to where they could have gone.

To judge by the leftovers in the icebox and a calendar with a slash through the date, people had been in this day, and then they'd all done a bunk. I'd found living quarters, perhaps belonging to Balsamo, examination rooms with the usual medical supplies and equipment, an office, and several hospital-style rooms where patients probably rested after their operations. I'd found the operating room, too, and it was a pip; this joint didn't seem to lack for anything except for a staff and patients—one in particular.

I got a fresh thought and went in search of the trash cans. Those were just outside the kitchen door. The second tin lid I lifted revealed that Opal had, indeed, been here.

Right on top was a pile of bloodstained white cloths. Table linens from the roadhouse.

My heart and hopes plummeted with sickening speed.

The idea I'd been pushing to the back of my mind since

I'd walked in shoved its way forward. It couldn't be ignored anymore. Maybe she'd not made it; maybe she'd died, and because of it they'd cleared out.

And if that had happened, then someone was going to *pay*.

10

"YOU found her discarded bandaging," said Escott. "That's not proof of her death. It's not proof of anything except that they've likely been changed for a proper dressing."

But he hadn't seen them, seen how much blood was on them. I stared out the front window of the Nash as the streets slipped past in one streaming gray blur.

Coldfield snorted. "Charles, if he wants to feel guilty about her being dead, go ahead and let him."

"We don't know that she's dead."

"Yeah, but he did spend half the night hauling those bags of money to his car instead of looking for her."

"He was filling in the time until the house was quiet so he could get Doc out."

"And if the money hadn't been there, maybe he could have done something *else* during that time that might have helped her."

"Now, that's quite unfair to—"

"Charles." I held up a hand. "Stop defending me. Shoe's right. Let's just leave it at that."

He opened his mouth like he wanted to say more, but the look I shot him shut him up tight. It didn't work on Coldfield, who was watching the road.

"Yeah, she's probably stone cold by now. Of course, if

you'd really worked at it last night and found her, everything would be different. She'd still be dead, but maybe you wouldn't be feeling so sorry for yourself for getting distracted.''

The flash of rage that shot through me was a physical thing. It seemed to roar up and envelop me like red flames. Escott reacted as if he saw and felt it, too, and flinched, his face going white.

"Jack . . ." he whispered. "No."

Coldfield ignored us. "On the other hand, if she's alive, then you're feeling sorry for yourself for no reason at all, unless it's something you *enjoy* doing. I know people like that, and I never do have much use for 'em."

I was trembling from it, from the sudden rush of adrenaline, trembling from the effort to keep myself from moving. I didn't dare, for then I might kill him.

"On the other hand, what happened is what happened and can't be changed or made better. I'd say you did the best you could at the time and you should let it go at that until we find out one way or another about the girl."

Escott held his breath for the longest time, and even over the sound of the car I could hear his heart thumping fit to burst. A few moments went by, and when it looked like I wasn't going to go berserk after all, the harsh pounding eased, and he let his pent-up air sigh out very slow and easy.

I imitated him, the slow breathing, had to shut my eyes and consciously work at it, but the action helped get me calmed down and nearly reasonable again. I wasn't ready to talk and be polite yet, but was past the point of being dangerous to anyone within shouting distance of me, myself included.

About five minutes later I looked at Coldfield. "You really are a son of a bitch."

He glanced over, chuckled once, and kept driving.

We were going straight to the roadhouse and only barely staying inside the speed limit. He skimmed under stop signals just as they changed and ran some when he saw the cross streets were clear. If there were any cops around, they weren't interested in us.

When I'd come stalking out of the clinic without Opal, he'd started the car and pulled forward, ready to brake when I stopped, only I'd not stopped, but kept coming, to vanish and reappear in the seat next to Escott so as not to waste time. Coldfield had nearly swerved off the road at this. I barely noticed, being too busy telling them where we needed to go next. Then I told them what I'd found—or rather not found—in the house on the corner and the dark conclusion I'd drawn from it.

As the miles passed under us my anger settled back into its box. There was no point being mad at Coldfield since he was only giving me the truth; I just wasn't so good at wanting to hear it. Guilt and self-pity were old, unwelcome acquaintances of mine, slithering in to smother me whenever I was dumb enough to let them get away with it. You'd think I'd know better by now. Coldfield certainly did and could recognize when a man needed a kick in the butt. So did Escott, though his way was usually a lot more diplomatic.

The trip to the roadhouse was a long shot. Sullivan probably wouldn't be there, but I was gambling someone would be left behind who could tell me where he'd gone or how to contact him. If gone, then he'd be in some place Maxwell didn't know about, but that the local muscle would. That's where I would put the pressure until something broke.

I looked up from studying the floor in time to call out the turn we needed and asked Coldfield to cut the lights and stop just before we came in sight of the house. We were all straining for a look ahead and made it out at the same time, a dense cloud of dark smoke rising high into the black sky.

"Holy hell," said Coldfield, and hit the gas.

The sight didn't get any better the closer we got; the whole joint was on fire and so far gone it'd be useless to call for help. The building was already collapsing in on itself. No more dance music, no more summer nights on the big veranda.

Coldfield made a wide, cautious circle of the place, giving us an eyeful of the destruction, and pulled up behind it. The parking lot was clear of cars, but we did see evidence that someone had been there and gone . . . leaving two of them behind. I boosted out of the Nash before it stopped and hurried toward the slack forms lying on the gravel. The fire created its own hot wind, and it plucked at my clothes.

Even at a distance you can tell the difference between alive and dead. The dead seem smaller, even when they aren't. The first man I came to had been shot in the back of the head and must have dropped right where he stood without trying to run or resist. Maybe he hadn't known what hit him. Some of his skull was gone, and I went sick at the smell of his blood mixed with the wood smoke from the building. A few feet from his body were three spent brass casings catching the intermittent light from the fire at my back—.45s. The killer must have stood about *there* with a semiauto in hand and . . .

I walked around to see the dead man's face, though I'd recognized his coat. He was in profile, his eyes were still open, and hadn't clouded over yet.

Baker.

The second man had tried running; he was sprawled flat, arms and legs thrown wide. There was a hole in his back, which may have stopped him, and another in his head, which had certainly killed him.

Calloway. Eyes also open. Mouth sagging, a thick line of spittle and blood flowing from one corner.

Still flowing. He was alive.

I bawled at Escott and Coldfield to hurry over.

Coldfield turned the car heater up as high as it would go; I
took the coat from Baker's body and wrapped it close over
Calloway, a futile attempt to keep him warm, then we put
him in the backseat and drove like mad to find a hospital.
None of us thought he had a snowball's chance of surviving,
but it was what you're supposed to do, so we were doing it.

"It had to be Angela," I said. In my own ears my voice
was a tired monotone. "When Doc got back he could give
her whatever information she'd need on the layout of the
place. She'd want to hit it to get back at Sullivan. She'd kill
these guys on principle simply because they jumped on the
wrong wagon when Kyler and then Sullivan came to town."

"That sounds right," said Escott.

"It is right. Blowing off the back of a guy's skull is her
specialty. I've seen her do it and not even blink."

"Sullivan could also do it just as easily."

"Why should he shoot his own men, burn down his own
place?"

He shrugged. "It seemed worth mentioning as an alterna-
tive. You did express suspicion that he was himself behind
the hit at the hotel, for reasons yet unknown. I also have
doubts on why she would attempt an attack on Sullivan knowing he has Opal as a hostage."

"She knows he doesn't dare hurt Opal since he needs her,
too."

"I'm just surprised she'd chance coming here."

"She's crazy like her old man."

"But not foolish, it's more likely to assume he wouldn't
be here. Knowing that you'd freed Doc, he might expect trouble to seek him out and not wish to linger. As with the clinic,
he'd make certain to be very much elsewhere."

"Okay, if that's true, then why should his pet cops loiter here being targets?"

Another shrug. "As decoys? Distractions? But we've not enough information to do more than speculate. We might be completely wrong. Sullivan and his companions could all be back there in *that*." He jerked a thumb in the direction of the roadhouse, now well behind us.

I hated the idea, for it meant that Opal could be there as well.

"But we need solid information. I would suggest making further inquiries with our reluctant guest in the trunk is in order."

"Yeah, but not just yet."

Coldfield grunted. "Gunshot wounds, Charles. The doctors are gonna bring in the police. Then when they see this is another cop . . ."

"Yes, you don't want to be hanging about when they start asking awkward questions."

"It's my life's ambition."

"Right, well, you'll just have to leave me at the hospital to deal with this bother and you two carry on. Jack also cannot afford to have too much official attention focused on him."

"How you gonna explain how you got him there? Or even why you happened to be at the roadhouse in the first place? You can lose your license over this. I say you just dump him and we drive like hell away from there."

"I'll stay and help," I said, before Escott could answer. "I can keep the cops from getting too curious."

Escott shook his head. "Thank you. While both your suggestions are worthy of consideration, I've already decided on my own solution to the dilemma."

"Which is?"

"I call Adkins. His name, authority, and hero status should

be able to smooth over any rough spots with the police. Besides, we can use the opportunity to present our other passenger to him.''

"He didn't strike me as the type to do anyone favors," I said.

"Then you should be available to persuade him to make an effort.''

The idea of wiping Adkins's face clean of all expression appealed to me enormously. ''Sure, count me in.''

I checked on Calloway. He was still breathing, barely, which was a miracle. How he could even be alive with a bullet in the head was past my knowing, though I'd heard of such flukes happening.

If Angela had done it—and I was sure she had—it was going to raise one hell of a stink with the New York bosses. They'd be out two valuable assets with Baker and Calloway gone, along with all the future revenue from the roadhouse, which looked to mostly be a legitimate business. They liked having those kinds of places, it was a great way to clean up their money from other, more dubious, sources.

But Angela wouldn't care about such details. She'd want to get back at Sullivan, and this was fast, direct, and brutal— her way of making a strong point. Just too bad for the dead men. I said as much aloud.

It wasn't the kind of thing to concern Escott. "Doubtless it will work against her in the sense that two undesirable elements in the police force have been removed. One may hope it will improve the overall standard.''

"Two more heads lopped off the Hydra?''

"Exactly.''

His cold attitude was understandable. He'd not spent any time with the men; they weren't much more than abstractions to him. Not that I'd liked them either, they'd both been bastards, but maybe they hadn't always been so. I'd seen enough of life to be cured of most forms of idealism, but not to the point of losing all hope for a person, any person—at least when I was in control enough to think about it—even Calloway, who had wanted to kill me. With that in mind I'd tried to open a door for them, to give them a way clear of the darkness. It looked like they hadn't ducked through in time. Someone had taken even that slim chance for redemption away from them.

As for Escott, I could see that Bobbi was right. One of these nights I just might try taking Coldfield's suggestion about him: get him stinking drunk and maybe then find out what dark thing had eaten away at his soul. Of course, I could just hypnotize it out of him . . . but that wouldn't be right. Better to do it the old-fashioned way.

Sudden bright lights in a bleak neighborhood. Coldfield pulled up to the hospital's emergency entry, and I hauled myself clear to go for help.

Coldfield opened the trunk and kept a lookout while I pulled Maxwell free and carried him fireman-style around to the front seat. The back might have been safer, but I didn't want to sit there. With the little overhead light on so I could work, I said Maxwell's name three times and clapped. He came out of it fast enough, and I put him under just as fast before he could do much more than widen his eyes in shock.

"Okay, Max, we've been looking for Sullivan, and he's not at the clinic or the roadhouse. Where else would he go?"

He struggled with that one for a while, then finally gave up. I knew better, or thought I did, and kept at him while Coldfield silently looked on.

Nothing. I started asking about the muscle from the roadhouse, trying to get at least one useful name, one place to search. I got a few of each, writing them down, but had a lot of doubts on whether any would prove useful. His best tip

pointed back toward New York, with the name of one of the
bosses there who Sullivan might call to ask for help if he
needed it. Just the name, though, Maxwell didn't have the
number in his head; Sullivan was always the one to deal with
the big boys. Maybe Escott could find a way to turn one up,
but not anytime soon, and I wasn't too excited at the prospect
of getting myself noticed by that crew, either. It seemed best
to keep things local.

"Doesn't sound like much," said Coldfield, looking at my
list.

"I'll have to make the rounds of the town, try to hook up
with anyone who could pass the message to Sullivan that I
want to talk to him."

"That'll take time."

"It's the only game left." Well, not quite, but I didn't want
him aware of the real ace I was holding back.

"You be careful. You thumbed your nose in a big way at
Sullivan, he's gonna figure you helped Angela with the fire
and killings and be on the defensive. That generally makes a
man a lot meaner."

"I'm not expecting him to be any too reasonable, so don't
worry, I'll watch my back."

"Good, 'cause scraping you off the sidewalk is a lousy
way to spend an evening."

He sounded like he wasn't intending to come along on the
hunt, which suited me. I'd already decided he and Escott were
going to stay out of the line of fire if I had to hog-tie them.
One down, one to go.

Not that I was actually going to make the rounds looking
up the names I'd gotten. They were useful, but mostly as
decoys to keep Coldfield and Escott busy should they decide
to trail after me. I didn't want them to know where I was
really going.

A few more questions for Maxwell, just so it looked like

I was working hard. When my head started hurting, I backed off, telling him to take another nap.

"Now, *that* is a handy talent to have," said Coldfield, all admiration.

"Handy like a dull knife," I muttered, rubbing my temples.

"How is it you can do that?"

Gave a shrug. "I just can, is all. It's sort of built in with the condition, like the teeth being able to slide back when they're not needed. I figure it's for keeping things quiet when I'm feeding." This was assuming Escott had mentioned to him how I usually take straight from the vein.

"Things—as in people? But Charles said—"

"Things as in animals. Charles told you right."

"What? Like rats, or maybe cats and dogs?"

I shot him an appalled look. "Not on your life. I *like* dogs!"

"Hey, no offense."

Waved a dismissal. "Forget it. The condition's gotten some bad press because of that movie."

"So it's cattle for you?"

"Cattle, sometimes horses. It needs to be something large to stand the blood loss without being harmed. I talk to 'em and get 'em calmed down using whatever this is. It acts on people like hypnosis."

He shook his head. "Damnedest thing I ever seen."

I stretched a bit in place, getting the kinks out of my neck and shoulders. "I guess I'd better find out how Calloway's doing and take this one in for Charles to toss to his federal friend."

"Keep him out of trouble, okay?"

"Charles? No problem."

It wasn't as bad as we'd anticipated, the part about having to deal with the police, anyway. No one had fallen over themselves to question me or Escott once we'd gotten Calloway checked in, so Escott took the opportunity to call Merrill Adkins and explain the situation. Adkins promised to come right over. Coldfield chose to wait in his car through it all, parking well away from the hubbub near the hospital. I kept him company for part of the time, me and Maxwell, though he'd not been aware of any of it.

A little break to give my head a rest, then I had one last session with him, this time issuing simple orders instead of making questions. When Adkins took him into custody, he would find him to be a remarkably helpful and talkative prisoner. Sure, my suggestions would eventually wear off, but by then it would be too late. Maxwell would have turned stoolie and have to keep at it to stay alive.

Leaving Coldfield behind—he was content to slouch low in the front seat and listen to the radio—Maxwell and I marched up to the front entrance of the hospital, and if his face was a bit blank and he seemed disinterested in his surroundings, no one bothered to comment.

I led the way to the emergency area, where I'd last seen Escott in a waiting room. He was still there and so was Adkins, who stood up as soon as he caught sight of me in the doorway.

"Fleming—I want to talk to you."

That made a change from the last time. "Sure, just a minute."

That got me a stern look, but I was way past the point of being intimidated by assholes. "How's Calloway?" I asked Escott.

"No news yet. They're still working on him."

"What about the cops, they come yet?"

"An officer did wish to talk to me, but Mr. Adkins here was most discouraging to him."

I'll bet he was. "Charles, Max here was wondering if there was any coffee in this joint."

"I'm sure I can find some. How is he feeling?"

"Oh, very quiet, a little sleepy, but otherwise just fine."

Escott offered a ghost of a smile, his eyes glinting with suppressed humor. He knew what I'd done to achieve that. "I'm glad to hear it."

Maxwell now received a close once-over from Adkins. His thin face was made for poker, but I got the impression he was curious. He'd find out soon enough.

The waiting room was small and four other people were there, a young couple huddled against each other in their chairs in one corner and two men in work clothes, one seated, the other pacing and looking out into the hall every few minutes, perhaps hoping to catch sight of a doctor with news. I noted them all and didn't try to meet their eyes. They all looked miserable, all very worried over their own troubles. I would have liked another place for Adkins to interview me, but this was as good as any.

Adkins wore the same clothes as the other night, short jacket, striped scarf hanging from his neck. The work gloves were off, but he kept the newsboy cap on indoors. Either his head was cold or he was starting to go bald and was shy about letting people know about it. His jacket was open, and when he sat down I caught a glimpse of a leather shoulder harness and the butt of the pistol he packed under his left arm.

"So how is it you and Escott came to find that cop?" he asked without preamble.

But Escott and I had already worked that story out. "It's connected to our earlier business with you."

One of the men paused in his latest trip to the door, obviously listening in on us. That's when I recognized him; he belonged with Adkins, as did the other. Great, I was surrounded.

"With those three you turned over? How?"

"I don't know how. Charles and I are trying to figure it.

He wanted to find out why they were trying to ace him, so we did a little digging. We got a tip in a bar about the road-house, that the guys were connected with the management there, so we drove out for a look-see tonight. The place was cooking when we arrived and we found the cop we brought in and his friend, who was dead. They were both in the parking area behind the building with no other cars around. I saw some shell casings but left 'em behind. You probably won't get any footprints or tire marks, it's all gravel.''

"Very neat," he said, watching me. He had pale eyes under those heavy lids, like ice under snow clouds. "Tell me about the cop. You know him."

"I got his name from his wallet for the nurse. Found his badge at the same time. Hard luck for him."

"They said he should be dead."

"Maybe he'll fool all of them. I've seen stranger things."

"Tell me about the hotel shooting last night."

"What about it?"

"You were there."

"I was?"

"Witnesses said there was a tall man at the scene with a short woman who'd been hit."

"This burg's full of tall men."

"They went off in a Cadillac with four men—three cops in uniform and a man in regular clothes. Why were you with them?"

"I wasn't."

"You're lying to me, Fleming. I don't like liars."

Big deal, I thought. "Escott and I were out checking a lot of places last night and didn't get back until—jeez, it was close to dawn. Don't know about him, but I slept the day through. I wouldn't even know about the shooting if he hadn't mentioned it. He's a nut when it comes to keeping tabs on city crimes."

He looked at me a very long time with those icy eyes, probably trying to unnerve me, but I'd faced worse and survived and looked right back. "You're lying," he finally said. It was a careful statement, spoken in such a way as to make an honest man want to take a pop at him. "You hear me, Fleming? You are a stinking liar."

He kept his voice low, but the feeling he packed into it was enough to carry to the others in the room. They were all noticing us, now, even the sad couple. It's what he wanted, I supposed. Maybe he was hoping I'd sock him in front of witnesses.

I matched him stare for stare again. Not long back someone like him might have intimidated me, now it was like throwing a bucket of water onto a rock. All it did was stream off, not really affecting the rock at all. "Everyone's entitled to an opinion," I said evenly. "I don't think I can help you anymore on this."

"We'll talk later." He made it sound like a threat.

"Great, if we're done for now—" I made to rise. He didn't object, so I stood up. His men still eyed me, all tense; from their combined looks they wanted to pulp me. They'd have to get in line behind their boss. "Gonna keep watch here on Calloway?"

"Maybe."

"What about the other men you took away? They helping you any in the gang-busting business?"

His full down-your-nose aloofness reasserted itself just then. "They're nothing you need to worry about."

I debated kicking his butt then making him forget, but decided it wasn't worth the trouble. "Let's go find Escott. We've got another one for you."

"What do you mean?"

"The guy with the specks I came in with is the secretary

to the man who replaced Vaughn Kyler. He's in a confessing mood. You interested?''

"How'd you get him?''

Better not to answer that one directly. "He's a volunteer. He's had it with the mob and wants to help you nail them, so be polite.''

That got me a sharp glare, but I was already turning away into the hall, forcing him to follow.

"Think you're smart?'' he asked, coming up behind me.

"I know I am. I just hope you're smart enough to take advantage of a prime gift horse when it comes your way. Maxwell knows all the dirt. Treat him right and you'll be the big name in all the headlines for the next year.''

"Headlines?''

I thought he'd like that idea. "You'll be getting marriage proposals, honorary degrees, invitations to all the best parties.''

"I don't care about that crap.''

"Suit yourself, but it'd be a shame to pass up now that it's legal to drink the booze again.''

"I don't drink.''

Again with the contemptuous challenge in the tone. I forgot about trying small talk with this one. On the same side or not, he didn't like me, and I had better things to do than try to change his mood. Like getting away from him as fast as possible.

Escott and Maxwell were in a badly lighted eating area that stank of old coffee and carbolic. It was even money which liquid was in their coffee mugs. Escott bounced a questioning eyebrow at me and I winked so he'd know everything was fine.

"Mr. Adkins,'' I said, pausing before their table. "This is Maxwell. I think you two will have a lot to talk about over the next few days.''

Maxwell stood up and politely put out his hand. Adkins didn't respond in kind. No big surprise there.

Escott also stood, excused himself, and without further word we hiked out of there, heading back to the waiting room. A young doctor with an old face trudged past us toward the dining area. I caught a whiff of bloodsmell coming from the surgical gown he still wore, though there were no stains to see. The whole place reeked of bloodsmell, carbolic, and things less tangible, but more potent: fear, sorrow, and death. I thought of Opal again. Worried.

"I take it things went well?" Escott asked.

"He'll always hate my guts, but we're square. How do you stand him?"

"It's not hard. Once you accept the fact he thinks we're little more than meddling amateurs, he's easy enough to work with—not that I welcome it. It's part of the price."

"For fighting your Hydra?"

"It's everyone's enemy, old man. We may not enjoy the company of our allies, but it's nice to know they're in the battle. Where's Shoe?"

"Out waiting in the Nash. I want to stop home to pick up my car, then I'm going to go hunting again. I got some names from Maxwell to look up and need to get started before the barflies are too drunk to help."

A cop, the first one I'd seen since coming in, followed in the doctor's wake and passed us, looking grim.

"We'll be glad to join you in the hunt," Escott said after the cop was out of earshot.

"Uh-uh. This is something I can do more quickly on my own, and you know it."

"What about checking the Paco house again?"

"That's next on my list if I don't turn up anything on Sullivan. First I'll start hitting the places where I know she's got business interests, like that brothel, the Satchel."

"You might need some help there," he said.

"I'll be talking to the madam and bouncers, not the girls."

"Just thought I'd make the offer," he said, all innocence.

Adkins's two men now passed by, all of us exchanging looks but not saying anything.

"This don't look so good," I said.

"Indeed." Escott kept walking. "Have you considered more area might be covered if Shoe and I go off in one direction and you take another? We do know the city rather well."

He was going to try talking me into it, and I was tempted to listen. He had ways of getting people to cooperate that were nearly as effective as my hypnosis, and here he was just getting started on me. "Thanks, but this is something I gotta take care of myself. I've had *some* experience at this kind of work."

"Escott! Fleming!" Adkins hurried up behind us, the doctor, cop, men, and Maxwell in tow. We waited for them. They delivered the news that Calloway had just died. I didn't have anything to say about it and just frowned like the others. For me, Calloway had been dead since I found him, the declaration only a formality, so I'd already had all the thoughts I wanted to about the waste of human life, no matter whose life it was.

"My condolences," Escott said to the cop, who made no reply, just stared at us.

Adkins's face was all frozen over, his voice just as cold. "It's a double-murder investigation now, maybe triple if it's connected to the other killing at the hotel. I want you two to come with us."

"To assist in your inquiries? Sadly we've already given you all the information we have."

"We need full, written statements."

I looked him square in the eye, knowing redemption when

I saw it. "Not from me, you don't. I gotta be someplace else."

Not a blink. Hard to tell if I got to him. Then: "All right. You can go."

"Myself as well," Escott put in.

But Adkins rounded on him. "No, you're staying here."

"Jack . . ." Escott's sharp gaze was on me. My conscience also gave me a good solid jab, but I endured the pain.

"Not this time, buddy."

I turned and kept walking and, with the idea of taking the sting out of it, didn't look back so he'd miss my grin.

No cops stopped me on my way to the front, though I saw several in the halls. Maybe Calloway and Baker would also be treated as heroes by their colleagues. It'd be good for the department to take that path with the public. No need to wonder what the papers would make of four cops shot in two days, three of them dead. There'd be plenty of editorials, every one with their own solution to the task of how to make our streets safe. Good luck to them; people had been trying to figure that one since streets were first invented. Once upon a time there'd been roving gangs of hoodlums running crazy in old Byzantium, terrorizing folks and generally having a good time committing murder and mayhem. When the emperor couldn't stop them, he started laying bets on which group would win their next fight with rivals elsewhere in the city. Nothing changes much.

The urge to write the whole present-day business up as a story and send it to the *Tribune* was very strong. I wanted someone to know the truth of what was really going on, of the gangs, the brewing war, of the corruption high and low. The urge would pass soon enough, though. It always did. I couldn't let myself get officially noticed in any way, shape, or form if I could help it. There was too much dirt on me to take that risk, and I had to protect those around me, Bobbi, Coldfield, Escott.

Another twinge about leaving him behind. I'd apologize to him later, take him to Hallman's an extra time or two. Bobbi could put on one of her drop-dead dresses and flirt with him over supper. He never did anything about it, pretending to be immune to her because she was my girlfriend, but you could tell he loved the attention.

I hoped she was doing all right. I wanted to toss all this in the nearest trash can and go see her, to get back to a normal life again.

Only one way to do that.

Of all the people in this town who would know how to find anyone, both Sullivan and Angela, Gordy was my best bet. He had more connections than the phone company and was the one name Maxwell had not mentioned. I'd been careful in my questions, phrasing them in such a way so that the subject of Gordy just didn't come up. It was part of the reason I got that touch of headache; I'd had to walk a tightrope on tiptoes. I didn't want Coldfield knowing and then passing the information on to Escott. He was busy now, but if he found a way clear of Adkins, I didn't need him to be involved.

It was complicated enough.

The suspicion I had that Gordy was the one behind the hotel hit and all the rest of it was pretty solid. Now Angela had plenty of motive for that kind of work and was still my first suspect, but Gordy could have done it just as easily. This was exactly the kind of thing to stir up the pond, to get Angela and Sullivan to kill each other off, then he could move into whatever openings presented themselves, and all with the beaming approval of the New York bosses no less.

I hated it; he was a friend to me, to Bobbi, had done us some outstanding favors, but above everything else Gordy was a businessman and more than capable of giving the orders. I'd have to see him alone and find out one way or another where he really stood in this mess, then somehow figure what to do about it if he was behind it all.

But that could wait just a little while longer. For now, the cold outside air was a relief after the hospital stink. I gulped it down gratefully, walking fast toward the Nash at the far end of some parking spaces. The idea was for privacy while I questioned Maxwell. It was between street lamps and plenty dark in that patch, but I clearly saw something was happening by the car and broke into a dead run.

No time to count them, and the numbers didn't matter, I'd have charged in, anyway, against two or two hundred. I couldn't see Coldfield, but knew he was there, somewhere in the middle of a knot of men. From the sounds, a couple of them were laying into him like pile drivers with their fists.

Three guys on lookout spotted my approach and stepped forward. I saw blackjacks and brass knuckles. I noted and forgot them, going semi-transparent just before the nearest man got close enough to do damage. His blackjack arced right through my near-invisible body, the force of his follow-through throwing him off balance. Ghostlike, I passed him and his two astonished friends, leaving behind a chill trail where I brushed by them.

Half a dozen of them, all circled around Coldfield. Another two held him in place while two more took turns hitting him. Bloodsmell everywhere, mixed with raw hate and the sound of dark laughter.

I burst into the middle of the circle, going solid and taking out a man before he could get his next hit in. His partner was next. I had time to drop a third holding Coldfield, then the rest moved in to stop me. Took some punches, hard ones, but didn't really feel them, too full of rage for it. I dug an elbow into someone's gut, something banged against the side of my head, but not enough to make an impression. I was pressed all around by their bodies, by the men trying to hurt me and failing. At one point I was completely lifted from the ground by the crush, and hands grabbed me from behind. Kicked out with both legs, sending a man sprawling. Lots of noise now, lots of cursing for me over spoiling their fun.

Hadn't even got warmed up yet.

Vanished just as we started to topple. Left them behind to be crushed under their collective weight and reappeared a few feet away. Glance toward Coldfield. Only one man held him now, and that one was watching the dog pile. Coldfield was bent double and not doing much of anything but retching, trying to cough air back into his body.

A man saw me and came fast. He lasted for as long as it took me to get my fist up. Two more, then three, as they got reorganized. Even three at a time, I could take them easy.

Gun.

Didn't see it, only heard.

Sure as hell *felt* it. Instantly knew that particular fiery burn as a bullet tore through my guts. When I dropped, my knees hit the pavement so hard my teeth rattled.

Pause in the madness. They must have thought it was all over. They stood still a moment, watching, waiting for me to crash at their feet.

Transparent again. Couldn't help it. When it came to re-covering from this kind of shock, my body rarely gave me a choice. I was there one second and not there the next and the hell with anyone who saw.

It didn't take long to return. I was still choked with rage; it gave me the will to come back a lot sooner than otherwise. Five, ten seconds later, perhaps, not enough time for them to even begin to figure out what was going on. The man with the gun was still gaping when I yanked it away from him and slammed the butt on his skull. He dropped as I'd dropped, only without the disappearing act.

Vanished again. Went solid a few feet to the left. Cracked another skull. And again, this time reappearing on the right.

Then it was over. I didn't catch on, was all set to bust more jaws, only the thugs that could still stand were now running off. Started after them, yelling.

Heard a hoarse shout behind me. Coldfield.

Last yell, triumph, defiance, rage, take your pick, then went back to him. He was on his side, trying to push the pavement away. He'd just managed to sit up as I came close. I put a hand out to help, but he snarled and batted it off. He started coughing, got some air, then spit blood. He puffed and wheezed and abruptly lurched to his feet, reeling over to lean on the car. The door was open, inside light on, throwing a pale glow across his bloodied face. Two shiners for sure, split lip, he'd need stitches for the cut over his eye, and that was only the damage I *could* see.

"Come on, let's get you out of here," I said, reaching again.

He reacted the same, this time with a curse. I knew it wasn't for me, his glare was strictly for the bodies left behind.

He doubled over, coughing, holding on to the car to keep from falling altogether. Every time he got enough breath, he swore. Take a breath, swear, take another, swear. Couldn't blame him.

A few of the men got up and shambled off. The bulk of their friends were heading for two cars parked farther down the road, looking nervously back to see if I was following. I stayed put in case another bright boy decided to try shooting again. Someone got a motor started.

Four men remained, casualties of battle, four of the ones who had been holding Coldfield, hitting him.

Before he'd quite caught his breath, he staggered to the first and kicked him once, hard enough to break ribs. I heard the crunch.

Got his balance, went to the next, and did it again, all the time calling him every name in the book.

Made a similar visit to all of them, cursing and cracking ribs.

I stayed where I was.

The first car moved past us, slowly picking up speed. One of the men leaned from the window, shouting. Couldn't make out the words, but they were full of hate. It set me off once more. He wasn't the only one who could hate. I ran toward them, all my attention centered on that one distorted face.

The car went full throttle and left me in its roaring wake. The second one was coming up. I waited as the driver hit the gas and steered right toward me, but he didn't have nearly enough speed yet. The vehicle was overloaded, sluggish. It came up; I dodged right and made a jump for the driver's-side running board. Yanked the door open. Grabbed the wheel and hauled it over. Nearly fell off when the damned thing swerved and jumped the curb, but I hung on.

The driver yelled, they all yelled. Fist on my face. Ignored it. The car rolled forward, then jerked to a stop when someone found the hand brake.

Gun. The driver.

My hand froze over his, squeezing. He couldn't pull the trigger. I dragged him from his seat. Momentum, balance lost, falling, hard impact. Rolling on frozen grass, his weight on top. More shouts from the others, but no one came to the rescue. The guy on the passenger side slid over the seat, slipped the brake, worked the gears, eyes wide, mouth open, making animal noises of fear. Ignored him. Rolled to get on top to see better. The car juttered away, sluing on the road, then straightening.

The man struggled to get his gun hand free. For the grip I had, it might as well have been buried in cement. His teeth were set, breath hissing. Made hits at me with his free hand, but no force in them; he was losing to his growing fear. I took the gun away from him. Got to my feet, pulling him up. Pinned his hands behind him. Marched him across the street to the Nash.

Coldfield, standing in the middle of the fallen, amazed look on his battered face. He'd seen what I'd done and didn't know why.

Brought my captive close, pushed him against the car into the faint light so he could see my face, my eyes. Wasn't going to hypnotize him, knew I was too angry for it.

"Where's Sullivan?" I hissed at him. I'd recognized some of the others. They'd been loitering in the carpeted hall of the roadhouse.

Shook his head. Wrong answer. Shoved the gun muzzle under his nose.

"Where?"

A long time, him looking at me. Long time. Then a head shake. He could see I wasn't going to shoot. He knew enough to be able to read my face, to know that even after all this, his death wasn't going to come from me.

I backed off.

Looked at Coldfield. Didn't have to ask.

He understood why now, and moved in, pure unholy joy lighting up his eyes.

11

BLOODSMELL in the car.

Some of it on me. On my hands.

Wanted to wash and change clothes, but it'd have to wait.

My turn to drive. Needed to, needed a simple mechanical activity to keep my hands from shaking from the unspent anger, from the aftershock of outrage. Held a heavy foot to the gas, wanting lots of distance between us and the battlefield casualties.

Coldfield sat partially curled around in the seat, knees drawn up, resting his back against the passenger door. He wasn't moving if he could help it. Since he'd had a chance to cool down, the knocks he'd taken were making themselves felt, and I'd hear him catch his breath every time we hit a bump. I tried to take it easy on the turns. I also tried to talk him into going to the hospital, but he nixed that.

"Trudence'll do better by me," he said, so I got us rolling toward her sanctuary in the Bronze Belt and didn't argue him out of it.

I drove for ten minutes before he looked up, squinting at me in the intermittent light as we passed under street lamps.

"You all right?" he asked.

"I'm fine."

"But they shot you. I saw."

"I'm indestructible, remember?"

"Saw you fall."

"Well, it hurt."

"You went away."

"I do that when it hurts too much." My voice sounded wrong. Tight. It takes time to lose a load of anger like that. I shifted my bunched shoulders and toned things down inside. "Don't worry about it. How're you doing?"

"I feel like how Charles looked the other night."

"You must feel a lot worse than that."

"I'll get better." He held an already well-stained handkerchief to the cut over his eye. His knuckles were scraped, but unlike the rest of him, their damage was in a good cause.

The thug I'd grabbed proved to be very informative, once Coldfield started in on him. It's one thing to gang up on a solitary man, and quite another for him to turn on you and you alone in a fair fight, to make you the special object of his attention. The thug hadn't liked it one bit and started talking after a very short time. Coldfield never asked why I'd not used the hypnosis; I doubt it even occurred to him once he got going.

The news of the fire, murder, and Calloway being brought to the hospital had been passed to Sullivan via one of his other pet cops on the force. Sullivan, who had indeed moved out of the roadhouse before Angela came calling, harbored no doubts that she was behind the shootings and the fire, once he heard about them. He'd dispatched two carloads of stooges to check the whole business out, some to ask questions, others to keep watch in case Angela's goons turned up to finish the job on Calloway.

His men got a description of the Nash from the people at the emergency-room entrance, and that there was a black man at the wheel. They learned about me and Escott, but couldn't get near either of us in the hospital, so they opted to find and

question the driver. They'd just located him and had started
in with the fun and games at about the same time I was leaving Escott in the hands of Merrill Adkins. Their question was
the same one I was asking: Where's Angela? Coldfield sure
as hell couldn't tell them, but even if he'd been able to, they'd
have kept at it with him. They were in a killing mood.

That's why it was important to bring one of them back for
him to work over in turn; getting news about Sullivan had
only been the second thing on my mind when I made the
grab. I'd done it for Coldfield.

Kicking unconscious men doesn't give you the same kind
of satisfaction as taking out someone who can hit you back.
By giving that man to Coldfield, I'd also returned his self-
respect to him. Neither of us said anything about it directly,
but after he was finished with the fists and questions and the
man was taking his turn at lying bloody, beaten, and gasping
on the ground, Coldfield looked up and nodded his thanks to
me. Only then was he ready to let himself be helped into the
car and driven away.

I found the right street, the right alley, and pulled in easy
does it. Lights showed in the kitchen windows, and as I set
the brake the back door opened up. The big man named Sal
came out.

I waved at him. "Miss Coldfield's brother is hurt and needs
help. Go find her, would you?"

He leaned down to peer in. He shot a look at me I couldn't
read, then nodded and went inside. I went around to help
Coldfield and we staggered toward the door like a couple of
drunks.

Trudence hurried into the kitchen and paused just as I eased
Coldfield onto a chair. Her face went all pinched like she
wanted to yell at him, but she swallowed it back and went to
work, issuing orders. People jumped to obey.

I got myself a corner out of the hubbub and settled against

the wall to look on. It gave me the chance to check myself over. The bloodstains were alarming, but nothing was leaking out now and most of it didn't belong to me, anyway. Had holes through my shirtfront and back where the bullet had gone through, but they weren't too noticeable if I buttoned the jacket. My clothes were a lot less than clean and sported some tears, but I didn't look too bad for a guy who had done what I'd done.

It was bad enough for Trudence. She caught clear sight of me and came over.

"What's the damage?" she demanded.

"I'm just a little bruised up, Shoe got the brunt of it. Worry about him."

"I do. Too much. What happened?"

"A few guys with fists bigger than their brains. They won't be coming back."

Her dark eyes were hard. The look in them could make a stone wince. "You kill any of 'em?"

"Not that I know of." The last man had been breathing when we'd left, so he had a better than even chance of crawling his way to the emergency entrance if he wanted. The others I wasn't quite as sure about, but maybe someone would find them and drag them in for treatment before dawn. The street wasn't all that isolated. "You won't be getting any trouble from this, I promise."

"I appreciate your promise, but there's always trouble. Always."

"This wasn't his fault," I said. "He was just trying to help me and got stuck in the middle."

She whisked away to see to her brother.

They'd eased some of his clothes off and went to work cleaning him up. From the practiced way they went about it, I wondered how often this sort of thing happened here, of hurt people turning up at the back door and being taken in without question. Probably far too often.

I left my corner long enough to wash off at the sink, scrubbing hard at the stubborn dried blood clinging to my fists. I didn't know how much, if any, was on my face or where. The sink was big enough, I put my whole head under the faucet flow and hoped for the best. Sal threw me a towel when I'd finished. I puffed a dripping thanks at him.

Someone put broken ice in another towel and gave it to Coldfield to hold on his swelling shiners and got hot water to wash away the gore from the eye cut. Trudence did the stitching herself. She must have been mad as hell from her set-in-stone expression, but her hands were steady as she worked. He wouldn't have much of a scar.

When things slowed down he thanked her and said he'd go off to the Shoe Box to get out of her way.

She glared down, a look of disdain mixed with triumph on her face. "I don't think so, brother of mine. You have a bill to pay."

"Well, sure, how much?" He made to reach for his wallet.

"Oh, it won't be in money."

"Come on, Tru—"

"The price is you stay here for the night."

That surprised him. "But I thought you didn't—"

"I don't, but I'm not having you slip out before I get the chance to say 'I told you so' to you a few hundred times. I'm thinking I'll sing you to sleep with it."

He choked and looked at me, a hint of desperation in his eyes. "Fleming?"

I gave an openhanded shrug. "It was your idea to come here instead of the hospital. Sounds to me like you're getting off easy."

"You gotta take me away."

"And look ungrateful? Besides, this strikes me as being a family matter, and I try to stay clear of those."

"You son of a—"

"Clarence!" she snapped. "You owe me."

He started to bristle back, but it must have hurt too much, for he subsided pretty quick. "Okay. But will you at least hear my side of it?"

She gave that one some thought. "Maybe. But only if you drink all your hot milk."

He groaned.

With Sal to steady him he was just able to go upstairs on his own feet. Trudence got the cleaning up started and turned to me again. "Your turn."

"I'm fine, really. I just need to go home for a wash and change."

"You look like you've been through a meat grinder."

"It's all from your brother and the other guys. I was moving too fast for them to touch me. I just got a couple of bruises, don't even need an aspirin."

"This is on top of what you had the other night."

"I was just cold then. I'm all better now."

A long study from her. "Well, I'd like to call you a liar, Mr. Fleming, but you do seem okay."

"I am. I also want to apologize for leaving so fast then. I had some things to do that couldn't wait."

"Must have been important to drag you out of here while you were still thawing."

"Yeah, pretty important, enough so I forgot my manners. I want to thank you for what you did. Could I make a contribution? Shoe said you—"

"I don't take mob money."

"This ain't mob. I worked for and earned every penny." And I had, too, helping Escott out on past cases. Before we left the house I'd grabbed some bills out of my half of the basement safe and stuffed them in my wallet. They weren't part of the stash I'd taken from the roadhouse, so I was telling her the absolute truth. I counted all of them, a hundred and ten dollars, into her hand. It didn't seem like a lot. I could send more later.

Her eyes popped. "This is too much!"

"You gonna say that the next time a woman comes in here with a hungry kid?"

Now her eyes flashed on me hot enough to scorch, then settled. "You know how to fight dirty, don't you?"

"On some things. Don't be too hard on Shoe, okay? He really was trying to fight on the side of the angels tonight, but there were just too many of the bad guys against him."

"What was it about?"

"It had to do with me, and he got stuck in the middle. I should have been the one there, not him."

"Where's Charles?"

"He's safe." Probably pretty annoyed with me, but safe out of the way.

"It's not over for you, is it?"

"No, but it will be soon."

"More beatings?"

"I don't think so. A little talk with a man I know should clear most of this up tonight."

A skeptical look, but she let it go. "You need a ride away from here?"

"I can find a cab."

"Not in this neighborhood and not without money you won't. I'll have Sal take you in Clarence's car."

"Thanks. That's kind of you."

"Uh-uh. Kind is you bringing Clarence here, giving me a chance to talk some sense into him before he gets himself killed doing what he does."

I wished her a silent good luck for that one.

*   *   *

Sal dropped me off at the corner nearest the house, and I quickly covered the rest of the way on my own power. Time was passing and I had to change and get my Buick on the road before Sullivan took it into his head to move again. His boys would have turned up by now with their tails between their legs and no doubt a weird story about fighting a ghost man. Whether he believed it or not, he might get nervous and decide to take another hike to safer pastures. And if he had a pet cop on watch at the hospital, he'd be wondering what the hell was going on now that Maxwell was with Adkins. That would make him more than nervous.

But I knew where he was for the moment, however long that moment lasted. No need to call Gordy for help, either.

Sullivan was with him at the Nightcrawler Club.

Should have figured it earlier. Gordy said he did what New York told him, and if one of their top boys turned up on the doormat asking for a room, like it or not, he'd have to take him in. If Sullivan had any suspicion about Gordy being behind the hotel hit, he'd have plenty of time to talk to him about it.

And then there was Opal. She'd be there with them.

She was alive. Thank God. The thug knew that much. One less anvil sitting on my head. Before another hour passed I hoped to shake another one loose by straightening things with Sullivan and then getting her out of there.

Trotted up my front steps. Dark night, and no lights left on in the house, the place looked haunted-house gloomy. Escott wanted it to seem like no one was home yet. I was tempted to just vanish and sieve inside, but spotted a couple of my neighbors coming along the sidewalk with groceries in their arms. We exchanged nods and said hello, and I used my keys like anyone else.

Just as well, for about five seconds later it eased a lot of potential complications.

I was aware of them the instant I shut the door. Froze in my tracks. The lights were out, but I saw all of them, all their guns. All pointed at me.

Slowly raised my hand and flicked on the hall light. No point in pretending the place was empty now. I had a houseful what with Angela and her friends making themselves so cozy.

Oddly enough, they seemed a lot more surprised to see me than the other way around. If I'd wanted to I could have shot out of there while they were still flat-footed with their jaws dragging on the floor, but this looked to be very interesting, so I stayed.

Doc was the first to speak. "Well, good night and little fishes, if you don't have more lives than a cat."

"You told me he was dead," said Angela, sounding accusatory. She was button cute in a red-and-blue striped hat that perched sideways on her head like a bird about to fly away. She really didn't need that .45 in her hand to stop traffic.

"He *was* dead! I know dead, and he was it!" Doc tried to look at both of us at once and it made him a little wall-eyed.

"That's what you said before they rolled me in the carpet with the weights," I put in. "But I forgive you."

That got me a long funny stare from him. "There's something not *right* about you, boy."

"I know, but no matter what, my mother still loves me."

"Knock it off," said Angela. "Newton, frisk him."

Newton stepped forward. He'd been one of the men who'd helped wrap me in the rug with the intention of dumping me into Lake Michigan. He liked milk, cookies, and reading *The Shadow* magazine. As he cautiously slapped me down I wondered if he'd had a chance to get the latest issue or if they'd all been too busy running.

He picked a gun out of my jacket pocket and put it in his

own for the time being. That was okay, I'd taken it from Chick the other night when *that* group had invaded the house, so it was no big loss. I made a mental note to talk to Escott about getting better locks put in. Maybe it would slow down the next army for a few minutes before they marched through.

Newton pronounced me clean—of weaponry, that is—and Angela had him back away.

"He was dead," Doc muttered.

"Well, he doesn't look much better now," she added. "What happened, someone drag you backward through a dog kennel?"

Doc continued, sparing me from thinking up an answer for her. "That little weasel friend of Sullivan's jabbed him with poison and I watched him die. It wasn't pretty, and he was *dead.*"

Angela frowned at him.

"It was some kind of drug," I said, finally deciding to let him off the hook. "Knocked me colder than mackerel . . . but I'm *much* better now."

He sneered contempt, not wanting to buy that one, kept shaking his head. Couldn't blame him, it was a lousy story.

Before he could make an additional comment, Angela stepped in. "At least we know now why Escott didn't call the cops when he came and found them, why he'd move a dead body instead and keep quiet. We couldn't figure it, but you being alive explains all that. So where is he?"

"Someplace else. Why do you want him?" I kept the worry from my tone. It should have been too soon for my suggestion about her calling off the hit on Escott to have faded yet.

"We don't want him, it's Sullivan's secretary. He'll know where Sullivan went with Opal."

"You're too late, for Maxwell at least," I said, spreading my hands.

"What? Did you kill him?"

"No, though Sullivan will wish I had."

"What do you mean?"

"Maxie's singing up a storm with Merrill Adkins about now. Maybe you've heard of him."

That got me a truckload of shocked disbelief from them all as his name hit home; they'd been keeping up with the newsreels.

"You're lying." said Angela.

I shrugged. "Suit yourself."

"How is it you know someone like Merrill Adkins?"

"Doesn't matter, but you'll have the proof of it soon enough. It'll be in the papers for sure." Adkins would probably see to that detail himself. "The federal boys will soon start busting up all the hidden businesses in this town, not just Sullivan's, but the ones he was going to take over."

Her businesses. "Wh-what are you saying?"

"That it's all over any way you look at it, sweetheart. Armistice has been declared. Once Maxwell is finished giving his life story to Adkins and his friends, Sullivan won't have anything in this town to run, and neither will you. What's left won't be worth having. So you won't need the books anymore." *Or a bookkeeper.*

I half expected her to put the .45 in my face and pull the trigger, but she just stood and stared, lips parted, eyes stricken. She'd get no apologies from me, though. After the load of grief she and her pop had dumped on yours truly, I figured she was coming out damned well on the deal, especially if she still had that carful of money. Of course, I planned to talk her into sharing some of it with me.

"Where's Opal?" she demanded after a moment; her voice sounded thin, shaken.

"Still with Sullivan the last I heard. She's alive, no thanks to the hit on the hotel—"

"I didn't do that!"

" 'S okay, I believe you, lady." Thousands wouldn't, but mine was a front-row seat and she was getting me convinced.

The phone rang in the kitchen. No one moved, they all seemed to hold their breath. I followed their lead and kept shut, figuring they wouldn't let me answer anyway. It rang a dozen times before stopping, then they relaxed.

"Who'd be calling you?" asked Newton.

"Could be anyone." Escott, Coldfield, Bobbi, even Gordy, or maybe someone else entirely.

"They must want to talk real bad. It's been doing that every ten minutes since we got here."

Which meant there was some problem. Escott and Coldfield knew where I might be found. If there was an emergency with Bobbi, Gordy would send people out to look for me, starting with this place.

"Let me get it next time and I'll let you know."

That made him laugh. I should have known better.

"Angela! You should have had someone catch the phone." Frank Paco's voice. From the front parlor.

"Another time, Daddy," she called in reply. "It wasn't for us."

"You don't know till you answer."

He sounded pretty lucid. My reaction must have been plain on my face. Angela gave me a smug look.

"Those head doctors had it wrong keeping him quiet. All the running around has done him good. Perked right up after the raid. Almost like he was before."

I didn't care for the sound of that. The last thing I needed was Angela thinking Frank was on his way to a full recovery. It'd give her a reason to stay in town. "May I?" I asked, gesturing toward the parlor. She stood out of the way and I walked in slow, mindful of all the guns centered on my back.

Frank Paco was on the sofa, listening to the radio, his hollowed-out face looking only slightly more animated than the last time I'd seen him. He'd been cleaned up, combed, shaved, and was in a decent suit, one cut to reflect the weight he'd lost since last August when I'd shattered his world. As I walked in I wondered if he'd know me and remember what had happened.

He glanced up once, eyes as empty as ever, and I felt a familiar chill on my neck. He was more walking dead than I'd ever be.

One glance, then he ignored me, staring with vast concentration at the lighted dial on the set as if trying to recall how to work it. Static came through the speaker.

My apprehension eased. He was in no shape to take over the running of a windup train set, much less what was left of his old organization. I took my usual chair opposite the sofa, getting comfortable. Angela, still holding her gun on me, sat next to her father, who didn't seem aware of her at all.

" 'Almost' doesn't cut it in his business," I said to her. "Look at him—he's nowhere close to being what he was and you know it."

Big brown eyes, snapping fire. "You son of a bitch."

Paco kept looking at the radio. "Hey, talk nice like a lady," he admonished her fondly. He sounded normal, but the blank look on his face didn't change. He reached across and played with the volume dial. The static rose to earsplitting levels. Without a word, Newton stepped forward and turned it down.

"You want me to find a station for you, Mr. Paco?"

"Always with the questions. Make up your own damn mind." Paco sat back and frowned at something past my right shoulder. I looked behind me, but nothing was there but the drawn curtains of the window.

"I rest my case," I said gently, almost whispering it. I began focusing on her, hardly thinking twice about it. It was safe enough even with all the chaperons watching. "Now, we need to talk, Angela."

She was falling into it. Not in a big way, but her grip on the gun eased and her expression softened.

"I need you to listen to me."

Then Doc stepped exactly between us. "Oh, no you don't."

Angela snapped full awake. "Doc, what are you—"

"I said there's something not right about him, and this is part of it."

"What do you mean?"

"You gotta take me on trust for this, girl, but he's got something up his sleeve what ain't normal. I seen him work it on Sullivan's men."

She didn't discount him. "Work what?"

"The stuff he was just starting on you. I once saw a side-show magician do like that, had a hypnosis act going for him. He'd pick a yokel outta the audience and have him thinking he's a chicken quick as scat. This mug's got the same thing going for him, only better. He's not too obvious on it, but when he wants something from you, he can get it, and you'd never know what hit you."

I shook my head, smiling. "Where'd you get your booze tonight? I want some for myself and my friends."

Dead silence. They weren't in the mood for a comedian. Doc was a drunk, but he still had plenty of influence with them.

"Okay, I'll go with you on this," she said after a moment. "You watch him, and if you don't like anything he does, plug him one."

"I am a healer, girl. I don't 'plug' people if I can help it, it ain't in the oath I took."

"All right, then you give Newton the high sign and *he* can do the shooting."

"That's more like it." Doc settled in on the arm of the sofa and Newton made a place on the other arm. They could look at each other over the heads of Paco and Angela.

This was the last thing I needed, and I felt like groaning, but held it in. I'd just have to persuade her without artificial help.

"You were talking pretty big last night," said Angela, addressing me. "Made a lot of promises. You remember the one I made you?"

"If I screwed up you'd hang me from a meat hook. It's kind of burned into my memory."

"Good, then you won't be too surprised when it happens."

"Uh-uh—I fulfilled my part of the deal. I got Doc out and you've got your payoff money. You shouldn't have any beef with me."

"Money?" she asked, looking innocent and blank.

Something lurched unpleasantly in my chest. This was no time to panic. I made myself speak. "Don't tell me you didn't find those bags in the car?"

The innocence turned cynical. "Yeah, we found 'em. I thought they were a joke."

Breath of relief. "A hell of an expensive joke for Sullivan."

"It's not Sullivan's payoff money, he wouldn't have that much cash ready at hand. It's the stuff Kyler skimmed. You were trying to keep it for yourself."

"How do you figure that?"

"Because you forgot to mention it to Doc."

"Of course I did. I've learned to nail my trap shut in this town, you live longer. Besides, for all I knew, he might have taken it and done a bunk on us both."

"Oh, yeah, sure, that was the first thing that crossed your mind."

She wasn't going to believe me, so I gave it up. I wasn't

believing me, either. "Okay, I won't deny I was tempted. It seemed a shame to leave it lying around for Sullivan to stumble on, so why shouldn't I make a try to get rich? I went to a hell of a lot of trouble to get it out of the basement and succeeded. Nothing left for me then but to get Doc out and make sure you and Sullivan settle up your own accounts— but Maxwell spoiled all that, so you've got your money and I'm out of luck."

"But what was in the car was not what I was supposed to get from Sullivan."

"Lady, what do you expect? You've got the cake, the frosting, the whole damn kitchen, now you want more on top of all that?"

"You better believe it. I want the money that was coming to me for selling the books to Sullivan."

Jeez. And I thought I was greedy. "And how much would that be? He'd have never given you anything near the amount you have now. It'd have been cheaper for him to kill you than pay you off with this kind of cash. Think it over. Put yourself in his place. Would *you* have paid *him* that much?"

That closed her down for a moment.

Doc snorted. "Balls and brains. Maybe you should marry him, girl."

We both shot him an annoyed look.

I picked up the thread again. "The way I see it, I've done my part of the deal. I got Doc back, you have your money, all that's left is your part of the trade, but now you give the books to me instead of to Sullivan."

"Why the hell should I do that?"

"Relax, it's not like I'm going into the business myself."

"Then what do you want them for?"

"So I can hand them over to Merrill Adkins."

"*What!* You're crazy!" She added a few other personal

observations about me that I let pass. She was entitled to an opinion.

When she wound down, I said, "You ready to hear why yet? You just might like it."

She jerked her chin. It looked like a nod. A hostile one.

"Here's the picture for now: Sullivan is set to take over from you, and it's going to happen with or without the books or Opal. He can glean what he needs from local sources; it'll take time, but he can do it, leaving you out in the cold."

"I thought you said I'd like it."

"Now picture this: Give the books over to Adkins. He starts doing his sheriff act and cleaning up the town. The newspapers follow him like hungry puppies while he feeds them gangbusters for real, closing down business. The kind of stuff Sullivan does can't take too much publicity, if any. The revenues drop to nothing, he'll be sending excuses to New York, but all they'll be seeing is that he's bungled the job. Before you know it, Sullivan's out in the cold—and without a carful of cash like what you've got."

"He'll find a way to cover himself."

"Maybe with the law, but not with his New York friends. And don't forget about Maxwell's vaudeville act backing up what the books will be telling all those busy little federal bookkeepers. It wouldn't surprise me too much if everything blows up in Sullivan's face like a two-ton bottle rocket."

"What made Maxwell turn stoolie?"

I shrugged. "Maybe he got religion. Who cares as long as Sullivan gets burned for it and you're in the clear?"

"Then I can move in."

"No, that's not the idea at all, Adkins will have done too much damage to what's there."

"I can always start in on new places."

Froze her with a look. "No, you *won't!*"

She gasped. Doc straightened and Newton brought his gun

up. I threw my hand out and was within a hair of vanishing. It'd be a mess, but I'd deal with it somehow.

No bullet, though. Newton held off as Doc glared, but did not give the high sign. "You just behave yourself, boy."

Gave him a thin spasm of a smile, no humor behind it. Too bad I couldn't hypnotize him, but you could smell the booze on his breath at two yards. It wouldn't take.

"If—" said Angela, all recovered from the push I'd given her. "If Maxwell is spilling his guts, then that should be enough for Adkins. He won't need the books."

"Oh, but he will. The courts like seeing things on paper."

"I need them more than they do."

"You're not getting the point—once they start investigating, the books will not only be useless to you, but pure poison. Whoever has them, whoever uses them will get caught. These guys know how to trace stuff, they'll find you."

"But—"

"And when they find you, they find your father. You want him to be turned over to one of their institutions while you're serving time? We already talked about this, and you weren't too happy about the idea."

She suddenly looked ready to boil over—onto me.

"On the other hand, giving the books to Adkins puts that many more nails into Sullivan's coffin. Maybe you won't have the business, but he won't get it either. He takes the fall instead, while you're home free with all that cash to play with. It sounds like a beaut of a deal."

She snorted. "And what do you get out of it?"

"I was figuring myself in for a small cut of the cash. Ten percent would be fine, I'm not too greedy."

This time she laughed out loud. "No, but you've got a hell of a nerve."

"Only for what I've earned."

"I'll have to disappoint you." She paused, waiting for me

to protest, but I kept shut to hear her out. "You talk a good game, Fleming, but if I do have to leave town, it's going to be with Sullivan's cash as well. I sell him the books and have a good laugh on him. Adkins I could care less about. If he wants to put Sullivan away, he's welcome to it, but I'm taking my cut first."

I sat forward. "What, you're actually going to meet with—"

"With Sullivan, yeah. Maybe I won't get what was in the car, but it'll look funny if I don't take some kind of a payoff from him, no matter how much or little it is."

"Quit while you're ahead, Angela. As of tonight, it would be a really lousy idea for you to try dealing with him."

"Oh, yeah? And why is that?"

"Because of your little fire out at the roadhouse. He knows all about it and the murders."

Blank look. "What fire?"

"Forget the Sarah Bernhardt act."

"What murders?"

"Come on, I know Doc told you where to find Sullivan, so you and your boys had a little country drive to the joint then set the bonfire."

The collective looks they exchanged were too real to be discounted. There's always one bad actor in a troupe who gives away the game, but I didn't see any of that here.

"You saying the roadhouse is burned?" she demanded.

"Down to the basement steps."

"When?"

"Tonight."

"You're lying."

"If you think that, then call the papers, they should be finishing the report on it about now. It's probably too late for the morning edition, but they might squeeze it into the afternoon—unless with the cop killings they decide to issue an extra.''

"Cop killings?''

"Couple of men named Calloway and Baker. Someone checked them out using your signature—a forty-five in the back of the head. They were working for Sullivan.''

"Fine with me, I never liked the bums, but I didn't scrag 'em.''

"She did want to go to the roadhouse, but I talked her out of it,'' said Doc.

I believed him, and the next few minutes really convinced me, since they had a few dozen questions about it that I couldn't answer. At the top of the list was who did do it and why? By then I was figuring Gordy was behind it, but kept the idea strictly to myself.

"It had to be Sullivan,'' Angela concluded.

My head was starting to hurt, and not from doing any fancy hypnosis. "You pick him for a reason or just because you don't like him much?''

"I don't know anyone else who would want to, including myself. That place was a real moneymaker, so why should I burn it? But I'm thinking if Sullivan does the job and puts the blame on me, then anything he does in reprisal gets full approval from his bosses.''

It sounded plausible if you discount the fact that it'd still be cheaper for Sullivan to just kill her instead of burn the place; I let her keep on thinking it.

The phone rang. Kept ringing. I counted to fourteen before it stopped. No one moved the whole time.

"Angela! You should have had someone catch the phone.'' The same words as before from Frank Paco, the same tone. Same lack of expression. He still stared over my shoulder with his dead eyes.

"It wasn't for us, Daddy.''

"You don't know till you answer."

Her face was all tight at she looked at him, bleak with heartbreak. It's hell when the kid has to become parent to their parent, and she was having a harder time of it than most.

"Angela." My tone was quiet, gentle.

"Go to hell."

"Look at it square. I know you wanted to hand the whole organization back to him, but he can never take it."

"Shut up," she whispered.

"It's not going to happen, not because of anything you did, but just because that's how things turned out. You've got to take the money you have and get away from this town."

"When I have the payoff from Sullivan—"

Held my hand palm out, calming gesture. "That's not going to happen either, because he's going to be thinking you torched the roadhouse, killed his men."

"But I didn't."

"But he'll think it, same as you thought he did it."

"If he didn't do it, who did?"

"It doesn't matter, but like you figured, blaming you is going to be his story. Shutting you up is going to be his next step. You won't get money from him, but a whole lot of bullets instead. If you get killed, your father—if he survives—goes to an institution."

She pushed off the sofa and stumbled clear. Her breath came fast, her hands shook.

"I know this isn't what you want to hear, but this is what you're facing. You and your father can be alive with the cash you have, or risk death for a chance to have a laugh behind Sullivan's back. I don't think Sullivan is worth it. Any money you might get from him would not be worth it. If it comes to a choice between pride and living, I'll take living any old day."

She paced now, back and forth, her face flushed dark. She

did this for a long time. Doc and Newton stayed where they were and stayed quiet. I did the same. The pacing finally, gradually slowed, and she turned to look at me.

"I suppose . . . I suppose I can already start laughing at the bastard," she said. "He never knew about the other money being in the basement. If he ever finds out about it and thinks that he burned up seven hundred grand . . ."

"He'd probably shoot himself—if New York doesn't do it for him. Then there's the other thing."

"What's that?"

"The money's clean now. If anyone should ever find out about it, that it ever existed, they'll think it went up in smoke like the rest of the joint. They won't be looking for it."

"Yeah, there's that." She liked that idea, warmed up to it real quick. "I guess you've done me a big favor, Fleming."

I let her smile over that one, it was a nice smile, for a killer. "Then lemme call it in."

"Your ten percent?"

"Forget that. Just give me the books, those useless to you, poison-in-your-hand books. You want a last laugh at Sullivan, then be the one who puts him in jail."

"Men like him don't go to jail."

"You never know. It's that or he takes a long walk off a short pier wearing cement galoshes. Either way, you win."

"What about Opal?"

"Let me take care of her. You don't have any work for her, do you?"

She shook her head. "Not anymore. Look, one thing about Opal? Don't play blackjack or gin rummy with her, she'll wipe the floor with you. You should find her a job at a casino. The odds favor the house, but guys never mind losing to a woman. She'd be really cute if someone taught her how to dress and do her hair. What do you think?"

I started to automatically object, but on second thought it

was a damned sensible suggestion. Playing cards were just numbers, after all, and the variables involved just might hold her interest. "I'll think about it. So will she."

"But how do you get her away from Sullivan?"

"That's my problem, but not to worry, I can do it."

"I bet you can, blue eyes."

"So—just where is that seven hundred grand?"

Another laugh. "Someplace else."

Well, I'd done my grieving earlier tonight. The money was gone and never meant to be mine. On the other hand, I'd already taken my cut from it with the cash I'd stuffed in my pockets. That was roughly ten percent. Nothing to sneeze at on its own. "You gonna take it to Switzerland?"

"Maybe."

"I hear they never ask a lot of questions on where money comes from. I also hear that most of 'em speak Italian."

"You sound eager to get rid of me."

"Only because all the guns pointed in my direction, but yeah, it would be a good idea for you and yours to leave. Sullivan could be the next one through the door, and if it's all the same to you, I'd rather the both of you just keep missing each other."

"What, he'd come here looking for Maxwell?"

"You got it. Look at me. . . ." I gestured at my scruffy appearance. "I got like this having a dustup with some of his boys. He'll know who to come looking for and where to start—"

"Okay, Doc, Newton, get Daddy out to the car."

"Not so fast, sweetheart—where are the books?"

For a second I thought I'd have to take a chance and give her a nudge, but she barked out a short laugh. "All right, they're at the dance studio."

"You figured Sullivan wouldn't search a place that was already raided?"

"Nah, we just didn't have time to get them out."

"Where are they?"

"Look in that stairwell. The trapdoor. They're inside it."

"Good place to hide something."

"I thought so. You just damn well better use them like you've said."

"Or it's meat-hook time?"

"It's a promise. Come on, you guys, let's go."

Doc and Newton were already helping Frank toward the back door.

"What?" I asked, all injured. "No kiss good-bye?"

She looked like she'd rather shoot me instead and held her gun steady on my heart as she backed from the room. When the door snicked shut, I dropped back in my chair and didn't do anything except feel like a wrung-out washrag for the next few minutes.

Then I felt it happen. Felt one of those anvils slipping from its previous spot on top of my head. It dropped fast and hard and made a satisfying clunk as it hit the floor. Jeez, but it felt good, just too bad about all the shit you have to go through before it falls off.

No time to celebrate, though. I still had a couple more firmly in place and had to get to work fast before I missed the opportunity of jogging them loose.

The phone rang. Whoever was calling was doing it every ten minutes or so, unless three people trying to call in were making a coincidence in their timing. I went to the kitchen and pulled the earpiece and said hello.

"That you, Fleming?" It was Gordy.

"In the flesh. Did you get the wires fixed?"

"Can it. Get over here to the club. Now."

12

"YOU been calling here before?" I asked.

"Yeah, get over here."

"What's the problem?"

"The front door will be open, use it. Come to the office."

"What's—"

He hung up.

Okay, something was seriously wrong. I assumed it had to do with Sullivan, and Gordy wouldn't or couldn't give me any other details. Changing my shirt would have to wait. I locked up—for all the good it might do—and hurried out to my Buick.

At other times when I'm in a rush, it always seems to take forever to get where I need to be; not so for this trip. I had no idea what to expect and so I wasn't all that eager to arrive. Perversely, most of the stop signals were in my favor, and I made my best time ever getting to the Nightcrawler Club. I didn't park right away, but circled the place, looking things over; that's how I spotted the two cars the thugs had used escaping away from the hospital. The driver's door on one of them wasn't properly closed. I must have wrecked it a little yanking it open.

The next interesting thing I noticed was a Packard parked within sight of the club's front entrance. Not too new and pocked with bullet holes; I was surprised at Gordy for taking such a chance. Of course, if he'd knocked off Calloway and Baker, then he was removing witnesses who could connect the car to him. I wondered if he had it in mind to try killing me, but not for very long. He knew better.

Not Sullivan, though. I had no reason to take him out of the running. Maybe they'd split the job, Gordy doing the hotel hit and Sullivan burning the roadhouse. All of that would put Angela out of the picture but good.

The club was dark, which was wrong. The raid a few nights back shouldn't have kept the joint closed for this long a time. Maybe Sullivan didn't like the noise.

I parked and thought about slipping into the building quietly just to see what might be lying in wait. Gordy's specific mention of the front door was too important to ignore, though. If he'd wanted me to sneak in, he'd have found a way to say so. Unless he had a gun to his head.

Walked fast down the street, eyes wide to take in every shadow, every window. Nothing to see worth seeing until I got to the front steps. There were grills on either side of the door. Men usually sat in little rooms behind them to check out the customers as they came in. I couldn't see past the grillwork too well, but did spot movement beyond each, so someone was on watch.

Opened the door, half expecting to see goons standing there with guns, but the outer lobby was empty. Only one light was on over at the hatcheck counter. I crossed to the next set of doors that led into the club.

The joint had been busted up, but cleaning had taken place since then. Chairs were piled onto tables, the tables shoved to one side, giving the floor cleaners room to work. The darkened stage and bandstand looked lonely. I hurried along to a door marked PRIVATE and pushed through.

The damage here was much more obvious. Every gambling

device from the slot machines to the roulette wheel to the blackjack tables had been thoroughly worked over by sledge-hammers. Nothing to do with the remains but haul them out to the junkyard and start over.

My shoes crunched against broken glass and splinters as I walked toward the back. Nobody here either. I was starting to get a good case of the creeps.

Another door marked PRIVATE; it opened to the back hall with the kitchen, various small offices, and stairs to the second floor, which was populated. Four men were hanging around the lower landing having a smoke. They all stopped talking and stared at me as I came through. I recognized them as regulars with Gordy. They knew me by sight and that Gordy had given me full run of the place.

"The boss in his office?" I asked.

One of them nodded. "Yeah, go on up."

"Sullivan there?"

"He's there."

"What about his boys?"

"Why do you think we're down here?"

"Don't like 'em?"

"What I like don't come into it."

Went upstairs. Heard several radios playing, each set on different stations. The floor was fixed out with bedrooms and some of the men lived here. Not a bad place to flop if you didn't mind the hours.

Three guys on the top landing. They looked a lot like me as far as their clothing went, with it being in less than perfect condition. One man had a black eye, another had his wrist bandaged; neither looked happy about it or about me. Though it seemed too late for it, I thought it best not to remind them of the riot by the hospital because they weren't hiding their guns.

They glared plenty hard, but didn't speak or make a move

to stop me as I took the few steps to Gordy's office. I knocked twice and opened the door.

I don't breathe regular, but still held my breath, all tensed, more than half expecting a bullet.

Nothing. Just Gordy's voice telling me to come in, so I did.

He sat behind his desk, playing out a hand of solitaire. Half a dozen more goons from the hospital fight were scattered around the room. It wasn't all that big, so they made for a good crowd. On the couch, the crease still fresh on his pants, was Sean Sullivan reading a magazine. He put it to one side and stood, looking me over.

"You've been busy tonight, haven't you, Fleming?"

I couldn't tell if he wanted an answer to that and knew if I opened my mouth it'd just annoy him. I shrugged. Shot Gordy a questioning look, but his face was way past being just deadpan.

Sullivan went on. "I heard you had a bit of an altercation with my boys. They were full of wild stories about you."

"How flattering."

He gave me a long dead stare, and during that time I got the impression he had some specific questions to ask about the fight, but didn't dare ask them, not in front of everyone in a well-lighted room. You can't start asking a guy how he kept disappearing and coming back, how he survived a bullet in the belly, and not lose face with the hired help. He wouldn't get any straight answer out of me anyway, and probably figured as much.

So he left that and tried a different tack. "Why did you pretend to be working for Angela?"

"What's with pretend? I do work for her." It seemed best to continue that fiction.

"No, you don't."

"I don't?"

"You're working for Gordy—or at least you were."

"Uh-huh." Okay, so Gordy had fed him some kind of story, but I wasn't sure how to go along with it just yet. I looked at him. He looked back, still deadpan, and put a red queen on a red king. His hands were steady, but either what was going on was distracting the hell out of him or he was trying to tell me something. "So I was working for Gordy and then what? I quit and worked for Angela?"

"No, you sidestepped all of us and went to work for yourself."

I shifted on my feet. The goons came alert. Two of them came forward and patted me down, but all they found were keys and an empty wallet. They looked disappointed as I put the items back in my pockets.

"So I'm self-employed?" I asked brightly. "The pay is lousy, then."

At a nod from Sullivan one of the goons rapped the back of my head with something hard. It wasn't too forceful, being meant to get my attention, nothing more. "Hey what's the idea?" I looked at the goon, who had a blackjack in his fist. He just grinned at me.

"The idea," said Sullivan, "is you planned to take the books and bookkeeper off on your own and go into business for yourself—that is, after Angela and I killed each other for you."

Gordy glanced up at me a moment, then went back to his cards. Now he put a black nine under a black ten. He held to the stone face, but had given a very slight lift of his chin, so small that it could have been a normal movement of his head. I was to go along with this line.

Sullivan continued. "Of course there were no guarantees we would be so cooperative, so you were setting things up to make sure the right people died."

"Like the hit in front of the hotel? I'd set a hit on myself and Opal?"

"No, that was the responsibility of this gentleman." He gestured at Gordy.

I didn't want to hear this. Thinking and suspecting is one thing, but it's quite another to have to face it, face the ugly truth. "Gordy? Were you behind that?"

"What do you figure, kid? That I'm gonna let you get away gypping me? I've had my eye on you for months."

My mouth dropped open. It was with vast relief, but Sullivan read it otherwise, as shock maybe, and that pleased him.

"Gordy has a lot of eyes and ears in this town. He got a tip you and Angela were at the hotel and sent some of his boys over thinking to do me a favor. They made a sorry job of it. Who did they think all those cops were, a girls' glee club?" He addressed the last to Gordy. It obviously wasn't the first time he'd needled away on the subject.

Indifferent, Gordy lifted his big shoulders a quarter inch. "They saw a short woman with a lotta guys that might have been bodyguards, and went in shooting. A mistake. Easy to make with the car moving so fast and it being dark. That bookkeeper could have been Angela."

"Too bad she wasn't."

"Where is she?" I asked. "Where's Opal?"

"She's all right," said Gordy, giving me another unblinking look. "We got a doctor looking after her. She's going to be fine."

He didn't absolutely have to add that last part. I was glad he did. "Good."

"Good for all of us," said Sullivan. "All but Angela, that is—and you."

"Hey, I—" Another crack on the head. A little harder than the last. The guy still grinned, daring me to try something.

Sullivan crossed his arms, cocking his head to one side. I'd bet money it was a trick he'd used on the old college debating team. "So when you come into my place you give me to think you work for Angela and can talk her out of the books. I took a chance on you, but you didn't meet your obligations. Instead you gave Calloway the slip so you could get that drunk doctor out and kidnap my secretary. By the way, where *is* Maxwell?"

I had to dish him anything but the truth. "He's okay. I got him stashed at a warehouse I know. It ain't the Ritz, but it's warm."

"We will discuss his release momentarily, then. Why did you take the doctor? What use was he to you?"

"He was my ticket to get close to Angela."

"You could have told me the truth instead of implying you had some assignation with her that would take all night."

"Yeah, I could, but I knew you wouldn't have let me walk out of there with Doc."

"No, but I could have gotten the required information from him by other methods."

"And maybe killed him before he talked. He's a stubborn bird and loyal to Angela. He'd have died before giving you squat. But by getting him free, he was ready to trust me and take me right in."

"Why didn't he?"

"Who says he didn't?"

That hooked his attention. "What are you saying?"

"That I finally got to her. She's not someone you need to worry about anymore."

"She's dead?"

"Leaving town. You've got a clear field to—"

"Not good enough."

"Huh?"

"That business with the roadhouse."

"What about it?"

"Gordy and I are agreed that Angela is responsible for the deaths and damage. I've informed some friends of mine about the incident and the decision is that there has to be an accounting. If she wants to play rough with the big boys, then she'll get a bloody nose and more, the same as anyone else."

If it came to a face-to-face showdown with Sullivan, my money would be on Angela—unless he got the drop on her. I shut up to think a minute, but nothing wanted to jump into my brain just then. All I could figure was one was lying to the other for his own reasons. Gordy didn't have anything to gain by destroying the roadhouse, though, but Sullivan did. He was probably playing some kind of a cute double game with New York to secure his place here. Set the fire, kill his pet cops, blame Angela for everything, get a contract on her, and . . . "So you've got permission to rub her out?"

"I've always had that as an option, should it become necessary, but it's nice to have it all official."

"Well, you can call it off. She and her mob are blowing this town for good—but she left the books behind."

He smiled, all tanned and true. He could have posed for a portrait of Jack Armstrong just then. "I was wondering when you'd get around to mentioning those."

"I don't have them—"

"You astonish me."

"But I know where they are."

That made him uncross his arms. "You'd have to prove that, and right now I've absolutely no reason to trust you with so much as a burned match."

I thought he was trying for some joke connected to the roadhouse, but he seemed unaware of it. "I guess not, but you've got nothing to lose—I do. The feeling I'm getting here is that I'm dead meat."

"That's for certain."

"I got a little ambitious, so you're gonna make an example of me, is that it?"

Gordy nodded. "That's it exactly, kid." Now he put a red three on a black four. He was square with me again, giving me a warning to watch my step.

"But—" I spread my hands. "Do I look like a man scared of being killed?"

"It just means you're a good liar." Lots of contempt in Sullivan's tone. He expected people to lie to him, it was part of the trade.

I snorted. "Before you think that, check with Gordy. He'll tell you what kind of poker player I am."

Gordy almost cracked a smile. "It's true. He stinks. If he says he has the books, listen to him."

"In which case," I continued, "we're going to have to work out something different from what you've got planned or you don't get the books."

Sullivan came within a foot of me, maybe hoping to intimidate. "Such as?"

I liked the way he met my gaze, it made things very easy. "Let's keep it down to simple basics: I give you the books, and you let me go free."

He went blank for as long as it took me to say it, then I backed off. He didn't move right away, just blinked a lot, as though trying to remember something. I couldn't do much more or his goons would notice and get uneasy.

"Sullivan?" Gordy asked. He'd been watching, saw what I'd done, had been looking for it. "What do you think?"

"I . . . I . . . don't like it."

"Neither do I, but let's play along just for laughs. It's not like the kid's gonna disappear on us."

I chose to not take that as a signal to do so and waited.

"He's a liar, he turned on you."

"Then he's my problem to deal with, not yours. If he's got

the books then take 'em and get outta my place. I got a business to run here and you and your boys are crowding me."

Sullivan gave me a sharp look. I returned it with care. "This is on the up-and-up," I said. "You can have the books, and I'll get clear of your business."

Release.

He shook his head, probably wondering what hit him. I sensed his men shifting on either side of me, ready for trouble. They were aware something was off, but not sure what.

"What's your answer, Mr. Sullivan?" I prompted.

He made an impatient gesture. "All right. But you even *think* of pulling a double cross . . ."

"Then hang me from a meat hook," I suggested.

The guy with the blackjack had an expression like he'd be pleased to do the honors.

"Let's get started," said Sullivan. "Where are they?"

I put a hand up. "Not until I see Opal."

"What for?"

"She's a friend of mine." I was ready to give him the eye again, but Gordy spared me the headache.

"Let him. It'll only take a minute. I'll send someone down to warm up the car."

"Cars," Sullivan added. "You want us out, we're leaving. I haven't had a decent meal the whole time I've been in this dive." I guess manners weren't part of the Ivy League curriculum these days.

Gordy produced another slight twitch around his mouth. It gave me the idea that maybe his cook for the duration of Sullivan's visit had been told not to make any special efforts at the grub. "I'll take him in to see the girl," he said, and rose. As he stood he swept his hands over the unfinished game of solitaire, gathering the cards together in a neat stack, wiping out their message.

"Come on, kid."

He took up a lot of space and Sullivan and his boys had to stand aside as he passed. No one stopped me as I went with him into the hall. Neither of us said anything because Sullivan was right behind us.

Gordy called orders about the cars to his men downstairs, then turned and led the way to the far end of the hall. The big bedroom there had belonged to his former boss, now deceased, Slick Morelli. His stuff was all cleared out and replaced, different wallpaper, different pictures. The bed looked the same except for Opal being in it. I made a beeline for her.

She seemed smaller than before. Her face was too white and reminded me of a crushed flower. I was scared to touch her.

"Here, now, what's this?" A fussy-looking man in sober dark clothes came out of the bathroom. "Mr. Sullivan, this simply won't do."

"Dr. Balsamo, I presume?" I muttered.

"And who might you be?" Neatly trimmed beard on his chin, dark features, not old, not young, a slight foreign accent I couldn't place. When I didn't answer he went to talk to his boss in hushed, but insistent tones. His theme was that visiting hours were over. Gordy came up next to me to look down at Opal.

I took the opportunity while I had it. "Did you really do the hit at the hotel?" I asked, barely moving my lips.

"Nope."

"Why say so?"

"Because it was a good idea at the time."

"You know who did do it?"

"Nope."

"The hit car's out front, a Packard full of holes. You can't miss it."

He made a small grunt of acknowledgment.

"You know I can get the truth out of you if I have to."

"I know, kid. Truth's what you're getting now."

"What about the fire? Who did that?"

"Angela, maybe."

No time to tell him different, Sullivan came over. "That's it. We're going."

It wasn't enough. I wanted her to be awake so I could apologize. Selfish thing to do, robbing her of sleep just to ease my conscience. Managed not to do it, but I did pause on the way out to talk with the doctor.

"Is she really going to be okay?"

"She should be, unless she develops an infection from having all of you in here breathing your germs into her air."

"She doesn't look so good. You sure? Why doesn't she wake up?" No one was being any too quiet.

"That's the sedative. She was up earlier and beating me at checkers. Now, everyone get out of here this instant."

He was fussy, but I liked that. It meant he was looking after her.

I said good-bye to her for now. Apologies would have to wait for later.

We trooped downstairs, Sullivan's men lording it over Gordy's, not enough to cause a fight to break out, but sufficient to drive their point home that they were with the winning boss, the man with all the power. I'd seen it before, but it's usually on a grade-school playground.

Sullivan's two cars weren't enough to hold us all; Gordy sent someone to bring around his Cadillac. He drove and Sullivan sat up front with him. I was in the back between two goons. None of Gordy's men went with us, which had a funny smell I didn't like.

"Where to?" Gordy asked.

"Flora's Dance Studio," I said.

Sullivan looked ready to choke. "My people went over that place, every inch."

"It's not my fault you've got a bunch of dummies on the payroll."

"Where are they?"

I assumed he meant the books, not the dummies. "Upstairs, not too far from the manager's office." If Angela hadn't lied to me, that is. I didn't think she had, but if so, then I'd have to take the hint from Gordy and disappear. I was planning to anyway. Once I had the books in hand, I'd get scarce and let Sullivan and his boys go chase themselves trying to find me. With any luck, Adkins could start working on their codes before dawn. As for Opal, she was going to stay well clear of the mess from now on if I had anything to do with it. Her part was over.

Our caravan trundled through the thinning traffic, Gordy holding to a nice comfortable pace, sometimes pausing if one of the cars behind got caught by a stop signal. The drab studio and its neighborhood was on the other side of the world compared to his swanky club, but both were linked tight as twins to the common need of people wanting risky distractions. Rich or poor, it went to all levels. I wondered if the mobs would go out of business if suddenly all the current vices became legal. Probably not; they'd just find a way to take their usual cut, only it'd be aboveboard.

Not my worry, though; Gordy found a spot across the street to park and slipped in. The other cars cruised forward to the end of the block and made U-turns, stopping in front of the studio. Everyone got out. Some of the bums hanging around the all-night theater stopped trying to panhandle tickets and turned to watch our particular show instead.

Our group waited until Sullivan's boys broke the doors open and went through. The building had been boarded up by the cops, but no one was on watch. The place was a dump, so why bother?

One of them came out and waved, then we started across the street. Way at the far end of it a car rounded the corner, the headlights flashing in the turn, then shutting down. No one else noticed because of the dark, but I recognized the Packard. Something was up, and I didn't know who was behind it, Gordy or Sullivan. Gordy might have lied to me when I'd asked about the hotel hit, knowing I couldn't seriously try getting the truth out of him in front of the others. Maybe all he'd wanted was some time to set up another one, and I'd provided a convenient way of having it take place far from his club.

Talking to him about it was impossible, of course. For the moment.

With Sullivan's men on either side like an honor guard, I was ushered through the studio doors with a lot more ceremony than on my last visit. Someone hit the lights, only half of them came on. The place looked cavernous with all the dancing couples gone. Overturned chairs lay here and there by the walls and on the floor were hundreds of torn ticket stubs. We walked over them and went upstairs, leaving most of the goons to cool their heels below. Sullivan must have been comfortable with just the two guarding me.

I took them down to the manager's office, passing wrecked rooms on the way. The damage was severe, a lot like the gambling area of the Nightcrawler Club, full of broken machines and similar litter.

The glass panel on the office door was smashed through. I went in and tried the light so everyone could see the wreckage, too. The bowling trophy still lay on the floor, but it was easy to overlook amid the smashed desk and pulled-out drawers. Not so easy to miss was the manager's blood. No one had had time to clean it up before the raid.

I went past it all to open the second door onto the back hall. It was freezing, the fire-escape window still gaped wide. The two goons outflanked me when they saw my interest in it, putting themselves in my way in case I got any ideas about leaving in that direction. It seemed best to ignore them.

The door to the janitor closet also sagged open. The thread-bare rug was all rumpled, but still pretty much in place covering the trap. Even the dim light worked. There wasn't much room for the others, but they crowded together on the threshold to watch as I yanked the rug back and pulled the door up.

"My boys already searched that place," Sullivan informed me.

I ignored him, too, for a closer study of the trapdoor. It was heavy, but not unexpectedly so, and a few inches thick. I ran my fingers along the front edge, looking for some way in. A board shifted under them. I gave it a push and it swiveled, revealing a cavity. Angling the door just right, I could see down inside, glimpsing the thin flat spines of ledger books.

"Bingo," I said by way of announcement, and leaned back so they could get a look.

After the first wave of satisfaction passed, Sullivan seemed disappointed. Now he'd have to let me go. Then again, my influence on him wasn't so firmly fixed that he couldn't over-come it if he wanted to badly enough.

"Get them," he ordered.

I tried reaching in, but my hands were too big. Not so for little Angela, or even Opal. "Have to fish them out with something unless one of your boys is on the dainty side."

"Don't be smart."

"Then have someone turn up a wire coat hanger so I can snag this stuff."

He sent one of the goons away and we stood around with

our hands in our pockets and not saying anything. There was quite a chilly draft coming from that window. It made the exit door at the bottom of the hidden stairway bump against its latch. I checked down there, but it was empty.

"Where's that go?" asked Gordy.

"Comes out in an alley. Opal and I used it the other night to get away from the raid." I might use it again once the books were out, just vanish and pop down the rabbit hole with them, leaving Sullivan with one hell of a mystery on his hands. It might be tough for Gordy, but he could take care of himself, probably pretend to be as astonished as the others. If it seemed necessary, I could always dump the books someplace safe, like the roof, then hurry back to help him. The chance might even come up for me to grab Sullivan for a little private talk. Then Maxwell wouldn't be the only guy telling his life story to Merrill Adkins. Now wouldn't *that* be sweet?

The goon was taking his time. Sullivan snarled at the remaining one to go find out what the holdup was. Another few minutes crawled by with everyone getting colder.

"They're not gonna find anything," he finally concluded. "Here—" He pulled a claw hammer off its peg and gave it to Gordy. "I'll watch him, you break it open."

Gordy shrugged, but the room was too small for both of us, so I eased out to give him space and he went to work on the wood joints, thumping away on them, then trying to pry them apart. It made a lot of noise and at first masked over what was going on below. I was barely aware of it, all my concentration being on Gordy. The sound only registered with me as a random banging that might have been a freak echo of Gordy's hammering coming up the narrow stairs.

Then Gordy paused and we all heard it, muffled by the many walls between but unmistakable: the sound of a machine gun stuttering.

It went on for only a second or two and stopped and was answered by some scattered individual shots from semi-autos.

"What the hell . . . ?" Sullivan must not have spent any time in the streets and didn't know the universal rule about always running away whenever you hear gunfire, preferably in the opposite direction from its source. He hauled out a shiny new .45 and rushed off toward the ruckus.

"What is it?" I asked Gordy. "Something of yours?"

He shook his head. "Damned if I know, kid." He left off with the hammer and pulled his own gun clear. I followed Sullivan's path, with Gordy behind me.

More guns going off, men yelling. Jeez, how they were yelling. The machine gun started up again, getting louder the closer we got—no, there were at least two of them, maybe others.

Gordy hung back out of sight of the main stairs while I pressed forward. Sullivan crouched at the corner, peering down, not moving.

"What is it?" I called.

He jumped and turned like I'd hit him with a live wire. His face was sheet white and his hands shook. He was better for giving orders to send his mugs in for strong-arm work than doing the work himself. "Th-they're shooting 'em."

I'd figured that much. "Who?" I got up next to him and peeked around the corner.

Couldn't see a lot, part of the stairs, a man's very still body on it. He'd fallen forward trying to run up; big bloody holes marred the back of his pale tan coat. Saw another body farther down, also not moving. The rest of what lay below was blocked off by architecture and smoke. Cordite stink filled the air; that and the bloodsmell.

It was enough for me, I pelted back and grabbed Gordy's arm, heading for the fire escape. I went through first and re-treated just as fast when I spotted a man below. He'd been waiting for someone to try using the window and fired off a couple rounds to cheat us of escape. Didn't recognize him beyond the fact he was a threat.

"In here," I said. But Gordy was way ahead of me, moving for the closet.

"Tight fit," he commented as he eased into the stairwell.

"The door at the bottom just might be watched. Stay in there until you hear from me."

"What're you—"

"I gotta see what the hell's going on."

"The books—"

"Screw the books, get 'em later."

As soon as his head was below floor level, I lowered the trapdoor on him. The top part of it wouldn't lie flat because of damage from the hammer, but I threw the rug over it, then pulled a rolling bucket and mop cart over on top of everything. It would survive an initial look-see.

I went back to the fire-escape window, this time putting only as much eye past the sill as was necessary. The man was still down there. Apparently all he had to do was make sure no one got out. Going invisible, I did exactly that, feeling my way along the metal framework until I reached the ground. I didn't go solid again until I was well behind him, and then only enough so I could see.

All alert, he was engrossed with looking up the stairs, gun out and ready to shoot. Not one of Gordy's men, and I didn't recognize him as being with Angela's crowd, but he seemed familiar nonetheless. Whoever he was with, he was dangerous, so I went completely solid and popped him one just as he turned to see who was making the fast footsteps. He dropped and I grabbed at the gun to keep it from landing wrong. A no-nonsense Thompson fitted out with a fifty-round drum. These boys meant business. I shoved it high on the fire stairs out of the way.

Gunfire. Echoes cracked off the buildings. A few spatters of it, then silence.

Down the alley, turn two corners, and I was out front. The bullet-pocked Packard was slewed across the path of the other cars, and had company with a year-old Ford, which similarly blocked the Caddie.

I saw movement at the front entry of the studio, a couple of men, postures tense, looking the street up and down for trouble. One of them held another Thompson at the ready. His gave the area one last look then went into the building, leaving his friend on watch. I ducked back to where I'd come from and slipped up the fire stairs the easy way, going solid once inside.

Listened. No more shooting, but who could say how long that would last. I worked slowly toward the front stairs. Sullivan was gone, maybe hiding in one of the rooms, or he'd slipped out the escape while I'd been away.

Couple more steps and look around the last corner. Dead man still sprawled on the stairs, only another man—machine gun in hand—loomed over him, checking him.

"Adkins?"

He reacted instantly, bringing the gun around fast enough to give anyone else a heart attack. I conquered my shock enough to put my hands up and told him to hold off a second.

"It's me—Jack Fleming! What the—what the hell are you doing here?"

He waited and two more men joined him, also with Thompsons. There was something strange and bulky about their clothing until I realized they were all wearing bulletproof vests.

"What is this? Some kind of raid?"

"Some kind," Adkins snapped. "Take him below."

"Hey, I'm one of the good guys, remember?"

"Sure, that's why you're so cozy with your friend Gordy."

One of them came up and grabbed the back of my coat, shoving me downstairs, ignoring my protests. Then I saw what was waiting below and couldn't talk anymore.

Cordite and bloodsmell. Lots of both.

Couldn't move, could only stare. It was too much to take in.

Blood flooded the floor. Bodies everywhere, all with that peculiar stillness of death hovering over them. Nearly a dozen men were scattered across the huge room. Dead. Except for the War, I hadn't seen anything remotely close to it, not even in the news photos of the garage that made the headlines on St. Valentine's Day.

Had to shut my eyes a moment and fight the rising nausea. Gulped it down until I was dizzy, then looked again. The sight hadn't gotten any better. Noticed one standout from the rest, a smaller man in an expensive dark coat I thought I knew. Walked over on wooden legs, knelt, and turned him over.

It was Maxwell. Had been Maxwell.

I looked up at the faces of the other men, of Adkins and the two with him. They stared back, their eyes full of darkness, the souls that should have been there long gone.

"What have you done?" I whispered.

"Just made the world a little cleaner," Adkins answered.

"You murdered them."

"They had guns. It was a fair fight."

"And him?" I pointed at Maxwell. "He had a gun?"

"He will before we're done here." He gave an order to the others and they split off to run upstairs.

I focused hard on Adkins, rage welling fast. Tried to damp it. "Stop them. You hear me? Call them back!"

He squinted a little like I'd blown smoke in his eyes, then shook his head.

"Stop them!"

Too late. I heard Sullivan's distant panicked shout before
machine gun clatter abruptly shut him down.

Took a step toward Adkins, but his gun was square on me.
I held off a moment, tried again to get past his darkness, put
on all the pressure I had. I let the rage loose, felt it leaping
forward. "You call to them and get them down here. You
listen to me and call them back now!"

But my anger, the same kind that had shattered Frank
Paco's mind, had *no* effect on this bastard. He was already
too far gone for my influence to touch him. "Like hell I
will," he said evenly, and lighted a cigarette.

I staggered back as if he'd been the one trying to do the
hypnosis. Fought the sickness again; this time it was more
emotional than physical. I'd heard about such monsters, had
done news stories on them, had even met a few, but not like
this, not in the middle of their handiwork while the blood was
still fresh.

"You did the hotel hit, didn't you?"

Adkins shrugged, puffing.

"You nearly killed an innocent girl."

"She works for scum, that makes her the same as them."

"She's a girl, not much more than a kid."

"Sometimes they grow up wrong. I heard about her, about
her not being right in the head, so it wouldn't have been any
big deal. There's too many freaks as it is."

This was like picking at a scab, knowing it would bleed.
"And the other two cops, the fire . . ."

"We had our eye on that bunch for a long time. Didn't
take a lot to get them out to the roadhouse, get some dirt on
Sullivan from them."

"Then shoot them in the back."

"They were crooked. Crooked cops are cancers, when you
find them, you cut them out."

"And what are you? Your world must be wonderfully

black and white. People are either good or bad with nothing in between, is that how it is for you?''

"We do what we have to do.''

"You didn't have to do any of this! That's why I gave you Maxwell. He could have helped you put them all away—without killing.''

Shook his head. "I know better. Months of courts and fancy talk with fancy lawyers, and even if some do go to jail it's nearly always a fluke. I'd rather have my taxes going to pay for new roads than buy room and board for this kind of garbage.'' He nudged Maxwell with his foot.

"The others that Charles and I turned over to you—they dead, too?''

"What do you think?''

Then I couldn't look at him anymore. If I did, I would kill him. Once started, I might kill them all. I held it in so hard it hurt.

One of them shouted that they couldn't find Gordy. "Must have used the fire escape. Conrad's out cold in the alley.''

"Then we'll catch him later. Let's get this organized first.''

Only now did they come down, dragging Sullivan's body along.

"Won't it look funny moving him?'' one of them asked.

"We're the ones who'll write the report. No one's going to question anything.''

"They never have yet,'' the other man assured his friend. They let Sullivan's body drop. The second man pressed the plated .45 into Sullivan's relaxed hand. I noticed the safety was still on, not that it would matter much.

Adkins kept watch on me while they went outside to retrieve Conrad and the other man out front. Conrad was groggy and uninformative about his attacker and very annoyed that he couldn't find his Thompson.

"Gordy probably took it," Adkins concluded. "We'll get it back, don't worry."

Now it was time for them to have a quick cigarette and make sure their stories matched up. They'd say they'd gotten a tip about a mob meeting from Maxwell and came to check it out, but it had been a trap. The shooting started, begun by Sullivan and his men and finished by Adkins.

"Does Charles know what you do?" In any other place or time I would have the answer, but here and now . . .

"Not yet. Maybe sometime later when he's ready to step up from his nickel-and-dime problem solving and do some real work. Then he'll be ready."

"What about your bosses?"

"We get results, they never mind those."

"But how you get them is wrong."

They looked at me, uncomprehending.

I struggled to find words to make them see, but my emotions kept choking me. There were no words for it, only feelings, and these men were past anything so human. "It's not just to clean up the world, Adkins. You want the headlines that made your name big before Repeal. The next one will be a real doozy: 'G-men Nail Hoods in Fiery Shoot-Out,' or do you prefer 'G-*man*'? You can be the spokesman for this fine group of outstanding law officers."

"So what if I am? I've done a lot of good work. We all have. It deserves recognition."

"You just murdered a dozen people!"

"Scum, Fleming. All scum—who would have murdered any one of us given the chance."

"Not this way."

"Of course, this way. You just don't get it, but then you're one of 'em."

"Oh, I am?"

Contemptuous laugh. "Remember those calls to Gordy?

Like tonight, him calling you to come help him out.''

"The wire on his phone."

"Easy as follow the leader."

"But you can't kill me."

A shrug. "Wait and see."

"Escott will know better. He won't believe any lie you feed him about me being with the mob."

"Then you'll be a tragic accident. You got curious, wanted to tag along with us, and got caught in the cross fire when all hell broke loose, very sad."

"He won't believe that either."

"If he doesn't, then accidents can happen to private agents the same as anyone else."

I bowed my head. I couldn't change his mind by any means. He was too far gone. With those words he'd made the decision for me on what to do. Like it or not, I was slipping into their darkness. I would have to kill, after all. Turn executioner. Watch my own soul slide away forever.

Hesitated. Wanted to hang on to who I was for just a moment more.

That wasn't going to happen. They'd have to finish up fast here before anyone else came.

"Stand him over there by the stairs," said Adkins. "We'll say he started going up and that's when they got him, that's what started it all."

"Don't think it'll work," one of them commented. "Why should they all come down here if they had the high ground? No need to get all dramatic, Merrill. Just say he lost his nerve when the shooting started and ran out in front."

"Okay. Get one of their guns and do it."

The man stooped and plucked a gun from someone's hand. Checked the clip for ammo. Raised it up. He hardly needed to aim at this distance.

I was set to vanish, to start my way to hell. The scene was

already burning itself into my memory. I'd carry this and
what I was about to do with me for the rest of my life.

Burst of fire above and behind me. The man staggered and
dropped. Strings sliced.

Before the others could react, another burst rattled the
room, it seemed to go on much too long. Could have been
only a few seconds' worth. Felt like eternity. Instinct made
me hit the floor and curl up as the slugs hammered overhead
and cut down Adkins, cut down all of them.

The last man toppled.

Silence.

I couldn't believe the silence. Shut my eyes against it for
a moment.

Didn't want to see, but looked anyway.

All dead.

Head shots. All head shots. To get past the vests.

Looked up the stairs.

Angela Paco stood on the top landing, that silly hat still
precariously clinging to her hair, her face new-penny bright.
She had Conrad's machine gun in her firm grip.

She laughed down at the slaughterhouse, then whipped
away.

Bloodsmell making me gag. I stumbled up the stairs to
escape it.

Past the office, down the hall to the closet. She was there,
pushing back the bucket and mop to lift the trapdoor slightly,
just enough so she could slip her hand inside and pull out the
first of the books.

She saw me and grinned. "You know how to throw a hell
of a party, don't you?"

"You came back for the—"

"Yeah, a double cross against you, but I got to thinking I
really should have them after all. Like insurance or some-

thing. I won't need Opal, though, so you play Salvation Army with her, okay? How's she doing?''

"She's fine. How long were you listening?"

"Long enough to know you were in over your head."

She was right about that in more than the obvious sense.

Before she could continue, Gordy surged up from his hiding place. Angela squawked and fell back, landing flat on her butt.

For a second no one moved, then: ''Hi, Gordy!'' she said, beaming.

'' 'Lo, kid.''

"I don't want any trouble." Her hand was on the machine gun, but it was too bulky to bring around in the confined space. Besides, Gordy already had his gun on her.

"Neither do I. How's your old man?"

"Getting better."

"That's good."

"I came to get some stuff."

He nodded. "So get it."

She cautiously reached forward and drew the books out one by one until five were stacked in her arms. "I'm going now," she announced.

We made no objection.

She stood, leaving the gun behind, and started walking.

"Where you going?" I asked.

She paused. Turned enough to smile at me. "I thought maybe Switzerland."

Gordy nodded at the books. "Think you'll need those there?"

"Probably not, but you never know."

"Maybe you'd like to cut a deal for them."

"Maybe."

"Call me at the club before you leave, we'll talk about it."

"Okay."

She continued toward the fire-escape window. I followed while Gordy struggled out of the stairwell.

She stopped at the window to look back. Big smile for me. She was a killer like the ones below, but unlike them, still strangely alive and enjoying that life.

She came back, snaked an arm up to pull me down close, then planted a solid one right on my lips. "You owe me, blue eyes," she whispered, then ducked through the window, her heels clattering on the metal escape as she descended. Her laughter, schoolgirl giddy, floated up to coldly tickle my ear like the wind.

Gordy had a look at what was downstairs and came back. Even he was shaken and suddenly in a hurry. He wiped the machine gun down and left it in the closet, then we followed Angela's route down the fire stairs, got in his Cadillac, and drove away, simple as that. The bums by the movie house, if any remained, were well out of sight.

He wanted to know what had happened. I told him.

"Will there be reprisals from New York?" I asked, after a long thinking silence.

"Not over this."

"I mean against you or Angela for Sullivan's death."

"Not after I give 'em my version of the story. She ain't even coming into it. Neither are you. So long as I'm running things, you and your buddy are strictly hands off from every wiseguy in this town. That's a promise. I owe you, Fleming."

"Uh-uh, we both owe Angela."

"They couldn't have killed you."

"But I would have had to kill them."

"You ain't cut out for that kind of work."

"I know. And I'd have had to do it. Then she stepped in. She can handle it a lot easier than I. I feel it, she doesn't."

He shrugged. "Yeah, she takes after her old man and then some."

I rubbed the spot on my chest where Frank Paco's bullet had cut through my heart and changed everything. My heart didn't beat anymore, but it was still there instead of a scraped-out empty space. The darkness hadn't taken it away just yet. Angela had spared me from that, so yeah, I owed her. I owed her big time.

I wondered if she'd ever try to collect.